TRAFFICK

Also by Ellen Hopkins

Crank

Burned

Impulse

Glass

Identical

Tricks

Fallout

Perfect

Tilt

Smoke

Rumble

The You I've Never Known

People Kill People

TRAFFICK

Ellen Hopkins

Margaret K. McElderry Books

NEW YORK LONDON TORONTO SYDNEY NEW DELHI

MARGARET K. McELDERRY BOOKS • An imprint of Simon & Schuster Children's Publishing Division • 1230 Avenue of the Americas, New York, New York 10020 • This book is a work of fiction. Any references to historical events, real people, or real places are used fictitiously. Other names, characters, places, and events are products of the author's imagination, and any resemblance to actual events or places or persons, living or dead, is entirely coincidental. • Text copyright © 2015 by Ellen Hopkins • Cover illustration copyright © 2015 by Sammy Yuen Jr • All rights reserved, including the right of reproduction in whole or in part in any form. • MARGARET K. McELDERRY BOOKS is a trademark of Simon & Schuster, Inc. • For information about special discounts for bulk purchases, please contact Simon & Schuster Special Sales at 1-866-506-1949 or business@simonandschuster.com. • The Simon & Schuster Speakers Bureau can bring authors to your live event. For more information or to book an event, contact the Simon & Schuster Speakers Bureau at 1-866-248-3049 or visit our website at www.simonspeakers.com. • Also available in a Margaret K. McElderry Books hardcover edition • Book design by Mike Rosamilia • Book edited by Emma D. Dryden • The text for this book was set in Trade Gothic Condensed 18. • Manufactured in the United States of America • First Margaret K. McElderry Books paperback edition January 2017 • 10 9 8 • The Library of Congress has cataloged the hardcover edition as follows: • Hopkins, Ellen. • Traffick / Ellen Hopkins. • p. cm. • Sequel to: Tricks. • Summary: Five teenagers struggle to find their way out of prostitution. • ISBN 978-1-4424-8287-6 (hardback) • ISBN 978-1-4424-8289-0 (eBook) • [1. Novels in verse. 2. Prostitution—Fiction.] I. Title. • PZ7.5.H67Tp 2015 • [Fic]—dc23 • 2015000095 • ISBN 978-1-4424-8288-3 (pbk)

This book is dedicated to all those committed to helping victims of trafficking—child or adult, sex or labor—become survivors.

Acknowledgments

Special thanks to those who shared their stories with me, opening up so freely about painful situations. You've chosen to remain anonymous, and I've pledged to respect your privacy. Here's to your future as survivors. Walk forward proudly.

A Poem by Cody Bennett
Can't Find

The courage to leap
the brink, free-fall
beyond the precipice,
hurtle toward

the abyss,

end the pain. Mine.
Mom's. Oh, she'd feel
the initial sting, cry
for a day or two, but it

would be

short-lived, a quick
stab of grief. Finite.
A satin-lined coffin
and cool, deep hole are

preferable to

walking a treadmill
over a carpet of coals,
enduring the blistering,
skin-cracking flames of

this living hell.

Cody
Awake

A slow swim toward the light, breaking
the surface to crawl back onto the beach,
here in the land of the living. It seems

like a worthy goal. So why do I wish
I'd died instead? Should that be the first
thought to pop into my head?

I open my eyes. Snap them shut again.
I've been treading dark water for . . .
I have no idea how long. I test the light

again, and the fluorescent glare against
white walls makes me bury my head
in the pillow. Bleach stink assaults me

immediately, fights the antiseptic smell
that confirms I'm in a hospital. Hospital, yes.
That information sinks through the fog

licking inside my head, syncs with
the onslaught of noises. Monitors
beeping. Ventilators whooshing. And

somewhere, there's a game show on
TV. Tubes jut from my arms, and some
sort of brace wraps my midsection, limiting

movement, but I manage to swivel my head
toward the rhythmic snore marking time
very near my right elbow. Mom's dozing

on a gray plastic chair beside the bed.
Her voice floats from memory. *Come back
to me, Cody boy. Don't you dare leave me too.*

And I remember her hands, oh God,
soft as rose petals, and fragranced
the same way, as she stroked my face

over and over, urging, *Please, son.
We'll make it through this. We always
make it through. But I can't do it alone.*

I want to help her make it through.
I want to go back to sleep. Except
I've finally accomplished what she's been

waiting for—resurrection. "Mo-mom?"
I have to force the word through
a thick soup of phlegm and it exits

my mouth a hoarse whisper. She doesn't
stir until I clear my throat. *Cody . . . ,*
she mumbles, and her eyes stutter open

to find my own staring at her. *Cody?
Are you really here?* She jerks upright.
Oh my God! She jumps to her feet,

rushes bedside, and grabs my hand.
Too hard. A wicked buzz, like a static
shock, zaps the base of my skull.

3

A Low Moan

Almost a growl, leaks from my lips.
Mom drops my hand like she's the one
getting shocked, backs away like maybe

> I'm contagious. *I'm sorry. I'm sorry.*
> *Did I hurt you? Hold on. I'll get*
> *a nurse.* She pounds the call button.

"It's okay. I'm okay." Except I'm not
sure I am. A shimmer of pain, muted
but present, radiates from my neck.

It spreads across my shoulders,
down into my chest, swelling to fill
the space defined by my rib cage,

finally settling in my belly. It stops
there, having traveled pretty much
everywhere. Everywhere, except . . .

Anywhere below my waist. Weird.
What the hell? I see Mom watching,
assessing me in some alien way.

With great effort, I reach down,
poke my right leg. Nothing. Left?
Numb. "What's wrong with me, Mom?"

My voice slurs. My brain is slow.
I'm drugged, yeah, that's it. A phrase
comes to mind: morphine cocktail.

I'll have another, please, bartender.
That cracks me up, and I laugh like
a madman. Mom looks terrified.

"Don't worry, Mom. I'm just loaded,
you know? They gave me some pretty
good drugs." She nods agreement, but

> her expression argues there's more.
> *Where's that nurse? I'll be right back.*
> She hustles off, calling for someone

to come right away. Wonder how long
I've been here, hooked up to these
machines. A day? Two? A week?

Logic argues it's probably been
a few days at least, or Mom wouldn't
have been so worried that I wasn't going

to wake up again. And now, duh, it hits
me that must be a big part of the reason
my legs feel so weird. They're still asleep.

Try, try again. I pinch my right thigh.
Hard. Pinch my left thigh. Harder.
Zip. Nada. Man, this is excellent dope.

Bet old Vince would go for this shit.
Vince. Wait. There's something about Vince.
I need to remember. I close my eyes. . . .

Tumble Backward

in time to . . .
Vince's apartment.
A poker game.

I remember that and . . .
winning for once.
Did I win?

Yeah, that's right.
Six hundred . . . no,
six hundred and fifty bucks.

Played it smart.
Left the table still ahead,
like smart gamblers do.

Ronnie.
Oh, Ronnie, Jesus,
I'm sorry. I never meant

to hurt you.
That day, after work
(work?), I was going

to see Ronnie.
She wasn't mad.
I thought she'd be mad.

Quick stop at the bank.
Deposited the cash,
half in my account,

half in Mom's
before . . . my date?
I dated Ronnie.

It wasn't a date,
it was a three-way meet.
Oh shit, no. Misty . . .

The thought of her
makes me sad.
Sad? Why? Misty.

Sweet Jesus.
Ambulances. Stretchers.
Misty, but where is her face?

Under the sheet.
Dead.
Misty is dead.

Before that, what?
Misty in bed
with some squeaky guy

      with a teeny dick
      telling me to hurry.
      Time is money.

Time.
Tick.
Bam.

Noise at my back.
Splintering wood.
A fist against my kidneys.

Down I went.
Crack-crack-crack.
The report of a gun.

Small. Sharp. Deadly.
You fucking whore.
You promised no more.

Chris. Misty's boyfriend.
But she didn't answer.
And you . . .

Addressed to me,
right before
his boots found my ribs.

Boom. Boom.
He took out two
just like that.

And then, *snap!*
Electric. Brilliant
sizzling white heat.

A shattering
splintering of bone
in my back.

My back.
I felt it go.
He shot me in the spine.

Chris.
Shot.
Me.

He was at Vince's.
I taunted him.
He was crazy mean

and I knew that.
Why take chances?
My fault.

My fault Misty is dead.
My fault I'm lying here.
My fault that I can't feel . . .

No! Screw that!
I'm okay. I'm fine.
Just a little numb.

I'm just fucked up.
It's the killer dope.
Killer . . .

Spontaneously

Tears spill from my eyes, track
my face. Spontaneously, one word
falls from my mouth, in quick

repetition. "No. No. No. No. No."
I'm still babbling when Mom
returns with a nurse the approximate

> size of a large gorilla. *Take it easy,*
> she soothes. *I've sent for Dr. Harrison.*
> *She'll be here as soon as she can.*

> *I'm sure you have questions and*
> *she can answer them better than I.*
> *Meanwhile, how's the pain?*

I dissolve into hysterical laughter.
Both Mom and Nurse Gorilla look
ready to flee. "Can't feel a thing. Hey . . ."

I reach down to the approximate level
of my pecker. "Am I wearing a diaper
or what? How am I pissing?"

I pat, pat, pat. "Nope. No diaper. Do
I still have a dick? 'Cause I for sure
can't feel it if I do." Jesus. H. Christ.

> Laughter segues to sobs. Mom shifts
> into Mommy mode, rushes to my side.
> *It's going to be okay, Cody. I promise.*

She starts to reach for me. Remembers
what happened last time, withdraws
her hands. Her soft, rose-petal hands.

> Nursilla steers Mom back into the chair,
> and when she moves closer, her badge
> tells me her name is Barbara. *Listen.*
>
> *You have experienced major trauma.*
> *Do you remember what happened?*
> At my nod, she continues. *I'd prefer*
>
> *Dr. Harrison explain in more depth,*
> *but I can tell you that you have a spinal*
> *cord injury. The good news is it's in*
>
> *your lower thoracic region, which*
> *is why you've got the use of your upper*
> *extremities and can breathe on your own.*

Barbara lets that sink in. Spinal cord
injury. Lower thoracic region.
I have no clue what any of that means.

But, hey, I can breathe on my own,
and should that become difficult
I can still use my hands to pick my nose.

That's the Good News

I'm about to ask what the bad news
is when two people bustle into
the room. The nurse introduces us.

Dr. Harrison, apparently my neurosurgeon,
is a tall, pretty woman, with toffee-colored
skin and striking blue-green eyes

that seem determined to look anywhere
but straight at me. Not a good sign.
The dude, who's Hispanic, stands a good four

> inches shorter, but man, is he buff.
> *Federico will oversee your PT,* explains
> Barbara. When I look confused,

> Federico clarifies, *That's physical
> therapy.* He extends a hand. *Awesome
> to meet you, Cody. We've got work to do.*

PT. Also not good. I shake his hand
anyway, wait to hear the information
I need, but am absolutely sure I don't

> want to know. Dr. Harrison delivers
> it. *I must be perfectly honest with you.
> Your life has been irreparably altered.*

Great bedside manner, Doc. I swallow
hard. "What do you mean? I'm not
going to get better or what?"

You will improve some as your body
heals, and we're not even sure
what the ultimate prognosis is.

We'll need to do some tests, now that
you're conscious. What I can tell you
is the most improvement you'll see

will be within the first six months.
That said, there are lots of promising
new treatments for spinal cord injury.

And SCI researchers are very close
to tremendous breakthroughs, for
quadriplegics as well as para—

"Are you saying I'm paralyzed?"
No, goddamn it! It's just the drugs.
I can move, and I'll prove it. I try

as hard as I can, but no amount of
concentration makes my legs so much
as twitch. "No. You must be wrong."

Finally, she looks directly into my eyes.
We can't tiptoe around the truth here,
Cody. Your spinal cord has been severed.

It's incomplete, so some function may
return. As I said, we'll have to run
more tests. But first, let me explain.

Thirty Minutes Later

I know a lot more. Hell, I'm
a walking, talking SCI textbook.
Let's see. The spinal cord is a soft

bundle of nerves, traveling from
the base of the neck to the lower
back through the spinal canal—

a tunnel in a person's backbone.
Electrical signals ping from
the brain down that pathway,

reminding body parts how
to move, or telling them to feel
pain or pleasure or whatever.

But sever the cord, or even nick
it, the communication stops
beneath the site of the injury.

Now let's get technical. She sure
as hell did. The spine has thirty-three
vertebrae, divided into regions:

cervical (neck); thoracic (upper and
middle back); lumbar (lower back);
sacrum (pelvis); and coccyx (tailbone).

There are twelve thoracic vertebrae.
The bullet struck my lower spine,
sending bone chips on an upward

trajectory. One or more dinged
my spinal cord between T(horacic)11
and T12, but didn't cut through it

completely. Still, it silenced the flow
of energy between my brain and
the body parts beneath my middle back.

Oh, but wait. This is where it really
gets good. Not only are my legs
confused, but so are my bladder

and bowel. Far fucking out. I'll be
able to piss and shit with the aid
of "specialized equipment."

Meaning, (one) stick a tube in the end
of my penis several times a day.
And, (two) . . . well, that is just too

disgusting to think about right now.
So, yeah, once I get out of this hole,
where they've got waaaaay underpaid

orderlies to drain my dick and
massage my anus, it's giant Pampers
for me until I learn how to make

myself take a dump. Make. Myself.
Crap. I know I'm guilty of awful sins.
But do I really deserve this kind of hell?

The More

The good doctor talks, the more
I just want to fold up and die.
But since that won't happen

right away, there's something
she hasn't told me. I need to know.
"Will I ever walk again?"

> *It's really too early to say. You might*
> *be able to, aided by leg braces,*
> *though you won't be running marathons.*
>
> *It depends on how much feeling,*
> *if any, returns. Meanwhile, your*
> *wheelchair will be your best friend.*

Wheelchair. The word slams
into my gut like a brick. I will be
confined to a wheelchair, at the mercy

of a caregiver? Someone to tell me
where to go, when to go, if I can go?
"What about driving? Can I do that?"

> *Absolutely, with a specially equipped*
> *vehicle.* She smiles. *That's usually*
> *the question I get* after *"What about sex?"*

Holy shit.

A Poem by Ginger Cordell
Will I Walk

Away from here, this dirty
city, where people come
in search of Lady Luck,
certain she'll guide them to
the fortune she owes them,

or

to shed their skins, reveal
the extraordinary creatures
beneath, aliens they struggle
to conceal from spouses,
ministers, their local PTA.

Will

I walk away from her?
My best friend turned lover
before our tumble from
enlightenment, if such a thing
ever belonged to me. Can

I

excise her from my heart
as easily as she deserted me?
If I opened my arms, begged
her to return, would she come
back, or would she turn and

run?

Ginger
How Can I Leave

Here without her—Alex, my sweet
Alex. At least, she was sweet until
Las Vegas claimed her, made her
its bitch. This city is a pimp, selling

fantasies. For a time, Alex and I
were a fantasy duet, working for
Have Ur Cake Escort Service,
despite being a couple of years

underage. "Eighteen" isn't necessary
to participate in a business that
props up the underbelly of Vegas.
It was not what I had in mind when

I ran away, but then again, I had no
plan, and sometimes it comes down
to survival. We survived, stripping
for pay in hotel rooms, mostly

working bachelor parties, two for
the price of one. I insisted on that,
refused to do more than take off
my clothes and dance. But Alex

couldn't care less about spreading
her legs and accepting foreign objects,
as long as the dudes were willing
to pay the going rate. Then she got

greedy, started working the streets
so she wouldn't have to kick back
Lydia's commission. I found her out
there, soliciting some guy wearing

ugly purple Bermuda shorts. That
pissed me off, but in hindsight,
looking for revenge by offering to let
him buy all he could eat, double-decker,

wasn't the smartest move. Turned
out, he was a cop on a trash run, prowling
for teen hookers. Vegas has issued
stern orders: get 'em off the sidewalks,

> bust their pimps and even their johns.
> Detective Bermuda Shorts was only
> doing his job. *Tell me who's sending
> you out, the court will go easy on you.*

Alex and I didn't roll on Lydia
or Have Ur Cake. Luckily, Judge
Kerry was sympathetic anyway,
an honest-to-goodness do-gooder.

> *Nevada considers trafficking
> children a serious offense.
> This is not a victimless crime,
> and you, young lady, are a victim.*

Nothing He Said

Made sense. How can a willing
participant be a victim? No one
tied us up at the end of the day
(although a few of our customers

offered). And we weren't trafficked,
as far as I knew then. No one kidnapped
us and smuggled us to the foreign
country of Las Vegas. Now, thanks

to my recent interaction with law
enforcement, the courts, and social
workers, I understand that three
things define trafficking: coercing

someone to turn tricks, transporting
them for that purpose, or in any
way threatening or encouraging
an underage person to sell their body.

Oh, and how good ol' Iris collected
money for allowing men to force
themselves on me? Uh, yeah. That,
too. Then, there's Have Ur Cake.

Since Alex and I haven't reached
the age of eighteen—that magic
birthday that supposedly makes
you an adult—Lydia was definitely

guilty of pandering minors for sex.
She arranged our "dates," and
collected a hefty fee for her trouble,
so technically she was our pimp,

though we asked for the work.
She never had to twist our arms.
But she totally knew how old
we were, and that we'd run away

with a minimal bankroll. Plus,
she did, in fact, put us in her debt
by letting us stay with her when
we first arrived in Vegas. When I

appeared before Judge Kerry, though,
I didn't understand all that. "I don't see
myself as a victim, Your Honor. I was just
trying to make enough money to survive."

He looked at me with such sadness
in his eyes. *I understand survival,
but this is not a good way to earn
money if you truly want to survive.*

I Guess I Was Lucky

I don't really know
what all Alex faced
when she did outcalls
solo. She refused to talk

to me about it. I only
did a few gigs alone,
and I never exactly felt
threatened. Together,

there were a few times
when I thought a client
might hurt us, and one guy
forced Alex to jerk him off.

More than once, we got
stiffed for payment, and
then we owed Lydia
anyway. She never really

bullied us. Convinced
is more accurate. She had
a way of doing that, although
she never could talk me into

stuffing condoms into my bag
and earning a hell of a lot more
money. I'm a dancer. A stripper.
But I'll never be a whore.

Now My Stripping Days

Are over, at least that's what Judge
Kerry said. After my advocate
determined Gram does want me
back in Barstow, they sent me

to stay in a group home until
Gram can arrange to come pick
me up. The law says I can only
be released to a "custodial adult."

Hey, at least I have one of those,
unlike Alex, who ended up in
a different group home—one that
accepts pregnant teens. Pregnant.

If she got that way, it means
she wasn't using protection, and
God forbid she picked up anything
else besides sperm. The father?

Some anonymous trick, and who
knows what color the baby will
be, or what defects it might inherit
from its paternal side? So sad.

Then again, everything about Alex
makes me sad—her childhood;
the things she's allowed herself to do;
the fact I might never see her again.

Our Goodbye Was Bittersweet

Bitter, because it *was* goodbye.
Sweet, because it meant she was
safely off the streets. I spent many
hours pacing our apartment,

pining for closeness and a return
to sweet adventures in bed,
wondering when she'd come home.
If she'd come home. She always

did eventually, but every time
another little piece of the Alex
I loved was missing. Tricking chews
you up from the inside out.

We had a few minutes together
while waiting to see the judge.
"Gram says she welcomes me
back, believe it or not."

> *I believe it. The one thing about*
> *you I've always been jealous of is*
> *how much your grandma loves you.*
> *No one's ever loved me like that.*

"What about me? I still love you,
Alex, don't want to live without
you. Please come with me. I'm
sure Gram will let you live—"

> *No. Are you kidding me?*
> *She's got six kids to take care*
> *of, plus your mom. You expect*
> *her to add me and a baby?*

"We can work out something.
Get jobs, our own place. I can
still help Gram with the kids,
and . . ." It sounded ridiculous.

> *Aw, Gin. I want you to go back*
> *to school, get your diploma,*
> *head off to college. You can*
> *legit make it in the real world,*
>
> *and do it all on your own. You*
> *don't need me holding you back.*
> She reached out, put one hand
> on my cheek. I directed it to my lips,

kissed each finger. "I don't know
what I'll do without you, and I'm
scared for you and the baby."
Her hand fell away, never there.

> *Don't worry about us. We'll be*
> *just fine. Besides . . .* She forced
> her voice cold. *I've been thinking*
> *and I've decided I prefer men after all.*

She Divorced Me

And though her remark was meant
to slice into me, sever the tie between
our hearts, I understand why she said
it so matter-of-factly. I don't believe

it, and the hurt she attempted hit
its mark square. I still have my cell,
and I've texted her dozens of times
in the two months I've been here

at House of Hope, where I'll stay
until Gram can get the guardianship
paperwork in order, take a day off,
plus find babysitting for the kids

and Iris, who is too sick to care for
herself, let alone her offspring.
Wonder if she'll let us call her "Mom"
now that men won't be coming around

and aging is the least of her worries.
She spent her youth on a slow death,
creeping closer for years, though
she was clueless until recently, when

a flu bug wouldn't go away. Tests revealed
advanced HIV-inspired lymphoma.
With her immune system compromised,
there will be no cure for her cancer.

House of Hope

Is a corny name, and I'm not sure
how much hope is actually here.
It's nice enough, and the food is good,
and the staff pretends like they care.

There are other sex workers here,
some younger than me, who happens
to be something of an anomaly because
my skin is white. The population is

largely divided by race, at least as far
as room assignments go. Hispanics and
black girls don't get along very well.
Their 'hoods are separate, and they stay

that way beyond those boundaries.
My roommate, Miranda, is Latina,
and pretty, though her plump face
makes her look younger than she is.

She says she'll be fourteen in two
weeks. She's thirteen, going on thirty.
Miranda was suspicious of me at
first, but after I told her my own

sob story, she decided to open up.
Right now, we're sitting on the lawn,
enjoying the mellow November sunshine.
After the god-awful heat of the past

few months, this feels like heaven.
The tale of horror Miranda's sharing
right now, however, is totally hellish,
and I have no doubt it's true.

> *My brother Ricardo runs dope*
> *for Los Sureños. He uses also,*
> *and too much on credit. He owed*
> *Papacito a lot of money.*

"Papacito," I interrupt. "That means
Daddy, yeah?" Lots of pimps insist
their stables refer to them as Daddy,
as if a father would sell them the same

> way. Truth is, I guess, some fathers
> do. *Sí*, she answers. *I don't know any*
> *other name, only he makes all the girls*
> *call him Papacito. One day after school,*

> *I'm talking with friends and a big car*
> *pulls up. Ricardo is inside with Papacito.*
> *He tells me to get in. I say goodbye*
> *to mis amigas, and we drive out of*

> *my 'hood, away from El Monte. I've never*
> *been so far from home. When we stop,*
> *I don't know where, Ricardo gets out.*
> *"Do what he says and you'll be safe."*

He closed the door, and I never see
my brother again, and not Mamá,
either. Papacito, he drive me all
the way to Las Vegas before we stop.

When we get here, he drives down
the strip. I never saw nothing like this
before. "Isn't it beautiful?" he asks.
"I know all the best places to show you."

He takes me to a house. It's nice
on the outside. Nice on the inside.
Except, what happens there is not
so nice. There are other girls, too.

This one, Belinda, she said she'd be
mi mamá now, she'll take good care
of me—buy me pretty clothes, teach me
makeup. Make me even prettier.

I say, "Mi mamá está en El Monte."
Papacito grab my arm and squeeze
real hard. "Your mamá, she doesn't
want you no more, so Ricardo give

you to me." I thought about that.
Mamá and I had a fight because
I told her about her man, how
he came into my room when

she wasn't home. How he touched
me. She said I was a liar. A puta.
But I didn't lie. . . . Her eyes water,
and it's the first time since I've been

here that I've seen real emotion in
the girl. "I believe you. It happened
to me, too." I don't add the part about
my own mother pimping me out.

Miranda nods. *It happens to many*
of us. Men are coyotes. I was eleven
the first time. Twelve when Ricardo
traded me for his debt. I found that

out later. But that day, I believed
it was Mamá's punishment. "But when
can I go home?" I asked. *Papacito*
tell me never, I'm his now. "Do exactly

as I say," he said, "and Belinda, too,
or I will hurt you so bad you'll wish
you were dead. But if you are a very
good girl, I will be your boyfriend.

¿Quieres un novio, no? Someone
who'll love you forever?" Every girl
wants a boyfriend, and I had no place
to go. The other girls seemed happy, so . . .

30

It isn't a unique story, but it *is* hers.
I think of my sister, Mary Ann, who's
about the same age, and pray it will
never happen to her. "Weren't you scared?"

> She nods. *But not so scared then*
> *as later that night, when Papacito*
> *come to my bedroom. "Such a pretty*
> *little girl," he said. "Now I will make*
>
> *you my woman." I knew what he meant*
> *and tried to say no. He slapped my face*
> *so hard I thought my head would snap off!*
> *Then he grabbed my neck and squeezed.*
>
> *I couldn't breathe. I begged him to stop*
> *but he choked me until I almost blacked*
> *out. I wore the marks from his fingers*
> *for many days. I had no fight left then,*
>
> *and he threw me on the bed, made me*
> *his wife for real. When he finished,*
> *he sent five friends to break me in*
> *better. After that, what did it matter?*

What came next, she says, is he pimped
her online or sent her out to work
truck stops, demanding a minimum
$800 per night. He kept every penny.

He Used Her

For almost two years, until a national
trafficking sting operation took
Papacito down good. Pandering
children under fourteen carries a life

sentence, if they can convict him,
which means they want Miranda
to testify against him, something
she's more than a little nervous about.

Men like that have a very long reach,
and his ties to Los Sureños make him
dangerous, even in prison. Miranda's
advocate has convinced her to do it, but

what will happen after that is anyone's
guess. Her mother's boyfriend says
she can't go back to El Monte. So, yeah,
I really am lucky. The court has freed

me, forgiven me, allowed me to go home.
Gram says her house will always be
my home, and she wants me there, safe
and sound. I guess, despite everything,

I'm mostly sound. But I wasn't safe
before, and I'm not sure there is such
a thing. All I know is, I'm happy to leave
Vegas. This city annihilates souls.

A Poem by Seth Parnell

My Soul

Has taken a vacation,
hitched a ride
somewhere cool and clean.
Maybe the mountains.

                                                    I

haven't seen it in months.
Perhaps it's deserted
me permanently.
I should feel bad, but I

                                              can't

muster sympathy
for the boy-become-man
who is me. Man. Gay
man. Kept man. You'll

                                              find

the ultimate meaning
of that term
in the eyes of every boy
forced by circumstance to

                                         sacrifice

the truth of himself.
I keep digging
for truth
but can't seem to find it

                                          in me.

Seth

I Swore

I'd never get used to living like this,
at the beck and call, and under almost

total control of another human being.
I say almost, because after Carl, my ex

sugar daddy when I moved in here
with David, I knew enough to find a way

to stash some cash in case I ever need
an escape plan. Carl, who brought me

with him from Louisville, a trophy
houseboy to decorate his Lake Las Vegas

luxury condo, allowed me no chance at
personal resources. He wanted ownership.

Slavery is alive and thriving in Sin City,
Nevada. Maybe that's why I gambled

on connecting with hot-stranger-in-the-gym
Jared—the growing need for rebellion,

or at least a taste of autonomy. Or maybe
it was simply because I'm only eighteen,

and still stashed inside is the belief
that love waits for me somewhere.

The Truth, However

If I'm to be perfectly honest with myself,
is that my attraction to Jared was totally

fed by lust. Well, lust and loneliness.
Carl may have provided well for me, but

he wasn't much for companionship.
Working out, lying by the pool, and

improving my culinary skills didn't exactly
tally satisfaction. Even the sex with Carl

(and sometimes an added friend of his)
didn't add much spice to our relationship.

So, yeah, I was pretty damn hungry when
Jared showed up in the gym, and that man

was something to look at. Ripped, not
an ounce of flab, and the chiseled face

of a god. I never suspected he was a ringer.
Carl baited the hook, and I bit. Hard.

When he reeled me in, I felt about like a trout
who knew that fly hadn't looked quite right,

but just couldn't help himself. And then,
Carl gutted me, threw me into the frying pan.

He Picked the Bones Clean

Disowned me completely, gave me
twenty-four hours to vacate his life,

not even a few dollars to help me
accomplish that goal. Luckily, I had

made a couple of friends online and
was able to convince one of them to pick

me up. Lake Las Vegas is quite a distance
from downtown, and the Mojave summer

temps are killer, sometimes literally.
I was ride-less. Homeless. Totally broke.

I did manage to stuff some very nice clothes
into a duffel bag. I figured I'd be the most

suave street person ever. But Jacques
was cool. He invited me to stay at his place

for a couple of days until I could find a more
suitable habitation, not that he didn't expect

a little *something* in return. I was happy
enough to oblige. Exchanging blowjobs

for room and board was nothing new.
There was one slight problem with that—

Jacques had a boyfriend. But I crossed
my heart that Morris would never find out.

As Far as I Know

He never has, which I'm happy about.
I like Morris. He's quirky and gentle,

and happens to be one of David's dancers.
In fact, it was Morris who introduced us

at one of David's infamous parties. My first,
but definitely not my last. It was a week after

I moved in with Jacques. Maybe Morris
felt a little threatened, and hoped I'd stumble

upon a different circumstance. I doubt
he expected what happened. It was late

> when he showed up at Jacques's. *Hey, boys.*
> *There's a party at David's. Wanna go?*

I had nothing better to do, and Jacques
goes along with anything Morris suggests,

especially when it's partying. "It's after
midnight. You sure it's still going on?"

> *Don't you know this city never sleeps,*
> *especially not on a Saturday night?*

> *But even if it did, the crowd at David's*
> *wouldn't. Staying up all night is a hobby.*

I Was Stunned

When we turned into the driveway
of David's amazing home in the Ridges,

a glitzy neighborhood, even by Vegas
standards. All lit up for the evening shebang,

the house looked like a five-star hotel.
Morris pulled his Prius right up in front,

where a hired valet took the keys. "You've got
to be kidding," I said, as I followed Morris

and Jacques up the marble stairs to the front
door. "How many people live here?"

> Morris laughed. *Officially, just David,*
> *although he keeps a steady supply of guests,*
>
> *plus a rather large staff. This place has,*
> *like, ten bedrooms or something. It takes*
>
> *three housekeepers just to keep it dusted*
> *and vacuumed. One day, Jacques darling . . .*

That house swarmed with men. Women.
Undetermined. Gay. Straight. Unspecified.

Everyone drinking. Everyone eating.
Everyone smoking. Snorting. Popping pills.

It was Sodom and Gomorrah under
a single roof. I was awed. Awkward.

Nervous. Bemused. Out of my element.
And also totally psyched to explore.

We maneuvered our way through
the house and out into the huge backyard.

Even at that time of the night, the air
was hot and still, and the Olympic-size

pool overflowed an assortment of noisy
guests, most of whom wore only their skin.

I trailed the boys to the bar, and no one
asked for ID when I ordered a mint julep.

I drew away from the tangle, to the edge
of the pavers, and lifted my glass. "Fond

memories, Carl," I whispered toward
the starlit sky. When I returned my focus

to the party, I noticed Morris and Jacques
had knotted into a small group listening

diligently to a compact man on the far
side of sixty, but decent-looking nonetheless.

Morris caught my eye, waved for me
to come join them. First, I took a big

swig of my mint julep, loving the burn
of exceptional bourbon. "Fuck you, Carl,"

I said out loud, before wandering over
to meet up with my friends. As I neared,

the group's attention turned toward
me. *Who's this?* asked David, although

I didn't know that's who he was until
Morris made the introduction that altered

my life yet again. *Seth,* repeated David.
Wonderful name. Are you a dancer?

"Not unless you count two-step, in
which case, I'm a hell of a dancer."

Everyone laughed, including David, but
his eyes were serious as they regarded

me, his interest quite obviously piqued.
Well then, not a dancer. What do you do?

I met his gaze square. "I am a top-flight
personal assistant. Currently unemployed."

The Crowd Began to Thin

As the earliest hours of morning
trickled toward dawn. David and I

hardly noticed, except the queue for
the bar grew shorter and shorter

and his personal entourage shrank
smaller and smaller. A few people

offered cocaine. At first I refused, but
David indulged and finally convinced

> me to try it. *Oh, but you should. It*
> *makes every bad thing better, and*

> *everything good the experience of*
> *a lifetime.* He winked. *Especially sex.*

I wasn't attracted to David, not in
the classic sense. But I was hypnotized

by the power of his wealth, and I knew
if I played the game intelligently the reward

could be well worth the effort. One snort
of what David said was damn fine coke,

I shed worry like rainwater. Two, conversing
came easier. Three, and the world righted itself.

At Some Point

Morris and Jacques wanted to leave.
I wasn't ready, but had no other ride.

       I must have looked anxious because
       David volunteered, *You two go on home.*

       I'll take good care of Seth and my driver
       can drop him off when he's ready to go.

The boys wandered off somewhere
close to two thirty. I can't say exactly

when because I was way too busy
mellowing the coke buzz with bourbon

and, conversely, fighting the alcohol
sluggishness with yet another line.

It's a great combination, one I've since
enjoyed fairly regularly, though David

doesn't keep a stash here at the house.
Most of it comes in with his guests.

That night we talked well into the morning
hours. Turns out, David was born in

Illinois, so we had neighboring home
states in common. I knew he was angling

for sex, of course. David doesn't try
to hide his attraction to pretty young men.

When he discovered I was still a teen,
though technically legal, he was intrigued

immediately. *So what's your story?*
How did you get to Las Vegas from

Indiana? I take it you're on your own.
Do you still have a family back home?

Without the cocaine stoking my mouth,
I would never have told him as much

as I did. "My mom died a long time ago,
but my dad still lives on the farm. When

I came out, he gave me twenty dollars
and told me to hit the road and stay gone

until I decided I wasn't gay. My boyfriend
was studying at the Louisville Seminary,

and I figured we'd just move in together.
But when I got to Loren's apartment, he told

me he was moving to New York to do
a field study with a congregation there.

> *Ah. And you weren't invited to go along.*
> *Queer rule number nine: avoid falling*
>
> *in love with members of the clergy.*
> *Even the best boyfriend can't trump God.*

"A very good rule. But what are numbers
one through eight? And is there a ten?"

> He smiled. *Maybe I'll fill you in one*
> *day. But you haven't finished your story.*

I didn't especially want to confide disgusting
details about Carl, so I gave an abbreviated

version. "I met an older guy in a club
and we hit it off. He was moving to Vegas,

asked me to come with him. When we broke
up last week, I had nowhere to go, so Jacques

let me move in with him temporarily. I need
a new living arrangement. If you have any

ideas . . ." At that point I was high enough
to be reckless. I looked him straight in the eye,

traced my upper lip with my tongue.
Needless to say, he didn't summon his driver.

44

I Wanted the Sex to Convince Him

To let me move in, so I offered anything
he wanted. Compared to Carl, who was all

about the kink, David's requests weren't
extraordinary. The thing is, he can have

whatever he wants with any of the cute
dancers in his stable who might be looking

to advance his career. But David doesn't want
easy sex, he wants affection. Okay, he wants

love, which isn't something I can give him,
though I profess to. I doubt it's possible

for someone my age to fall in love with
a man old enough to be his grandfather,

no matter how good that person is to him.
I want to experience real love again,

wrapped around sex and infusing lust
with meaning. But that won't happen here,

won't happen today, and I don't dare go
searching for it elsewhere right now.

It's enough that I can barter my body for
a lifestyle most people only dream of.

La Dolce Vita

That's what I'm living here with David—
the sweet life, and I can't discount that.

But neither can I count on it to last, as that
asshole Carl so aptly proved. So I'm bartering

my body on the side, via Have Ur Cake
Escorts. People travel to Vegas specifically

to create memories to leave here, and I'll stay
in Vegas with them. When Lydia interviewed

me, I was clear about the parameters—only
clients willing to pay premium rates for a top-

of-the-line barely adult. I won't risk losing
life with David for anything less than a grand—

five hundred in exchange for my company,
another five for invading it, condoms required.

Sometimes couples want three-ways, and that
costs a third more. For fifteen hundred,

I'll get it up for a woman, too. With limited
hours available plus a relatively high price

tag, I've had five dates, plenty to open a bank
account. That should multiply quickly.

I'm on My Way

To an outcall now, meeting the guy
at Picasso, one of the Bellagio's finest

restaurants. David's in L.A. for a couple
of days, so I don't have to fabricate

an excuse. I expect my client to be
older, but when the maître d' brings

me over to the table, the decent-looking
man who stands is in his early thirties.

>   *I'm Joe,* he says, and that may or
>   may not be the truth. *Thanks for*

>   *joining me. Would you like a drink?*
>   he asks, knowing I'm underage,

not that it matters. Carding is rare
in these situations, and should a waiter

get too nosy, I have a forged ID. I request
my favored mint julep, and Joe springs

for the prix fixe dinner. Four Five-Diamond-
Award courses, accompanied by wine.

I sit, staring at actual Picasso paintings,
while Joe tells me about himself.

I can't imagine he's lying. The details
are too specific. He's an art dealer, in

Vegas on business. His wife, three kids,
and two golden retrievers wait at home.

> *You must be wondering why a married man*
> *would arrange to meet someone like you.*

I shrug. "Everyone has fantasies or fetishes,
but few are brave enough to act on them."

> *When I was a kid at summer camp,*
> *there was this teenage counselor, Rob.*
>
> *He wasn't exceptional, really. Still, I*
> *used to daydream about him holding me.*
>
> *Touching me. Using me. The first time*
> *I masturbated, I pretended it was Rob*
>
> *jerking me off. It's strange, because I'm*
> *really not gay. I love my wife, and having*
>
> *sex with her. But once in a while, this need*
> *rises up, and I want Rob to jerk me off.*

After dessert, we go upstairs—Joe and Rob,
who does a whole lot more than jerk Joe off.

A Poem by Whitney Lang
Need Rises Up

From a bottomless well
of longing,
a whining so insistent

           no

amount of willpower
can force
it silent. They say the

           way

to be strong
when confronted with
the siren's song is

           to shutter

your ears,
fight the darkness, reach
for the light, but

           the windows

are draped
with memories
of ecstasy.

Whitney
A Chat

With the Grim Reaper
should be enough to scare
away any thought of relapse.
Wish it were that easy,
but not even days conversing
with death can disintegrate
the claws of addiction.

My memory banks
are foggy, misted by months
held fast in the arms of the Lady,
squeezed by need
you can't describe, can't relate
to unless you've experienced it.

I barely remember that last fix,
Mexican black tar instead
of my usual China white.
The Lady, she took me on
one hell of a ride
before we dove over the cliff,
falling, falling, falling.
Falling in slow motion.

Overdosing on Heroin

Is ugly business.
Well, the initial rush
is truly incredible. Similar,
I imagine, to a military jet taking
off, throwing you back in your seat
as you climb, almost perpendicular
to the ground. Yeah, close to that.

But then, the noise, a hurricane
inside your head, blowing.
Pounding. Exploding.

You try to fight the bad wind,
and everything slows.
Your breathing.
Your heart.
Slow.
Slower.
You
    can't
       find
          air
             as
                you
                    drift
                        toward

                              darkness.

Withdrawing from Heroin

Is a whole lot worse.
When you OD, you have no idea
you're tumbling toward death.
When you withdraw,
you have no doubt about it.

It's like being underwater,
and really, really needing to breathe.
You swim as hard as you can,
but you're too deep
and it's taking too long,
you won't break the surface
in time. If you inhale,
you'll drown, but there's no oxygen
left and your body's on fire
and your lungs ache with trying.

Then, there's projectile puking
and green water squirts.
Your joints throb and there's no relief
for three days because you can't sleep
without help from the poppy.
It's all you can think about.
Just one more rig to kill
the pain and rescue you
from the black depression,
knowing you're helpless,
smashed flat into the ground
beneath the feet of the Lady.

Unbelievably

The person helping me weather
those first few days
was the very woman I blame
for chasing me away from home
and into the arms of the man
who would become my pimp.

I expected my mom's scorn,
not her apology. *Oh, Whitney.*
Thank God you've come back
to me. I'm so sorry. If I had
lost you forever, I don't know
what I would have done. Please,
Whitney, whatever your reasons
for leaving, for . . . for . . .

She couldn't finish, could
not bring herself to put into
words the things the cops
must've told her, the awful
things their evidence showed—
that I'd been turning tricks
in a stinking apartment
in a disgusting neighborhood
in America's filthiest city.

I still don't feel even close
to dirt-free five weeks later,
despite the pristine living conditions
here at Clean Slate, a five-star rehab.

As Rehabs Go

I doubt you could find a better
one, or one with a higher
maintenance fee. That's what
they do here—maintain our sobriety.

You get what you pay for, yes
you do, and as the Clean Slate
brochure describes this place:
The buildings are sleek modern,
with big, open rooms flooded
with natural light gleaming
against polished ceramic tile
and walls painted in rich earth
tones. Client bedrooms are all
private, with windows that open
to invite the Pacific breezes inside.

Right. For a quote-unquote
lockdown rehab, the shackles
and bars are mostly invisible.

Clean Slate *is* close to the beach
near Santa Cruz, which used to be
where I lived. Those Pacific
breezes smell like home, and
the perfectly manicured grounds
remind me, too often, that I'll go
back there once they decide
I'm capable of reentering
mainstream teenager-hood.

My Day

Consists of group and
individual therapy.
Schoolwork to catch me
up to where I was when
I nose-dived into the bottomless pit.
Exercise, to keep my mind off
the ever-present craving
for the Lady. Exercise!
Man, after doing little but trolling
for johns for so long, my body
was slack. I chose yoga,
and have to admit it's helping
both muscle tone and relaxation.

Everyone on staff here, from
teachers to trainers to therapists,
looks like they stepped out
of a TV soap—cute, fit,
with pretty smiles they offer freely.

Most of the residents match
that description, too, minus
the smiles, which we're stingy
with. Of course, drugs of one kind
or another are largely responsible
for our collective willowy-ness,
which for many is exacerbated
by eating disorders.

Drug-free but fucked up—
that's the umbrella we share.

I'm Told

By rehab regulars that some
facilities encourage the use
of maintenance meds—
methadone or suboxone,
which allow substitute euphoria
without later withdrawal.

> But Clean Slate expects
> a total system scrub.
> As Guru Naomi says,
> *Relying on a substance*
> *to keep you off another*
> *substance won't make you*
> *self-reliant, and that's our*
> *goal. Weather the pain,*
> *the gain is greater.*

I am currently one-on-one
with so-cute-she-gags-me Naomi
who, if her looks accurately
represent her age, must be
right out of Therapist School.
Not the smartest woman, but
I think she thinks she cares.

> *Can we talk about why*
> *you first started using?*
> *Too much stress at home?*
> *Unrealistic expectations?*
> *Why your perceived need*
> *to escape reality?*

Perceived?

Escaping reality wasn't
a choice. It was necessity.
I've avoided opening
this box of memories,
but now that I can sleep
again, nightmares visit
regularly. Maybe talking
about it will help.

"I didn't use before I went
to Vegas. Well, a little weed
and alcohol, but everyone
I knew got high once in
a while. No big deal.
It was just having fun."

> *But it became a big deal,
> and when it did, it almost
> killed you. Do you think
> you might've made better
> decisions had you avoided
> substances completely?*

Ack. I hate when she asks
questions with obvious
answers. I know I shouldn't
respond, but my resident
interior smart-ass (RIS) has
a big mouth. "Do *you* avoid
substances completely?"

*No, I don't, Whitney. But I'm
thirty, not fifteen, which is how
old you were when you embarked
on the journey to nowhere,
right? Fifteen years makes a huge
difference, as does experience.*

Thirty? No way. Talk about
well-preserved! "What do you
want me to say? Of course I
would have made better decisions
had I not gotten high to begin with.
Or was that a trick question?"

Shut up, RIS. You aren't
being very helpful. "Look.
I wasn't hooked on weed
or booze. I don't even have
an addictive personality or
whatever. You can't *not* get
hooked on heroin, you know?"

*Some people can use it once
or maybe even a couple of
times without developing
an addiction, but it's rare.
Obviously it didn't work like
that for you. Are you ready
to talk about Las Vegas now?*

I Look at Her

All goofy-eyed and pertly
ponytailed. How can I admit
to *her* the raw things I've seen,
the slimy things I've done?
She only wants to obtain
my confession because it's her
job. Wonder if it will earn
her a bonus. Still, what have
I got to lose? It might even
be fun to freak her out.
"What do you want to know?"

> She looks surprised. *Everything.*
> *According to the police report,*
> *you were likely prostituting*
> *yourself. Is that accurate?* At
> my nod, she asks, *But why?*

"For love, at least at first."
I reward her with a shortened
version of how I met my former
pimp outside the Gap. How
he rescued me from a party where
my so-called boyfriend was groping
another girl. How he promised
to put me to work modeling,
convinced me to run away
to Vegas with him, set us
up in an apartment. How
modeling segued into sex
in front of a webcam, then . . .

I think I've heard this story.
He needed you to earn some
money so you could have
a nicer place. "Just once,
for me. Oh, and try a little
taste of heroin. That will make
everything easier." Before
you knew it, you were hooked,
and doing whatever you had
to do to keep supplied.

She *has* heard this story.
How many girls like me
there must be in the world!
And some of them leave it
in awful ways. At least
Bryn didn't hurt me, not
physically, the way some

pimps do. "That's pretty
much it," I admit. "Then I
found out he kept a whole
stable of 'models.' I was just
another one of his girls."

That stings to say. And while
he never beat me, he scarred
my heart. I doubt I'll ever be
able to trust a guy again.
As for love, what's the point?

I Don't Expect Sympathy

Okay, maybe a little. Instead,
Naomi's jaw stiffens like cement
setting up, and her eyes take
on a serious chill. Total

> transformation. *Let me ask*
> *you this. Why would you leave*
> *a cushy life in a nice home,*
> *with a family who supported*
> *you? Why would you let them*
> *worry for months that you might*
> *be dead? A little selfish, yes?*

Whoa. She can be downright
mean. Come on, RIS, think of
something to say. "You don't
know anything about my family.
All my mom cares about is her
country club and taking my sister,
Kyra, shopping. All my dad cares
about is work. They probably didn't
even notice I was gone for a week."
And Kyra no doubt threw a bon
voyage, good riddance party.

> *Sometimes there's a decent bit*
> *of distance between perception*
> *and fact, especially when it comes*
> *to teenagers and their parents.*
> *Did you ever stop to consider*
> *you might have been wrong?*

Not until Mom's barrage
of apologies in the hospital.
Of course, Dad showed up
all pissed and disgusted.
And Kyra, my loving sister?
All she cared about was
her reputation. *How could*
you do this to me? What
happens if my friends find out?

So, "No, Naomi, I'm pretty
damn sure I was spot on.
No one noticed me when
I was there. Why would they
miss me when I was gone?"

> *The universe doesn't revolve*
> *around you. Me, me, me.*
> *Tiresome. I've talked to your parents,*
> *and your sister. If you'd died,*
> *they would've been devastated.*
>
> *Did you know your mom spent*
> *hours and hours e-mailing*
> *your photo to law enforcement*
> *agencies? That's how the police*
> *knew who you were when they*
> *found you, lying there frothing.*
> *Had you been just another hooker,*
> *who knows how hard they would*
> *have tried to resuscitate you?*

Derailed

By dimpled blond Naomi.
So much for sympathy.
So much for trying to justify
the dumb moves I made.
I'll try to pacify her, paint
my face with contrition.

"You're right. I was totally
selfish, and I'm sorry I hurt
my family." As the words
fall from my mouth, I realize
they're maybe true. "I'm just
a stupid girl who fell in love
with the wrong man."

> Tell me about him. What
> was so special about this
> guy that made every ounce
> of common sense desert you?

"Br—Bryan is to die for.
Cute. Smart. Drives a cool
car. Mostly, he treated me
like I was the most amazing
girl he'd ever met. He swore
I was beautiful, and made me
believe it. No one else has
ever done that for me."

Okay, that sounds lame. Totally TV.

I Don't Out Bryn

To Naomi—I call him
Bryan. Bryn is a peculiar
name, one that stands out,
and even as hurt and pissed
as I am, getting him in trouble
(he could go to prison
for a very, very long time)
isn't on my "to do today" list.

Don't ask me why not.
Part of me would genuinely
enjoy seeing him locked up
in a cell with some beefy guy,
looking for a little action.
I'd probably pay to watch.

Despite that, the biggest
piece of schizo me remains
head-in-the-clouds in love
with the bastard. How is that
possible? I'll never forget
hours and hours, curled up
in a corner, stomach knotting,
body shaking beneath beads of salt

sweat, waiting for him to bring
powdered relief, cursing the day
I met him, weeping at my need
for him, screaming into the silence,
"Please come, Bryn. Please
come and make love to me!"

A Poem by Eden Streit

Screaming into the Silence

No one to hear
the brittle cries
but shadows thrown
against the walls and

                                              I

burrow my face into
the quilts to shut out
the demon dance.
This nightmare I

                                            can't

escape walks and breathes
beyond the confines
of sleep, and with it
a monster impossible to

                                            forget,

grinning. Leering.
Whispering lust-infused
ballads through serrated
teeth. He carries in

                                            his

hand a perfect strawberry,
offers it like treasure,
and when I bend to taste
it, he smashes it into my

                                            face.

Eden
Walk Straight

Was a godsend to me, maybe
even literally. I'd been sleeping
on the streets, crashing behind
Dumpsters, offering myself up
to passersby for meager money,

barely enough to eat. I would
say "survive," but that requires
being alive, and I was one of
the walking dead when I threw
a plea skyward, "Please, God,

please, if it's your will, show
me the way out." It wasn't God
who actually answered, but
a priest in the Catholic church
I had sleepwalked into.

How can I help you? he asked,
trying not to look disgusted by
the odor clinging to the awful
Salvation Army clothes I wore.
I didn't know how he could help,

but once he had no doubt about
my circumstances, Father Gregory
knew exactly how. He sent me here
to Walk Straight, a rescue for teen
prostitutes intent on a better life.

Teen Prostitute

How can I ever reconcile that
title in front of my name? It's so
contrary to everything about me—
the straitlaced daughter
of an evangelical preacher and his strict,

overbearing wife. Mama. At least
she was until she sent me to hell on earth,
a reform school of sorts called
Tears of Zion, where they isolated me
in a tiny room, only a Bible for company.

Barely fed me. Rarely bathed me.
Forced me to meditate on my sins—
chief among them falling in love
with Andrew, the Catholic boy with
attitude and spiritualistic belief beyond

the ken of my hellfire and brimstone
parents. With love as my sin, it was
only proper that my redemption
would come at the hands of a devil,
my savior Jerome, a Tears of Zion

apostle with a sick appetite for sex
with young girls like me, who he wanted
to own. I did what he required in trade
for an escape route across the desert—
my path to prostitution when I fled from him.

I've Confessed None

Of that to the great people here
at Walk Straight, a place founded
by an ex-prostitute determined
to help reshape the tomorrows
of teens who want out of "the life."

My caseworker, Sarah (who still thinks
I'm "Ruthie") has been after me for
information. To live here, my legal
guardian has to sign off on it. I was
never arrested, so I'm not in the juvenile

justice system, therefore not a ward
of the state. When I first arrived
here, I told them my parents
were dead. That lie is catching up
to me. Walk Straight has been patient—

their goal is to take kids off the streets
and give them a safe place to live.
But there are legalities involved.
I'm scared to return to Boise and live
under my parents' rule again. I'm also

terrified of seeing Andrew, who I love
more than anything in this world,
because he'll want to know why—and
where—I vanished last spring.
I just don't know how to tell him.

I've Been Courage Building

For weeks, and today is the day
I'll give Sarah the information
she needs to ruin my life the rest
of the way. But it's the only real
roadway into the future. I truly wish

Andrew could be there, too, but
he deserves someone better than me.
Someone clean. Unbroken. Worthy
of a love so intense it will leave her
breathless. Suddenly, my eyes sting.

>*You okay?* asks Shayleece, noting
>the onslaught of tears. She's one
>of thirty-two Walk Straight girls—
>about my age, with dark-chocolate
>skin and huge espresso eyes.

We haven't talked much, but then
neither of us is the talkative type.
"I'm all right. Just thinking
about someone back home."
We are at lunch, which today

is a delicious (not) tuna salad
sandwich. I never cared for tuna,
anyway, but in this setting, with
everyone eating it at the same
time, the fish smell is nauseating.

Shayleece doesn't seem to notice.
Someone special, huh? Bet it's a guy.
She waits for my nod before
continuing. *Like a real boyfriend?*
Ooh, girl! I want one of those someday.

Okay, maybe she *is* the talkative
type. I remain tight-lipped, except
to say, "He's the most amazing guy
in the world." If I think one more
time about him kissing me beneath

the broad Idaho sky, I'll go completely
crazy. It's the best memory I own,
but when it rises, smoke, I choke
on the knot that forms in my throat.
I'm suffocating at this moment.

I don't want to talk about Andrew,
so I refocus the conversation,
which I guess is what we're having
between bites of yucky tuna sandwich.
"You never had a boyfriend?"

> *Oh, hell no. My mom, she would*
> *have killed me. Sex for love, which*
> *means for free? Nah, she wouldn't*
> *have put up with that for one second,*
> *and Daddy would've killed the guy.*

70

Now That She's Opened Her Mouth

It's going to be hard to slam it
shut again. Because when I ask,
"You mean your mother knew
you were turning tricks?" she has
no compunction about sharing

> her entire life story with me. *Oh,*
> *yeah. My mom's the one who put*
> *me out on the track. Well, she did*
> *it for Daddy. See, she was one of*
> *his "wifeys," too. And know what?*

> *Daddy was maybe my real daddy,*
> *ain't that a hoot? Mom was fourteen*
> *when she started tricking, and he was*
> *her man, so she didn't use no protection*
> *with him. She was fifteen when she had me.*

"Wait. Your mom *wanted* you
to prostitute? How old were you?"
My own mother insisted I had to
get married before I even allowed
a boy to kiss me, let alone . . .

> *We needed the money for rent and*
> *stuff. I was thirteen, but no big deal.*
> *One of Daddy's friends broke me in*
> *when I was nine. As Daddy says,*
> *tight pussy costs a pretty penny.*

71

Unless You Can Coerce It

Crush what's left of a little girl's
childhood into dust. I know
it happens, but it's hard to picture,
and she doesn't even seem that upset
about it. How can that be possible?

       Shayleece finishes her sandwich,
       chases the last swallow with a big
       gulp of chocolate milk, starts on
       her giant oatmeal raisin cookie.
       Who broke you in? she asks bluntly.

"You mean who did I give
my virginity to?" I realize few
enough girls here actually gifted
it to someone. Maybe only me.
"My first time was with Andrew."

       He your boyfriend? Her voice
       drips incredulity, but when she
       assesses my body language and
       finds only truth reflected there,
       she asks, *So how you end up here?*

"Want my cookie?" I shuttle
my tray across the table so she can
enjoy the second dessert. "This will
probably sound stupid, but I think God
sent me here. See, this priest—"

No. I don't mean here at this table.
I mean in Vegas, in the life. I never
saw you out on the track. Daddy
woulda loved getting hold of you.
He's always scouting for white girls.

I don't really want to talk about
Tears of Zion with Shayleece,
so I tell her, "It's a long story. Let's
just say I had no choice but to run
away, and the trucker who picked

me up hitchhiking was headed
in this direction. I've got a question
for you, though. How did *you* wind
up at Walk Straight? Does your mom
know you're here?" I watch her stuff

the last bite of cookie into her mouth.
My mom's dead. A few crumbs fall
from her lips. *Daddy makes his girls give*
him five hundred every day. Mom was
short too many times. He got mad, beat

her down. I got home right as he put
the gun to her head. I ran 'cause Daddy
saw me, but didn't know where to go.
A girl out on the track told me 'bout this
place. She said they'd keep me safe.

The Sex Trade

Is a violent business. Pimps
competing. Pimps keeping their
girls in line. Big city, small town,
makes no difference. "Did the cops
ever find out who killed her?"

> *Oh, hell yeah. Word got around*
> *on the street, and you know, one*
> *person said something to someone,*
> *probably someone who runs other*
> *girls, and eventually it reached*
>
> *the police. Plenty of Daddy's DNA in*
> *that place. Then my counselor here*
> *made me fess up about my pimp, so*
> *now they've got him for murder and*
> *for trafficking children. I still qualify.*

That busts her up, and the way
she laughs, head thrown back
as she squeals and snorts, makes
me grin, despite the fact that it
isn't funny. Am I still a child?

> *Okay, well, it looks like lunch*
> *is over. Thanks for the cookie.*
> She pushes back from the table,
> stands. *If your boyfriend really*
> *loves you, he'll forgive you.*

On Weekdays

We're required to attend classes
both a.m. and p.m., the goal
being to earn our high school
equivalency certificates so we can
move on to productive jobs and

become solid members of society.
That's assuming we stay long
enough to make all that happen,
and I don't think I will once Sarah
contacts my parents. Then again,

I can't imagine returning to Boise
High, pretending to be an ordinary
junior, a little behind on credits
because . . . Exactly why? Beyond
school, what about church? Papa's

church, where he preaches everlasting
hellfire for infractions as insignificant
as divorce or using birth control. How
can I sit there and listen, all the while
remembering the things I've done?

How can I bask in the glory of God
when I've trolled the streets on Satan's
arm? Shayleece claims Andrew will
forgive me. But how can I forgive myself,
or expect the Lord to offer redemption?

These Thoughts

Intrude on my concentration
this afternoon. I'm happy when
I can leave US Government behind
in favor of library hour. I requested
computer time yesterday. I don't know

if they bother to monitor what
we view online. Probably. Doesn't
matter to me. My tastes are benign.
I check e-mail first, always hoping
for some little word from Andrew.

I'm not disappointed. Hello, my heart,
he writes. *Hope you are well and
that you're coming home soon. Wherever
you are is too far away. God, I miss
you. I dream about you every night.*

*Sometimes those are good dreams.
You and me, here on the ranch,
playing with Sheila (who's not
a puppy anymore . . . funny how
fast they grow into dogs!), or just*

*sitting on the porch, watching
the cottonwoods flicker in the breeze.
But then come the nightmares
where I see you in the distance, faint,
but no matter how hard I try or how*

fast I run, I can't catch up to you,
and when I reach the place where
you were standing, you're gone.
Vanished, just like you disappeared
from my life. Please come back to me,

or at least tell me where you are so
I can come find you. I promise, no
matter what has happened, we'll make
things right again. I don't care what
your parents think. All my love, Andrew.

Beautiful words. I want to believe
them, need to trust in him. But how?
The love we shared ran marrow deep,
but the Eden he knew died behind
the walls of Tears of Zion. "Ruthie"

is who I am here in Vegas. Walk
Straight needed to call me something,
so I offered my middle name, Ruth.
Sarah added the "ie" to make it feel
"friendlier." Less biblical, for sure.

But I don't want to be Ruthie
anymore. She represents a short
chapter of my life I'm determined
to edit out. And if I'm no longer Eden,
who'll I be if I return to Idaho?

Heart at War with Head

I think about how to respond.
At some point, I'll have to break
down and tell him the truth. Not
possible to construct a solid future
on a foundation of dishonesties.

Doing it this way would give him
time to consider the implications
and change his mind about wanting
me back in his life. He wouldn't
even have to write a reply to say

goodbye, he could simply excise
me from his life with his silence. Plus,
I don't have to look into his eyes,
absorb the hurt and anger that will
surface there if I admit the ugliness

face-to-face. I'm a coward. Too
cowardly, in fact, to come clean
right now. To keep moving forward,
I have to maintain at least a minimal
amount of hope that Andrew and I

can be together again. Still, I need
to give him something, so maybe
a bare-bones explanation of why
I simply evaporated one day.
The story begins with Mama.

Backward in Time

That's where I take him, not so
far back, not really though
it feels like years ago, and what
has transpired between then and
now has aged me more than months.

"Dearest Andrew. I am safe, for
now, in a shelter in Las Vegas.
I do hope to return to Boise, but
I'm not sure when, because I told
them my parents were dead,

something I plan to rectify today.
I won't tell you everything now,
but want to confide some of it.
Remember the last time I saw you?
My family was at church, at least

I thought so. But when I got home,
Mama was there, and I was sure
she'd beat me again. Instead she brought
me into the kitchen, made tea laced
with sleeping pills, and as I passed

out, she blamed Satan for me falling
in love with you. I woke up eleven
hours later, out in the middle of
the Nevada desert, at a rehab
center called Tears of Zion. . . ."

I Describe

My routine, the lack of sustenance
and human company. Underline
the hopelessness I felt when I learned
my time there had no set termination
point. Now comes the hard part,

but without it there's no explanation
for how I got here. "All I could think
about was finding a way to escape,
to get back to you. One of the orderlies
had a crush on me. God forgive me,

but I promised he could be my boyfriend
if he helped me get away." I won't give
Andrew the disgusting details; he can assume
them or not. "It worked. When we stopped
for gas, I hid from him. A nice rancher

gave me a ride and I wound up in Vegas.
I tried to call you, but your phone was
disconnected. I didn't know my parents
had you arrested until your mom told
me. I'm so sorry. For everything."

I spend a few minutes stressing over
how to sign off. "Love" isn't strong
enough, and he used the preface "All my."
I choose, "I'll never stop loving you,"
hit send before I change my mind.

A Poem by Cory Bennett

The Disgusting Details

Of life in hard-core juvenile
lockup don't really need
to be repeated. My brother
Cody would never let me
live it down. I won't argue
the system got it wrong, that

                                                    I'm

not qualified to be here.
Break into a home,
then whup the owner's
ass until she's lying

                                                    still

on the ground,
they'll put you away
if they catch you. Problem
is, there isn't

                                                    a kid

in this place
who won't walk away
tougher, meaner, calloused,
no hint of child left

                                                    inside.

Cody
Imprisoned

I thought a lot about being locked up
when they first sent my little brother
to jail. Not saying Cory didn't deserve

it, or that it didn't maybe save his life.
The path he was headed down
could have ended with him slamming

face-first into a brick wall. But it made
me a little crazy to consider the day-
to-day of containment in a little cement

room, only let out for meals, classroom
bullshit (like anyone there gives a fuck
about school), and an hour of exercise.

Yeah, that pretty much seemed like hell
to me. But, with luck and good behavior,
Cory will be released one day. He didn't

manage to kill the woman he knocked
senseless, and since she recovered, he'll only
be incarcerated until he turns eighteen.

The cost of my indiscretions, which
should've resulted in nothing but pleasure,
was life, in prison in a useless body.

One Day Blurs

Into the next, a huge brown smear
of hospital shit. There's nothing to do
but watch TV, hour upon tedious hour.

The food sucks, but even if it was gourmet
I'd avoid it because eating only means
someone's gloved finger massaging

my anus to make me take a dump. Not
that I can feel it, but knowing that's what's
going on is more than enough to drop

me into a cavern of depression, a place
I fall into regularly, with or without
a latex-sheathed pointer exploring my ass.

Mom brings me books, and the unread
pile continues to grow, along with a stack
of magazines. *Sports Illustrated. People.*

National Geographic. No *Hustler*, not that
it would do anything but remind me
what a worthless excuse for a man I've become.

No, my life will never be the same,
and worse, my future as a complete human
being was stolen by that low-life fucker, Chris.

Federico would tell me to shut the hell
up, cancel the pity party and get to work.
His idea of work? Learning to sit up.

Equilibrioception

That's another word for balance,
and apparently I've got a problem
with that. First of all, I've been lying

here for weeks, rolled side to side
from time to time so I don't get these
nasty things called pressure sores—

wounds caused by staying in one
position for so long your bones
poke through your hide. I've seen

pictures. Disgusting. The worst thing
is, since I can't feel the wear and tear,
they could get infected before I even

realize my skin is rotting away.
But there's more. To keep from falling
over, your eyes, ears, and proprioceptors

have to work together. Proprioceptors
are sensors that tell you where your limbs
are positioned in space. Like, your right

arm is over your head, or your left foot
is two inches off the ground. And since
my legs don't have a clue where they are,

things get a little tricky. Federico insists
it gets easier with practice. Too bad
sitting up isn't on my to-do list at all.

This Will Be the Day

That's what he said, and I do
believe he meant it. Best of luck
with that, old buddy. He's yanked

the sheets back, exposing most
of my uselessness, slack and pale
as the Cream of Wheat they tried

        to make me eat for breakfast.
        Okay now. The process is fairly
        simple. Put your elbows flat

        on the bed beside you and push
        down, bending your head and
        shoulders forward. He stands there,

waiting, but I don't bother to try
and move. What's the point?
"Don't feel like it. Maybe tomorrow."

        His expression is priceless.
        Look, Cody. Time keeps ticking
        forward, and the rest of the world

        isn't on hold waiting for you to
        get on board. You're not going
        to die, and the quality of your future

        living is entirely up to you. I believe
        you want to get up on your feet
        again, and I also believe we can

absolutely make that happen.
Scratch that. You can make that
happen. People with worse injuries

than yours have made that happen.
But it takes heart and courage.
Out of breath with the effort of not

convincing me to budge an inch,
he lingers there, hands on hips,
with such genuine bewilderment

on his face I almost feel sorry
for him. But not anywhere near
as sorry as I feel for myself.

"Look, dude. I'm lying here with
a tube hanging out of my dick, leaking
piss into a plastic bag. That dick,

by the way, is totally useless for
anything worth getting excited about.
Yeah, yeah, Dr. Harrison told me

ninety percent of men with incomplete
injuries, T12 and lower, get it up, and some
higher than that, too. But that's not the real

problem, is it? Not like I want to go
above and beyond, just to whack off.
How many girls go looking for cripples?"

86

Half-Sad

Half-annoyed, that's how
he looks now, like he needs
to dig for words of wisdom

>   but the shovel needs sharpening.
>   *It's "disabled," not "crippled," and
>   so you know, there are millions*
>
>   *of couples living with disability.
>   Not only that, but there are plenty
>   of perfectly healthy partners who*
>
>   *don't have sex regularly.* He winks
>   conspiratorially. *You could ask
>   my wife, but she'd probably lie.*

That actually makes me smile,
and I almost consider rewarding
him with the behavior he's seeking.

>   But then he has to go and ruin
>   the moment. *So, do you have
>   a girlfriend? Someone special?*

With a stunning burst of memory,
the face of an angel materializes
from the ether. "Not anymore."

>   He's gone too far, and backpedals
>   quickly. *You don't know that, do
>   you? Have you talked to her?*

Are You Out of Your Mind?

That's what I want to ask him,
quite loudly, but yelling is too
much effort. "Not since before . . ."

> *Look, at the very least, let's work
> on mobility. You don't have to do
> anything but roll onto your side.*
>
> *I'll handle the heavy lifting, and
> while I do, why don't you tell me
> about your girl? What's her name?*

"Ronnie," I answer without
even thinking. "Well, Veronica,
but everyone calls her Ronnie."

Federico rolls me onto my left
side, begins manipulating my right
leg. This isn't new, but I sense more

> movement than before. *Ronnie.
> Is she pretty? Bet she is.* Bend.
> Lift. Backward. Forward. As

he continues the routine, I find
myself describing the girl who
still possesses my heart. "She's not

pretty. She's beautiful. Her hair
is the color of obsidian, and shiny
like it, too. And her body. Man,

it's amazing. You've never seen . . ."
I skid to a halt before I mention
her glorious tits. "But there's so

much more to her than that.
She's—was—my rock." My rock,
when my stepfather, Jack, got sick

and died. My rock when Cory melted
all the way down into a puddle
of booze-inspired anger. My rock.

And then I went and fucked it all
up with drugs and gambling and
financing those by offering myself

up for sale. Invincible, that's what
I believed I was. Untouchable.
Such conceit! And now, look at me.

Hard to maintain an air of vanity
while being posed like a nude mannequin—
bend, lift, backward, forward, flip,

and repeat. Federico finishes each
side by massaging my legs and feet,
all for the sake of circulation. Too bad

I can't feel it. Ronnie used to do that
for me, and boy, did I love . . .
Next thing I know, I'm sobbing.

Even Better

Suddenly, my right foot jerks. Ouch!
But, wait. Movement? "Hey, what
was that?" Does that mean more

> brain connection than we supposed?
> The action was involuntary. Federico,
> it seems, missed it. *What was what?*

"My foot just twitched. Hurt like
hell, too. That's a good sign, right?
Like, maybe you're all totally wrong

> and my spine just had to heal more?"
> But Federico shakes his head.
> *That's called spasticity. We've been*
>
> *wondering if it would affect you.*
> *It usually doesn't first occur until*
> *several weeks post-injury. See,*
>
> *your muscles have memories, and*
> *even without an intact circuit board,*
> *they try to repeat learned behaviors.*
>
> *The bad news is, it can be painful,*
> *or at the very least, annoying.*
> *The good news is spasticity*
>
> *can actually be helpful with bowel*
> *and bladder behaviors, and many*
> *SCI patients utilize it to help them*

90

stand and even walk. One day
at a time. If it becomes a real
problem, there are drug therapies,

so be sure and let a team member
know if the pain is too much.
Team member: one of the nurses,

doctors, physical therapists,
psychologists, and social workers
assigned to my case, just a number

among many on their busy lists.
Federico waits to see if I'll spasm
again, but when that doesn't happen

right away, he spreads the sheet
back up over me. "So, if spasticity
is nothing but my foot remembering

how it used to move, and I'm still
paralyzed, why could I feel it? And
how could it possibly be painful?"

He shrugs. *With incomplete*
injuries, it's always possible some
feeling will return. Besides,

the brain is an incredibly
complex machine. Sometimes
its will trumps common wisdom.

Go Right Ahead

Burst my fucking balloon.
The truth is a sharp pin,
and I tumble back down

to earth. "Hey. My brain
tells me I'm hurting. Can
you give me something

for that? You must've
worked me too hard. Or
maybe it's just spastic me."

> He looks unconvinced,
> but then he decides, *Tell*
> *you what, Cody. I'll send*
>
> *in a nurse, but only if you*
> *give me your word that*
> *tomorrow you'll cooperate*
>
> *and help me get you sitting*
> *up. We've got a long way to go,*
> *and it starts with you upright.*

I'd say anything for the key to
oblivion, and besides, as my Kansas
kin might say, my word ain't worth

a pile of manure, so it's a no-brainer.
"I solemnly swear if you eradicate
my pain I'll try to sit up tomorrow."

Nurse Carolyn

Who remains my favorite filly
in a stable of Thoroughbred
caregivers, tries to rip me off

at first, offering acetaminophen,
but I'm not going for that.
Federico isn't overseeing,

so I'll use my latest, greatest
excuse. "Please, Carolyn.
Did Federico tell you? Spasticity

has reared its nasty head, and
I'm in a lot of pain right now.
I need something stronger

than Tylenol!" I wait for her
stern face to soften, and it does
almost immediately. Score.

> *Oh, all right, as long as*
> *the on-duty physician concurs.*
> *I'll check and be right back.*

She isn't gone long, and
when she returns it's with
a healthy (or not) dose of codeine.

> *Dr. Cabral gave the okay*
> *this time around, but there are*
> *better pain management methods.*

I understand spasticity can
cause quite a bit of discomfort,
but so can opiate dependency.

As your rehab progresses,
I'm sure your doctor will
recommend alternatives.

Pill swallowed, agreement
is easy. "I understand. Thanks
for caring, Carolyn." I reward

her with my very best smile—
the one that swears all will be
well, though that, of course, is a lie.

Okay, then, I'd better get back
to work. You aren't the only
needy patient around here.

As she leaves, the codeine kicks
in and I find myself inexplicably
drawn to the pendulum of her narrow

hips, thoroughly disguised by baggy
powder-blue scrubs. "You're an idiot."
I scold myself for the transference,

which is also impotent transference.
Obviously, the will of my brain
is trumping its common sense.

Rocking

In the cradle of the poppy,
all the bad feelings slip away.
Why am I lying here again?

Where am I, anyway? White.
Everything's white, and quiet,
like a winter-quilted mountain

meadow, except it's warm. I like
it warm, and now I know this
can't be snow, because the air

doesn't sting my nose. Inhale.
No sting, but there is perfume.
Apples. That's it. Baked apples,

rich with cinnamon and brown
sugar, and I realize I'm dreaming.
Weird, when you're aware

you're not treading time in the real
world, but rather wandering
another dimension. A drift of apples

fills my nose, and a satin caress
(surely not Federico's!) slides
along the skin of my legs. Legs.

Why does that word bother me?
Not important. What is worthy
of my attention is the force field

rising up around me, a halo
of well-being that can only be love.
I search for the source. Nearby,

she must be nearby. My rock.
There, in the mist, a shadow,
approaching, and growing as

it nears, solidifying. "Ronnie?"
It's no more than a whisper, and
escaping the fog, comes an answer.

> *I'm here, Cody. I waited for you,*
> *but almost gave up hoping that*
> *you'd come back to me. Wake up.*

> Her voice is smooth and rich
> as frosting. But I still can't see her.
> Now she urges, *Open your eyes.*

I do and the dream dissolves.
Bedside, in the flesh, is, "Ronnie."
I start to throw back the sheet,

remember where I am, how I am,
who I've become. "Go away. I
don't want you to see me like this."

> *Too damn bad. I have no clue*
> *why you decided to throw "us" away,*
> *Cody, but I won't let it happen.*

A Poem by Alex Rialto
The Dream Dissolves

Every dream does,
but hope saturated this one,
and a tiny piece
of me tries very

                                        hard to

believe my cards
have been re-dealt.
The thought of nurturing
an innocent soul makes love

                                    rise

in me like nothing else
ever has before, not even
lying next to Ginger, wrapped
in the warmth of her sighs.
I am lifted high

                                    above

the landscape of my life.
But now I fall again, desert
scrubbed of sustenance,
without the promise of
my baby, who chooses

                                surrender

in favor of time with me.

Ginger
Time Drags

Here at House of Hope,
where everything is regimented,
little variation to any given day.
They say that sameness

is necessary to meeting
expectations, that it's good training
for real-world situations like
keeping a job. Up at six thirty a.m.,

dress for the day, make our beds,
straighten up our rooms. Breakfast
at seven, finish by seven thirty.
Load the dishwasher, if it's your day.

If not, lucky you, fifteen minutes
to read or stare into space before
chapel, where you'll stare into
space even longer. House of Hope

is a Christian home, and morning
prayer meeting attendance is mandatory.
Saving souls. That's what they believe,
and hey, if it works that way, more

power to the Power. The concept
of God is foreign to me. Not even
Gram subscribes to the notion,
at least, she's never mentioned it

to me if she does. Personally,
I'm just happy House of Hope
has rescued my body from abuse.
If there's anything resembling a soul

residing inside me, it probably
does need a little assistance, but
I'm pretty sure listening to Pastor
Martin yak at us won't make

that happen. Doesn't matter.
It's easier than scrounging a living
taking my clothes off, and for the girls
who somehow still *do* believe,

his words seem to offer comfort,
don't ask me why. He sits on
a stool in front of the group, as if
standing would be too much effort.

> *The amazing thing about our Lord,*
> *Jesus Christ, is his bottomless*
> *supply of love, and all you have*
> *to do to receive it is ask.*

That doesn't sound so bad, but he
won't stop there. He never does.
Because, although he would argue
this, Pastor Martin's all about judgment.

And ... His Engine Fires

First, he straightens his back,
builds himself real tall, tilts
his chin toward his nose. Red
alert: serious stuff headed this way.

> *Now, you probably think*
> *you've experienced love,*
> *but unlike the men many*
> *of you have known, Jesus*
>
> *doesn't ask for favors in return,*
> *at least not that kind of favor.*
> *All he requires of you is to*
> *accept him into your heart,*
>
> *and to pray for forgiveness*
> *for your sins. You can do that,*
> *can't you? The robots group-nod.*
> *Then let us pray. Heavenly Father,*
>
> *please search our hearts, and*
> *find repentance there. We admit*
> *we have sinned. Forgive us and*
> *allow us to walk forward cleansed*
>
> *of our transgressions. Infuse us*
> *with your light. Fill us with your*
> *love. In Jesus's blessed name, amen.*
> We. Us. Our. All-inclusive.

Why Does Everyone Insist

On lumping us all together
under the "troubled youth"
label? I guess our stories
might sound similar,

but to us, they are unique
and personal, despite
the ugly things we have
in common. Most of our

childhoods were marred
by rape, often by older men.
But those might have been
a stepfather, grandfather,

older brother, neighbor,
teacher, priest, doctor,
foster parent, policeman,
or complete stranger.

Faces. Bodies. Odors.
Skin textures. Voices.
Mannerisms. Methods
of attack. All different,

and scratched into our
memories and, worse,
our psyches. We are who
we are because of them.

Post Prayer

We attend classes. I balked
at first, knowing I'd be leaving
House of Hope before I'd complete
a semester, but my counselor

did her job and convinced me
I shouldn't get any more behind
than I already am. She even got
hold of my high school in Barstow

and found a way for me to finish
up the classes I was most of the way
through when I ran away last spring.
I worked a little magic. That's how

she put it when she told me I could
complete geometry, world history,
and sophomore English and receive
credit for them. When I go home,

I'll take online classes, work at
my own pace and hopefully complete
my junior year pretty much on schedule,
or at least by the end of next summer.

I could then, if I wanted, go back
to high school for my senior year
and graduate like a regular kid.
But how do I pretend to be normal?

To Be Perfectly Honest

I've never exactly felt "normal,"
thanks to the circumstances
of my life. And, to be even more
honest, I actually feel more

normal now, knowing how many
other girls' lives don't fit the usual
definition of the word and yet
share so many strange facets.

There are more imperfect diamonds
than flawless stones. So, what
the hell? I'll give it a try, and do
my best to keep moving forward.

Hey, with luck, maybe Pastor
Martin's shtick will rub off and
I'll make the journey "cleansed
of my transgressions." Wouldn't

that be brilliant? Meanwhile,
I'm working diligently to finish
my assignments quickly and earn
decent grades. It's the first time

since I was a little kid that I've
felt compelled to excel at something,
and I'm discovering my mind
is every bit as important as my body.

My Love for Language

Has been rekindled. I first found
it back in Barstow, in Ms. Felton's
creative writing class. The one
where I met Alex—all spiky hair

and heavy eyeliner and I thought
she was amazing before we ever
hung out together. And maybe
I'll have to write that memory

>for Ms. Cox, who teaches English
>with a heavy lean toward creative
>writing. *Every one of you has stories*
>*to share with the world,* she says,
>
>*and you must tell them the way only*
>*you can. If I asked you all to write*
>*the same story, still it would be*
>*different from one another's because*
>
>*each of you will tell it in your own way,*
>*choosing specific words and syntax.*
>*That is your voice, and it's as unique*
>*to you as the voice you speak with.*

In reply, most of the girls groan,
but they claim to hate writing,
anyway. A few of us take up
the challenge, and I embrace it.

We Write

Happy memories. I struggle
to come up with one of those,
and find it buried beneath
a deep pile of resentments.

It was the first Christmas
we spent with Gram, and there
was a tree—a real tree, our first!—
with ornaments we made ourselves.

Not beautiful by any means,
but spending that time as a family,
stringing popcorn and cranberries
and making paper chains, was new.

We also write sadness,
and I don't have to look too hard
to pull a short chapter from
my personal history. I only had

to go back a few weeks ago,
to the day Alex and I parted
ways. Although, as I admit
in my paper, she and I had truly

split quite a while before our
formal goodbye, and that's where
I found the true wellspring
of my sorrow. Faded love.

This Morning

Ms. Cox has a new assignment.
Today let's write about fear.
First, an exercise. I want you to
concentrate on sensory details.

So take out a piece of paper
and tell me how fear smells.
How it tastes. How it sounds.
How it looks. Feels. One or two

sentences for each sense, and
be creative. You are artists,
painting pictures with words.
Fear isn't pastel. Be bold. Brave.

This should be easy. For all
the sadness I've experienced,
fear is a more present companion.
I have to take a couple of deep

breaths to breast stroke through
the recollections. Now I pick up
my pencil and write. Fear smells
like nicotine-tainted fingers, playing

with an unwashed pecker poking
from piss-damp boxers. Bold?
I think so. I continue. Fear tastes
like the whiskey-soaked lips of your love,

whispering a long goodbye.
That one is fresh, and personal.
Fear is the sound of fingernails,
scratching linoleum, seeking escape

from the monster clawing behind.
Nothing brave about that,
but it's something I know well.
Fear looks like a crow, circling closer

and closer until its black pearl eyes
come even with your own. Heavy
with symbolism, but also drawn
from experience. Fear feels like

waiting for the phone to ring,
certain the caller will inform you
that your little brother is dead.
Definitely not pastel. That memory

is bloodred, and though I try
really hard not to let it surface,
sometimes it does—a sharp photo
of Sandy lying in the street after

being hit by a motorcycle.
I should have been there, watching
him instead of hanging out downtown.
Thank God he survived, and healed.

We Go Around the Room

Sharing what we've written.
Some girls clearly didn't get
it, and their papers are mostly
blank. Others scribbled madly.

From Lena: *Fear is the sound*
of my father's belt, unbuckling.
Plenty to think about there.
Sometimes I'm glad my father

didn't stick around long enough
for me to get to know him well.
If he was married to Iris, he must
be the world's biggest loser.

From Brielle: *Fear tastes like*
the oily, smoky barrel of a gun.
Another bold picture for you,
Ms. Cox. Is that what you expected?

And from my roomie, Miranda:
Fear feels like a snake, wrapping
around and around your throat
and squeezing tighter and tighter

until the light goes all the way
out. And after that comes a gang
rape. Wonder if Ms. Cox might
prefer something more in sepia.

If So

She doesn't mention it, or
even look surprised at the things
she's heard, including what
I wrote. The other girls aren't

shocked, either, although
my "fear smells like" sentence
does elicit a fair amount of laughter,
mostly because the majority

of girls here have been in that
exact situation. Which makes me
wonder about Ms. Cox and her
relative lack of reaction. Was she

ever in the life? Thinking about
it, I'm guessing no, or she probably
would have changed her last name.
That makes me giggle, so I'm glad

     the other girls are still laughing
     about unwashed pecker and piss-damp
     boxers. But now, Ms. Cox reins us in.
     Okay, since you've got solid

     sensory details to bring this story
     to life, I want you to write about
     a time when you were frightened.
     Make your readers feel your fear.

Won't That Depend

On who my readers are?
I mean, if I wrote about
my "breaking in" by one
of my mother's men,

the story wouldn't bother
these girls, though it might
scare the hell out of some
innocent virgin somewhere.

Oh, well. Ms. Cox never
mentioned audience, so I'll go
with whatever first comes
to mind. I have to think for

a few minutes. Fear. I close
my eyes, fall backward in time.
Way, way back into childhood.
I was a kid once, wasn't I?

And there was a time long
before moving in with Gram
when Iris was still "Mommy."
We moved around, spent lots

of time on military bases,
living with a lineup of men,
and I find myself on a lopsided
sofa, watching cartoons.

I Start My Story There

Mommy says I'm a big girl, so I'm in
charge while she's gone. Mary Ann's
asleep in her dirty old crib. Her diaper
smells like poo, but it's dark outside,

and the light is burned out so I can
only see by the TV. _Scritch-scratch._
What's moving across the floor? Ew!
Giant brown bugs, two of them, with

clicking shells and antennas that twitch
sideways. I pull my feet up onto the couch,
which smells like cigarettes and beer
and something I don't have a name for,

but it stains the cushions crusty white.
Suddenly, there's banging on the door.
Iris! Let me in! It's Wes. Where's his key?
I start to get up, but with a loud crash,

the door flies open. _Where the fuck is Iris?_
That makes Mary Ann wake up, crying.
Wes stomps closer, eyes wide and weird,
reflecting the TV's glow. His mouth leaks

booze-stinking spit and he screams, _I said,_
where's your fucking mother? I draw back
against the arm of the sofa, try to crawl
into the crack there, but Mary Ann's wailing

makes Wes mad. <u>Shut up!</u> he yells, shaking
the rail, which only makes her cry harder.
He reaches into the crib, but I know he'll hurt
her. "No! Stop. I'll take care of her. Mommy's

next door at Steve's." Ken spins, and I think
he'll leave us alone, but he grabs hold
of me, tucks me under one arm, and now
I smell onion sweat. I'm facedown, watching

the ground move below, dizzying. Tread
the steps, across the dead grass, toward
the neighbor's, Wes's anger beating palpably.
<u>Hey, Iris! I've got your little girl!</u> Bam!

He kicks in the door, and there's Mommy,
and now I notice the knife in his hand.
<u>You been screwing around, whore?</u> He puts me
down, but doesn't let go. Instead, he holds

the blade to my throat. <u>Come here, Iris. It's you
or her.</u> I see Mommy smile. Feel a sharp sting.
Look down as red dollops fall onto my shirt . . .
The story ends with shirtless Steve, who

went out the bedroom window, around
the house, and sneaked in from behind,
resting his pistol against Wes's temple.
Iris laughed and laughed and laughed.

A Poem by Bud Parnell
My Story Nears Its Conclusion

Not quite two years
since my sweetheart let go
of her pain, emptied
these rooms of love, and

still hear her whispers
fall soft against my pillow
in the deep indigo sea
of night. How do I ignore the

I

hunger

to hold her again, spend
just one more hour together?
And my son, my Seth.
If I could change a thing
it would be the need for you

to leave

the path to damnation
you chose. I sit, drowning
sorrow in a bottle, look out
over the fields, harvested
and soon fallow, consider
the coming freeze and

this

I wonder: is the blossoming
pain in my chest more than
just a broken heart? I pull
a weary breath, knowing
my time is short in this

world.

Seth
Choreographing a New Show

Is apparently time-consuming.
David has been working overtime,

which bothers me not at all. I enjoy
his company, but I'm not lonely

without it, and when he comes home,
despite the long hours he puts in,

he seems energized. Maybe it's just
passion for creation, or maybe it's got

everything to do with white lines
snorted in dressing rooms. Probably both.

I'm glad he refuses to maintain a stash
here, or I might be tempted to indulge

far more often than I do. I like the cool,
numbing escape; love the delicious rush

of goose bumps and shivers. But not
enough to lose the "me" I've worked hard

to find and encourage in a more positive
direction. Coke is more addictive than

alcohol, and that's saying a lot. I'm trying
desperately to keep a handle on both.

At First

I thought the reason David won't keep
drugs in this place was because he worried

about getting ripped off by his staff
or me. Turns out, he's just paranoid

about losing the house in a raid. But,
if he were to think about it logically,

law enforcement must have some idea
about what goes on here at the parties.

Seems like all the city's movers and
shakers attend them, and that probably

includes a politician or ten, and maybe
even a keeper-of-the-peace or two.

Even without actually witnessing
him use, it's not much of a stretch

to conclude famed choreographer
David Burroughs has a tidy drug habit

himself. Ah, show business, especially
Sin City show biz! Sexy girls. Sexy boys.

And enough stimulation to keep both
going all hours of the day and night.

To Keep

From falling into the same trap,
I have to stay busy, and not just with

Have Ur Cake entertainment. I need
something wholesome in my life, so

I'm volunteering at a center serving
LGBTQ youth. At eighteen, I'm old

enough to work here, but young enough
so queer teens will feel comfortable

hanging out with me. I can't officially
counsel them, but I can share my own

experiences and try to help them become
more at ease about living in their unique

gay skins. For kids sleeping on the street,
there are showers and food, as well as

an Internet café and ways to have
fun, including movies and games.

Not all YouCenter clients are homeless.
Many have parents, the majority of whom

have no clue how to talk to their kids
about what it means to be gay.

Some of our teens haven't yet confessed
their sexuality to anyone beyond

these walls. They come, looking for
answers, but more often, they come

in search of communion with people
like themselves. People like me, and

most of the staff. The great thing for
me is, I'm actually building friendships

with gay people who aren't bartering
their bodies to survive. I almost feel . . .

Dare I think it, let alone say it out loud?
It's only when I'm here, not at David's,

not while sitting in a bar, waiting for
a "date." Only here. Normal. There.

Thought it out loud. The last time I felt
anything close to this was so long ago

I didn't know enough to consider myself
different. Once I did, however, it became

pretty much all I could think about.
I'm different. I'm weird. I'm damned.

One Excellent Thing

About volunteering at the YouCenter
is it doesn't bother David at all, so not

only can I come here at will, I can also
use it as an excuse when Lydia calls.

Today, however, I'm really at the center,
and currently playing a game of pool

with Charlie, aka Charlene, who is not
only one pretty cute lesbian, she's also

kicking my butt. "Hey, man. Who taught
you to shoot pool? I think I need a lesson."

> Bam! She sinks another one. *My dad.*
> *Back when we still used to talk.* And . . .

> Ka-blam! In goes the eight ball. Game
> over. She looks up, smiling. *Had enough?*

"Hell, no. Rack 'em up, woman.
But I get to go first this time."

> *Sure. Like it will do any good.* She dances
> around the table, collecting balls from

the pockets. "I don't talk to my dad, either,"
I tell her, drawing a bead on my break.

*You don't talk to him, or he won't talk
to you?* She watches me spectacularly

miss the shot. *Don't choke up on the cue
so much. You shoot like a girl, by the way.*

That makes me laugh. "I want to shoot
just like you do, and you're a girl."

*Some people would argue with that
observation. And don't change the subject.*

"Fine. My dad kicked me out last year,
two months before I graduated, in fact.

So instead of finishing high school,
I ran off to Las Vegas with my partner

at the time. . . ." No need to confess
the lurid particulars. "Now, Dad refuses

to talk to me. I've tried calling several
times. He asks if I've decided I'm straight,

and when I can't tell him yes, he suggests
a heart-to-heart with God, and hangs up."

*I'm sorry. My parents, at least, will let
me stay until graduation. We don't converse*

much, but we quit talking before I came
out. You're not from Vegas, then?

I shake my head. "Indiana born and
raised right there on the farm . . ."

The last word lifts a cloud of nostalgia.
Were the crops good this year? I tilled

the fields right before I left. Did Dad
get the harvest in by himself okay?

I have to stop thinking about home.
"But is *anyone* actually *from* Vegas?"

> Charlie raises her hand. *Yup. Believe*
> *it or not, one or two of us came into this*
>
> *world right here in Sin City. It's funny,*
> *because everyone assumes anyone living*
>
> *here must be liberal and morally bankrupt.*
> *Well, they haven't met my dad, who's about*
>
> *the most conservative asshole who ever*
> *lived. Not one hundred percent sure*
>
> *about his morals, but I think he's got*
> *at least a few left intact. How about you?*

What Is She Asking?

"How about me, what?
Do you mean, am I liberal?

Or morally bankrupt?"
Her answer is a massive shrug.

Okay, then. I have to think
about how to respond. Let's see.

Gay? Makes me a liberal,
at least in Indiana, where

leaning left is not exactly
celebrated. Gun rights? Used to

go hunting with my dad, and
target shooting with a black

powder rifle kind of turns me
on. Probably conservative.

Enjoys a good buzz?
Could go either way.

"Politically, I suppose I'm
a white line kind of guy. . . ."

Oops. Freudian slip. "Uh,
meaning middle of the road.

Call me an Independent, I guess,
not that I'm registered to vote."

      She bristles. You are eighteen,
      yes? Because, left, right or

      "middle of the road," you have
      a voice, and damn it, we need

      more queer voices shouting
      that we won't be ignored, and while

      we might be underrepresented,
      we're no less consequential

      than all those straight, white
      evangelical voters who somehow

      believe they matter more than
      anyone who doesn't look or think

      or dissect biblical scriptures
      exactly the way they do. Get it?

"Jeez, Charlie, catch your breath
before you turn blue. I know

you're right. I just haven't gotten
around to it, but I promise I will."

Passionate

That word describes Charlene
Tate, and it's only one reason

I like her so much. Maybe
the biggest one is because

she likes me, and has zero
ulterior motive for palling

around with me. It's been a long
time since I've had a friend, and

now I second-guess myself. "Hey,
Charlie. We're friends, aren't we?"

> She glances up from the table,
> confused. *Well, sure. Why?*

> *You're not going to ask if you
> can borrow money, are you?*

"Do you have any?" God,
she's funny. "Just kidding.

No, I was just thinking how
nice it is to make a new friend.

Then it struck me that you
might not feel the same way."

Especially Not

If she actually knew everything
about me. Which brings us back

to moral bankruptcy. Who am I
really? Indiana Seth, or the Seth

I've forced myself to become?
I realize suddenly that Charlie

is standing there, waiting, hands
on her hips, as if I missed something

important. "I'm sorry. Lost in
my thoughts. What did you say?"

> *I said friends are hard to come by,*
> *so I'm happy we met, as long as you*
>
> *realize I'm pretty much always broke.*
> *So . . . what were you thinking about?*

I retreat again into half-truths.
"Unlikely friendships. Chance

meetings. Getting my butt whupped
at pool by a girl. And home." That

is the complete truth, and I know
I've got to try harder to reach Dad.

124

Unlike Charlie

My wallet is comfortably fat,
so I invite her to get a bite with

me, which turns out to be a good
thing because by the time I get home

the Friday night festivities have already
kicked into gear. This time, the party

is relatively small—mostly the cast
of David's new show, I'm guessing,

plus significant others and hangers-on.
Immediately, I climb out of my "regular

gay kid" disguise, move into the role
of party boy. As usual, David holds court

poolside. I grab a drink from the bar,
head over to say hello, working hard

to look like I absolutely belong here
after questioning that idea for the past

several hours. David's entourage
consists of dancers—men and women,

and all stunning. Handpicked as much
for beauty as for the talent they must

possess to have made it this far
in such a cutthroat market.

The show's producer is also here,
so David is distracted, entertaining

his moneyman, and that's all good
by me. I let him know I'm home,

withdraw to a quiet Adirondack chair,
away from the revelry, where I can

better meditate with my bourbon.
I'm looking up at the auburn night

sky, wondering where the hell the stars
are hiding, when a husky voice behind

me inquires, *Want some company,
or would you rather be alone?*

He materializes from the shadows,
and I think he must be a Greek god,

with copper skin and topaz eyes
and soft waves of burnt-sienna hair.

"Please." I gesture toward the adjacent
chair. "Make yourself comfortable.

I'm Seth." I offer my hand, and
when he accepts it, we both smile

>at the exchange of energy. *Great
>to meet you, Seth. I'm Micah. You*

>*sure I'm not interrupting communion
>with the universe or something?*

"Nothing as lofty as that, and I'm
happy to have someone to talk to

besides God, who I'm pretty sure
disowned me a while ago, anyway."

>*Oh, I doubt that. God tends to favor
>the most beautiful of his creations.*

I've never before experienced
instant mutual attraction, but I'm

pretty sure that's what this is, unless . . .
I don't want to sound paranoid.

How do I ask? "So, how do you
know David? Are you in his show?"

>*I am. I'm a principal.* There's pride
>in his voice. *What about you?*

127

We Talk

Until the party breaks up—hours.
Micah's twenty, and from California,

where it's mostly okay to be gay.
He's confident. Strong. Straight-up

gorgeous, and for whatever reason,
he's impressed by me, despite

> the fact I have no real direction.
> *You're only eighteen. You don't have*

> *to know where you're headed yet.*
> *Maybe I can help you find your passion.*

Little doubt about that, at least
if we get the chance, and I'm certain

we will. The chemistry between us
is palpable. I'll have to be careful

that it escapes David's notice. I wait
for him to go inside before inviting

Micah back into the shadows.
I haven't kissed a boy, lips on lips,

since Loren. But I'm kissing one
now, and it's soaked with promise.

A Poem by Kyra Lang
Into the Shadows

That's where Whitney
needs to fade,
like the vampire she is.
People might think
it cruel that I can find

       no

sympathy for the sister
who was once my playmate,
if never quite my friend.
But, while I do

       hope

she can claw her way
out of the pit she jumped
into, eyes wide open,
I see little need

       for

offering my hand,
only to have it bitten
again and again and again.

       Whitney's

a hungry bloodsucker,
willing to drain this family
dry in her misdirected search
for love, and any expectation of

       redemption

dissolves like a rainbow
in burgeoning sun
when I look into her eyes.

Whitney
One Thing About Rehab

You're pretty much guaranteed
to meet new dope connections,
in case that happens to interest
you, considering why you're here.
The funny thing is, if you want
illicit substances, you don't have
to go very far. They're on-site.

Rumor has it they come in with
one or two members of the staff,
but more often on our weekly
Sunday visiting day. And when
they arrive that way, they might
be hidden in flower wrappers
or the hem of someone's skirt.
Mostly they're pills, but I hear
every now and again the Lady
will make an appearance. I can
leave the pills alone, but I'm afraid
if I see heroin I'll give in to temptation.

Of course, I'd need money, at least
after the first time, and I have no
available cash. So maybe I'll be
okay. I really don't want to take
that ride again, but I'm not the strongest
person in the world, and just thinking
about dropping down the shaft
into purgatory makes my mouth water.

I've Tried

Talking to Naomi about it,
in fact asked for a meeting
today to discuss it specifically,
but she can't bring herself to
agree that there could reasonably
be a problem. Her response:

> *Have you actually seen drugs
> in this facility? No? Then I suggest
> you keep quiet about that possibility
> until you do. We work extremely
> hard to maintain a drug-free
> program, and even a hint of
> impropriety could make our job
> a lot more difficult. Understand?*

"Sure." I say it, knowing that's
what she wants to hear. But when
her expression turns smug, I change
my mind. "It's just, I'm worried
if someone offers me powdered
goods, I won't be able to say no."

> *That's why you're here—to learn
> how to say no. What happens
> when you leave? Do you think
> all drugs will magically disappear?
> You have to want to stay clean,
> and you have to reach deep down
> inside to find strength of character.
> Let's give you some tools to do that.*

A Half Hour Later

I've got "tools in my recovery
toolbox," as Naomi put it.
They sound pretty basic to me,
and I'm relatively sure I could
have written this list on my own:

One: Find a trusted acquaintance
I can confide in, especially
when I feel like backsliding.
Programs like Alcoholics or
Narcotics Anonymous would call
this person my "sponsor."

Two: Join one or both said programs.

Three: Avoid old friends who might
tempt me down the rabbit hole.

Four: Make new, wholesome friends,
who'd never, ever use and abuse.

Five: Work very hard on rebuilding
relationships with my family.

Six: Keep in mind the times I'll
be more likely to succumb—when
I'm tired, lonely, hungry, or angry.

Seven: Find fun in simple things.
Dancing. Biking. Swinging.
Singing. Long walks on the beach.

There Are Problems

With all seven tools.

One: Who the hell might
that be? I don't trust one single
soul on this pathetic planet.

Two: Sit around confessing
my history and feelings to strangers,
most of whom are just as messed
up as I am? Not going to happen.

Three: If I do that, I won't have
any friends at all. Everyone
I'm comfortable around hangs
out through the looking glass.

Four: See three.

Five: Rebuilding relationships
is a two-way street. Only Mom
seems interested in reconstruction.

Six: Even if I force myself to
eat three massive meals every
day and get the requisite eight
hours of sleep, I'm almost always
lonely, and regularly pissed off.

Seven: Long walks on the beach
will forevermore remind me
of how very much I miss Bryn.

Not Sure

How it's possible
to miss the person
who brought me down
in such a profound way.

He lied to me, and not
only that, but he lied
about loving me, and
that is unforgiveable.

He used me, almost
all the way up. Pimped
me out for his own
selfish purposes. Hurt
me by allowing me to
be abused by a long
parade of johns.

He hooked me on
the vicious Lady, to
keep me at his mercy
completely, and within
that addiction, he made
me suffer. He swore
I was beautiful, and
then he made me ugly.

I won't forgive him.
But how do I forget
him when I can't fall
out of love with him?

I Don't Mention That

To Naomi, who's heard it
before, and won't accept
my emotional attachment
to a man she views as evil.
She isn't totally wrong.

Neither do I argue tools and
toolboxes with her.
She's only doing her job,
and it doesn't include
convincing me, just repeating
the stuff she tells everyone.
Before I can leave, however,
she tosses a wrench at me.

> *One last thing that might*
> *help your recovery, especially*
> *in the early stages, when*
> *things are likely to be most*
> *difficult. Find a purpose, and*
> *I don't mean just returning*
> *to school and getting decent*
> *grades. Try volunteering*
> *somewhere—at an animal*
> *shelter, or maybe mentoring*
> *a child who needs help learning*
> *to read. Retrain your focus*
> *away from yourself, toward*
> *others. Happiness requires*
> *cultivation. I'm here to show*
> *you how to plant seeds of change.*

Planting Seeds of Change

Sounds good, and that's what
I tell her, right before I go.
But the truth is, I'm scared
of change. Every time I try
it, something goes wrong.

Still, I'll be out of this place
in a few days. I've only been
here three months, and I'm not
sure I'm ready to go, but there
it is. Rehab costs a ton, and while
Mom would probably like to see
me stay longer, Dad's paying
the bill, and I don't think
he believes seeds of change
have actually been planted.

Maybe he's right, because
the idea of going home scares
the crap out of me. What if I
go ahead and relapse right here
instead? Would he have to let
me stay then? Wow. I might
have found the solution.

There's still the problem with
having no cash. What could I
barter? The answer comes rushing
at me, slams against my gut.
Duh. My body is a commodity.
I just have to find the right dealer.

Now That a Different Seed

Has burrowed into my brain,
it sprouts and grows quickly.
I've overheard this girl, Dana,
talking about disguising
her highs. I seek her out, hoping
Naomi et al. will be happy
I'm making a new friend.

I find her, just finishing breakfast,
plop down across the table.
"Hey. Delicious cardboard
pancakes, yeah?" She looks up
from her plate, offers a smile.

> *Frisbees, you mean?* Dana
> swallows what's left of hers
> anyway, then asks, *Did you
> need something from me?*

"I was wondering if you might
happen to know where I could
score something to help me sleep.
Every time I actually doze off,
these goddamn nightmares wake
me back up. I'd give just about
anything to stay out an entire night."

> She looks me right in the eye,
> trying to figure out where I'm
> coming from. Whatever she sees
> seems to satisfy her. *I might.*

But that's all she says, so I go
ahead and add, "The only problem
is I don't have any money, so I'd
have to work out a trade."

        She studies me harder. *What*
        do you want, and what can
        you give in exchange for it?

I shrug. "Powder or pills,
doesn't really matter. What
I've got is a talent for great
sex." Still, she makes me wait.

        How old are you, anyway?
        And are you really sure you
        want to fuck up your rehab?

"I'm sixteen. Age of consent
in California, so whoever is safe
that way. And yes, I'm sure, or
I wouldn't be asking. Will you
help me, or point me to someone
else who will? I'll be generous."

        My delivery arrives on Sunday.
        She reaches her hand across
        under the table, rests it on my knee.
        So have you ever been with a girl?

The Unexpected Question

Gives me pause.
I figured she'd hook me
up with a male staff
member who'd cut loose
with a finder's fee.

The truth is, though
I've been with more
men than I want to
consider, I haven't ever
had sex with a girl.
But how hard could
it be? "Of course."
The lie slips past
my lips like custard.

> *You're pretty. I can*
> *spare a couple of pills.*
> *No powder. Too risky.*
> *Sunday night, my room,*
> *after lights-out. I promise*
> *you'll sleep like a baby,*
> *no dreams, good or bad.*
> *Until then . . . She flicks*
> her tongue, serpentlike.
> *You can dream about me.*

Now That I've Determined

A course of action,
I can hardly wait to put
the car into gear, even if
it might mean motoring
over a very steep cliff.

I've chosen a dangerous
route, and yet I feel safer
than I did an hour ago.
Not like my morals
are going to take a hit.
Guys. Girls. What can
it possibly matter?

I suppose I might have
believed I could put
Las Vegas all the way
behind me. But something
like that tails a person,
teeth bared for the bite,
doesn't it? Guess I'll have
to develop a tough butt.

God knows the rest of me
is tougher. I think back
to Lucas, how devastated
I was learning he never
cared about me at all.
I was just a little girl
seven months ago.
What am I now?

I Don't Feel Guilty

Until Sunday, when I, too,
have a visitor—my mom,
who arrives all excited about
the prospect of my coming
home at the end of the week.
We sit out on the patio,
bundled against the chill.
The sun does its best, but
it's no match for the sharp
November breeze.

> Mom doesn't seem to notice.
> *So, I've talked to your school,*
> *and it's no problem for you to*
> *start midterm. They'll bring*
> *you in for an assessment next*
> *month to see how far you've*
> *managed to catch up, okay?*

I nod, robotlike, knowing
it doesn't matter at all what
they've got planned. Safe.

> *You won't believe this, but*
> *I'm actually going to attempt*
> *to cook Thanksgiving dinner.*
> *I've been taking some culinary*
> *classes, and I think I can manage*
> *it, with your and Kyra's help.*
> *She's flying home for the weekend.*
> *I want us to feel like a family.*

Yeah, well, good luck with that.
I half listen to her talk about
everything she's got planned for me,
though she frames it with the word
"us." Through the window, I see
Dana talking with her visitor,
who might be her sister. They
look alike. All I can think about
now is what's coming later,
and anticipation creeps along
my spine, manifesting itself
in a huge crop of goose bumps.

> Mom notices me shiver. *Cold?*
> *Let's go inside. I should probably*
> *think about leaving anyway.*
> *Whitney? I want you to know*
> *how proud I am of you for*
> *hanging tough in the program*
> *and digging yourself out.*
> *I was so scared for you. And me.*
> *I know I haven't told you enough,*
> *but I love you very much, and*
> *I promise to do better as a mother.*

She gets to her feet and I join
her for the short walk to
the front door, noticing
Dana's wink as we pass.
Despite guilt, game on.

142

Fortuitously

Dana's room is only three doors
away from mine. I wait almost
an hour after lights-out before
venturing down the hall and
slipping inside. She waits for me
in bed, two little tablets in hand.
"What are they?" I ask, hoping

> for the exact answer she gives.
> *Oxycodone. You into opiates?*

Oh, darling, if you only knew.
"I'll try anything once." I pop
one, put the other into my pocket
to save for right before our next
drug test. Tonight I'm going to
sink down, down, down. It's a slow,
lovely drop, and oh, how I've longed
for this feeling! Denial is pointless.

> *Okay, baby. Payment required.*
> *Take off your clothes. Sex is better*
> *naked.* She watches me strip, pulls
> back her covers, and I shimmy in
> beside her already nude body.
> *There's a pretty girl. Kiss me.*

The one thing I never did with
a john was kiss them, or let them
kiss me. But, even as a form of payment,
kissing Dana isn't so bad. In fact, it's nice.

Maybe it's the oxy, or maybe it's
because she's a girl, not in spite
of that fact, or maybe it's just because
I've missed being intimate with anyone,
but the heat of her skin, which is satin
soft, and the rich perfume of her
femaleness turns me on completely.

No, I've never been with a woman
before, but everything feels familiar,
from the curves of her heavy breasts
to the invitation between her slim thighs,
and my mouth and tongue and fingers
know exactly what to do to pay my debt
in full. She signals the end with a shudder

> and quiet moan, then draws me
> into her arms, laying my head
> against her chest, where I can hear
> the stutter of her heart. *That was*
> *outstanding. I'll expect you back*
> *tomorrow night.* When I start to
> question her, she shushes me.
> *Those are eighty-milligram oxys,*
> *and go for thirty a pop. How*
> *much do you think you're worth?*

Good question.

A Poem by Andrew McCarran
How Much Is It Worth

To discover the girl
who infuses every day
with light, even when
she's not here—it's enough
to know she's woven into your

life,

a luminous ribbon.
A promise of happiness.
How much can be forgiven,
when the excuse

is

existence, no other way
to reach tomorrow?
Morality becomes

meaningless

when you're wandering
the streets, the way home
lost to you. Forbidden.
What is the future

without

hope for a rainbow
on the far side of the storm,
no hint of sunshine
to shimmer through the gray
in a world emptied of

Eden.

Eden
Last Week

I chickened out. I swore to
myself I'd tell Sarah everything
she wanted to know about
my background: Boise; Pastor
Streit, Assembly of God minister,

not to mention my father; evil, in
Mama disguise; my younger sister,
Eve. I hope she's okay. She always
was smarter about dealing
with our parents than I. She'll be

a freshman this year, at least
if she pretends to do exactly
what Mama tells her, and
wouldn't our mother be surprised
to know that my little sister

is every bit as rebellious as I am?
Was. The rebellion has kind of
been shaken out of me. Damn.
That thought makes me sad,
because it means Mama won.

So yeah, I took the coward's way
out. Kept my mouth shut, and
now I regret it, mostly because
I just got another e-mail from Andrew.
He's the only person in the whole

world who can help me rebuild
my confidence, which makes
perfect sense, since he was the one
who built it for me in the first place.
Knowing he thought me worthy

of his love was all I ever needed.
And now, he cyber promises
he'll love me, no matter what.
My beautiful Eden. Desperation
drives people to places they'd never

ever go otherwise. Whatever
horrors you suffered in the desert,
whatever lengths you decided
were necessary to remove yourself
from that place, I stand firmly

in your corner. You don't need
forgiveness. The person I must
learn to forgive is myself. I could
see trouble brewing, and I chose
to love you selfishly. I won't make

that mistake in the future. I promise.
I'd give everything I own to hold
you again. Tell me how to find you.
Tell me what I have to do to get
you back in my life. Your Andrew.

My Andrew

Straightforward, like Andrew
himself. I wish I could believe
it can be as easy as telling him
where to find me. Come to Vegas.
I'll meet you just off the strip,

where I once gave a tooth-impaired
guy a BJ for twenty dollars.
Of course, if *you* want oral sex, no
charge other than your continued
misplaced faith in me. In us.

I need to be pragmatic. Believing
in miracles is what led me here
to start with. "Hey, Almighty, giving
source of love, please bless the unlikely
love I've found with Andrew.

Remember how I asked you that,
not even a year ago? Remember the faith
I invested in you, despite the example
my father, 'your representative on
earth,' demonstrated on a daily basis?"

Am I actually talking to God, and
not only that, but talking out loud?
Glad there's no one close by to hear me.
Pretty sure everyone at Walk Straight
has given up any notion of him, if they

had one to begin with. Little
evidence of God in the backseat
of a john's car, or some seedy
motel room, and even less in
the eyes of your pimp when he's

beating you while ranting about
your failures as a good little
prostitute. Almost every girl here
tells a similar story of being scooped
up by some predatory man when

it was obvious they had nowhere
else to go. Runaways, most of them.
I suppose if I'd been on the street
for very much longer, some smooth-
talking guy would have latched

onto me, convinced me I'd be safer
in his care than on my own. A few
more days, struggling to eat and
clean the ugliness from my body,
I probably would have been grateful

for the intervention. Instead, I found
a helpful priest. So maybe God was
watching out for me after all. I whisper,
"Father, forgive me. And if it's your
will, please bless Andrew and me."

My Counseling Session

Is after lunch, which I can't eat
because of the nerves tap dancing
in my stomach. I practically crawl
to Sarah's office, coaxing myself
the whole way to go ahead and tell

my entire tale of woe. I knock on
the door, hoping something has called
her away, but no such luck. Instead,
she invites me in with that chirpy
voice, and I have no choice but to

      comply. A whooshing fills my ears
      as I sit across the desk from Sarah.
      She takes one look at the way I'm
      shaking and gushes, *What's wrong,*
      Ruthie? Did you see a vampire?

That makes me giggle. "A vampire?
Don't you mean a ghost?" I must look
as pallid-faced as I feel. "Anyway, no.
I didn't see either. It's just . . ." Go on.
Reach deep for the courage you need.

"I think it's time for me to tell you
some stuff. First of all, my name
isn't Ruthie. It's Eden. Eden Ruth Streit,
and my parents aren't dead (at least,
I don't think so), and I'm from Boise. . . ."

Ice Broken

It all comes gushing out,
as if a dam breaks inside
me. I rush the telling,
sure if I slow down I'll grind
to a complete halt. I notice

Sarah nodding, but she stays
silent, like she intuits my fear
of stopping before the climax.
I know this can't surprise her,
that she's heard plenty of awful

things before, but when I get
to the part about Tears of Zion
and Jerome, her eyes grow
wider and wider, and when
she finally gets the chance to

      speak, she says, *I've just been*
      reading up on teen boot camp
      horror stories. Your Tears of Zion
      wasn't mentioned, but there are
      several similar places that

      invoke conservative religious
      values to abuse their clients.
      Most parents, however, don't have
      any idea about their practices,
      which include isolation, denial

of food, water, and the ability
to use the bathroom. Sometimes
they get shut down, but usually
they just move and set up shop
somewhere else. It's very hard

to regulate them because often
they operate as "private schools,"
which have a whole different
regulatory process than, say,
rehab facilities or public entities.

Thank you, God! She believes
me! A huge knot of tension
tumbles from my shoulders,
and a warm wave of relief
washes over me. Still, tears

spill onto my cheeks. "I thought
everyone would think I was
lying. The only thing is, Mama
knew what was going on, and
she left me there anyway."

Are you sure, Ru—I mean, Eden?
From everything I read, parents
rarely have a clue about what
goes on in these places. Why
would your mother leave you if . . .

She Trails Off

Noticing the way my face
turns to marble. "I guess
you'll have to ask her that.
I assume you'll need to be
in touch with them. But

do you really have to?
I'm so scared that if you
send me back to Boise,
they'll make me return
to Tears of Zion. Mama

says I'm possessed, claimed
by Satan, and she really,
truly believes that. Please,
please, find a way to keep
me at Walk Straight. I'll do

anything—work here for free,
or go to work somewhere else
and pay you to let me stay.
Whatever it takes. I can't go
home!" But now, she's shaking

> her head, no. *I wish I could*
> *tell you okay, Eden, but the law*
> *is very clear that I must report*
> *your whereabouts to your legal*
> *guardians, who happen to be*

your parents in this case.
They have a right to know
you're alive and safe. Besides,
what about your young man?
She's completely missed the point.

Still, I knew this was not
only possible, but probable.
I'll find a way to make it work.
And she's right about Andrew,
if nothing else. "I understand.

Do whatever you have to do.
But is there a way for me to
maybe talk to a judge about
emancipation?" The word swims
out of my subconscious.

That is a possibility. As long as
you're at least sixteen, as per
Nevada law, you can petition
the court. You're seventeen, yes?
And when will you be eighteen?

"I just turned seventeen
last month. Right before I
came here, in fact." A birthday
to remember, alone on the street,
sleeping behind a Dumpster.

154

I Learn

The requirements
of emancipation,
which are pretty
much the same in
Idaho as in Nevada:

Must be at least sixteen.
Check.
Must be living away
from your parents.
Check.

Must have the financial
security to be independent.
Almost check.
Walk Straight can
help me find a job.

Must stay in school
until you're eighteen.
Check.
And this is where
things get tricky.

Both mother and father
must agree to let the child
emancipate.
Guess there's only one
way to find out.

I Also Learn

The pros and cons
of emancipation.
Pro: You can enter
into contracts without
a parent's signature.

Con: You can be sued
if you violate said contracts.
Pro: You can also sue
someone, if that's a priority.
Yeah, me? Sue who?

Con: Cannot drop out
of school without written
permission from
the school board. No problem.
I want to be educated.

Pro: Can go to the doctor
of your choice and parent
doesn't have to okay
treatment. Wonder if that
includes mental health.

And just FYI: Still can't vote
until age of majority; can't drink
till twenty-one. And worst
of all, can't marry without
parental consent until eighteen.

Which Brings Me Back

To Andrew. Everything seems
to. Six months ago, I believed
we would marry as soon as I
turned eighteen. Yes, I knew
that was young to make such

a momentous decision, but
the overwhelming love we felt
for each other trumped common
sense. Now, I don't know if
even the deepest affection

can overcome the reality
of who I am, what I've become.
This isn't a romance novel,
not that I've ever read one.
Mama would have gone off

the deep end had she ever
found me in possession
of a steamy confessional.
Wonder what she'll say when
she finds out what's become of me.

If she suspected Satan's handiwork
in my relationship with Andrew,
she'll have no doubt at all that
he's holding court inside me
once she's privy to why I'm here.

I Look at Sarah

Who stares back at me, and I see
something in her eyes. Something
dark. Hidden. Something like
a secret. Suddenly I know. "You
were in the life once, weren't you?"

> No hesitation. *Yes, Eden, I was,*
> *although the circumstances were*
> *somewhat different from those*
> *of most of the girls here. Once*
> *upon a time, I was a world-class*
>
> *gymnast, used to having all eyes*
> *on me. After a horrible fall,*
> *I could no longer compete or*
> *perform, but I still had a great body,*
> *and I was only nineteen. I did get*
>
> *a few TV commercials and stuff,*
> *but not enough to cover the drug*
> *dependency I'd developed after*
> *the injury and beyond. Someone*
> *suggested escorting with a high-*
>
> *priced service. Believe it or not,*
> *many failed athletes end up there,*
> *and celebrity has its advantages,*
> *including the level of clients who*
> *are willing to pay top dollar for it.*

She's so open about it, it's scary.
Why didn't I suspect it before?
"How long did you do it? And
what got you out? And why are
you here?" So many questions!

Sarah takes a deep breath.
*I escorted for a little over three
years. I can't say it was an awful
experience because, like I said,
the men who pay upwards of*

*a thousand dollars an hour for
your company tend to be looking
for exactly that, with fringe benefits,
of course. For the most part, they're
respectful, even kind, if a little kinky.*

*What got me out was two things.
The first was my boyfriend, who
found out what I was doing and
issued an ultimatum: Stay where
I was, or stay with him and he*

*would support me through rehab.
The second was watching younger
and younger girls being moved into
the business, and really coming to
understand just what was at stake.*

159

Which doesn't exactly explain
how she ended up here. "But why
did you get involved with Walk
Straight? You were already an
adult when you started escorting."

> *Yes, and there was some rather
> ugly lobbying being done by adult
> sex workers who don't like the term
> "sexual exploitation" because they
> say there's no coercion involved.*

> *But I saw teens who were promised
> the world and forced out on the streets.
> Maybe not where I was, but nearby.
> I decided to get my degree in social
> work and lobby on the other side.*

I glanced at her left hand, find
no telltale ring, ask the question,
though I'm afraid of her answer.
"So, what happened with your
boyfriend? Are you still together?"

> *No. But I'm with someone different
> now. He fell in love with me despite
> knowing about my past. It's all about
> the man. But trust me, you can't hide
> from the truth. It's persistent.*

A Poem by Veronica Carino
The Truth Is Persistent

Once, I believed it possible
to hide lies behind a wall
of plausibility, but the facade
always crumbles. The only way to

                                        help

rebuild any semblance
of trust's to come clean and
plunge into apology, hoping
you don't drown. I've always
managed to float, but that's

                                        me

and the depth of Cody's
deception is hard to reconcile.
When the details first became clear,
I thought it would be impossible to

                                        find

the compassion to go on
caring. But when I saw him
leaning into the opened arms
of death, a fierce sort of

                                        forgiveness

surfaced, transcending anger
and resentment, buoyed
by the tenacity
of my indestructible love

                                        for him.

Cody
How Do I Believe

Love is still possible
for a creature like me?
It's not just the half-man

that I've become who's
undeserving of the devotion
of someone like Ronnie,

or anyone at all. It's the person
I already was—the one
responsible for the rest—

whose right to even exist
I question. He's a liar.
Cheat. Hopeless addict.

Always seeking the easy
way out, and unable to admit
the horrible mistakes he was

making, despite the evidence
mounding right under his nose
and stinking like dog shit.

And now. Now there's no way
to turn back the clock and
choose another path, let alone

fix what he's done to his family,
his beautiful girl, his so-called
friends. Himself. All ruined.

Busting My Pity Bubble

Mom walks through the door, and
for once, all smiles. In fact, she's
humming. "What's up with you?"

> She comes over, kisses my forehead.
> *Your social worker has accomplished*
> *some magic. Apparently, Jack's*
>
> *medical insurance is still in force for*
> *you and me, and with Nevada expanding*
> *Medicaid under the Affordable Care Act,*
>
> *your bills here are pretty much covered.*
> *Plus, she found a rehab hospital*
> *with some charitable giving "angels"*
>
> *willing to take care of whatever costs*
> *insurance won't cover. You can move*
> *there and start your rehab as soon as*
>
> *your doctors say you're ready. It's*
> *supposed to be an amazing place, and*
> *I hear the food is a lot better, too.*

She laughs as if that's the funniest
thing ever. Hate to burst her own
bubble, but, "What if I don't want rehab?"

Her mouth snaps shut, and suddenly
she looks about seventy years old. "Can't
you just put me in a home or something?"

> *Yes, she can. Your* own *home, but not*
> *till after your inpatient rehab. After*
> *that, there will be more rehab, so shut*
>
> *your mouth and for God's sake, quit*
> *feeling sorry for yourself.* Ronnie stomps
> into the room and across the floor,

looking every bit the part of a pissed
little girl. Man, she is something.
Why did she have to come into my life

just as it was ending? She reaches the bed,
nods once at Mom, and plops her cute
little behind right down on the mattress.

It strikes me that she and my mother
have never met, except for in passing
at Jack's funeral. "Mom, this is—"

> *Your mom and I have met,* interrupts
> Ronnie. *In fact, together we have*
> *formed the Cody Bennett Fan Club*
>
> *and Two Woman Cheer Squad.*
> *Our mission is to get your ass out*
> *of that bed and on your feet again.*

Mom's Expression

Changes to smug.
I really don't get it.
I will never stand on

my feet again. My
head begins to twist
side to side. "Not

going to happen and
you know it. Why
don't you just leave

me alone? Go find a real
man. Someone who'll
love you the way you

deserve to be loved.
Seriously, Ronnie. I'm
a sinking ship. Don't

go down with me when
the lifeboat is empty
and waiting for you."

>Ronnie turns to face
>me straight on. *Last
>time I looked, assault*
>
>*was a crime punishable
>by jail time. Consider
>yourself lucky I'd rather*

not experience lockup,
or I just might slap you.
Instead, I'll do this. . . .

With zero regard for
my mom's presence,
Ronnie leans into me,

covers my mouth with
hers. Her lips are sticky
with cherry-flavored gloss.

The kiss is a slow ride
to heaven, and transports
me back to the post-funeral

afternoon we spent in bed,
sponging comfort from
the heat of our intertwined

bodies. If Mom wasn't
watching, I'd try to assess
the boner I must be wearing.

Muscles have memories,
right? Hey. What happens to
a catheter when your dick

gets hard? The sudden
thought makes me pull away.
Still, I say, "Thank you."

Hurt Surfaces

In her eyes, and her face grows
taut in response. *Thank you?*
That's the best you can do, Cody?

I know exactly what she wants
to hear, but if I say it, if I make
it real, I'll just open us both up

to disappointment. Mom looks
almost as eager as Ronnie for me
to admit it, and that makes it harder

yet. "Mom, could you please give
us a few minutes alone?" Her nod
is reluctant, but she leaves the room.

Once she's retreated, I hold out
my hands and Ronnie takes them
into her own. "Veronica Carino,

you are the most amazing girl
in the entire universe. And the fact
is, I fucking love you more than life

itself, which is why I want you to
find the person you deserve, and
that is so not me. . . ." She tries

to interrupt me again, but I shake
my head vehemently. "Listen to me!
It's not just because of my legs."

I pause to gather the courage
to continue the sordid confession,
and Ronnie actually sits there

patiently, not saying a word,
eyes glistening. "Please don't cry,
or I'll never be able to do this.

Look, it isn't just my 'condition.'
it's the stuff I was doing that
resulted in my being here. I told

you things that weren't true, and
didn't tell you things that were true,
and all I did for months was lie to you.

I didn't mean for any of it to happen,
but I was gambling, and couldn't stop,
and when I tried to dig myself out,

the only way I could come up with
was . . ." Goddamn it, how can I tell
her this? Fuck it. Just go for it. Push

her totally away. "The only way I could
come up with was working for an escort
service. That's what I was doing when . . ."

> I let my voice trail off, certain I've said
> more than enough to make her run.
> Instead, she looks me in the eye. *I know.*

Okay, I Did Not Expect That

Her acknowledgment is a complete
surprise, as is her calm acceptance.
"How?" Does Mom know, too?

> *From Vince. He told me everything,*
> *at least everything he knew, and*
> *the police, too. That guy, Chris,*
>
> *was at the poker game, remember?*
> *He followed you to that hotel room.*
> *Killed his girlfriend, and the other*
>
> *man. They said you were lucky*
> *you didn't die, too. He definitely meant*
> *to kill you. Oh. I'm not sure you know,*
>
> *but the other guys at the game were*
> *all called in as witnesses. It wasn't hard*
> *to track Chris down. When the cops*
>
> *knocked on his door, he went out*
> *a window. There was a high speed*
> *chase out into the desert near Red Rock.*
>
> *Finally the dude ended up stuck*
> *in the sand. He jumped out of his car,*
> *shooting. The cops took him down.*

"He's dead?" Her nod brings
relief, and also elicits a small sense
of satisfaction. Extremely small.

He Got What He Deserved

But you couldn't exactly call it
an eye for an eye. It was a two-
for-one deal, and that doesn't touch

what he did to me.
I hope it hurt.
I hope he screamed.

Most of all,
I hope he didn't die
quickly. I close my eyes,

picture him lying
on a bed of hot sand,
bleeding out slowly,

listening to the cops
discuss the relative merits
of glazed versus jelly

doughnuts while a dozen
buzzards circle above him,
edging lower and lower as the cops

move into the shade to wait
for the coroner, who's sitting
in an air-conditioned office—

Earth to Cody

Ronnie's gentle urging elevates
me out of my trance. "Oh. Sorry.
I was just thinking about . . . him."

Let's talk about you and me instead.
I'll admit I had a pretty tough time
when I found out about the stuff

you were doing. But then I started
thinking about me, and where I was
then—getting high, cutting school,

hanging out on the strip with my
friends, and fighting with my parents
when they called me on it. Who knows

how far I might have gone if I'd kept
down the same path? Not to say
I'm perfect now, but it was a wake-up

call, and one I seriously needed.
I love you, Cody. I should've seen
you were in trouble. Should've asked.

You probably wouldn't have admitted
it. Forthrightness (that's a word, yeah?)
isn't your best thing. That has to change.

I'm Speechless

Is she really going to stay with me,
despite my treachery, not to mention
my disability? "Does this mean you'll

give me another chance? That you
forgive me?" I can't believe she'll jump
right in and agree, and she doesn't.

> In fact, she sits for way too long,
> silently studying my face. Finally,
> she says, *I'm not sure forgiveness*
>
> *is possible, Cody. Trust is the core*
> *of commitment, and my faith in you*
> *has been shattered. Whether or not*
>
> *it's repairable will take time for me*
> *to decide. But if I walk away now,*
> *I'll never know for sure, will I?*

She, at least, could walk away.
Which kind of brings me back to,
"What are you, some kind of saint?"

> Ronnie spits laughter. *You know*
> *me better than that.* Now she turns
> serious. *What I am is in love with you.*
>
> *What I've learned is just how resilient*
> *love can be. You can beat it, pound it*
> *into pulp, but killing it is hard to do.*

Little flickers of hope sizzle
like sparklers inside me. Can it really
be possible to move forward from here,

finish school, build a career, with
a girl as perfect as Ronnie by my side?
Can love even survive, let alone thrive,

immersed in the dreary details
of living with someone like me?
"But what about . . . about . . . ?"

> *I don't know, Cody. I've never*
> *considered myself especially strong,*
> *and I'll have to be, won't I? This*
>
> *isn't just a storm. It's a freaking*
> *tornado, and it's doing its best*
> *to blow our world apart. I guess*
>
> *the question is, do we kneel down*
> *and let it wipe us out, or hang on*
> *tight and work our asses off to rebuild*
>
> *what we can and start again?* She stops
> to draw breath, and I'm struck by
> the way the curves of her breasts expand
>
> and contract, expand and contract.
> *Hey. What are you staring at? Good*
> *to know your eyes work okay, I guess.*

173

Yeah, My Eyes Work Fine

But other things don't work at all,
and the truth is, sex with Ronnie
was an important part of who "we" were.

"I so want to believe it's possible
to have some kind of future with you.
But you have to understand that

my legs aren't the only things
that might be lost to me. I mean . . ."
I take a couple of deep breaths.

"My favorite memories are lying
in bed with you, holding you close,
touching you, and you teasing me,

making me hard, but making me wait
so it would last a very long time.
And then, being inside you, God!

You are just so incredible, all I want
is to make you feel half as good as
I feel, remembering. What if I can't?"

> She has listened patiently, those
> pretty eyes never veering away
> from mine. Now she says, *I liked*
>
> *that, too. But it isn't what made me*
> *love you. Besides . . . She grins.*
> *Abstinence makes the heart grow fonder.*

We Laugh Together

Warm. Soothing. Remembered.
And that invites another kiss.
Honeyed. Luscious. Reinvented.

> She puts on the brakes too soon. *Better*
> *stop before someone takes a picture.*
> *Besides, we've got work to do.*

Déjà vu. "Uh-oh. I don't think
I like the sound of that. That's what
Federico says every time I see him."

> *I know. And he swears you refuse*
> *to cooperate. Just to be clear, with*
> *me you have no choice, and from*

> *what I hear the PTs at the rehab*
> *hospital don't take crap from patients,*
> *so you'd better be prepared to give*

> *it your all. I've been doing some*
> *research, and I want to share a few*
> *videos with you.* She reaches into

> her backpack, extracts a tablet, and
> turns it on. *First, there's a website*
> *you should check out. It's got a ton*

> *of interviews with people with spinal*
> *cord injuries, both paraplegia and*
> *tetraplegia—that's the new word for*

　　　　quadriplegia, did you know that?
　　　　Apparently she thinks I haven't heard
　　　　anything these people keep telling me.

Mom hustles back into the room
just as Ronnie starts touring the site.
She pauses to show us several short clips

of SCI patients, doctors and therapists.
Visiting hours officially end during
the marathon, but apparently my team

thinks this is more important than
rules. Maybe they're right. My biggest
takeaway from the session is knowing

I'm not alone with either my injury
or my reaction to it. It's normal
to feel like a freak when that is, in

fact, what you've become. Still,
every single one of them insists
it's possible to move on and create

a fulfilling future. It's a regular
SCI house party. Wonder how much
is bullshit. Hey. Wait. What if

they're all ringers, not paralyzed
at all, just paid to say they are, and
no worries because hey, it gets better?

Go Ahead, Label Me Cynical

Okay, considering that website
is an SCI resource clearinghouse,
they're probably mostly legit.

> *I've bookmarked that site for you,*
> *but now I want you to watch this*
> *video. It's by this amazing woman.* . . .

It's a long glimpse into the rebound
of a lady who broke her neck in a car
crash. They told her she'd never so

much as move her fingers again,
but by sheer strength of will, and
forcing herself to tap into her muscle

memory, she managed not only that,
but using swim therapy, taught herself
to walk unassisted in water, where gravity

can't interfere. Ronnie holds my hand
until it's over. "That's incredible.
Only problem is, I'm not that strong."

> *Don't say that. You are, and I'll be*
> *here to help you.* She places the tablet
> on the table next to the bed, stands

and pulls back the sheet, not even
wincing at the too-obvious tube. *First*
things first. It's time for you to sit up.

177

A Poem by Iris Belcher
Sitting Up

Who'd have thought this
simple thing would become
an impossible chore?

very sure I managed it
while in my crib,
when my bones were still
pliable, my muscles soft.
Yet here I am today,

able to prop myself upright
for more than an hour at
a time. I'm only thirty-four
and being tugged toward
a distant doorway I'm not

to enter. My mother
won't say it to my face, but
I notice the blame in her eyes,
know when Ginger comes
home I'll see it in her, too, only
magnified, and I will carry that

the cold sandy pit
they'll lower me into
without forgiveness when I

                  I'm

                  not

                  ready

                  to

                  die.

Ginger
I Keep Thinking

About Iris dying, withering
into the dried-up flower she's always
aspired to be. I keep thinking
I need to manufacture the tiniest

spoonful of sympathy—elixir
for me. No amount of medicine
can help her now, and I don't feel
the slightest bit bad about that.

Instead, I keep wishing she'd go
ahead and take that long, scary walk
before Gram can manage to pick
me up. Gram tells me it's a matter

of days now, that the final paperwork
giving my grandmother custody
of all of Iris's children will arrive
any time. Does our mother have any

regrets, other than doing the guy
who infected her, obviously without
protection? Considering the state
of her deterioration, that had to have

happened seven or eight years ago,
probably soon after Porter was born.
Baby Sandy was carried in her HIV-
infected womb. Luckily, the stats

were in his favor, at least that's what
Gram told me when I asked why
he wasn't born positive. *Only one
in four babies will pick up the virus*

in utero if the mother goes untreated,
Gram said. Iris didn't even suspect it.
Ob-gyns don't test for HIV as standard
procedure, but even if they did,

Iris wouldn't have known because
she never was one for prenatal care.
I remember her whining when she
was twin-carrying Honey and Pepper:

> *All those tedious office visits,*
> *and the outcome will always be*
> *the same. It's just a way to take*
> *money from people who don't have*
>
> *enough to start with. You're healthy,*
> *right?* Somehow, all six of us
> mostly were, despite the fact that
> Iris smoked at least a pack a day.

Well, healthy except for Mary Ann's
asthma and Porter's heart murmur
and my ridiculous attraction to the very
substances I hated to smell on Iris.

Iris Has No Regrets There

I'm sure. She loved smoking.
Needed to drink. But what
about any of the rest? Does
she realize Sandy might have

come into this world cursed
with a shortened life span?
Does it bother her at all?
What about leaving her kids

behind when she heads on
down to the brimstone-heated
whorehouse? Oh, and how
does she feel about putting me

up for sale? Does she carry
even the smallest thimbleful
of remorse for that at all?
My guess is the only thing

she's sorry about is having
cut her life in half. I suppose
it's a little sad that she'll die
before her thirty-fifth birthday.

Wonder if the kids even know
she's dying. Wonder if they'll miss
the mother who's been nothing
but a negative presence in their lives.

I Only Hope

She never auctioned off my sisters.
Mary Ann would tell me if it happened
to her, not that I can do one damn
thing to change it. And now a big

old knife of guilt rips through me.
Running away accomplished zilch,
especially considering where Alex
and I ended up. It was totally selfish,

and what if it only opened the door
to one of the kids being traded
for cigarette money? I could probably
forgive the fact that Iris was a sex

worker, but making one out of me,
and profiting from the rapes
that ground my childhood into
oblivion? What do I say when

I see her? "Hey, Iris, I'm home.
I'd like to tell you I'm sorry
you're dying, but that would be
a lie. Could you hurry the process,

please?" And how much do I confess
to Gram? I haven't said a word to her
about why I ran off. Do I want her
to hate her daughter as much as I do?

Play It by Ear

That's what I'll do, like every
girl here, pretty much. One day
feeds the next, and the routine
grows exponentially more boring.

I never really learned how to deal
with routine. We've always moved
around a lot, never put down roots
in a town or school, Iris chasing

dreams with penises, one after
another. You can't keep friends
like that, which is why I'm so close
with my sisters and brothers.

Alex was the first outside person
I'd ever truly connected with. God,
I miss her. But I guess she's moved
on with her life, totally independent

of me. For all the texts I've sent her,
she's only bothered to answer a few.
I try one more time now. HEY GIRL.
STILL PUKING IN THE MORNING?

BEEN THINKING ABOUT U AND
HOW WE MET. DID I EVER TELL
U I NEVER HAD A REAL FRIEND
BEFORE U? MISS TALKING TO U.

NOT THE SAME SWAPPING
STORIES WITH STRANGERS.
HEARD SOME GOOD ONES
THO. WELL, SO BAD THEY'RE

GOOD. ALWAYS THOUGHT
I WAS STREETWISE, BUT I
NEVER REALIZED JUST HOW
DIRTY THOSE SIDEWALKS

CAN BE, SPECIALLY FOR KIDS
EVEN YOUNGER THAN U AND
ME. PEOPLE WANT TO CLOSE
THEIR EYES TO WHAT'S GOING

ON JUST OUTSIDE THEIR DOORS
OR ONE BLOCK OVER. HEH. NOT
LIKE I'M TELLING U SOMETHING
U DON'T ALREADY KNOW.

DO ME A FAVOR? TELL ME
SOMETHING I DON'T KNOW.
LOVE YOU. TALK TO ME!
I leave it there, with the less-

than-subtle plea to stay connected,
if only virtually. Despite it all,
how can she toss "us" away so
easily? Did she totally forget me?

I guess this is the downside
to loving someone. When they cut
you loose, pretend like you don't
even exist, how do you say goodbye?

I Tuck My Cell

Into my pocket, go on inside.
It's Saturday—no homework, so
most of the girls are busy doing
crafts, which House of Hope

sells online to help finance
their programs. Next Thursday
is Thanksgiving. The cornucopias,
scarecrow wall hangings, and pumpkin

and turkey candles were finished
in September. We've been working
on Christmas decorations since
I've been here. I'm not really

the crafty type, but pasting sequins
on glass ornaments is easy enough,
and it's better than hanging out
in my room. I slip into a chair

next to Brielle, one of the few girls
I've bothered to get to know. I'm leaving
soon, so have done my best to avoid
making friends. But there's something

special about her, and you can't
always silence attraction. "You've
got glue stuck to your head." It clings
to the burnished copper waves

like ice. Brielle tosses her hair
back over her shoulders, looks
at me with striking gray-blue eyes.
Good thing it's Elmer's, huh?

*But remind me to wash it before
I try and brush it. Hard enough
to keep my ends from splitting.*
Her ends are perfect. Her hair

is definitely a vanity, but that's
not a bad thing. Every girl here
struggles with self-confidence,
which is how pimps and other

masters of violation maintain
control—by beating it out of us,
verbally and/or physically.
"Are you kidding? I'd kill for hair

like yours. If I try to grow mine
out, I kind of resemble one of those
dogs with fur like a mop, which
is why I keep it cut short."

She laughs, and I love the way
it sounds. Gentle. Sweet. Pure.
*I think those dogs are cute, but
I happen to like your hair short.*

The Chime

Of her laughter touches a place
inside me. Half of me wants to
hug her. The other half tells me
to run before I get hurt again.

But I'm just so, so lonely. I need
to feel like somebody cares,
and not because they're related
to me, which, with the obvious

exception of my mother, means
they pretty much have to care.
Of course, I'm probably totally
wrong to think Brielle might be

interested in hooking up with me.
I've caught her staring a few times,
and when I smile at her, she always
smiles back. Is that meaningful?

We both turn our attention to glue
and sequins and ribbon and beads,
but as we work, I slide my leg
over so it's barely touching hers.

Nonchalantly, of course. Game
on. Her move. It comes swiftly.
She tucks her shin behind my calf,
shimmies it softly up and down.

Exquisite little shivers trill
through my body. Man, it's been
a while since I've experienced
anything even close to this.

When I first got together with Alex,
I questioned whether it was sexual
identity or just the need to be held
tenderly by someone. I think I just

found the answer, cleared up
any sense of confusion. I still can't
be sure it doesn't have a lot to do
with the way I've been mistreated

by men, and maybe one day I'll change
my mind, so for now I'll just consider
myself bi, leaning toward women.
Right now I find myself leaning

toward the girl on my right. "Want
to take a walk later?" I ask, sure
despite our tangled legs that she'll
say no. "It's gorgeous outside."

> *No.* The word deflates my happy
> bubble. But then she qualifies,
> *Not later. Let's go right now.*
> *I'm feeling claustrophobic anyway.*

We Put Away

Our craft supplies, clean the table.
There aren't a whole lot of rules
here at House of Hope, but respect
for others is required, and this qualifies.

We can take off if we want; the doors
are unlocked during the day and
only bolted at night against danger
outside them. Brielle and I sign out,

so the staff understands we're gone.
Should we not return, the proper
authority will be informed,
but very few girls who leave

don't come back. For most, there's
nowhere better to go. Right now,
a test-the-waters stroll is in order.
"See? Isn't it great today? I think

November must be the best month
in Vegas. Still warm, but not melt-
your-makeup hot." We start along
the sidewalk, and before very long

> Brielle reaches for my hand.
> Our fingers link, and we don't care
> who sees. *Do you wear makeup?*
> *I've never noticed it before.*

"I used to wear it all the time, but
there's no reason to here, you know?
Besides, it reminds me of a place
in my life I'd rather not revisit."

We are beyond sight of the House
of Hope windows. Brielle stops,
turns so we're facing each other.
I understand. I've got one of those

*places, too. But I think it's good
to talk about it. My grandpa always
used to say that keeping secrets
chews you up from the inside out.*

*I'll tell you about my place if you
tell me about yours. But first . . .*
Her kiss, like her gentle demeanor,
is so different from Alex's—soft,

sweet. Tempting. It doesn't last long—
not close to long enough—but we are
very aware of traffic, some of it
slowing to gawk. One guy even beeps

and yells encouragement. Brielle
pulls away, face slightly red. *Sorry.
Hope that was okay. I just wanted
you to know how I feel. Was it okay?*

190

I Love That She's Worried

I love that she cares enough to ask
permission rather than expecting
me to respond the way my body
most definitely has. "It was more

than okay. It's been a long time
since I've kissed anyone. The last
person I was with quit kissing me
before she tore us apart. Thank you."

She shakes her head, and her eyes
insist she does not understand.
"Thank you for showing me
there is still beauty in the world.

All I've seen for most of my life
is ugliness. So, okay. Let's walk
and I'll share my story with you."
We tour the neighborhood, finally

come to a park with shade trees
and a playground that seem out
of place in Las Vegas. By the time
we settle at a picnic table, sitting

very close, and comfortable that way,
Brielle knows the circumstances
of my arrival at House of Hope. When
I finish, she boosts herself up on

191

the table, facing me and putting
my eyes level with the full curves
of her breasts. She leans forward
until her eyes are even with mine.

> *God, that so sucks. I can't believe*
> *your mom is that evil. And I'm*
> *sorry your girlfriend left you like*
> *that.* She kisses me again, and this

time there's no one watching,
no reason not to escalate into
the red zone, all the way to
breathless. "Holy crap. You're hot."

> She smiles. *Ditto. So, fine. Guess*
> *it's my turn for confession. I didn't*
> *know my dad, either. But my mom,*
> *she was pretty cool. She worked hard*
>
> *to take care of me, but then she got*
> *sick. I was fifteen when she died,*
> *and they sent me to foster. The first house*
> *was okay, pretty nice, really, but they*
>
> *decided they didn't want to take care*
> *of teens so I got moved. I don't know*
> *how people like Rick and Claudia*
> *manage to pass background checks.*

The Rest of Her Story

Is about what I expected. Seems
Rick had quite a thing for teenage
girls. When he got too friendly,
Brielle told him she was a lesbian.

One night he decided to "fix her
little problem," and to help convince
her he brought a gun into her room,
forced it into her mouth and gave

her the choice. Suck the thirty-eight,
or suck him. Then he proceeded
to do his best to "turn her." Acutely
aware that the pistol was nearby,

Brielle didn't fight, but she ran
away later that night and was on
the street for a couple of days
when a proactive cop picked her

up before one of Vegas's numerous
pimps could. Her caseworker
believed her tale, and she ended up
at House of Hope, better off than

many girls in similar situations.
Unlike me, she'll be here at least
a year, until she turns eighteen.
Which complicates things.

A Poem by Micah Lerner
Complications

Rarely have I allowed
myself to tumble
for someone, but it
appears I've taken a

          hard

stumble, and finding my feet
again is proving difficult.
It's not that I don't want
the experience, but

          time

is a luxury I have no way
to indulge, and why
did it have to be this guy
I was destined

          to fall

for? I mean, Seth's kept
by the very man who gave
me a chance to jump-start
my career, here

          in

a place where dreams too
often die, sucked dry
of hope by a city that
celebrates sin in favor of

          love.

Seth
I Didn't Expect

To fall in love again, and definitely
not here in Vegas, here in David's care,

here where I must be careful not to
expose that fact to anyone. Not even

Micah. Not yet. I mean, he has to suspect,
and if I dared trust my feelings, I'd swear

he's in love with me, too. When we're
together, the outside world melts away,

and it's just the two of us there. Despite
our different backgrounds, we have so

much in common, from our taste in movies
and books, to our favorite cuisines.

And where our opinions differ, we're willing
to compromise. For instance, I'll put up

with Broadway music and he'll take a listen
to country. Not sure we've totally swayed

each other, but we do agree broadening
horizons isn't a bad thing. He makes me

feel—dare I say it out loud?—hopeful.
Like there's a real future available to me.

Of Course, As Soon as I Think

That way, the reality of my situation
slaps me upside the head. To have

a real future with Micah would mean
deserting David, which could very

well lead to problems for Micah, unless
David was willing to let me go, and who

knows when he might get sick of me?
But then I'd need a place to live, which

would require an income. And if I were
to commit to Micah, I'd have to leave

escorting behind. What else can I do?
I didn't even graduate high school.

I suppose a minimum wage something
would be possible, but I'm used to living

well. I'm sure I could get my GED, but
then what? College? Paid for how, and

to study what? I'm just a gay hick farm
boy loser. So who am I fooling? There's

no hope of escape for me. For now,
I'll just pretend to believe in possibilities.

It's Thanksgiving

And I'm helping out at YouCenter,
which is hosting a big turkey dinner

this afternoon for kids with nowhere
else to go. David doesn't especially

care about the holiday, other than
the fact that most people spend it

with their families, rather than in
casino showrooms. Hell, even Have

Ur Cake expects a slow evening.
Guess L-tryptophan and pumpkin pie

bloat aren't especially conducive to
the desire for paid sex. Tomorrow,

Black Friday, johns will probably be
looking for deals. Meanwhile, kitchen

work is mostly keeping my mind off
my future. I've always enjoyed cooking,

though I've never attempted anything like
an entire Thanksgiving dinner. Good

thing Charlie's here to help. "This stuffing
smells incredible," I tell her. "My mom

makes plain old cornbread with onions.
I bet the sausage really spices it up."

Sausage. The word entices a memory—
Dad and me joking about venison

sausage and haute cuisine. Wonder
who's sharing Dad's table tonight.

Wonder if I should try calling him
one more time. Charlie stops humming.

> *Sausage, my dear, makes the stuffing.*
> *That, and fresh rosemary. Of course,*
>
> *I prefer it cooked inside the bird,*
> *but I would have had to be here by*
>
> *six a.m. to make that happen. Baked*
> *in a casserole will just have to do.*

"Is your mom a great cook? Where
did you learn your way around a kitchen?"

> She snorts. *My mom is the frozen*
> *food queen. No, my grandpa taught*
>
> *me. But I love it. In fact, I've been*
> *thinking about a culinary arts degree.*

198

"You mean like go to school to learn
to cook? But you already know how."

> *I don't know everything. Besides,*
> *you can also take restaurant*
>
> *management, which basically*
> *gives you a business degree.*
>
> *With the right credentials, you can*
> *make bank, especially if you get hired*
>
> *by a big casino or something. I'm*
> *not going to be a doctor or a lawyer.*
>
> *But that doesn't mean I don't want*
> *to earn a good income. Why not*
>
> *make it doing something I love to*
> *do anyway?* She slides the big pan

of stuffing into the oven, closes
the door with a satisfied smile.

Huh. I like to cook. "Is a culinary
arts degree, like, major expensive?"

> *Depends. Le Cordon Bleu is pricey.*
> *But College of Southern Nevada isn't.*

Think Outside the Box

Mom used to tell me that. Still,
she probably would've laughed

at the notion that a person might
be able to make a decent career

out of cooking, and Dad would
have chuckled right along with her.

I'm sure a short-order cook's paycheck
couldn't approach what I make on

a single night escorting. But what
about overseeing a five-star kitchen?

Definitely something to think about,
especially if things get serious between

Micah and me. And if not that, at least
I'm thinking outside the box, rather

than flinging myself into a big pond
of pity. Funny how when I think about

home any culture I managed to absorb
from Carl and David dissolves and rural

Indiana takes over. Home. Back home.
Home sweet home. No place like home.

Around Two P.M.

People start trickling in, knowing
dinner is supposed to be served at three.

I'm familiar with many of the faces,
but some are new to me, and some

interest me for whatever reasons.
There's a butch girl who can't be

more than twelve. Surely she's not
homeless, right? Surely she has family

somewhere who cares? I asterisk
a mental note to ask Charlie about her.

Ditto the girl, maybe a year younger
than me, coming through the door now.

She's pretty enough to model, except
she looks so scared. Not sure there's

a market for that. Oh, but wait. What is it
about her? She's lanky, and wearing heels

that make her even taller. Is that why her gait
is awkward? I nudge Charlie. "Who's that?"

> *Pippa. Born Philip. You should talk
> to her. She could use a friend like you.*

Born Philip

That explains a lot. But transitioning,
or just cross-dressing? Only one way

to find out, at least if she feels like
sharing the information with me.

Once dinner is on the table, I make
sure to take the seat next to Pippa.

It isn't hard. No one else has chosen
it. "Hi. I'm Seth. Mind if I sit?"

She looks at me nervously, with dark
eyes enhanced with expert makeup.

> *Uh . . . No. I mean, I guess so. If you
> want to.* Her gentle voice is more

male than female, but it belongs
to a boy, not a man. "I'd like to . . . ?"

> She understands the implied question.
> *Philippa, but you can call me Pippa.*

> She passes a big bowl of cranberry
> sauce, skips it herself. *You work here?*

"Volunteer," I correct. "I haven't seen
you here before. Are you new to Vegas?"

202

Not really, but kind of new to YouCenter.
I ran into Charlie downtown. She told me

about it. It's nice to be around people
who don't think you're a freak, you know?

"I do know. So, where you from?
I mean, if you want to tell me. Oh,

and please pass the gravy." I notice
she skips it. "What? Don't like gravy?"

Love it. But I'm watching my weight.
I'm from Provo, which explains why

I'm in Vegas. Other than Salt Lake City,
which is more open-minded than most

people realize, Utah isn't exactly trans-
friendly. Las Vegas was a cheap ticket.

We take a few minutes to stuff food
into our mouths. "Man, Charlie, you can

cook for me anytime!" Everyone nods
and murmurs agreement, and Charlie

beams. You ain't seen nothing yet,
she replies. *Wait till you taste the pie.*

Pippa Skips the Pie, Too

But seems content enough watching
me devour pumpkin cheesecake.

Afterward, everyone helps clear
the tables, and a few step forward to

wash the dishes. Pippa and I grab cups
of coffee and wander outside to sit

on a bench haloed by the duskish light.
"The days are short. Almost December."

> *I hear they've already had snow
> in Utah. It definitely fell early.*

"I used to like the snow, but we only got
four or five inches a year in Perry County.

Sure did get cold, though. Not like here,
where they think fifty degrees is cool.

So, anyone missing you in Provo? Do
your parents know where you are?"

> Incredulity spikes her laugh. *They
> couldn't give two fucks about where*

> *I am. They stopped worrying about
> me years ago, when I wouldn't quit*

>insisting God put me in the wrong
>body. My mother says God doesn't make
>
>mistakes, but I identified at three. All
>I wanted was to play with my sister's
>
>Barbies. All my father wanted was to
>beat the girl out of me. Couldn't do it.

Different fathers. Different states. Different
religions, I'm guessing. Similar attitudes.

"My dad didn't beat me when I came
out, but he completely disowned me.

I can't imagine what he might have
done if I'd told him I was a girl in

a boy's body. Gender dysphoria is not
in his vocabulary. Are you transitioning?"

>Pippa nods. *Started hormones, and
>I've done a few rounds of electrolysis,*
>
>*but that's so expensive. I want to go
>all the way at some point, though.*
>
>*A girl doesn't need a penis. In fact,
>it's counterintuitive to who I'm becoming.*

"Do you have a safe place to live?
How are you supporting yourself?"

Let alone affording estrogen
supplements and facial hair removal.

*I have a little studio, yes. Not much,
but it's cozy and clean enough. As for*

*how I pay my bills, you can probably
guess. No back alley blowjobs, not*

*anymore. I'm not proud of it, but I've
no other way to make that kind of money,*

*and I'm saving up for procedures.
Besides . . .* She smiles. *What better*

*excuse to shop for pretty clothes?
I'll quit someday, once I've become*

*the woman I was meant to be. In
the meantime, I'm surviving. But mark*

*my words. Philippa Young will make
something special of herself one day.*

"I believe you. Until then, never
apologize for doing what you have to."

I Don't Mention

My personal connection to "doing
what you have to do," but I do offer

Pippa my friendship. "Anytime you
need to talk, you can call me, okay?

Be really careful out there. This city
is crawling with creeps, and some

of them are dangerous." I take time
to study her face really closely.

"You're lucky. You have amazing
bone structure. You won't need

surgery there. In fact, you could
model. Have you considered it?"

> *What girl hasn't? Actually, I'd love to*
> *find work dancing. The one real gift*
>
> *my parents gave me was dance classes,*
> *and my teachers told me I have talent.*

"Believe it or not, I might have an in
for you. And not pole dancing, either."

> She smiles. *I'd do that, too, except . . .*
> *Yet another reason I don't want a dick.*
>
> *But I'd give my left nut for a chance*
> *to dance. Nah. I'd give both of them.*

Which cracks me up. "I can't promise
anything, of course. But I do know

some people." I don't mention names,
nor my living arrangement. "I should

go. You've got my number." I head
on inside to say goodbye to everyone,

then call for David's driver to pick
me up around the corner. No one here

knows where I live, or with whom.
Once we're on our way home—scratch

that, back to David's house—I call
Micah, careful not to say too much

within earshot of Percy. "Hey. Hope
you've had a great Thanksgiving.

Would love to hear from you. Please
call me later." Way to be ambiguous

when what I really want to be is in
his face, followed by him in mine.

And what I wish is I was on my way
back to a home Micah and I share.

Home

I check the time. Six p.m. here in the Pacific
zone, two hours later in Indiana. Dad will

probably still be awake. Hands shaking,
I dial the number I committed to memory

years ago. One ring. Two. Three. On four,
a machine answers. *Can't answer the phone*

right now. Please leave a message. Dad's
voice. Strong. Clear. Loved. Now, the beep.

"Hi, Dad. Happy Thanksgiving. Hope you
spent it with Aunt Kate or someone. Sure

do miss you. How did the harvest go?
So you know, I'm thinking about going

back to school. Maybe getting a degree
in culinary arts. Las Vegas is in dire need

of decent venison sausage. Love you." Huh.
Aunt Kate. Dad's sister. Haven't thought

about her in a while, but she always was
decent. Kind. Wonder if she'd talk to me.

As we pull into the driveway, I make a
note to track down a way to reconnect.

A Poem by Renée Lang
Reconnection

How do you glue
back together
a relationship torn into
scraps like paper?
Where do you find

                          trust

buried in a stinking heap
of epic past failure?
Losing a child
to illness or accident

                          is

a bitter tonic to swallow,
but losing one
to personal indifference
would be too

                          hard

to reconcile, and I've come
much too close—
within the width
of an eyelash—

                          to

doing exactly that.
I've been given a second
chance with my Whitney.
But how do I

                          rebuild

her faith in me?
How do I prove my love?

Whitney
Free

From the confines of rehab, and
scared through and through
to be without overseers, unless
you count my family. Yeah,
and how did that work out
last time? Okay, they're doing
a good job of pretending
to care about how I'm feeling.
Well, Mom and Dad are, anyway.

Kyra acts like I'm a dark cloud—
something to draw the blinds
against. She's probably said
two dozen words to me over
the past two days, and those

she barked. *Don't talk
with your mouth full.
Get out of the bathroom.
Put some decent clothes on.
God, look at your arms.
How could you?*

Except for that, nothing.
I'm glad she's flying back
to Vassar on Sunday.
Long-distance silence
is preferable to
the in-your-face kind.

My Arms Are Tattooed

With long silver scars—damage
from shooting up over and over
in the same general location, once
I forgot to care about hiding it.
What did I know? Not like drug
programs teach you how *not* to inject,
when they're warning you about
using at all. Not like I thought
I'd ignore that advice and go walking
with the Lady. She calls to me,
and I'm terrified. I'm weak.

I didn't take that second oxy
back in rehab, not because I
tried to be strong, but because
I lost it somewhere, and figured
that must have been a sign.
It made me take a long look
at myself, and I hated the view.
Once a junkie, always a junkie,
that's what I keep hearing.
But the dope doesn't have to win.

And I can reclaim my body,
abused and broken as it might
be, I can take ownership of it.
Dana thought it was hers for
the price of two pills—pharms
that would slide me back into
the arms of the Lady. Instead,
I pulled away. That time.

It's Weird

Being back in my room.
My room, but not like I left
it. Apparently, Mom thought
I needed a fresh start, so she had
it painted a pale lilac with purple-
and-crimson paisley borders.

It's pretty enough, but not
something I'd choose. Given
free rein, I'd likely pick black,
to match my mood. It's hard
to come home, be confronted
with rules, most of them meant
to keep me from making the same
mistakes that almost killed me.

I understand the need for them,
but they're suffocating me, and
I've only been here a few days.

Yesterday was Thanksgiving.
Talk about strange.
Mom did do the cooking,
and did ask for help from
my sister and me. Way back
when I was just a little kid
we worked in the kitchen together.
But it's been years, and since
then holiday meals have either
been prepared by hired help
or, more often, eaten out.

So, the Turkey Was Dry

The dressing was bland.
And the rolls were underdone.
The best thing was the pies,
apple and pumpkin,
and they came in a box from
our favorite bakery—
Dad's contribution.

Hey, at least he was here,
not hiding out in San Francisco,
his Turkey Day habit
for the past couple of years.
He was even nice at dinner,
and managed the entire meal
with only two glasses of wine.
Mom needed three, but
stayed pleasant enough.

It's like my parents decided
the only way to save me
was to save themselves.
Not that I'm at all sure
it's possible for their marriage
to be resurrected. It was dead
and buried before I left.

Sobering thought.
Maybe that's how
they should've left
it. If it all nose-dives
again, will that be on me?

Today Is Black Friday

A day when any sane person
stays holed up at home, or goes
to the gym to work off a few
calories. But not the Lang clan!
We're going to the mall, and
calling it an adventure.

At least, that's what Mom's
calling it. Dad, who's driving,

> says, *You realize this is insanity?*
> *Look at this parking lot. How*
> *far are you ladies willing to walk?*

Kyra (speaking to the family
in general, not to me specifically)

> claims, *This is a total nightmare.*
> *I bet Coach is already sold out.*

Me? I'm just going along
for the ride, and because
they're scared to leave me
alone in the house, not
that I blame them.

The stores opened early,
but none of us is the type
to rise before dawn so we
can stand in mega-lines,
just to fight the inevitable
crowd, which might actually
thin out later in the day.

We did skip breakfast
instead of working out
to make up for calories
consumed yesterday. Fueled
only by coffee, we hit the mall
a little after ten, including
a six-minute walk in from
the far edge of the parking lot.

Dad was right. This is insane.
The sheer number of people,
all in one place, threatens
to overwhelm me. It's like Vegas
on steroids, only for all its nasty
underbelly, Sin City's facade
is beautiful. Nothing particularly
attractive about Capitola Mall
even without all the jostling.

A guy walking by turns to stare
with eyes that don't quite track
and suddenly I'm carried back
to another day here. I came with
Paige, and we went on a weirdo
watch—that's what we called it—
and ran into one hot creeper
loitering outside the Gap, looking
for stupid girls like me to recruit
into his stable. Wonder how many
pimps are hanging out here today.

I Spot a Possible Few

As we push and shove
our way into the throng,
a determined Kyra carving
a path to Coach, I'm pulling
in air as if through a pillow.
"Mom," I try, but it's a weak
attempt, and she can't hear it
above the clamor. "Mom!"

> It's Dad who falls back,
> takes a long look at me.
> *What's the matter?* Now
> he grabs my hand, and his

skin is hot and I can't stand
the touch of a man—any man,
really, but especially not this Vegas
wolf, who rushes me and I feel his grasp
at my throat, and he's telling
me that he doesn't pay for sex
and now he's cursing,
> *Fight, you goddamn whore!*
> *Fight or I'll kill you.*

"Leave me alone!" I scream,
and even above the din,
people hear. People stare.
People think Dad is hurting
me. Dad. The realization
of what just occurred punches
me and I fall to my knees.

"I'm sorry. I'm sorry. I'm so
sorry." It's a chant. "I didn't
mean it. I'm sorry. I'm sorry."
Finally, I chance looking up.
People are still staring, but
they've pushed away,
forming a wide circle, giving
me space. And now I see

> Dad encouraging the crowd
> to *please move back. Can't
> you see she needs air?* His
> mask is calm, assertive, but
> his voice trembles, denying
> the disguise. *Are you okay?*
> he asks, and I know he wants

to help, but he's definitely scared
to touch me again, so I stretch
my hand toward his. "Please?"
Still, I have to reach deep inside
for the courage not to recoil
when his fingers close around
my wrist and gently pry me
up from the dirty tile floor.

> Once I'm on my feet, he lets
> go of me immediately. *What
> just happened, Whitney? Do
> you want to talk about it?*

Before I Can Answer

A security guard wades in
between us. *Is this man
bothering you, young lady?*

"No, sir. This is my father.
I just had a bit of a panic
attack, that's all. Sorry for
causing a scene." The guy
looks unconvinced, but nods
and returns to patrolling for
shoplifters, dine-and-dashers,
and maybe the odd flasher.

Now that I'm so obviously
safe, the crowd goes back to
scouring stores for bargains,
despite the fact that most of
the good ones are long gone.
Which reminds me, "Kyra
must have found something
good at Coach after all. She
and Mom have been gone
a while." Thank God Kyra
didn't witness my little scene.

Don't change the subject, says
Dad. *Was that a panic attack?
Have you had them before?
You about gave me a heart
attack, Whitney. Are you okay?*

How Many Times

Is he going to ask me that?
Maybe until I answer?
"Yeah, Dad, I'm okay."
Sure I am. For the moment.

"It's just when you grabbed
my hand, it reminded me of
something that happened in
Vegas." I've been mostly silent
about the stuff that went on
while I was working for Bryn.

The focus has been the H, and
fighting addiction. My parents
know I'd been lured into the life
by a panderer—Vegas Vice was
clear about that. But no one's
asked for the details, and I sure
haven't volunteered them.

"I think it was a panic attack.
First, I couldn't breathe. It was
all the people, all the noise.
And then . . . I don't know.
No, I haven't had one before.
I think maybe I just need fresh
air. Is it okay if I go outside?"

> *I'll go with you if you want.*
> *And anytime you need to talk,*
> *please know you've got my ear.*

I Haven't Talked to Dad

In a very long time.
I wouldn't have any idea
what to say to him now.
Would he want to know
that I met Bryn, the phony
"fashion photographer"
who convinced me to run
away so he could pimp me out,
right here in this very mall?

No, probably not. I attempt
a joke to lighten things
up. "I don't have your ear,
Dad. I can see both of them,
one on either side of your
head, and they look firmly
attached." I smile, signaling
humor, but he doesn't get it.

> All right then. Let's go
> outside for a while.

"You don't have to come
with me. I'm fine on my own.
I'll just go find a place to sit
in the sun and watch people
behave badly for a while.
Catch up to Mom and Kyra,
and text me when you're ready
for lunch. I'm getting hungry."

He's Reluctant

To leave me on my own, but
I convince him a few minutes
solo are just the medicine
I need. Awkward thought:
What I wouldn't give for that
oxy right now, or better yet,
a ticket to the Land of Nod.

Stop it, Whitney. Guess I'd
better consider finding a sponsor
after all. Weak moments like this
are exactly why they invented
them. I step out into the cool
coastal morning, where the sun
hints at its presence behind
a gray mist. There's really
no place to sit, except on
the sidewalk—too dangerous
today. So I lean back against
the side of the building, take
deep breaths of sea-flavored air.

Suddenly, a familiar laugh
comes floating toward me from
the parking lot. The annoying
nasal giggle belongs to Paige,
my onetime best friend. I squint
to find her. Yes, there she is,
and she's with . . . Skylar?

Okay, I Get

That it's been almost eight months
since Paige and I went to the party
that basically ruined my life—
the one I left, destroyed by finding
Lucas cemented to Skylar. The one
Paige was too busy making out
with some random guy to take me
home from, so I called Bryn, who
was all too happy to use the excuse
to worm his way into my pathetic life.

But Paige and Skylar are as different
as blue and red. Or at least they were.
Can people change so much so quickly?

Backpedal.
Of course they can.
I pretty much define the concept.
I've been to hell and back.

As they near, it's easy to see who
did the changing. Paige, who always
carried a spare few pounds, is thin
enough to wear those skinny jeans
well. Her hair's styled into short
spikes, and her makeup is plastered
on. Head to toe, she's Skylar's
twin, except if anything, despite
the weight loss, her boobs are even
bigger. Skylar, it pleases me to witness,
has yet to grow an observable pair.

I Hold On to the Thought

As they hit the sidewalk
together, almost straight
in front of me, yet somehow
don't seem to notice I'm here.
Better fix that. "Hey, Paige.
Long time no see, huh?"

> Her jaw totally drops.
> *Whitney? Oh my God,*
> *girl, where have you been?*

> Skylar can't help herself. *Yeah.*
> *And what happened to you?*
> *You look so . . . so rough.*

Rough? My hair has grown
out. My skin's mostly clear.
And I'm wearing a cute long-
sleeved sweater, which covers
the tracks. I ignore the bitch.
"Most recently, I've been in rehab.
Before that, I was in Las Vegas.
With Bryn. Remember him?"

> Paige wrinkles her forehead.
> *You mean the photographer*
> *guy? The one who was stalking*
> *you here last year? What were*
> *you doing with him all that time?*

224

I have to be careful. Whatever
I say *will* get around. "Modeling,
of course. He had a lot of contacts
in Vegas. But you know it's a dirty
business. Lots of drugs and stuff.
I kind of got in over my head,
so I ended up in rehab. Old story."

> *Wow. Sounds exciting. I want
> to hear more. Are you coming
> back to school?* asks Paige.

"That's the plan." I wince at
the hard nudge Skylar gives her.
Before they escape, I have to dig,
"How's Lucas? You two still together?"
Not like I don't know the answer.

> Skylar shakes her head. *Nah.
> I decided he's not my type.
> We have to go. See you around.*

Call me, says Paige, turning
her back. As they walk away,
I hear her say, *Wonder what
kind of drugs she got into.*

> *Wonder what kind of modeling
> she was doing,* responds Skylar.

Wouldn't she like to know?

A Poem by Eve Streit
Not My Type

That's what I told him.
Did he believe it was a lie,
or could he look through
the windows of my tears,
see beyond the words to

the truth

behind them? I wanted
to know what it was like
to fall in love, conveniently
forgetting the facts

of my

sister's disappearance.
Incorrigible. That's what
my parents called Eden when
they tossed her to the jackals,
where her limited

experience

did not equip her for what
followed. I know because
they've done the same to me—
forced me into isolation
at Tears of Zion, where Father

is

the heavy hand of God,
or so he claims. All I did
was give my heart away.
Punishment like this is

incomprehensible.

Eden
Thanksgiving Is Weird

On a personal level, it is the first
I've ever spent away from home,
where the pattern never deviated.
Papa hates turkey, so Mama
put a huge ham in the oven

at ten a.m. exactly. Then the Streit
family went visiting faithful church
members to remind them that thanks
is better shared. We prayed together,
Papa collected a Thanksgiving

offering, and often we left with
food, too, most generally homemade
rolls or pie or maybe even a sweet
potato casserole. By the time we'd get
home, the ham was ready and Mama's

cooking was finished. It was brilliant,
really, and, of course, the whole
plan was Mama's idea. Cooking,
especially baking, isn't her favorite
pastime. And after all that earlier

praying and talking and collecting,
we'd sit at our own dinner table
in silence, which is how most meals
at our house are experienced.
Quietly communing with ourselves.

But Here at Walk Straight

Noise fills the dining room—
girls talking and laughing and
sharing stories of Thanksgivings
past. The majority of those aren't
beautiful, yet they are comforting

because of experiences they have
in common. For many, the best
thing about the day is their pimps
understand that men usually spend
it with their families, rather than

trolling for sex. Fewer customers,
less money, not the girls' fault,
they get a pass. By the time we
get to dessert, everyone's guard
is down, and Rhonda, who's

     usually standoffish, offers
     a memory. *My mama, she all into*
     skag and she spend a lot of time
     in jail, so I had to take care of
     my little brother. That's why I'm

     on the track. I don't know nothing
     else. Quit school in sixth grade.
     Had to, you know? Never had no
     pimp, only me. Mama, when she not
     locked up, she work the streets,

and she told me what to do, and
where to find johns, and how much
to make 'em pay. It's not so hard,
not usually, but you know sometimes
a guy go a little crazy or whatever.

So one time, one Thanksgiving,
Mama was gone and Oscar was
hungry, no food but stale cereal
in the cupboard. I tell him to watch
TV, I'll be back soon. I go out,

and yeah, it was real slow but after
a while along come a black-and-white,
and this old cop stop to see what's what.
"What you doing out here?" he ask.
"Don't you know what day it is?"

I tell him, yeah, but I gotta feed my kid
brother, hoping maybe he let me go,
maybe for a blowjob or whatever.
He say, "Get in," and that made me
scared, but you know what he did?

He drove to Denny's, bought four
turkey dinners, two pieces of pie,
gave it all to me, and a twenty, too.
Didn't ask for nothing. "Feed your
brother," he say. "Happy Thanksgiving."

After That

A lot of cop stories are passed
around, few enough as feel-good
as Rhonda's, though there are some:
Cops who looked the other way.
Cops who offered numbers to

services and rescues like Walk
Straight. One cop who played
protector when he saw a john
on a rampage. But mostly, we hear
about cops who were quick to haul

the girls in. Cops who let them off
in trade for squad-car sex. Two girls
told of cops who chose the role of
pimp, both eventually busted and
made to leave the force. Across

the board, what the girls learned
was not to trust men who wore
badges. Back home in Boise, most
cops I met were fresh-faced hometown
boys, and friendly enough, at least

on the surface. Wonder how many
were hiding dark secrets. I go back
to my room, plop into bed, thinking
about the lies people carry, and
what's to gain by shedding them.

Such Thoughts

Lead to a night of underwater
dreams—struggling to swim up
from the deep without drowning,
finally sputtering to the surface
just about daybreak. On the far

side of the room, my new roommate,
Hana, snuffles softly. Tia, my last
roomie, snored like a bulldozer.
She's been gone two weeks now—
decided the straight and narrow

wasn't for her, and went back to her
pimp, despite the fact that she wore
the scars of his cigarette burns and
his tattoo on the back of her neck,
signifying his ownership. We weren't

close, but I hope she'll be okay, or at
least as okay as you can get, renting
out various parts of your body.
Hana is a soft-spoken Korean American.
She's been here four days now and

I still don't know her whole story.
We're just getting used to seeing each
other in the mirror, and to the unique
sounds of our voices and breathing
patterns. The rest will come with time.

Except, I'm Not Sure

How much time I have left
here. Just got unhappy news
from my counselor, who finally
heard from Mama. Apparently,
she's decided to arrange a reunion.

> *She'll arrive tomorrow.*
> *Sarah's eyes hold sympathy.*
> *I tried to ask about emancipation.*
> *She told me her relationship*
> *with you is none of my business.*

"Of course she'd say that."
Dread drops into my stomach.
"I'm not ready to go, Sarah. Oh
God, I'm so afraid. Will I have
to leave with her if she insists?"

> *Unfortunately, you would.*
> *Walk Straight can't keep you*
> *if either of your parents wants*
> *you with them instead. Not unless*
> *we can prove extenuating*
>
> *circumstances like sexual abuse*
> *or neglect. But from what you've*
> *told me, there was neither in*
> *your home. As for Tears of Zion,*
> *that's a different can of worms.*

If my parents couldn't send me
back there, could I deal with living
at home for a year? If I had to,
yes. "What about Tears of Zion?
What if I brought charges?"

> *After we last talked, I did*
> *a little research. Tears of Zion*
> *calls itself a religious retreat*
> *center, not a boot camp or*
> *rehabilitation facility, which*

> *complicates things. The easiest*
> *way to shine a spotlight on*
> *the place would be to allege*
> *that one or more staff members*
> *were responsible for abuse.*

> *The problem with that is, unless*
> *the director—what's his name . . . ?*
> *She opens a file to check her notes.*
> *Oh yes, Samuel Ruenhaven. Unless*
> *he was personally involved, he could*

> *simply fire whoever was accused,*
> *and it would probably be business*
> *as usual. That said, there were prior*
> *allegations of neglect against him,*
> *though in Idaho, not Nevada.*

Hope Surges

First, because she believes
me enough to dig deeper.
Second, because maybe there
is a solid answer. "Really?
Against Father? What happened?"

> I rethink the question before
> she can answer it. Nothing
> happened. *He settled out of*
> *court, then dismantled his*
> *Idaho operation and moved*
>
> *to Nevada, where his name*
> *hadn't been blasted all over*
> *the media. This was years ago,*
> *of course, before the Internet*
> *made finding information so easy.*

Hope abates. "So no one
will take me seriously
if I come forward?" Beyond
my personal fate, Father and
his disciples need to be stopped.

> *I wouldn't say that, Eden.*
> *For all we know, someone*
> *else might find the courage*
> *if you go first. Or maybe*
> *someone else already has.*

Just cueing in law enforcement
would be a good thing, and
if the media gets hold of it,
at the very least there will be
public scrutiny, something

I'm sure Mr. Ruenhaven would
not appreciate. But he'll have
to change the way he conducts
his business. The question is,
do you want a spotlight on you?

Okay, I hadn't considered
that. I won't be publicly outed,
will I? I'd have to give
details about Jerome, and
the things I accepted, even

encouraged, to escape Tears
of Zion. And I'm sure, should
I accuse my mother of spiking
my tea, she'd be more than happy
to tell the world about her daughter,

who is not only incorrigible,
but also a harlot, in every sense
of the word. I don't know
if that's necessary yet. "I'll think
about it." And decide tomorrow.

Sarah's Phone Rings

I start to leave, but she gestures
for me to stay. *Are you sure?*
Urgency shades her voice. *When
was she supposed to be there?
I see. Okay, I'll ask around.*

She replaces the handset. *Have
you seen Shayleece? She had
a dentist appointment, but never
showed.* Worry creases her face.
Do you remember if she was at lunch?

"Actually, I haven't seen her
since yesterday. But she planned
to go to the dentist. She was excited
about getting that hole in her front
tooth filled. She hated it."

*That's what I thought. Maybe
the bus broke down? But then
she would have called, right?
Will you help me poll the others?
Maybe someone saw her go.*

A half hour later, all we know
is the last person who talked to
her was her roommate, Rhonda.
*That was last night. She was
going outside to have a smoke.*

Rhonda Was Asleep

Before Shayleece came back
in. *If* Shayleece came back in.
No one has seen her since.
Sarah goes to call the police
and report her missing.

A few of us volunteer to canvass
the neighborhood. We go in two-
person teams, in four directions.
I partner with Hana. We head east.
It's afternoon, post-school, and

we pass parents walking with
their children. A few older people
are walking their dogs, and there
are bunches of kids sitting
on car hoods or stoops, smoking

or making out. We ask every
person we come across if they've
seen our friend, with little luck.
It's starting to get frustrating.
It's starting to get worrisome.

One elderly woman asks for a
description, nodding her head.
*I think I might have seen her
just a few minutes ago. She got
in a car with some other youngsters.*

Hana and I look at each other.
A few minutes ago? Couldn't
have been her. Still, I ask, "Do
you remember what kind of
car, or what color it was?"

> The lady scratches her thin hair.
> *I was all the way over on the far*
> *side of my grass, and I don't see*
> *so good anymore. But it was a big*
> *car, and I'm sure it was gray. Or blue.*

> We thank the woman and, as soon
> as we're down the block, bust up
> laughing. *Probably didn't need*
> *to worry,* hiccups Hana. *Bet her*
> *hearing isn't so good, either.*

But now the heavy gravity of
the situation sinks back in.
"Shayleece wouldn't run off.
Where would she go? Besides,
she likes it at Walk Straight."

We keep going until the light
begins to pale, then circle back,
the chances of finding out anything
useful fading with the sun. Dinner
this evening is unusually quiet.

Sleep Is Evasive Tonight

Playing tag with worry
about what the morning
will bring. Usually, I fall
straight into dreams but
an odd slant of moonlight

through the blinds disturbs
the darkness, and the silence
is punctuated by Hana's gentle
snoring. I haven't noticed it
before. Now I can't not hear

it, even with a pillow over
my ears. It reminds me
of my sister. I've thought
about Eve a lot lately, and
now, with Mama coming

tomorrow, a collection of
images mash together in
my head: Eve and me giggling
together in church; Papa
halting his sermon to chastise

us; Mama glaring, Mama
accusing, Mama handing
me a cup of tea; Mama's
face smearing, blurring;
the face of Father Samuel

Ruenhaven swimming
into view; Father staring,
Father chastising, Father
forcing me to pray; Jerome
leering; Jerome coaxing;

the luscious taste of ripe
strawberries; calloused
greedy hands touching
places meant for no one
but the boy whose face

I cannot find. I sit up,
lean back against the wall.
Something's wrong.
Really wrong. Every
nerve in my body tingles,

on full alert. I don't know
what this means, except
there'll be no sleep at all
tonight. Quietly, I slip out
of bed, search for clothes

in the dark, take them down
the hall to the bathroom,
and get dressed. The entire
building is asleep, so I tiptoe
to the rec room, wait for morning.

By First Light

My intuition is shouting a warning,
but can't give me details. I skip
breakfast. Can't possibly eat. When
Mama finally shows her face,
I look every bit as ragged as I feel,

> and the door to Sarah's office barely
> closes behind us before she attacks.
> *Look at you. Hmph. Ended up exactly*
> *as I predicted. You were determined*
> *to prove me right, weren't you?*

The old Eden would find an excuse,
even knowing she wouldn't be believed.
The new Eden has nothing to lose.
"*You* are responsible for my being here.
I didn't deserve what you did to me."

> *Of course you'd try to blame me.*
> *God will punish you for that, too.*
> *I had to see for myself just how far*
> *you fell. One thing's for certain, you*
> *can't come crawling back home. Stay*
>
> *among the filth, where you belong.*
> *It will probably please you to know*
> *you infected your sister with your*
> *disease, but Samuel will reform her,*
> *and she won't escape the way you did.*

A Poem by Vince Carino

Blame

Is a bullshit game,
and I'm a world-class
expert at gaming.

                        Some

are easy, some not so much,
but you need rules to play
competently, and one of the

                        things

you learn very quickly
about the blame game
is there

                        are

no guidelines, no
predetermined directions
to an exit strategy. What's

                        worse

is when the guilt
that evolves continues
to grow longer and deeper

                        than

the original stab
of remorse. Had I been
responsible for Cody's

                        death

I'd probably be over it
by now. But this will haunt
me until I go to my own grave.

Cody
You'd Think

Sitting up is something easily done,
and for most people, from the time
they're six or seven months old, it is.

Learning the skill is baby's play.
Relearning it has been one of the hardest
things I've ever attempted, not only

because I'm mostly numb from the waist
down, but also because my muscles
are seriously considering atrophy.

The most I've accomplished in some
twelve weeks is pushing the buttons
that call for the nurse or raise the bed,

and lifting silverware to my mouth,
when I feel like eating, which isn't all
that often. Federico's manipulations

keep me limber, but nothing close to
toned, let alone strong. We've mostly
managed to avoid bedsores, a plus.

But when Ronnie tried to help me
sit the first time, I couldn't. She enlisted
Federico, who showed me the ropes.

After several days of practice,
I can bring myself upright, unaided,
and move myself to the edge of the bed,

use my hands to swing my legs over
the side and stay there, mostly balanced,
for several minutes. I can't believe

such a little thing can give me such
a huge sense of accomplishment.
The determination to succeed doesn't

spark inside of me, however. Without,
as Ronnie calls them, my personal
cheerleading squad, I'd still be prone.

But between her, my mom, Federico,
and Nurse Carolyn, my free will has
been compromised, and truthfully,

sans Veronica Carino, the team would
not have near the influence as they do
with her spearheading my therapy.

She is a force to be reckoned with.
I just wish I knew why she's still by
my side after everything I've done.

A Stark Reminder

Of everything I've done walks
in the door this morning,
in the hulking form of Vince Carino.

Not sure why, considering his sister
is here practically every day, but
I never thought I'd see him again.

His approach is tentative, almost wary,
and so is my reaction to it—up come
my hackles. I feel like a caged coyote,

though the reason is watery. Vince never
did anything bad to me, except get
the best of me in poker on a regular basis,

and use me for my dope connections.
But I did exactly the same thing to him.
"Uh . . . Hey, Vince. What's up?"

He glances at the wheelchair parked
beside the bed. It obviously makes him
uncomfortable. Same for me, dude.

> *I thought I should drop by and have*
> *a conversation that's overdue.*
> *First, I'm sorry about what happened.*
>
> *Not that it's my fault or anything.*
> *Assholes like Chris are a dime a dozen,*
> *and he got no more than what he had coming.*

"Hey, you know, I don't blame you.
In the end, I'm the only responsible
person, not that I felt that way at first.

At first, I blamed everyone—Misty,
Lydia, my mom, my dead stepdad, and
even you, I guess. But when you wake

up to your life, changed forever in this
way, blame is easy. Figuring out what
to do next is the hard fucking thing."

> He nods as if he can relate, which is,
> of course, impossible. *Ronnie tells us*
> *she wants to help you, that she's willing*
>
> *to forget all the shitty stuff you did*
> *to her, and in spite of her being a very*
> *special girl. I want you to know that,*
>
> *two-legged, one-legged or legless, if*
> *you hurt my sister again, I will be*
> *happy to kill you the rest of the way.*

One thing about Vince, he's blunt. Cool.
I'll return the favor. "Even in the midst
of all the bullshit, I never stopped loving

Ronnie. Truthfully, one of the *only* things
I feel guilty about is letting her down.
I won't hurt her again. Not if I can help it."

He Studies Me Closely

Looking for hints of dishonesty,
ready to call my bluff. But this is
a solid bet. I mean every word.

> *Well, that's good, then. Because if*
> *I think for one moment you're playing*
> *her, just so she'll hang around until*
>
> *you get whatever support you can*
> *wring out of her, then decide to dump*
> *her . . . I told you what would happen.*

"Look, Vince. I never asked for her
help. In fact, I gave her every reason
to make a graceful exit from my life,

including coming totally clean
about the sewer I'd been swimming
in. I don't want her here because

she thinks it's the right thing to do.
I don't want her pity. I want her love,
something I don't deserve. But if

she's willing to give it, wants to invest
time and effort into what's left of me, I will
love her back, with all my heart. I can't

say what that means as far as the future.
I have to take it one day at a time, but every
day is a million times better with Ronnie in it."

His Grin

Is lopsided. Is it the first time
I've seen him smile, other than
his big-ass leer when he claims

> a giant pot at the poker table?
> *That's good to hear because*
> *it means I can offer my help, too.*
>
> *One, I have a friend who customizes*
> *autos, and he's willing to look at*
> *your car and see what he can do*
>
> *to make it work for you. I know*
> *buying another one is probably*
> *out of the question financially.*
>
> *Leon is talented. He'll get you on*
> *the road. Two, I don't know what*
> *your house is like, but I'm sure it'll*
>
> *need some alterations for accessibility.*
> *One of our cousins is a damn good*
> *handyman, and he'll work for cheap.*
>
> *I hear you're moving to a rehab*
> *hospital soon. How long will you be*
> *there? Do you know? Maybe he can*
>
> *have everything finished before*
> *you go home. And three, anytime*
> *you need to talk, man, call me.*

What the Hell

Just happened? We went
from murderous threats
to offers of help in less

than five minutes. "Jesus,
Vince. I have no idea what
to say, or how to thank you."

> Keep your mouth shut and
> stay good to my sister, we can
> be friends. I treat my friends right.

My eyes sting suddenly.
Can't cry in front of Vince,
or he'll change his mind.

No one needs a friend who
spontaneously bursts into
tears. But that's exactly

what I do, and he looks
petrified. "S-sorry. It's just,
no one except maybe Jack,

my stepdad, has ever been
so kind to me. Not even Mom,
and that's supposed to be her job."

> Yeah, well, don't let it get
> around. I've got a reputation
> to uphold, and "kind" isn't it.

Okay, then. One question,
though. "This isn't because
you feel sorry for me, is it?

'Cause I don't want pity
from you, either. I'd be happy
to accept your respect, though,

and I'm more than willing to
earn that, whatever it takes."
He's quiet, thinking it over.

Finally, he says, *Since we're friends
now, here's a story I don't tell
many people. My high school*

*sweetheart was this amazing
girl. Smart. Gorgeous. Going
places. A week after graduation,*

*a semi hit her car. She survived,
but lost a leg, and her face wasn't
ever going to be as beautiful*

*again. I did everything I could
to persuade her life was still
worth living, but she killed herself*

*that summer. You want respect?
Get your ass up out of that bed
and onto your feet again. You can.*

Add Vince

To my cheer squad. Weird.
So goddamn weird. "Sucks
about your girlfriend, dude."

> *It was a tragedy. What about you?*
> *You've thought about suicide,*
> *yeah?* He looks at me intently.

"Strangely, no. I mean, I did
ask the Great Squash to please
haul my ass home to the pumpkin

patch in the sky, but he ignored
me, and I'm way too much
of a coward to do the deed myself."

> He laughs, but then grows
> serious. *But . . . All right, I know*
> *this is really personal, but any*
>
> *chance you can have children?*
> *Not that you need a dozen*
> *next month or anything, but*
>
> *historically the Carinos are big*
> *on offspring—you know, like*
> *populating the planet with Italians.*

"I don't need a dozen, ever,
and I'm not sure I'll even want
one or two. But I felt that way

251

before this, and if I change
my mind, apparently the semen
factory is still functioning. It's

the delivery method that's in
doubt. Anyway, you're not saying
you want me to knock Ronnie up?"

> His amusement grows. *You do,
> and I'll kick your ass. Unless
> that's what she wants one day.*

"Just so you know, my ass can't
feel a thing, so kicking it would be
irrelevant." Am I really joking

about this? "As for the rest,
I guess it's one step at a time
(figuratively, of course) for now.

Tomorrow is a long way away.
The challenge is figuring out
how to get through today."

> *Fair enough. Listen. I'm happy
> to get hold of your mom about
> your car and the house renovation.*

> *But would you please let her know
> I'm going to call, so she doesn't think
> I'm out to scam her or something?*

252

I Agree

And Vince says goodbye, and as
I watch his retreat an odd sensation
settles over me: contentment.

Not at my condition, or the things
that led me here, but at the vague
possibility of a meaningful future.

The first step is acceptance, that's what
they keep telling me, and I understand
that my only real choices are to accept

or take the quick way out, like Vince's
girlfriend. My seventeenth birthday
is still a month away, three days after

the current year melts into the next.
I should be thinking about football.
Junior prom. Geometry, chemistry,

and American history. Psychology.
I should be worrying about Christmas
and what to buy for Mom and Ronnie.

Those things are lost to me, but what
remains is more important, and vital
to my struggle to, as Vince said,

get my ass up out of bed and onto
my feet again. I've got love. Support.
And at least a couple of friends.

253

Funny, but I never really thought
about my friends—or lack of them.
I had lots back in Kansas, and I

probably would have qualified
some of the people I knew from
school here in Vegas as buddies,

but no, not really. And of the girls
I went out with, only Ronnie
qualified. As for Vince, I saw him

as a means to an end. I had it all
bass-ackwards, and in hindsight
I see everything I did, every damn

goal I set, revolved totally around
me. Why did it take something like
this to clear my vision, shine

a spotlight on what's truly important—
not money or dope or winning a bet,
but treasuring the people who love

you? Figuring that out is the upside.
The downside is I didn't get it while
Jack was still around, or before I could

step in and stop Cory's downslide.
But any chance of that has evaporated.
Ditto the happiness I felt moments ago.

A Sudden Jolt

Zaps my spine, electric pain
just south of my disconnection.
"Jesus!" I fling the word toward

the wall, and it bounces back, too
loud in the hospital silence.
The effort sends another bolt

down, where I have no feeling
to speak of. How is it possible?
My finger starts working the call

button again and again. Overkill,
and I know it, but I want relief now!
Footsteps come pounding and Nurse

Carolyn hustles in. *What's wrong?*
She hurries to the side of the bed.
Pain? What kind, and where?

I'm familiar enough with the vocab
to tell her, "Lumbar region, neuropathic."
The kind initiated by my short-circuited

nerves, rather than musculoskeletal,
which is muscle or joint discomfort,
caused by overloading them. This is not

overwork. "It's bad. Real bad. Please,
can you give me something?" She nods
and goes to get permission while I sit

here wondering if the source of this
searing static isn't my stressed-out
brain informing my body that I

deserve to hurt. Maybe I should
keep my appointment with the shrink—
the one I've been avoiding, as if I

don't need a psyche adjustment.
Carolyn returns with both meds
and my mom in tow. Mom watches

me swallow a dose of relief, and
waits for the nurse to go. *I need
to talk to you about the house—*

"Hey. Ronnie's brother, Vince,
stopped by. He says he has a cousin
who can help with the alterations. . . ."

Another sharp stab in my lower
back makes me wince, and Mom's face
creases with concern. "Don't worry.

I'll be okay as soon as this pill
kicks in. Anyway, Vince says maybe
he could have it done by . . . what?"

She pulls a chair over close to me.
Takes my hand. *I didn't want to worry
you about anything outside of here, but . . .*

But There's a Lot

To worry about, starting with Mom
hasn't been able to put in very many
hours at her already low-paying job.

She's behind on bills, chief among
them the mortgage. Jack's life
insurance kept her head above water

for several months, but she can't see
a way to satisfy the bank. She's thinking
about letting the house go to a short sale,

> which means we'll have to live
> somewhere else. *Uncle Vern will
> let us move in for a while. There isn't*
>
> *a rehab hospital close by, but there's
> a gym not far away. Hopefully we can
> find a decent physical therapist.*

"Go back to Kansas? No fucking way!
What will I do there? I can't farm. I can't
fix tractors. Hey, I know. Maybe I can

find work as a scarecrow." Anger carves
into me, a white-hot blade. "No, Mom.
I won't leave Ronnie or give up on my rehab.

I'll figure something out." Where can I
find a big wad of cash? Is there a market
for sex with a guy in a wheelchair?

A Poem by Brielle Scott

Scarecrow

That lovely name
is what I was called
in elementary school.
All it took was one

vile

boy informing everyone
on the playground
that my clothes were Goodwill,
and my face was

ugly

enough to scare
crows dead off a high
wire, and the other kids'

laughter

inspired a whole line
of barnyard jokes. It took
years to understand how that

defined

the way I looked at myself
and perhaps explained
why I changed myself so
drastically. I became one of

the painted

women I saw on TV,
and that inspired
all the wrong people to steal
piece after piece of

me.

And then Ginger came along.

Ginger
Stealing Time

To spend with Brielle has totally
been a challenge. You're not
supposed to hook up with other
residents here, and since we're all

girls, that isn't a problem for most.
At first, it wasn't an issue for us, either.
But kissing led to touching led to
the overwhelming need to explore

each other in the most personal ways.
And that means sneaking around,
something I hate. I'm an in-your-face,
this-is-me-take-it-or-leave-it kind

of person. I'd rather just let everyone
know that Brielle and I have connected
because this feels like we're living
a lie, and dishonesty sucks most of all.

Still, after dinner, rather than follow
the group down the hall to watch TV,
I go to my room, wait a few minutes
for the others to settle in, then I slink

the opposite direction, to Brielle.
She's waiting for me on her bed in
a fuzzy blue robe. She opens it, and
there is nothing underneath but

toasted-oat skin stretched over soft
flesh. She is all curves, a complete
contrast to Alex's taut, straight lines.
Turn off the light, Brielle whispers.

Darkness shades the room, but
not completely. The moon is bright
through the window, offering just
enough illumination so we can see

each other's silhouettes. Brielle
coaxes me closer. I'm nervous,
but more about someone finding
out than about what we want to make

happen. I approach slowly, peeling
back my blouse and dropping
my skirt to the floor. "What about
your roommate? Should we worry?"

> *No need to rush,* she purrs. *Sonya*
> *is cool, and I asked her to please*
> *give me an hour alone in exchange*
> *for some help with her algebra.*

"Good. I do appreciate a smart
woman, not to mention excellent
planning. But I've got something
more exciting than algebra in mind."

I Climb into Bed

Beside her, open my arms, and
she settles into them like a warm
mist. Her lips seek mine, and our kiss
is sweet and gentle at first, but quickly

blossoms into passion. Brielle rolls
onto her back, urges me on top
of her, and the skin-to-skin contact
lifts the rich scent of cocoa butter.

"Mmm. You smell like chocolate.
Hot chocolate." We giggle softly,
like little girls, though the response
of our bodies is all woman. With Alex,

I was never in control, something
that always bothered me. I take charge
now, and it's a feeling like no other
to give pleasure before asking for it

in kind. Emotion wells up, seeking
release along with the rise and fall
of her breasts. I don't dare admit
to having fallen in love, though,

not to her or to myself, so I find
other words, hope they convey
how very much I care: "You are
beautiful, do you know that?"

Unreasonably, her muscles contract
and grow tight. *Don't say that.*
Don't lie to me. I'm ugly enough
to scare crows dead off a high wire.

My initial reaction is to laugh,
but I stifle it, knowing she means
what she said. "When was the last
time you looked in a mirror?"

She sighs. *Every time I look in*
a mirror I see that girl—the one
my classmates made fun of. I can't
find anyone else there. Just her.

"That is so wrong. Whoever told
you that you were ugly was obviously
blind. I wish he—or she—could see
you now. You are amazing."

I kiss her to prove it, and she relaxes
again. "That's better," I soothe, then
spend thirty minutes convincing
her how wrong that person was.

I Only Think About Alex

Four or five times.
I try to keep my mind
solidly here with Brielle,
but comparisons seem

to be inevitable. Alex
made me take, take, take.
Brielle opens herself to
my giving. Truthfully,

I have always been on
the receiving end, whether
by invitation or because
I had no choice. This is so

new I might have no idea
how to enjoy it, except it's
instinctive. My own joy
comes from making Brielle

sigh with pleasure, and at
last cry out that yes, this
is right, and yes she feels
beautiful. And I love

that I can do that for her
when I couldn't manage it
for Alex. I am turned on,
alive, because I am powerful.

Post-Pleasure

No time to revel in afterglow,
we slip back into our clothes
before Sonya can return to claim
her bed. "I wish we could sleep

together." Thinking about it,
I've rarely slept alone. Before
I left Gram's, there was always
at least one sister tucked in beside

me. And then there was Alex,
who I loved to snuggle up against,
though as time went on, she pulled
away from me more and more.

> *That would be nice,* says Brielle.
> *But that will probably never*
> *happen, and it makes me sad.*
> *Why did we have to connect now?*

"The natural cussedness of things,
that's what my gram used to say.
It's like the good stuff always hits
at the exact wrong time. Sucks."

> She comes over, slides her arms
> around my neck, kisses me sweetly.
> *Are you really leaving day after*
> *tomorrow? Why do you have to go?*

I push her gently away, look
down toward the floor so I can't
see the sadness in her eyes. "Gram
needs me. And I have to figure

out who I am. I don't know who
that is, or who I want to become.
I only know who I was, and this place
is a constant reminder of yesterday's

Ginger, the one I have to leave
behind. I just wish I didn't have
to leave you, too. I never expected
to care about someone again."

Brielle pushes closer, lifts a hand,
and her fingertips flutter against
my cheek. *I'll go you one better.*
I never expected to care for anyone,

period. I've worked very hard to
avoid it, in fact, which is why
everyone thinks I'm cold. Maybe
I am, but it's because I'm afraid

of getting hurt. Love wasn't meant
for people like you and me. You
have to be strong and brave to fall
in love. And maybe a little stupid.

Before I Can Figure Out

How to reply, we hear footsteps
outside the door. Brielle pops up
onto her bed and I hustle over
to the cracked vinyl chair near

the window, making sure my
clothing is straight and buttoned.
My butt is barely planted when
Sonya comes in, humming

> a Maroon 5 song I recognize
> from back when I still listened to
> music. She stops when she sees me.
> Considers. Smiles. *Oh. Hey, Ginger.*

I don't really care if she suspects,
so I meet her expression head-on.
"Hi, Sonya. Thanks for giving us
a little space. We were just talking

about how you have to be brave
to fall in love, or maybe stupid.
What do you think?" I address
Sonya, but give Brielle a wink.

> Sonya laughs. *I think you have
> to be stupid to hook up in a place
> like this. And if that leads to love,
> well, you get what you deserve.*

That Makes Me Laugh

Because I'm not sure if she's being
serious or totally sarcastic or even
if she means it in a bad way or good.
However she spun it, it's accurate.

"Know what? You're right. Okay,
I'll let you two tackle that algebra.
I've got some reading to do." I stand,
then turn to Brielle. "Gram says love

lives inside every one of us. We just
have to accept that it's there. Don't
believe it wasn't meant for you and
me. We deserve it more than most."

Deserving and accepting are two
vastly different things, of course.
I go back to my room, digesting
the past hour. There was making

love, yes, and it was new and
satisfying, in a whole different
way. Surprising. Something
I want to experience again.

But I think there was a fair
amount of love, the emotion, too.
I wish I was better acquainted with
it. How do I know if I'm right?

How Does Anyone Know

If they're right about love?
Pretty sure there's no way
around trial and error, and
hopefully learning from

your mistakes when it comes
to things like listening to
the arguments of your heart.
Argh! I'm so totally absorbed

in thinking about what just
happened with Brielle that it takes
several minutes for the scene
in my own room to solidify.

When I go inside, I notice
Miranda's presence. See,
from the corner of my eye,
that she's sitting on her bed.

But it isn't until I turn to look at
her that it becomes apparent
she's in shock, her Latina face
the color of oatmeal. "What is it?"

She doesn't say anything, but
offers whatever she holds in her
hand. It turns out to be a printed
page, ripped from the local newspaper.

MISSING TEEN'S BODY FOUND

That's what the headline screams.
I skim the story, which shares
the grisly details in lurid
tabloid fashion:

Shayleece Reynolds just turned seventeen.
She should have been struggling with chemistry
and reading Jane Austen novels. Instead,
the former child prostitute was found beaten,
raped, and left to die in a remote stretch of desert
north of Las Vegas. In a highly publicized trial
last week, Ms. Reynolds testified against

Lawrence Reynolds, her pimp and alleged
biological father (court-ordered DNA testing
has yet to return results) for murdering her mother,
another prostitute. Ms. Reynolds disappeared
on her way to a dental appointment and was
reported missing by staff at Walk Straight,
a child prostitute rescue group home.

It is believed her death was retaliation for
her testimony, which resulted in Lawrence
Reynolds's conviction for first-degree murder
and pandering a child under the age of fourteen,
which in itself carries a life sentence in the state
of Nevada. This case highlights the growing problem
of trafficking children for sex in Las Vegas and
across the US. Just last year, an FBI task force . . .

I Stop There

"Where did you get this?"
I've never seen any of the girls
look at a paper. Few enough of them
keep up with anything newsy.

> From Belinda. I was outside
> reading when she drives up, stops,
> and opens her window. She doesn't
> say anything. Just throws the envelope
>
> with this inside. I don't know how
> she knows where I am, Ginger.
> How did she find me? The message
> is clear: Keep your mouth shut.

Miranda is supposed to testify
against Papacito in a few weeks.
They've been building a case against
him and want to go to court before

the end of the year. "Did you tell
anyone?" She answers with a shake
of her head. "Why not? You have to!
They should take you somewhere safe."

> Where? If Papacito can find me
> here, he can find me anywhere.
> He'll kill me, just like that other
> girl. I have to leave. I need to hide.

"No, Miranda. Where can you hide?
You can't go home. Papacito knows
Ricardo, and your family would be
in danger. You don't have anywhere

else to go, do you? Better to let
your caseworker know, so . . ."
Her head swivels side to side.
"Listen. If you don't tell, don't

follow through and testify, Papacito
will get out of jail and go right back
to working those girls. You don't
want that to happen, do you?"

> She thinks it over, but not very
> long. *Doesn't matter who goes
> to jail, someone will make the girls
> work. Today, Belinda, tomorrow . . . ?*

Her eyes shimmer with frightened
tears. "Listen, I know you're scared.
I'd be scared too. But someone
has to make them stop—"

> *Not me! Why me? I'm just a kid.
> I can't change it. I can't change
> anything.* Rather than dissolve
> as expected, she goes totally blank.

It's After Hours

Only a single staff person here.
It's Bethany tonight. I'm afraid
to go looking for her and leave
Miranda alone, so I open the door,

call down the hall toward a couple
of girls headed toward the rec
room. "Hello? Can someone
please find Bethany right away?"

One of them waves assent,
and I turn back to check on
Miranda, who definitely looks
all "kid" right now. It's striking,

really. I mean, we just threw
her a fourteenth birthday
party, complete with balloons
and cupcakes. But turning

tricks makes you ancient
inside. I think it ages your soul.
If there's such a thing as
reincarnation, Miranda will

come back as a thousand-
year-old newborn, and in this
life she's already an elderly
woman wrapped up in a child's skin.

At the Sound

Of footsteps approaching, I step
out into the hall to intercept
Bethany and give her a heads-up.
I offer the basic info, then add,

"She's thinking about running.
You have to call her caseworker
or she'll be gone by morning."
And probably disappear forever.

> *I'll see if I can get hold of her,*
> agrees Bethany. *Meanwhile, keep
> an eye on Miranda. I'll be right
> back.* She scurries away and I

return to my room as requested.
Miranda looks catatonic, but at
least she's staying put. I decide
to check my messages, not sure

why, and I'm surprised to find
one from Alex. My heart stutters
happily. At least, until I read it.
MY MORNING SICKNESS IS OVER.

*THE BABY DECIDED HELL WAS BETTER
THAN LIVING WITH ME. I MISCARRIED.
AND I DECIDED LIFE ON THE STREET
IS WHAT I DESERVE. DON'T TEXT ME AGAIN.*

A Poem by David Burroughs
Living with Me

Is a privilege, one I reserve
for boys with exceptional
talents. It is well within

                                 my

power to make or break
not only careers, but also
the very lives of young

                                 men

and women, here in a city
spun on a web of connections.
The partners I choose

                                 represent

my taste, and I handpick
them carefully.
Intellect is high on

                                 the

list of requirements,
though I don't want them
better educated than me, and a

                                 beautiful

body like Seth's trumps worldly
experience. In fact, I prefer
schooling them. Some

                                 people

might disagree,
but breaking in a novice
definitely pleasures me.

Seth
Winter Approaches

Back home, it arrives, jacketed in ice.
Here, the only change of seasons

is sizzling to lukewarm and back again.
People tell me Las Vegas is no stranger

to snow, which makes me laugh. A few
flurries blowing down into the valley

from the surrounding mountains does
not a blizzard make. Still, even a pitiful

few snowflakes might shake me out
of this mood. I know it has everything

to do with Christmas coming. I've
never spent one away from the farm,

and nostalgia is suffocating me.
Familiar carols play in endless loops

in every store I happen into. It's almost
enough to keep me sequestered at David's.

But I'm even more uncomfortable there.
The parties have grown old. It takes

ever larger quantities of drugs to get
high. Ditto alcohol to dull the buzz.

Sex with David has become worse
than routine. It's how I imagine it must

be for couples together for decades—
a series of excuses followed by a single

let's-just-get-this-over-with encounter,
repeat the cycle. Even David must be

totally bored by the process. It feels
like things here are coming to an end.

But I don't dare make the first move
to disintegrate our relationship until

I've sorted out the far side. My bank
account is healthy, but won't last long

if I have to invest in a place to live
in Vegas, where a decent apartment

will set me back a minimum grand per
month, and I'd really prefer something

better than decent. I guess I've become
spoiled by living comfortably. Scratch

that. By living extremely well. How do
I give that up? Do I even dare try?

The Main Thing

That makes me want to try is Micah.
Our relationship has grown beyond

infatuation all the way to serious love,
and it's killing me because I just want

to be with him. If his show was dark
tonight and circumstances were different—

yeah, right—I could spend the entire evening
with him. Nice dinner. Take in a movie.

Go home and straight to bed, where sex
would be anything but boring. Fall asleep

in each other's arms. But he's dancing
and David's entertaining, and as for me,

the sex I'll have, but not enjoy, will be paid
for by Peter from Kansas or Oklahoma

or New Mexico, who's here for a roll
on the wild side. We're connecting at

Liaison, a relatively mainstream gay
nightclub housed inside a major casino

right on the strip. One thing I've learned
is to meet these guys somewhere very

public first, to gauge demeanor
and hopefully avoid problems once

we go upstairs or next door or down
the street to wherever they're staying.

A couple of times I hooked up with creeps
who wanted rough play and figured

since they were paying premium rates
I'd be happy to accommodate. I will,

to a point. But I do have limits, and stuff
like fisting or asphyxiation are high on

my no-can-do list. It's another good
reason to maintain a certain level of

muscle mass. I may be gay, but I can
fight my way out of a bad situation

if need be. Luckily those two men
weren't interested in getting *that* rough.

We compromised instead. And while
I didn't get the hefty tip they promised,

I still got paid for my time. There's
a learning curve to the escorting business.

Intuition

Becomes your best friend, and mine
tells me Peter from Wherever is safe

enough. The slender fortyish man is sitting
at a table for two, looking a bit unnerved

by the hunky guys dancing onstage.
I know it's him by the Stetson he wears—

our prearranged sign—and greet him
confidently. "Hello, Peter. I'm Seth."

> His eyes swing my direction and assess
> me curiously. *Oh. Yes. Hello. Um . . .*

> He stands and offers a weak handshake.
> *Please. Sit down. Drink?* At my request

for bourbon, he goes to the bar, returns
with two whiskey sours. It's well liquor,

which suggests that the bundle he'll drop
to spend time with me is beyond his budget.

Or maybe he's already dropped a wad
investing in slot-machine play. Either

way, I'll request payment up front.
I sip my drink and he gulps his, gaining

confidence and growing bolder.
You're different than I expected.

"Really? You're not disappointed,
are you?" He drains his glass to ice

before he answers. *Oh, no. Not
disappointed. In fact, I'm pleased.*

*I kind of thought you might be more . . .
effeminate, I guess. I mean, I did*

request a . . . He lowers his voice.
A top. But you're exactly right.

Okay, a little strange. There's some
kind of story here. Another drink,

and he tells it, slurring slightly.
See, when I was a kid, there was this

*guy who lived around the corner.
He looked a lot like you, except older.*

*I used to ride my bike by his house
and one day I got a flat out in front.*

*He was working in his yard and
offered to fix it. I followed him around*

*back to his shed. There were lots
of pictures on the wall—not naked*

*ladies, like most men have, but guys
in the buff, doing unmentionable things.*

*While he fixed my tire, I kept staring
at them. I didn't even know penises*

*were meant to do anything but pee.
Finally, he says, "You know, it feels*

*really good to have someone touch
your wiener. I'll show you if you want."*

*He showed me, and it did feel really
good. I kind of knew it was wrong,*

*but that made it even better. I went
back a few times. At first it was just*

*hand jobs. Then he taught me oral.
One day, he wanted to demonstrate*

*"the very best way." I was only ten,
and penetration hurt like hell. Plus,*

*it made me bleed. My mother noticed
my underwear, and that was that.*

What Peter Wants

Is for me to play dirty old neighbor.
Hey, it's his cash, and I do ask for it

up front before we head to his room,
which happens to be at the Mandarin

Oriental, a short walk from the club.
We go up to the twelfth floor, to superb

accommodations. Apparently Peter
is flush after all. Maybe he just likes

cheap booze. He pours two deep
glasses of Jack Daniel's before going

to the bathroom to get ready. I return
most of mine to the bottle, turn on

the TV and find a country music
channel. I'm betting Peter is a country

kind of guy. If not, I am, and I get
to be in charge. I take off my shirt,

leave the jeans on so I can order him
to unzip them. I also take a quick whiff

of powdered encouragement from
a little bottle hidden in my sock.

By the time he wobbles back,
I'm ready to go. Ready to play dirty

neighbor who has gay porn hanging
on the walls of his shed. "Come here,

kid. Get down on your knees." And,
we're off, Toby Keith warbling in

the background. Peter has come prepared
with a number of toys, including his favorite

vibrator. If I wasn't buzzed and expecting
a very good tip, I'd have a hard time

stomaching the coming play. Instead, I
jump into the game and an hour passes

before I know it. Little boy Peter finishes,
completely satisfied. "If it's okay, I'd like

to clean up before I go." He nods mutely,
and doesn't even put on his underwear

again before shuffling over to say hi to Jack
Daniel's again. I take a quick shower,

       and as I'm leaving, Peter says,
       I'm not even gay, just so you know.

Could Have Fooled Me

Then again, who knows? I've read
that a lot of men who don't identify

as queer enjoy a good male-to-male
romp once in a while. Apparently,

some of them don't believe it's cheating
on their partners if they have sex with

a man instead of another woman.
I guess you can justify anything, as

long as you have psychological
parameters firmly in place. Whatever.

As far as I'm concerned, cheating
is cheating. And suddenly, I'm struck

by a fierce attack of guilt, despite
the eleven hundred dollars in my pocket.

No way can I go home to Micah
after performing the way I just did

with someone else. I've got to get out
of this business before I lose any more

of Seth. Wonder if I can regain what
I've lost of him already if I do quit.

In Need of Fresh Air

And time to eliminate Peter from
my mind, I wander down to the far

end of the strip, then cut down a side
street to the monorail station, where

I'm sure I can catch a cab. I'm almost
there when I hear a couple of male

voices yelling and, just underneath
them, soft pleading. Shit. Last thing

I need is to get involved in a row,
but someone is getting pummeled.

I move closer, and sure enough, back
up against a building, a female form

is on the sidewalk with two large men
standing over her, and I can see her arms

        raised to try and protect her face.
        Fucking fag! screams one of the dudes.

        I don't let no queer touch my dick.
        I'm gonna kill you, fucking whore.

Ah, shit. Now I have to do something,
don't I? First thing is pull out my phone

and dial 911 to report an assault
in progress. Now I hear the victim

> wheezing. *Please. I'm sorry. Take
> my money. Please. Leave me . . .*

Oh, man. I recognize her voice.
"Pippa!" I yell. "Is that you?"

> *H-help me.* Now she falls silent
> and her body slumps, motionless.

Still the men beat her. Kick her. Stomp
on her. Goddamn it! "Hey, assholes!

You like beating up girls?" They
straighten, turn toward me.

> *This ain't no girl, dickwad,* says one.
> *Besides, what business is it of yours?*

"She happens to be my friend.
But even if she wasn't, I'd have

to kick your ass." Two against one.
Bad odds. But I have no choice,

so I wade in, hoping they don't rob
me when they're finished wasting me.

Adrenaline Pumping

I hold my own for a while, and
barely feel the blows that connect.

Luck is with me in a couple of ways.
One, neither man seems to have

a weapon. And two, by the time
I'm actually losing the battle, a siren

is closing in. A huge set of knuckles
opens my forehead just above my left

eyebrow. The dudes take off running
as I drop to my knees, blood dripping.

I crawl over to Pippa, pull her skirt
down over her exposed crotch

before the cop can see it. She's
unconscious, breathing shallowly,

and bleeding a lot worse than I am.
I'm glad she can't see her face.

Son of a bitch! The cruiser pulls up
parallel to the sidewalk, and an officer

> gets out, strolls over to take a peek.
> *You call this in? What happened?*

"Can you, like, possibly arrange
for an ambulance or something?

In case you haven't noticed, they
messed her up pretty good."

     He actually bends over to check her pulse
     and see if she's breathing. *I probably*

     should. You stay right here. I'll need
     you to give me a statement, okay?

He saunters—yeah, that's the word—
back to his car. I sit, pull Pippa's face

off the sidewalk and into my lap,
try to stroke her hair smooth. I know

she'd be mortified for anyone to see
her like this. "It's okay, lady," I soothe.

"You're safe now." She moans softly,
so maybe she hears me. Suddenly,

I remember the bottle in my sock.
The cop is busy reaching for something

so I take the opportunity to remove it
and roll it off to one side. Just in case.

That Proves

To be a wise move. When the EMTs
arrive, one of them takes a look at

my face and decides I should go in
for stitches, which means I get to ride

with Pippa in the ambulance. They haul
her into the emergency room immediately.

I, on the other hand, get to wait for a while,
filling out paperwork, both for the hospital

and for the cop who impatiently followed
to bug me for that statement. Pretty

sure he thinks I was more involved with
the incident than happening onto it

by accident, but tough. What I write
is a truthful account of the facts as I know

them. By the time I finally arrive home,
forehead sewn back together and bandaged,

it's almost three in the morning. I expected
David to be worried. But he's fast asleep.

I, on the other hand, won't sleep tonight.
I go outside, call Micah, disturb his dreams.

A Poem by Bryn Dawson
Disturbed

That's what everyone
called me when I was a kid,
and truth is, they were

                           right

though they didn't know
just how screwed up I was.
I believe the correct word
is sociopath. I was born in the

                           wrong

century. Ancient Rome
would've been perfect for me,
as long as my circumstances
were royal. I mean,

                           who

wouldn't celebrate having sex
with any number of slaves,
then trading them in
for newer models as soon
as boredom sets in? I

                           really

wish I'd been born into
money, instead of having
to create an income stream.
Think of the opportunities, no

                           cares

in the world except having
an exceptional time just being
alive and getting laid by pretty
young girls like Whitney.

Whitney
Despite It Being Saturday

I'm plugged into my computer,
where online learning is boring
me to tears. Yes, I've got lots of
catching up to do, if I'm to start
school again after the winter break
and reintegrate with my classmates,
now halfway through their junior year.

But even if I log in hours upon
hours, read every entry, learn
every math trick, pass every test,
how do I manage going back there?
What's the point? To pretend
I'm a regular kid again?

Even trying to reconnect
with Paige has been strange.
Yes, because she's friends
with Skylar, and that bitch
hasn't changed one little bit.
But it's more than that. For
as much as Paige has altered
her appearance, dropping
poundage and tinting her spiky
hair pink, once you get past
the Skylar-inspired conceit,
she's still the same inside as
before I left. Goofy. Girly.
She likes shopping. Texting.
Dreaming about the perfect guy.

But me? Oh, I'm different.
Once you've immersed yourself
in ugliness, wallowed in it,
sponged it up and internalized
it, you can't cough it back up
and spit it out. It becomes hard
to find beauty in anything.
No matter where I look, I find
evil lurking. A monster sleeps
inside every man. Cop. Mechanic.
Minister. It doesn't matter. I can
see the beast he hides. I won't let
one of them sneak up on me again.

How am I supposed to sit in
a classroom, hurry through
the hallways, change for PE?
How am I supposed to have
fun goofing around with friends
who have no concept of reality?
How am I supposed to stay clean
when the truth of what I've done
closes in around me, squeezing
hideous memories from the deep
recesses of my brain, and what
I really want is the kind of sleep
only the Lady can provide?

How am I supposed to trust
enough to fall in love, knowing
every guy is defective?

I Keep My K12 Program Open

(Still logging those online learning
hours!) while surfing the Web for
more exciting discoveries
than what chemistry can offer.

My news feed is full of them,
and the first story that catches
my eye is about a teen prostitute
whose body turned up rotting
north of Las Vegas. You know,
that could have been me, except
Bryn wasn't exactly the murder-
his-girls type. He was more
the help-them-OD type. Guess
I got lucky. The word makes
me snort. Yeah. Lucky. That's me.

Wonder how many girls just
disappear, sucked into the life
one way or another, only to die
at the hands of a pimp or a john,
no one to mourn them, or if there
is, those people have no idea
that their loved one met death
in such a brutal way. Is anyone
mourning Shayleece Reynolds?
Did anyone mourn her mother?

If I would've died there on that
stinking carpet, wonder how long
my family would have mourned me.

I Invest Four Hours

In schoolwork. Blow through
English and American history,
which aren't as boring as chem.
Dad says homeschooling isn't
a good path to college, but I
can't think past today, let alone
start plotting my future.

Mom pops her head in once
in a while to make sure I'm
performing, and when I finish
she has a surprise for me.

> You've been working so hard.
> I thought you might like to go
> to the boardwalk. The rides
> are closed this time of year,
> of course, but there's Neptune's
> Kingdom and the big arcade
> and tonight is the holiday lights
> train. What do you think?

She's letting me escape
the house? Surely not without
supervision. "You mean, go
alone or with you or what?"

> No fun to do it alone. Why
> don't you call Paige and see
> if she wants to go along?
> I'm happy to spring for it.

294

The Santa Cruz Boardwalk

Is right on the beach. In summer,
it's really fun, but during the winter
months the rides close down and
you're left with indoor amusements.
Still, there's music and food and
arcade games, which I used to love.
At this point they seem pretty silly.

So, of course, Paige wants to play
them. When I invite her to come,
I think for sure she'll turn me
down. Skylar, apparently, is tied
up elsewhere, however, because
Paige is quick to say okay.

Mom drops us off a little after
three. We watch her drive away.
"Before we go inside, can we take
a walk on the beach? My feet
haven't touched sand in months."

> *Las Vegas has sand,* she whines,
> but then agrees to a short stroll.

It's a crackling cool, clear blue
day, and the sound of waves in
the distance lifts a mist of nostalgia.
The last time I was near the surf
was the day Bryn took pictures
of me. How can I possibly miss him?

Paige must be psychic because
she chooses this moment to say,
*So tell me about modeling. Did
you make bank, or what?*

I'm good at off-the-cuff lying.
"Not really. I was still building
my portfolio by doing local shoots.
I was also partying a lot. It goes
with the territory." That part, at
least, is accurate enough.

*Skylar says you were probably
doing porn. You weren't, were you?*

"Skylar's a jealous whore. Tell
her I said doing porn would be
preferable to listening to her rude,
nasty comments. You can also
tell her she couldn't qualify to do
porn. She couldn't pass an audition."

*I can't believe your mom would
let you go to Vegas with that guy.*

"Mom's more open-minded
than you'd think. Okay, my feet
have touched the sand enough.
The train's at five. Let's get tickets."
I'm finished talking about Vegas.

296

We Could Skip the Train

Except Mom was really clear
that it should be part of the evening.
I think it's her own nostalgia.
We used to ride it every year
when Kyra and I were little.
Dad used to come along, too.

"You don't mind riding the train,
do you? Pretty sure Mom would
be disappointed if we didn't."

> *Are you kidding? Santa Claus*
> *and candy canes are two of*
> *my favorite things.* See?
> That's the old Paige right there.

We have to wait almost an hour
to board. As daylight fails and
the lights glitter on, I start to feel
pretty good. Like maybe I don't
really need a romp with the Lady
after all. But soon enough, we run
into a few people I used to know
at school. They all ask where I've
been and I feed them the same
tired story I shared with Paige.

After a while I kind of want to tell
them I was doing porn, if only
to see the shock in their eyes and
determine the velocity of rumors.

My Mood Improves Again

Once the locomotive gets
rolling through town. It chugs
through neighborhoods
where many people have
decorated their homes to
the max for the enjoyment
of the entire city, including
us holiday train passengers.

It's fun to watch the children,
especially the young ones,
whose eyes grow wider and
wider as they wait for Santa
to vacate the caboose and make
an appearance in the cars. Funny,
but I've never even thought
about having kids of my own.
I'd probably be a crap mother,
but, hey, you never know.

Was that just me, thinking
I might be able to have
something approaching
a normal life, after only
a few hours ago being very
sure that wasn't possible,
because of a train ride?

Maybe my mom knows
a thing or two after all.

The Arcade

Is crowded with families
enjoying everything from
pool to bowling to pinball,
plus a huge variety of electronic
games. Christmas carols loop
in the background, and the whole
place is done up with ornaments
and tinsel. It's fake, fake, fake.
But still, it's very pretty. I think
I'm starting to define "bipolar."

Before long, one thing starts to
stand out. I noticed it on the train,
too, where several women ignored
their excited children while vying
for the title, Crap Mother. "Why is
everyone so in love with their phones?"

Paige quickly stashes hers. *What
do you mean? Oh, look. There's
a MyBoardwalk kiosk. Let's get
some cards. They use those instead
of tokens here now, so you know.*

I hand her some of the cash
Mom gave me, thinking about
people and their cell phones.
I guess maybe I used to text
a lot. But in Vegas I only used
my phone for business, and after

299

a while I hated when it rang.
Sometimes when it blares now,
it plops me right back in that
shit-hole apartment with Bryn.

We spend a couple of hours
on games. Bowl. Shoot pool.
I'm miserable at all of them,
but have fun, anyway. "Hey,
are you hungry? I'm starving."

> *Get something. I already had*
> *a candy cane, and if I eat I'll have*
> *to go puke it up. I need to lose*
> *five pounds before winter break.*
> *We're going to Hawaii and I want*
> *to look good in my new bikini.*

"You're kidding, right? If you
lose any more weight you'll dry
up and blow away. What are
you now? Size three?"

> *Exactly. I don't think my bone*
> *structure will let me get down*
> *to size zero, but I'm trying.*

"I think you're being ridiculous
but I can't force a cheeseburger
down your throat. I plan to eat one,
anyway. Fries, too. My modeling
career is on indefinite hold."

300

It's a Damn Fine Burger

And I take pleasure in eating
it slowly, watching Paige
salivate. She does swipe a few
of my fries. Hope she doesn't
feel the need to vomit them.

Fed, full, feeling pretty good,
I go throw my trash away and
when I get back, find Paige flirting
with a couple of guys who have
joined her at the table. Their faces
are vaguely familiar. I'd peg them
as seniors, and jocks. "That was quick."

> Paige laughs. *They're stalkers.*
> *Actually, this is Gary and James.*
> *You guys remember Whitney?*
> *She just moved back from Vegas.*

Gary seems to be connected
to Paige. So much so, in fact,
that I suspect she made sure to let
him know we'd be here tonight.
James, who's sandy-haired and
obviously built, turns assessing
dark eyes toward me and grunts
something resembling a hello.

Next thing I know, we've become
a foursome, which is irritating, but
at least it keeps Paige off her phone.

Gary, who is much better-looking
than the guys I've seen Paige with
before, keeps an arm wrapped
around her shoulders as we head
back toward the arcade. James
measures my stride and adjusts
his accordingly. "You a senior?"
I ask because one of us should

> say something. *Yep. Five more*
> *months and I'm out of here. Not*
> *sure where I'm going yet, though.*
> *Did you like Vegas? I hear it's ugly.*

"Oh, baby, you have no idea.
I mean, if you like lots of neon
and phony facades, the strip is kind
of pretty. But underneath all that
it's filthy. And goddamn hot, too."

> *So, are you in school or what?*

"Right now, I'm homeschooled."
I give him a very short version
of the modeling/rehab story.
He's surprised when I tell him
I'm only a junior. "Why? I look older?"

> *Yeah. Drugs can do that to you.*
> *My sister got into that shit. Hope*
> *you can stay clean. She couldn't.*

302

His Concern Seems Genuine

Some people look at rehab
like it's for losers. Others,
like it's a badge of honor.
James sees it as a necessity
for someone who's chosen
to play with fire. His sister
got scorched. She OD'd.
"I'm really sorry to hear that."

> Thanks. It sucked. What a waste.
> She was special, too. And it
> was all because of some dude.

"Usually is." I don't elaborate.
It's been a long time since I felt
this comfortable around a guy.
He's different somehow. Sweet.
That's the word. At least, on
the surface. Which makes me
wonder what, exactly, he's hiding.

Gary, however, is obnoxiously
obvious. The arm that was
around Paige's shoulders now
circles her waist, and once in
a while his hand falls to test
the muscle mass of her butt.
Doesn't bother her at all.
Not sure why it's bothering me.

Finally, the Two of Them

Brake to a stop in front of
the laser tag entrance. Damn.
I was hoping to avoid it, but
Paige and Gary are hot to play.
I shake my head. "I'll wait for you."

> *Come on. It'll be fun. We used
> to do this all the time, remember?*

I'm not brain-dead. Of course
I remember. She's right. We
did, and it was fun. Besides,
they're all looking at me like
I'm totally lame. "Okay," I
agree reluctantly. "I've just
been a little claustrophobic
lately, so I might quit early."

We pay, go inside. Strap on
vests, choose our weapons.
James and I play blue; Paige
and Gary go red. The game
begins and everything goes
dark and my stomach starts
to churn. Now neon streaks
the shadows and, as I feared,
I'm back in the black alleys
of Las Vegas, and there's
movement signifying faces
I can't see and don't want to.

And this is nothing like fun.

Now Someone Yells

Behind you!

I spin, heart stammering,
and a laser beam lights my chest.
Inhale. Exhale. I breathe in stutters.
"You're fine, you're fine," I chant.

It's a game.
No danger here.
Kids are playing.
Danger loves kids.
Danger seeks kids.
Danger leaves kids
to die in the desert.

Exit.
Where's the exit?
There. Over there.
I run for the door and feel
someone running behind me.
"No!" I scream. "Leave me alone!"

> *Whitney.* He's there. Right
> there. Reaching for me. His
> hand falls against my shoulder.
> *Whitney. It's James. It's okay.*

James? James! I turn into him,
sobbing, and he takes me gently
into his arms, guides me to the exit,
my pendulum swinging toward crazy.

A Poem by Andrew McCarran

Reaching for Me

Finally, Eden's found
the courage to tell me
where she's been hiding
these long, lonely weeks,
and today—today!—I'll see

                    her

again. The mirror
reveals a different man
than the one who last held
her. It's not just that my hair
is longer, or that my

                    face

has grown winter pale
beneath a full beard.
No. It's the deep
trepidation that

                    haunts

my eyes, despite the surfacing
joy. What if we've moved
too far beyond the halcyon
days we share in

                    my

recollection? What if
she isn't real at all, but only
something I imagined,
or the invention of overactive

                    dreams.

Eden
It's Been a Nightmare Few Days

First, my mother informed me
that she has condemned my sister
to the dungeons at Tears of Zion.
She caught your disease, that's
what Mama said, as if falling

in love is a contagion—a virus
of the heart. I vowed to find a way
to get Eve out, and know transparency
is the only way to make that happen.
I have to confess before I can accuse.

But before I could take my story
public, we got the news about
Shayleece. No one stepped forward
to claim her body, so the counselors
here pooled enough money to bury

her properly. All the girls went to
the funeral, so at least she had people
there to say goodbye, whether or not
they wanted to. Most of us did. Most
of us realized it could have been one

of us lying in that coffin, which
remained closed. The speculation about
why turned into some interesting,
if macabre, gossip. Hard to think
about what the buzzards managed.

The Best Thing

To come out of all the bad
is I get to see Andrew today.
My decision to talk about Tears
of Zion freed me to let him know
where I am. He's catching the first

available flight. My stomach
is doing flip-flops. I'm scared
and happy and crazy excited,
all knotted up together. I wish
I had something nice to wear,

instead of the thrift-store clothes
in my drawers. When I told him
that, he said he couldn't care less,
he'd be looking at my face, not
my jeans. That's good, because

I've gained a few pounds since
the last time I saw him. Will
he look the same? It's been almost
eight months. Not a lot of time
in the scheme of things, but enough

to change our appearance. What
matters is what's left inside.
Right now, my heart is buoyant
with love. I just wish I knew for
sure that's how he feels, too.

Speaking of Feelings

Mine are in upheaval because
my parents cut me loose. That's
a relief because going home
is unthinkable. But what Mama
said is I'm no longer their daughter.

I've been orphaned, and that hurts
more than I could have guessed.
And what will I do about Boise?
Andrew still has solid ties there,
and it's not a very big city.

If I go back, I'm sure to run into
my ex-family, plus people from
church, where ugly rumors must be
circulating. Once I make a big stink
about Tears of Zion, that's bound

to get worse. Some pills are worth
swallowing, I guess. At least I'm
moving forward. I can't change
a single minute of yesterday.
But I can take charge of the future,

and at the top of my list is saving
my sister and hopefully playing
a role in the demise of Tears of Zion.
It's anyone's guess what will happen
once I report Father Samuel Ruenhaven.

I Wanted to Do It

Before I see Andrew, so
I can't change my mind.
Right now, I'm sitting
in the offices of the Nevada
Investigation Division.

Tears of Zion is in a different
county, and it will be up to
a detective here whether or
not to inform Elko County
that they might want to take

a look at this so-called religious
retreat center. Sarah is with
me, sensing I could still bolt
at any time. I'm relieved when
the detective who calls me in

> turns out to be a woman.
> It would be harder to look
> a man in the eyes and relate
> the horror stories I have to
> tell. *Come in,* she says. *I'm*

> *Detective Finnegan. But you*
> *can call me Marlene.* She must
> see the sudden rush of fear.
> *It's okay,* she soothes. *Don't*
> *be afraid. I'm on your side.*

A Half Hour Later

I almost believe she might,
in fact, be on my side.
She listens intently to every
word, and I find no disbelief
in her body language.

> First off, I want to thank
> you for bringing this to our
> attention. We take allegations
> of child abuse quite seriously
> in this office. I do have a couple
>
> of questions for you, though,
> as I'm sure the Elko County
> DA will be asking them, too.
> One: Why did you wait so long
> before coming forward?

"Humiliation, for one thing.
Before all this happened I'd
had exactly one boyfriend,
and we never did anything
like . . . that. I had no idea

people *ever* acted like that.
And then, what I did here
on the streets, just to eat . . ."
Emotion wells up, uninvited.
"I'm sorry. I didn't mean to cry."

Marlene leans forward,
hands me a box of tissues.
Please don't apologize.
Memories like that are hard
to relive. Any other reasons?

"I didn't want my mother
to know where I was, so I gave
Walk Straight a made-up name
and told them my parents were
dead. Eventually, though, I had

to come clean. I'm a horrible
liar and besides, the people
at Walk Straight are so good
to me, I couldn't risk them
getting in trouble on my account."

    Okay. Two: I understand this
    Jerome fellow assaulted you.
    What about Ruenhaven himself?
    I could make something up to
    implicate him. If I don't, he might

just walk. Still, I can't lie. "Not
sexually, no. But he was completely
responsible for the isolation,
and lack of water, food, and
opportunity to use the bathroom."

When she asks how I know
that, I tell her, "Because he was
very clear that he had personally
written the Tears of Zion rule book,
and deviation meant punishment.

He straight-on informed me that
my parents sanctioned whatever
actions he saw fit to provide,
and let me know they didn't want
me to come home. They still don't."

> *Okay, then. I'll type this up
> into a formal complaint and
> have you sign it. One last
> question before I do. Why
> choose to come forward now?*

"Because they sent my little
sister there, too. She's only
fourteen, and doesn't deserve
to be hurt the way I was. I need
you to help me save her."

Marlene winces, and I know
she's thinking the same thing
I have over and over for the last
eight months: How could any
parent do this to their child?

313

I've No Clue

What the outcome will be,
but I leave reassured that,
at the very least, Nevada
law enforcement has Tears
of Zion on its radar. Marlene

swears that's the case. "Also,"
I add, "my counselor did some
independent research. Samuel
Ruenhaven has had charges
brought against him personally

in Idaho. That's Sarah, waiting
for me, in case you want to talk
to her. I mean, I know you'll be
thorough and all. . . ." Come on,
Eden. Don't irritate her now.

> But she's not mad. In fact,
> she laughs. *I promise our*
> *investigators can dig deeper*
> *than Sarah can, but thanks*
> *for the heads-up. And, Eden?*
>
> *I know you're worried about*
> *your sister. We'll do everything*
> *we can to make sure Eve's safe.*
> *The Elko County DA is a good*
> *friend of mine. Try not to worry.*

Worry? Me?

But that's all I can do at this
point. I despise feeling helpless,
can't stand spending every day
being reactive. How do I change
that? How can I become proactive?

On the ride back to Walk Straight,
I broach the subject with Sarah.
"I believe Marlene is on my side.
But how long will it take before
we hear something from Elko?"

> Sarah's sigh could sink a life
> preserver. Not a good sign. *Longer
> than you'll want it to, I'm afraid.
> Bureaucracy, you know. One
> hand has to wash the other.*
>
> *It's good that Marlene knows
> the DA personally. That will
> help speed up the process some.
> And any extra time between now
> and when this thing blows open*
>
> *will benefit your emancipation.
> Once your parents sign the papers
> and they're filed, it won't be easy
> for them to change their minds.
> Hopefully this stays quiet till then.*

We decided emancipation
is the best way to go, for
the very reason that once a judge
agrees, no one can decide otherwise
except the court itself. Walk

Straight is instrumental to my
qualifying, as they've "hired" me,
so I have a job that includes room
and board plus necessary transportation.
But Mama and Papa have to agree.

Riling them up now could be bad.
"You mean because my mother
might decide to get even."
That revenge trumps disowning
her demon-possessed daughter.

> *She seems like the type, yes.*
> *I'm expecting the notarized*
> *papers any day now. Once I get*
> *them, we file the petition and*
> *secure a hearing date. Then*
>
> *we still have to serve notice*
> *on your parents, and that's before*
> *you even see a judge. It's not really*
> *complicated. It just takes time.*
> *But don't worry. We'll make it happen.*

Don't Worry

Everyone keeps saying that,
but nobody tells me how
to make myself quit. Every
facet of my life is stressful.
Thank God I've got such great

support at Walk Straight.
Without this place and these
people, especially Sarah,
where would I be living today?
Would I even be alive,

let alone have a solid chance
at a decent future? Which
brings me back to Boise and
Tears of Zion. Because if
Elko County closes it down . . .

"Question. What happens
to Eve if Father packs up
his disciples and moves on?
She'd go home, right?" Yeah,
and if she does, then what?

> *I'm afraid that would be up*
> *to your parents. As I said before,*
> *usually parents are clueless*
> *about what actually*
> *goes on at these facilities.*

It would be very hard
to prove they knew what
went on at Tears of Zion,
and even if you could, it
wouldn't be enough to make

the state step in and take
custody of your sister. Not
unless they actually took part
in the activities, or somehow
inflicted physical abuse.

But let me ask you a question.
Are you absolutely certain
your mom and dad do know?
Did you talk to your mother
about it when she was here?

"She never gave me the chance.
You don't talk to my mother.
She tosses words at you,
or in my case, insults. Besides,
no way would she admit it."

Sarah shrugs. Probably not.
But you never know, and I'm
big on communication, if
for no other reason than to
let the bad thoughts escape.

Once We Get Back

I've got around an hour
to kill before Andrew
is supposed to arrive.
I spend it helping Sarah
file paperwork. Earning

my paycheck, and letting
the bad thoughts escape
through mindless office
activity. I can hardly believe,
after this long, I'll see

my Andrew in just a short
while, and I keep watching
the time. *Click. Click. Click.*
The hands of the old-fashioned
wall clock barely move at all,

then suddenly it's twelve
thirty, the appointed time.
But no Andrew. *Click. Click.*
Twelve forty-five. *Click.*
One o'clock. He's not coming.

I keep working, pushing
back tears. 1:10. 1:20.
And suddenly there's a male
voice outside the office.
The door opens, and . . .

319

We Stare

At each other for several long
seconds. Oh my God. It's him.
It's really him. "Andrew."
He opens his arms, and I'm in
them, and he picks me up,

> spins me round and round
> until my head is spinning, too.
> Now he stops, looks down
> into my eyes. *My beautiful
> Eden. I finally caught you.*

Our kiss is tentative at first,
and not just because he's wearing
a beard, but then it's like our lips
remember, and no amount of
facial hair can interfere with

this connection. It's sweet. And
passionate. And soaked in love.
It lasts for a very long time, until
finally I have to say, "Oh, Andrew,
I love you. Don't let go of me."

> He keeps his arms wrapped
> tightly around me. *I'll never
> let you go again. Can this
> really be you? I thought I'd lost
> you forever.* Tears fill his eyes.

And I'm Crying, Too

I can't bear to pull away.
I lay my ear against his chest,
listen to his heartbeat, which
sparks delicious memories of lying
together under the Boise sky.

That scene fades into another,
out on his ranch, inhaling alfalfa
green while we made love for
the first—and only—time.
And that makes me think of Mama.

I extract myself from his arms,
reach up to touch the hair curling
softly around his chin. "You
grew a beard. I like it. Makes
you look so Idaho rancher."

> He smiles and his eyes glisten.
> *That's what I am, ma'am. Or, I*
> *should say, miss. Have to remember*
> *polite talk. I spend an awful lot*
> *of time alone. Not anymore, though.*

"Oh, Andrew, there's so much
to talk about. Some of it's good,
some I'm scared to tell you. But
I'm strong enough with you here."
It's a three-hour conversation.

A Poem by Veronica Carino
Some Conversations

Just don't happen, no
matter how important
they are.

keep putting them off—
let's talk tomorrow, Cody,
or next week or next year—
because, think as hard
as you're able, you

have the right words
to launch them. Or,
you withhold pertinent
facts because you don't

how the person across
the table might react.
But sometimes,
despite everything,

must be conveyed erupts
from your mouth
like a geyser you dare
not cap, and once that
happens, there's nothing left

You

don't

know

what

to say.

Cody
Been Practicing

Transferring myself from bed
to wheelchair and back into bed again.
The first few times were pretty damn

lame. Without Federico on my ass
to show me the ropes, I never
would have figured out the trick,

which has to do with weight shift
and lean, and compensating for what
my legs have lost with the strength

of my arms and core. Both were in
miserable shape until I decided I'm not
going to lie around grieving for the rest

of my life. Screw that. So I asked
for weights I could use in bed, and I'm
looking forward to time in the gym.

Tomorrow I move over to the rehab
hospital, where I'll work my butt off
every day, gaining what I can. If I wind

up back in Kansas, something I'm real
determined not to let happen, I want
to be the strongest wheelchair jockey

around, in case I need to kick some
farmer's ass for hitting on Mom or
something. I mean I could always use

a gun instead. But where's the challenge
in that? The game would be two viable
limbs conquering four. Not great odds,

but that's where the bluff—playing
the disabled card—comes in. Once
a gambler, always a gambler, I guess.

I'd probably be a better gambler
in the sticks, too, playing poker with
country boys. In Vegas, everyone knows

the rules of the game. Just, please God,
if there is a You, don't let me go back
to Kansas. "Hey, Jack. You up there?"

I hiss out loud. "Could you please put
in a good word for me? And if you
happen to be looking down, check this out."

I pull the wheelchair over, very close,
angle it so I don't have to push up
over the wheel. Lean forward, scoot

my butt back, which puts my weight
forward. Feet flat on the floor, arms
close to my sides. Grab the bed frame

with one hand, the chair with the other,
and lift . . . The wheelchair rolls back
and in one sudden motion, fuck! I find

myself on the floor. *Did someone forget
to put on the brakes?* Federico sweeps
into the room. *How many times have*

*I told you to do that first? It's the most
important part. Oh, well. Why not
work on floor-to-wheelchair transfers?*

"Really? That's the best you can do?
Aren't you even going to ask if I'm okay?"
I'm not really pissed, and he knows it.

*Will that make you feel better? Okay,
you okay, Cody? Now shut up and get
to work. Pull the chair up behind you,*

*and lock the wheels this time. Right
hand on the chair frame, left flat on
the floor. Remember, the farther*

*forward your head goes, the higher
your ass goes. One. Two. Three.
That's it! First try. Now, the other way.*

He Makes Me Work Hard

For ten minutes. Floor to chair.
Chair to floor. When he says I
can quit, my arms are sore and

I'm winded. "Damn, man. I need
aerobic exercise. I feel like a smoker
on a bad air quality day in Beijing."

> *I hear that's every day in Beijing.*
> *Until you get there, you'll be able*
> *to work out your lungs at the new*

> *hospital. By the way, I went to school*
> *with one of the PTs there. Mandy's hot.*
> *I figured you'd appreciate it if I made*

> *sure you'll get to work with her.*
> *She doesn't take shit, either.*
> *You're a match made in heaven.*

"Are you saying I give you shit?
Okay, maybe I do sometimes.
But no more than you deserve."

> Federico tsks. *Listen to you. That's*
> *the thanks I get for the vast amount*
> *of hard work I've invested in you?*

"Dude. Who's doing the work here?"
Wow. Despite his grumbling,
I think I'm going to miss this guy.

After Lunch

Carolyn comes in dressed in zebra-
striped scrubs. "Interesting pattern
there. Enough to cross my eyes."

> *I thought it might distract you
> while I take out the Foley. You
> still want it removed, yes?*

I nod. Since I've been here,
a Foley catheter has resided
in my penis, automatically

draining urine into a bag beside
the bed. After an SCI, two things
can happen to your bladder. Either

it will empty itself, all on its own,
and whether or not you want it to
(jeez, just picture *that*, out on a date

or something!), or it doesn't know
when to go, and you've got to remind
it. After a thorough workup, my doctors

concluded my bladder is the second
kind, and I've got to encourage it to
empty several times a day. I want to be

mobile, which means I'll have to insert
a tube into my joystick (not that it's so
joyful anymore) so I can use a toilet

instead of wearing a piss bag on my leg.
At least, I'm going to give it a try.
Carolyn extracts the Foley. Not sure

if it would hurt if my urethra could
feel something, but it can't, so there's
zero pain. Once, the process would

have embarrassed me, but I've kind of
gotten used to health-care professionals
poking, prodding, manipulating,

and otherwise studying my not-so-
private parts. Once upon a time,
that might have turned me on.

Maybe it still does, not that I'd know
without looking, and that would be
perverted. Carolyn gives nothing

> away. *Okay. Now I'll show you*
> *the do-it-yourself routine. Always,*
> *always, wash your hands before you*
>
> *touch anything. That's good advice*
> *for everyone, but for you, it's imperative.*
> *Last thing you want is an infection.*
>
> As always, she is matter-of-fact, and
> that's exactly how she demonstrates
> intermittent catheterization.

So Much to Learn

So much to understand
about the myriad ways
my life has changed.

I'm still swinging between
denial and acceptance, but
the former comes less often.

Before the incident, I knew
a little about SCI—I watched
Superman movies when I was

a kid, and heard the guy
who played him fell off
his horse and wouldn't ever

go flying again. Now,
the Christopher & Dana
Reeve Foundation is a font

of information on SCI, not
to mention a funding stream
for nonprofits that provide

services to people like me.
So thank you, Superman,
for your personal sacrifice.

I've learned a lot from
the foundation's website
and others like it, and what

the best of them offer
is not only resources, but
the knowledge that I'm not

alone, and that other people
with injuries much worse
than mine have risen above

denial, and even acceptance,
all the way to proving common
wisdom about spinal cord injury

wrong. It was Ronnie who
introduced me to them. Ronnie
who brought me a laptop

to investigate them. I'd pawned
my own when things began
to cartwheel out of control.

I asked if she didn't need
her laptop for school.
She said not to worry, her dad

would get her another one.
Wonder if he'll get pissed.
Wonder if he knows what

happened to the old one.
Wonder if he knows
what happened to the old me.

Almost Time

To check on out of here—my hospital
home away from home for months.
Ronnie comes in with some clothes.

> *Got these from your mom. She'll be*
> *here in a while to sign you out.*
> *She would've brought them herself . . .*

"Is there a 'but' attached to the end
of that sentence?" Ronnie moves
closer, looks at me with concerned

eyes. Eyes the shade of . . . violets?
"Purple contacts? That's, um, unique."
Ronnie changes eye color regularly.

> She grins. *Yeah. They make me look*
> *exotic, don't you think?* Now she grows
> serious. *Anyway, I guess they're releasing*
>
> *your brother from detention. Your mom*
> *had to take care of some paperwork.*
> *Meanwhile, I can help you get dressed.*

Cory. Man. I've been so focused
on myself, I've hardly even thought
about him. "Jesus. Has it been that long?

Poor Mom. Like she deserves something
else to worry about." Hospitals. Lockup.
Paperwork. Bills. Her job. And now,

trying to keep Cory in school,
and out of the liquor cabinet.
"Mom's going to need my help."

> Yep. And the best way to help
> her at the moment is for you to get
> dressed and check into the new
>
> facility. This is prime time for you
> to get stronger, and they are experts
> at that. By the way, Vince dropped
>
> your car off and Leon says he can
> have it finished in a couple of weeks.
> You'll be on the road again in no time.

On the road. Freedom. A measure
of independence. Except . . . "Ronnie,
I don't know how we'll pay for it."

> Don't worry. It won't be that much,
> and I've been looking into grants.
> If all else fails, we'll crowdsource it.

"Have I mentioned you're an angel?
A stubborn, demanding, purple-eyed
angel? And have I told you lately

how very much I love you? More
and more every day. Kiss me. Please?"
My angel kisses like she's possessed.

By the Time

I'm out of the ridiculous hospital
gown and comfortably dressed,
Mom hustles in, worry evident

on her face. "Everything okay?
What's up with Cory?" Ronnie
excuses herself in case the conversation

> should remain private. Mom waits
> for her to go, then says, *He's out, in*
> *an intensive supervision program,*
>
> *meaning he has to wear a monitoring*
> *device and submit to regular drug tests.*
> *To qualify, he has to reside within*
>
> *GPS range and attend school at*
> *the detention center, plus there's*
> *a community service requirement,*
>
> *so it looks like you're safe from*
> *Kansas, at least for the near future.*
> *I don't know, Cody. Cory's distant.*
>
> *Sullen. I'd hoped the experience would*
> *make him appreciate what he has,*
> *but I think it only made him colder.*

Yeah, lockup will do that to a kid.
"Give him time, Mom. He'll come
around." I hope. "Where is he now?"

Home with his ankle bracelet.
I asked if he wanted to visit you,
but he said no. He's scared to see

you, not that he'd admit it. Under
that tough exterior, he's a child,
and the idea of your disability

is hard for him to accept. In his
eyes, you've always been invincible.
If you're not, he isn't either.

"Makes sense, I guess." Little shit.
If I can put up with it, he'd better.
"You sure he's okay alone?"

>   *Not really. But life has to go on,*
>   *doesn't it? Best I can do is support*
>   *him, and let him know I love him.*

Man, she looks beat down.
I wish I knew how to help her.
"Hey, Mom? As soon as I get out

of the rehab hospital, I'll find
a job. We'll make this work, one
way or another, okay? I want you

to be able to rely on me, the way
I've relied on you." No pressure
there, Cody. None at all.

334

We Are Interrupted

By Carolyn, Federico, and Doctor
Harrison, who's taken time from
her busy schedule to say goodbye.

I demonstrate a bed-to-wheelchair
transfer, brakes on, and everyone
seems suitably impressed, including

Ronnie, who has joined the farewell
party. She helps Mom gather my few
belongings as Carolyn hands me

       a paper sack. *Disposable catheters*
       and a cupcake. I peek inside the bag.
       She isn't kidding. *I expect updates.*

          Federico hugs me. *I'll be stopping*
          by to check up on you, not to mention
          Mandy. Did I tell you she's hot?

"Hey, dude. My girlfriend's standing
right there, you know, and she's got
one hell of a temper." The mood is light,

but the implications of my leaving
are sobering. I've largely been taken
care of here, and while I'll still have

plenty of help in the coming months,
I have to stand up (figuratively, if nothing
else) and take responsibility for my future.

Tailed by Federico

Who's determined to show me
wheelchair-to-automobile transfers,
I maneuver said chair down the corridor

and through the door into the parking
lot. "Oh, man. It's bright out here!"
I've been under artificial illumination

for so long, my eyes fight accepting
the mild December sunlight. City
fumes hang heavily in the tepid air,

but beneath them is a the smell of
desert, much better than antiseptic.
Mom's cramped car won't accommodate

me comfortably. Ronnie's new SUV
is a better fit, not to mention a surprise.
"When did you get this? It's sick."

> *Three weeks ago. Daddy said*
> *my old car was an embarrassment.*
> *What was I going to do, argue?*

> Federico laughs. *I want a daddy*
> *like yours. Is he into adoption?*
> He oversees the transfer, watches

> me buckle myself in before
> shaking my hand. *You're gonna*
> *do great. Go kick some ass.*

Kick Ass

It's a phrase tossed around
thoughtlessly, but as we weave
through streets, familiar and not,

I ponder it. Cory kicked some
woman's ass for no real reason
other than he could. I doubt

getting his own ass kicked by
the system mitigated the wide
stripe of mean inside that boy.

That bastard Chris kicked my ass
before his bullet kicked it worse.
Kicked it forever numb. Ronnie

pulls up in front of a modern
stucco building, rolls my wheelchair
around the side of her new car.

I manage the transfer unaided
and we go inside, where it smells
like fresh fir thanks to the tall

Christmas tree in reception.
After Mom signs the admission
papers, a plain-Jane blond (not

hot, not Mandy) tours us around
the well-appointed facility,
where I'll learn to kick some ass.

A Poem by Alex Rialto

Christmas

Has no place in Vegas,
where Mr. Claus plays slots
and elfettes walk the streets
in Santa hats and crotch-short
skirts. You can count me

one

of them—just a sad, skinny
girl hustling a slender living.
Honestly, Christmas wasn't
a whole lot better in Barstow,
but then, for at least a month or

two

I thought I had a chance
at happiness with Ginger.
Stupid me. What I've learned
is yes, some people born into
shit holes can rise from
the cesspool and come to

enjoy

a decent existence, free
from the stink. The rest
of us surrender to sinking
back under, and I've embraced

the view

that it's all a matter of fate.

Ginger
Going Home Tomorrow

That's the plan. Gram's driving
over this afternoon and will stay
the night, then pick me up in
the morning. So I've got today

to find Alex. I wake early, despite
the silence in my room. They
moved Miranda last night—both
because they knew she was primed

to run, and also for the safety of all
the House of Hope girls. Security
has been tightened, just in case,
which will make getting out of here

kind of tricky. We're not exactly
on lockdown, but I'll need a good
excuse. At breakfast, I sit beside
Brielle, listening to the buzz,

which is louder than usual this
morning, everyone speculating
about Miranda and why she walked
out of here with her caseworker.

> Brielle nudges me. *What happened?*
> After I explain, she says, *Why don't*
> *they just make an announcement?*
> *The gossip is getting crazy.*

339

Good Point

Girls and gossip!
They're thinking:

> She must be pregnant.
> Yeah, but how? In here?
>
> Who could it be? One
> of the teachers? A janitor?
> Someone she sneaked in?
> Hey! Pastor Martin!

"Crazy barely covers it.
Do they really believe
we'd have a security guard
at the front door because

Miranda got pregnant?"
Not like the guy isn't obvious.
He's about the size of a grizzly
bear, and almost as hairy.

"Listen." Under the table,
I slide my hand into Brielle's.
"You have to help me figure
a way to get out of here after

prayer. I got a text from Alex
last night. She's back on the street.
This will be my last chance to—"
Brielle pushes my hand away.

That's right. Last chance,
and today is our last chance
to be together. Instead, you want
to find your old girlfriend?

Wow. I think this is called
jealousy, something I've never
experienced, at least on
the receiving end. Is love always

jealous? The noise level around
us has dropped. People tuning in.
"Shhh. Listen, Brielle. I'm afraid
for Alex. She's headstrong, and

impulsive, and pretty much lacks
common sense. But she's good
inside. I don't want her to end
up like the girl in the paper.

This takes nothing away from
what I feel for you. I'll always
love Alex as a friend, but there's
nothing left of what we were."

> Brielle softens immediately,
> reaches for my hand again.
> *I'm sorry. I don't mean to be*
> *selfish. It's just . . . Let's go.*

341

Ten Minutes

To morning prayer, Brielle
and I come up with a plan
for my escape. It's brilliant.
But first we have to suffer

> through Pastor Martin's usual
> badgering. That's what it is,
> and today it's directed toward
> me. *I understand one of you*
>
> *left House of Hope last night,*
> *and that another of you will*
> *be leaving us tomorrow.* His
> gaze falls on me. *I pray both*
>
> *of you girls will continue to*
> *walk in God's light. Go forth*
> *and sin no more, that's what*
> *Jesus would have you do.*

I wish circumstances would
allow me to kiss Brielle right
here. But that would cause
a stir and I don't need that kind

of attention right now. Still,
since I won't have to deal with
his condescension anymore,
I feel the need to say something.

342

I Raise My Hand

But don't wait for him to call
on me. "Excuse me, but I was
wondering if you understand
the reasons why most of us are

here. Because sin implies will,
and if you cared enough
to know our stories, you'd quit
accusing us of it. I appreciate

you worrying about our immortal
souls or whatever, but if there
is an all-knowing God, he must
be aware that we were coerced

into the life. That word is even
written into the definition of child
trafficking, and is why every one
of us has to listen to you remind

us of a past we're struggling
to forget. I doubt any of us wants
to return there. Maybe, through
considered prayer, the Lord would

grant you a bit of compassion
for girls whose childhoods have
been stolen and whose futures
are in doubt. Think about it."

Lecture Over

I stand up to leave,
surrounded by gasps,
yeahs, and one *Holy
shit,* not to mention

an outbreak of laughter.
"I'm sorry," I mutter,
heading toward the door.
"I didn't mean to interrupt."

I wink at Brielle, letting
her know it's almost time
to put things in motion.
She'll have to stay until

the good minister invokes
his benediction, but I'll be
ready as soon as the room
clears. I chance a glance at

Pastor Martin, expecting
the evil eye back. Instead,
he looks confused, as if I
was speaking in tongues

or something. And as I
take my leave, I think
I might hear him say,
You're right. Forgive me.

Probably My Imagination

The only thing more surprising
would be if the sky opened up
and belted out thunder, as if
someone-on-high was yelling, "Amen!"

> Brielle finds me in my room,
> reaches for my hand and slips
> a twenty-dollar bill into it.
> *Cab fare,* she explains. *Unless*
>
> *you can cover it, and I know*
> *you can't. That there is from*
> *Sonya, by the way. I'll be doing*
> *her algebra for a week.*

I don't ask for details. A few
of the girls have managed to
stash a little cash, but most of us
are flat broke. "Thank you. I'll get

it back to you when I can. Kiss
for luck?" Her lips are sticky
with maple-flavored syrup.
Delicious. "Okay. You ready?"

> She nods and picks up the thick
> government textbook from
> my desk. *Be careful. And . . . go!*
> We decided she'd count to ten

345

as soon as I'm out of the room.
I'm halfway to the front door
when there's an awful crash of
glass, followed immediately by

Brielle's scream. The security
guy, who's half dozing, jumps
to his feet and hauls balls right
past me. With all the commotion

behind me, no one notices when
I slip out across the threshold,
into the morning. Just in case,
though, I run up the block, smiling

at the scene unfolding inside,
where Brielle is explaining there
was a black spider the size of a
golf ball on the window, at least

till she smashed the book through
it. No sign of Los Sureños outside,
Grizzly Bear Dude will relax
and the on-duty house parents

will be so busy with glass repair
they won't even notice I'm gone
until my English teacher lets them
know I wasn't in class today.

And to Think

It only took ten minutes
to come up with the plot.
Maybe Brielle should be
an author, too. We could

cocreate amazing books
and live a life of luxury.
Okay, there's a novel.
Lovely fiction. Will I ever

be able to write my own
future? On one hand, it's been
good at House of Hope, where
everything is regimented.

Boring, but safe, because I
wasn't allowed to make
decisions for myself. As of
tomorrow, I'm free to screw

everything up again. How
do I chisel a better path?
Guess I'll figure it out later.
Meanwhile, I need to focus

on Alex. The first thing I do is call
Lydia. Makes sense she'd go back
to her. But when I dial the familiar
number, a generic woman's voice

tells me it's been disconnected.
Huh. I try the Have Ur Cake
business line next. This one
asks me to leave a message. I don't.

I walk a decent distance toward
what looks like a main road.
House of Hope isn't anywhere
near the heart of the city. Not sure

twenty will get me that far in
a cab, but this looks like a bus
route. It is. There's a stop. While
I wait, I consider my next move.

I could call Alex, but I'm sure
she'd just hang up on me. In
fact, I have no idea what to say
if I do find her. All I know is

I have to try. Not sure why,
but I scroll through my contacts,
and when I get to the L's, my
eyes settle on a name. Lenny—

Alex's and my favorite cabbie,
when we were working for Lydia.
Lenny. Yeah. The bus squeals
to a stop, and I board. The trip

downtown costs me four eighty
and takes twenty-five minutes,
plenty of time to give Lenny
a call. His hello sounds sleepy,

and it hits me he used to work
nights. "Uh, sorry to wake you.
It's Ginger. I know it's been a while,
but you used to drive Alex and me—"

> *Yeah, yeah. I remember you.*
> *I don't have dementia. And it*
> *has been a while. So now I'm*
> *awake, what can I do for you?*

"I'm looking for Alex, actually.
I'm leaving town tomorrow, and
have some of her stuff. Would you
know how I can get hold of her?"

> *What makes you think I might?*
> *And if you don't know, there's*
> *probably a reason. Now if you'll*
> *excuse me, I'm going back to bed.*

Now what? I get off the bus near
the Stratosphere, not far from
the strip club where Alex and I
got busted. This area is ripe for guys

on the hunt, and despite it being
just approaching noon, working
girls in all colors and shapes decorate
the sidewalks. All of them look tired,

and this time of day is the easiest.
Fewer creepers prowl before dark.
Still, as I show some of the ladies
a photo of Alex, ask if they've seen

her, a couple of men inquire about
my rates. One actually dares to touch
me. I wheel and push him backward.
"Fuck off. Do I look like a hooker?"

I'm dressed in jeans, a long-sleeved
crew-necked tee, and my face
is scrubbed. Hardly the wardrobe
of a girl working the sidewalks.

> *Uh, no . . .* he sputters, *sorry.*
> *I just thought . . . well, looks like*
> *you know these ladies. Happen to*
> *know any younger ones?* Sicko.

"You do realize that paying
for sex with an underage girl
is not only illegal, but also feeds
child sex trafficking operations?"

He Looks Confused

Eighteen is okay by me. He thinks
again. *Hey, wait. You a cop?*
Then he reconsiders one more time
and laughs. *No, you're too young.*

"Yeah, and you're a fucking
pervert. Why don't you go whack
off and call your fist Sweet Little
Miss, you disgusting piece of crap."

Too far? Usually I can tell how much
is too much, but this guy seemed
like a mouse until he turned into
a badger. I've seen it before, but not

often. He bottles his anger, stuffs
it inside. You can see it in the way
his face blooms red, and his fists
begin a slow clench-unclench.

Now the crazy billows in his eyes.
As he starts walking toward me, people
scatter in a wide circle. *No goddamn
whore's gonna talk to me like that.*

This one will. The voice I know so
well falls over my shoulder. *It's two
on one, in case your math isn't good.*
I don't dare turn away from the guy

to confirm who it is, but I don't have
to. Alex moves up beside me, locks
my arm, elbow to elbow, plants
her feet. The badger stops, assesses.

"You don't want to mess with her. I
hear she keeps a razor blade 'up
there.' I know she's got Mace
in easy reach. Better back off."

> *It's pepper spray, actually, and
> it's evil.* She points a small canister
> at the man, who flees. *How'd you
> know I had this?* she asks, laughing.

"Good guess?" I turn to hug her.
"God, it's so great to see you."
I want her to melt, but she freezes.
"How'd you know I was here?"

> She pulls out of my arms. *Lenny.
> I figured you'd return to the scene
> of our crime and was on my way
> to the club when I noticed trouble.*

I smile. "Funny. It's usually you
attracting trouble. You look good.
You okay? I'm sorry about the baby."
I am. It was her ticket out of the life.

That Realization Strikes

And suddenly I understand that
this mission will fail. "Gram's picking
me up tomorrow. You can still change
your mind and come with us. Please?"

> She avoids looking into my eyes.
> *Ginger, listen. There's nothing for*
> *me in Barstow but painful memories,*
> *and you are among them. We have no*
>
> *future together, not even as friends.*
> *You deserve love. I can't give it.*
> *Sex work is the best I can do, and*
> *not only am I good at it, I like it,*
>
> *at least most of the time. Some of us*
> *are meant to live this way. It's the world's*
> *oldest profession for a reason—there's*
> *a demand. Someone has to supply it.*

"It's not the best you can do, Alex.
You're brilliant. Please come home
with me. Don't you get it? You gave
me a reason to live. You saved me."

> *Maybe. But you can't save everyone,*
> *and that includes me. Come on. People*
> *are staring. Let's find some coffee, then*
> *get you a cab back to House of Hope.*

A Poem by Kate Carville
You Can't Save Everyone

But not every loss is weighted
equally. When it's someone
you respect, you examine
your own achievements, or

                                            lack

of them. What if it was your
time? What would you leave
behind? Conversely, if you
don't really care for the one
who's given an early out,

                                            perspective

argues maybe he deserved
to go. But when it's a person
you care deeply for,
hovering so close to

                                            death

you can hear the flicker
of the harbinger's wings,
knowing he'll leave this earth
weighted with regret and there

                                            is

nothing you can do
to lighten his burden,
it's hard to accept
that all your attempts
at reconciliation are

                                            meaningless.

Sad that Bud never even
gave poor Seth the chance.

Seth
Drowning

In dreams—some violent, some worse,
because in them, I'm sinking into a slime

of sadness—I come up for air midmorning.
A fist is thumping my face, just above

my left eyebrow, and that eye is swollen
most of the way shut, and now the details

spring from the ether. Shit. Pippa. I have
to go see her. And then, I need a big helping

of Micah. Something beautiful to mitigate
my overdose of hideousness last night.

The world teems with hatred and I think
it gestates in fear of what is different.

But if that's true, how do you explain
the human fascination with the freakish—

sideshows and circuses and even porn,
to some extent, capitalize on and monetize

it. Is it only when you stumble across
the unusual, free, and obviously happy

(maybe even happier than you) that it's
threatening? Is the difference chains?

A Long Steamy Shower

Makes my body feel better, but it
can't do anything for my face,

the left side of which has swollen up
to the approximate size of a grapefruit.

Ugh. Lovely. No way to disguise it,
I go find David, who is poolside on

a lounge chair beside a hard-bodied
young guy, both wearing nothing

but Speedos and a thick sheen of
suntan oil. The implications are crystal

clear, and what can I do? The word
"celebrate" comes to mind. "Morning."

        David lowers his sunglasses. *Holy*
        shit. What the hell happened to you?

I have a story, mostly true, prepared.
"Last night was movie night at the center.

We were most of the way through
The Birdcage when we got a call

from one of the kids that two guys
were following her, and she was afraid

they were going to rape her. By the time
I got there, they were mid-assault,

and when I tried to stop them . . ."
It's a good story, and I expect sympathy.

> Instead, David attacks. *Are you stupid*
> *or what? Who do you think you are,*
>
> *the cavalry? Why didn't you just call*
> *911? In fact, why didn't she? Why*
>
> *would she expect you to rescue her?*
> *You're lucky they didn't kill both of you.*

His companion nods agreement,
which is the most he's moved

since I got here. David reaches over,
settles a hand on the guy's chest.

> *This is Marco, by the way. I'd thought*
> *maybe we could enjoy a game of tag*
>
> *team. We waited up for you, but when*
> *you didn't come in by midnight, I was*
>
> *afraid Marco's magic spell might wear*
> *off. And now . . . I'd try ice if I were you.*

Dismissed

And though he didn't say forever,
it sure seems that way. I should be

scared, or at least, torn. But I feel
infused with hope, even if I've no clue

where I'll be tomorrow. One thing I do
know is I won't accept playing tag

team anymore, at least not unless I
initiate the game. David, bless him,

has just unshackled me. I watch him,
fingers combing Marco's chest hair.

Once, that might have turned me on,
made me want to jump in. But now,

it kind of sickens me. "I think icing
my face sounds like a good plan.

And then, if it's okay with you,
I'd like to visit Pippa in the hospital."

> David's free hand waves me away.
> *Go play Good Samaritan. I've got*

> *other plans.* He leans over to find
> his stash, hidden beneath a towel

under his chair. He takes a huge
whiff, offers the small plastic bag

to Marco, ignoring me, which is
totally fine. I'm sick of that shit,

too. Time to make some positive
changes. Resolved, I start toward

the house, then turn back to offer
David two words, well deserved.

"Thank you." I'm sure he has no
clue why I say them. If he'd bother

to ask, I'd explain: Thank you for
taking me in, for seeing something

in me worthy of rescue. Thank you
for helping me grow closer to being

a man. Thank you for teaching me
that independence is more valuable

than a cocaine-and-caviar lifestyle.
Thank you for allowing me the time

to understand that sex is undervalued
as barter, and that I am worthy of love.

Back inside, I take a few minutes
to absorb the magnificence of the house,

something I've taken for granted
for quite a while, and I know David

must have forgotten what attracted
him to this place originally. Sad, and

what a waste—all these gargantuan
rooms boasting lavish furnishings

and art, yet emptied of the emotions
that make those things truly valuable.

Wonder if all palaces feel this way,
if royals throughout time have always

favored hedonism and narcissism
over love, or if there have, in fact,

been epic romances among the chosen
few. I wander from room to room,

my footsteps the only sounds disturbing
silence so thick it seems to breathe.

Yes, I admire this place. But it embodies
loneliness, and could never truly be home.

I Leave David's

Marginally better off than when I
arrived. I stuff an upscale wardrobe

and four pairs of pricey shoes into
my old duffel, along with a nice

electric razor, a decent supply
of expensive toiletries, and the finest

plaque-removing toothbrush money
can buy. My only real valuables—

my phone and laptop—go into
a leather satchel I bought David for

Christmas. Glad this happened now,
before I got the chance to wrap it.

I've got a bank account, and a lot
of cash in my pocket, thanks to last

night's lucrative play. Better make
a deposit, in fact, and I will on the way

to see Pippa. I call for a cab; no more
limos and drivers in my near future.

Then I text Micah to let him know
I'll be stopping by this afternoon.

The thought elicits shivers,
anticipation threading my veins.

We have a chance at a normal
relationship now, but I don't say

so in my message. Don't dare jinx it.
Scares me enough just to think about

it. I consider writing a goodbye note
to David, but ultimately don't. What

if I change my mind? Is it already too
late? Endings are daunting, but every

irrevocable bridge burning initiates
a beginning, and a new direction.

I light the figurative fuse, prepare
to torch this chapter of my life, move

forward, build momentum. As I get
into the cab, carrying all my earthly

possessions in two bags, a strange
word pops into my brain, "strange"

as it applies to me, that is: purify.
That's it. I'll work on purifying Seth.

After a Quick Stop

To make my bank deposit, the cab drops
me off at University Medical Center.

UMC is the go-to hospital in Vegas for
ER patients who look like they might

be uninsured and/or on Medicaid.
At reception, I ask for Pippa Young.

       The silver-haired woman studies
       her computer. *Pippa? No record*

       of a Pippa here. Are you sure you have
       the right hospital? She peers at me

over the wire rims of her glasses.
"Maybe it's under Philippa? Or Philip?"

       Now she looks annoyed. *You don't know*
       if it's Philippa or Philip . . . oh. I see.

       She tries again. *Oh, yes. Philip. And*
       what is your name, young man?

She's awfully nosy, isn't she? Still,
I'll be polite. "Seth Parnell."

       Her head bobs up and down. *Very well.*
       Since Philip named you as his liaison,

you may visit him anytime. If I
might just see some identification?

Apparently, Pippa told them I'm
her partner, something they sanction

as a legitimate spokesperson for
a patient. How progressive! I find

her in a regular room, no ICU, despite
a whole lot of damage, mostly repaired

by some talented emergency room
doctors. If I tried not to look horrified,

I'd fail, so I embrace what I see. "Holy
shit, those fucks did a number on you!"

She wheezes through a rib-shrapnel-
punctured lung. *You don't look so hot,*

either, big boy. Her tiny smile reveals
a missing front tooth. *Except to me.*

Thank you. I mean . . . If not for you . . .
Resilience isn't always easy. She reaches

deep inside and finds a little. *I'm afraid*
it might be a while before I can dance.

Oh Man

"Yeah, well, about that. I might have
just cut off ties with my choreographer

friend." I pull a chair over to the side
of the bed, tell her why I've brought

two bags with me. "My mom used to
tell me things happen for a reason.

I'm sorry it had to be something like
this to open my eyes. I'm worth more

than this, Pippa, and so are you, no matter
how bad our families make us feel about

ourselves. Perhaps we're approaching the true
Age of Enlightenment. Maybe not everywhere,

but in more and more places, including
here. Excluding assholes like the ones last

night, people are starting to understand
that gender is something you're born with.

We can be who we are, follow our dreams,
succeed on our talents, celebrate falling

in love. But if we buy into the bullshit, believe
our only option is submission, we're doomed."

Pippa has listened quietly, sponging
the words, but now she says, *I wish*

I could believe that, but people are
basically mean. Survival of the fittest

or whatever. Hurting others gives
them a small sense of power, and

that includes verbal abuse. And
men like the ones who did this . . .

She lifts her hand, not quite touching
her pulped face. *Want people like you*

and me to disappear completely. They
want us on the endangered species list.

"Yeah, but they'll be extinct someday.
Until then, we can't cave in to fear."

The tears, expected, begin to fall.
How do I keep from being afraid?

"You have to stop living in isolation.
Find an accepting community. Jump in."

She thinks it over. *And where is your*
community, Seth? Excellent question.

I Chew on It

All the way to Micah's. Other than
the YouCenter kids, I belong to no real

community. I don't fraternize with other
escorts, and even if I did, I plan to quit

the business ASAP, because now I'm
free to move in with Micah and living

with someone you love negates having
for-pay sex with others, at least in my mind.

Who knew I had any moral sense left?
What little I have totally disintegrates

the minute Micah opens the door,
wearing nothing but a pair of blue

silk boxers. It's been a few days
since we've seen each other, and lust

attacks fiercely, at least for me. Micah,
however, jerks backward as if looking

> at a monster. *Jesus. What happened
> to you?* My face. Forgot about that.

I set down my luggage, close the door.
"Is that any way to talk to a superhero?"

I repeat the grisly details, hoping
my manliness will impress him.

　　　　Unfortunately, it seems to have
　　　　the opposite effect. *Seriously, Seth.*

　　　　You should have called 911, then run.
　　　　Those guys might have killed you.

"You sound like David. I couldn't
let them annihilate Pippa, could I?"

　　　　His shoulders relax. *I guess not.*
　　　　So, you really are *a superhero.*

"Nah. Just a regular hero. Now,
where's my reward?" I push him into

the bedroom, kiss him hard as I lay
him down, all the right muscles tensing

between us. He looks up at me with
those amber eyes, and a confession

spills from my lips. "I love you, and
I want you." I show him how much,

and what we share isn't sex, it's making
love. Micah becomes my community.

Somewhere Mid-Event

My cell phone rings. I ignore it, though
the thought briefly crosses my mind

that it could be important. No way
as important as this, though, and

when we finish I'm in no hurry to get
up. We lie tangled together in mute

satisfaction. Finally, I ask, "What do
you think about me moving in here?"

It's the first time I mention leaving David.
Micah's muscles (all the wrong ones) tense.

> *You can stay for a while, of course.*
> *My main concern is David. If he finds*
>
> *out, what would that mean for me?*
> Sucker punch. I'd hike hot coals for Micah.

I roll out of bed, go to find my clothes
and check to see if that call was critical.

> There's a voice mail from Aunt Kate.
> *Thank God I found you, Seth. You have*
>
> *to come home right now. Your father's*
> *in the hospital. He doesn't have much time.*

A Poem by James Buckman
Coming Home

To judgment is a concept
I'm familiar with—
being that person

                                    everyone's

analyzing, without
ever once asking straight
up where you've been
or why you were gone.
I understand self-medicating,
playing hide-and-seek with

                                    a

personal monster. In my case
(not to mention my sister's),
our father, who returned
from the Middle East
conflicts tweaked. So, yeah,
I indulged in more than a

                                    little

booze and pills and powders.
Anything to shut out
the noise of his waking
nightmares. Until I, too,
went most of the way

                                    crazy.

It was a long, hard
journey back, but if I
could do it, Whitney can, too.

Whitney
Getting Used To

Flipping out at random
intervals, for reasons sometimes
obvious, and other times
anyone's guess. I knew
laser tag was a poor choice,
all that neon cutting through
the darkness too reminiscent
of my time with Bryn and the Lady.

If not for James, don't know
how deep into memory-
driven insanity I might've sunk,
clutching shallow breath
as I went under. He saved me
that night, and I still can't figure
out why, let alone the reason
he wants to see me again.

Today, I was scratching for a way
out of the house to escape
the dual energy of my mom
and Kyra, who's home on winter
break. So when James called
and asked if I wanted to see
a movie, I jumped at the chance.

He's picking me up at one.
As long as I can talk Mom into
letting me out of the house.

Mom's in Her Office

With Kyra, looking at plum
pudding recipes online.
They're planning to cook
Christmas dinner, too.
But seriously. Plum pudding?
Better play nice.

"What's wrong with gingerbread,
or maybe chocolate cream pie?"

> Kyra cocks her head, points
> her chin in my direction.
> *I happen to like plum pudding.*
> *You got a problem with that?*

"Nope. Whatever you want
is fine by me. But can we please
have gingerbread, too? Maybe
Dad can pick it up from the bakery
if you don't want to make it."

> *Why should I make it? You can*
> *follow a recipe, can't you?*

Why is she always such a bitch?
Back away, Whitney, back
away. "I'm happy to give it a try,
but it probably won't turn out
very well. Baking is not my thing."
Change the subject . . . now.
"Hey, Mom. Can I go to the movies?"

*Well, we're kind of busy here,
and I thought we might go out
to dinner later.* Finally, she pulls
her eyes away from the computer
long enough to notice I'm dressed
to go somewhere. *Oh. Did you
already make plans with someone?*

"Well, yeah. See, I met this kind
of amazing guy at the arcade
the other night." I never told her
about the incident. No need to
mention it now. "You'll like him.
He'll be here any second."

*You told him you'd go without
asking Mom first?* blasts Kyra.

"I know I shouldn't have,
but I really like him a lot,
and when he called I was so
surprised, I just blurted out okay."
Okay, Whitney, make it good,
or Mom will never say you can go.
"Is it okay, Mom? He'll come
in and you can meet him.
You don't have to worry,
by the way. He's straight edge."
I won't mention it's because his
sister OD'd. Mom might worry
about the genetic factor.

When the Doorbell Rings

Mom's still considering. I let
James in. "Come meet my mother.
She's all worried about me going
out with you, so put on your best
perfect gentleman disguise."

> He grins. *What disguise? Mom*
> *says I was the perfect gentleman*
> *at conception. No morning sickness,*
> *short labor. And I've only gotten*
> *better with practice.* Sweet. Yep.

Sweet enough, that in less
than five minutes, he's got Mom
wrapped around his little finger.
Kyra is tougher, but even she mellows
and I'm allowed freedom.

James drives a new-model
Camaro, burnt orange and spotless.
He opens the passenger door
for me, and as I slide into the seat,
I wonder again what he's hiding.
No guy is quite this perfect.
He's probably a serial killer
or something. Wonder if he's ever
raped someone. Wonder if
he's ever hired a whore.

Wonder if I'll ever quit
thinking like a whore.

He Takes Me

To the Del Mar, an amazing
old Art Deco–style theater
downtown that plays a lot of
off-the-wall indie films.
The one today isn't new,
but it is really good. It follows
a boy from kindergarten
through high school, and is
really about relationships—
how they change with time.

I don't freak out when the lights
go down, so that's good.
I like sitting next to sweet James,
who totally acts the gentleman
role quite naturally. I'm surprised
he doesn't come on to me—don't
all guys use a dark theater as
an excuse to run a hand along
your thigh? James doesn't,
sensing, I guess, my need
for trust. Is it that obvious?

After the credits, there's still
light left outside. "Want to take
a walk? I'm not ready to go home
yet. My sister's making me crazy."

> The words are barely out of my
> mouth. *Wish my sister was still
> around making me crazy.*

"Jeez, man, I'm sorry. I'm an
idiot." Without even thinking,
I reach for his hand and our
fingers lace. It's the first skin-
on-skin contact I've had with
a man in months, and my initial
instinct is to pull away. Instead,
I force myself to hold on, even

> when he takes my other hand,
> too, and coaxes me nearer. *It's
> okay. No need to apologize.
> It was an observation, nothing
> more. Besides . . .* He smiles.
> *It brought us closer together.
> I didn't want to rush you.*

I study his eyes, seeking hints
of serial killer, but find none.
"Why did you call me? I mean,
after what happened the other
night, most guys would run
screaming in the other direction."

> *Let's take that walk.* He lets go
> of one hand, keeps hold of the other.
> After a few steps, he says, *This will
> sound weird, but from the moment
> we started talking, I wanted to reach
> inside you, grab hold of whatever
> is haunting you and smash it to pieces.*

Haunting

Funny verb to use in that
sentence, but accurate enough.
"Is it because of your sister?
Do I remind you of her?"

> *To a point. You're tough like*
> *her, on the outside. But she turned*
> *tough inside, too. There's more*
> *vulnerability in you, despite*
> *what you show the world. Besides . . .*
> He stops, turns to face me again.
> *I never wanted to do this to my sister.*

He leans toward me, but stops,
and his eyes ask permission,
which my eyes grant. His lips
are soft for a guy, and this kiss
is gentle, as if he's afraid to chase
me away. His instinct is good.
As nice as the kiss is, it's all
I can do not to yank back and run.

> This he senses, too. *It isn't me,*
> *though, is it? What happened*
> *to you in Vegas, Whitney?*

Before I can manufacture a word,
at the end of the block, a pickup
screeches around the corner. I cower
at the noise, and that's when the man

riding shotgun sticks his head
out the window. *Hey, lovebirds.*
Want a beer? A bottle comes flying,
smashes into the building beside me,
as the truck vanishes down the street.

It all happens so fast, I don't feel
myself go down until I land, hard,
in a pile of brown glass. I do hear
myself scream. The sound echoes
along the walls of an invisible tunnel.

Whitney. The voice finds me
in the tunnel. *Let me help you up.*
James reaches out, and the hand
that finds mine is familiar. I was
just . . . holding it? Yes, that's right.

He pulls me up and into his arms,
and I let myself stay there until
the trembling stops. "I'm sorry.
I'm a fucking freak." Passersby
stop to see what's going on, and
someone comes out of the store
we're in front of to investigate
the crashing noise. James handles
everything, but refuses to let go
of me. Eventually, explanations
made, we walk back to his car.

Again, James opens the door
for me and I fold into the soft
leather seat. He comes around,
settles in beneath the steering
wheel, where he rests his hands.
I have to tell him something.
Just not the whole truth.
"I . . . I . . . what happened
in Vegas is that I was sexually
assaulted, and more than once.
You can take me home now."

He doesn't move. *Thank you
for telling me. I know that's hard
to admit. It wasn't your fault,
Whitney. Stop blaming yourself.
And you're not a fucking freak.
If I were to guess, I'd say you
have PTSD—post-traumatic
stress disorder. My dad has it,
too, though it was war-induced,
and it manifests differently.*

*Dad's disorder-fueled rages
drove my sister to the boyfriend
who destroyed her, and pushed
me toward self-medication. Yeah,
I get addiction because I was right
there, too. I fought my way through
rehab two years ago. It does get
easier, but only with support.*

379

I Thank Him

For understanding. For offering
his support. Still, the fact remains
that, PTSD or whatever you call
it, I'm abnormal. Freakish. Crazy.

He drives me home, walks me to
the door. It's comforting to know
he does these things, despite
understanding enough of what
I experienced to drive most guys
far, far away. I could never tell
him the rest. Never admit it to
anyone, ever. Not even my parents.

Under the yellowish porch light,
we say goodbye, and I accept
his kiss, knowing in my heart
he'll never call again. Why would
he? Why would anyone as sweet
as James want to spend a single
second more with disgusting me?

I go inside to find everyone gone.
A note informs me they went out
to dinner and will be home by nine.
That gives me two hours alone
to find a way to fill the hollow space
inside my shell. Music, yes, but
I don't want to think. I want to fly,
and I find my magic carpet inside
a bottle in Dad's medicine cabinet.

Ambien

As if someone taking it needs
to know, the label says to take
one tablet immediately before
bed, but only if you have a firm
seven to eight hours to sleep,
and to expect dizziness in
the morning. It comes with
a stiff warning: *Do not exceed
recommended dose.* I've never

been real good at following
directions. Let's see. I have nowhere to be tomorrow but here.
It will be eight o'clock before it
kicks in, and I can sleep till noon
if I want to. That gives me sixteen
hours. So yeah, I'll take two. I do,
then replace the bottle exactly
where I found it before going

to my room. Screw it. What good
is staying clean? Your brain has
too much time to work. Mine
needs a vacation, especially from
these lilac walls. What was Mom
thinking? I strip off my clothes,
and the air hits my skin, cool.
I dig through my drawers for
some warm, comfy clothes,
choose some soft PJ pants and
an old favorite sweatshirt.

About the time I slip beneath
the covers, plug headphones
into my phone and turn on
my music, the Ambien kicks
in, and hard. My head spins,
hopefully quickly toward sleep
because I'm also feeling a bit
nauseous. Don't want to throw
them back up. I close my eyes,

lie back, thinking about many
trips to the bathroom in that
stinking Vegas apartment,
happily puking and crapping
right before crawling back
to the other room to nod off
into the land of oblivion. Talk
about a love/hate relationship.

As I turn onto my side, there's
a crinkling noise. Something in
my sweatshirt pocket. I reach
in and my hand closes around
a small piece of heavy paper.
A business card? Through thick,
drooping eyes, I read: *Perfect
Poses Photography.* Bryn.
Remembering the day he gave
me this makes me smile. How
quickly I fell in love with him.
He was the only one who ever

made me feel beautiful. Those
days, shooting gorgeous photos
on the beach. Photos of me. Me!
This amazing warmth creeps up
my spine, and on a total whim I dial
his number. Will he answer? Will—

> *Hello? Is this really you, Whitney?*
> *Oh, girl, I'm so happy you called.*

He remembers me. "Hey, Bryn?
I can't talk very long . . . kinda messed
up. Gonna sleep soon. Jus' wan' you
to know I miss you. It's crazy, cuz,
I mean, you fucked me up good.
But I do miss you. 'Member the beach?"

> *Sliding in and out now, still I hear,*
> *I'll never forget the beach, Whit.*
> *God, you were stunning, all long*
> *brown legs in that white skirt.*

"Hey, Bryn? I don' wan' back
in the life. But could you maybe
bring me a li'l taste of the Lady?
Jus' a li'l. I could meet you. . . ."
Jus' wanna see his face
one more time.

It's Early Afternoon

By the time I ascend from
a deep pit of sleep, head
pounding and disoriented.
What did I do again? Guys.
Right. The movie. James.
Thump-thump. Agh! Make
it stop. Thinking hurts. Why?

Now it all whirls back.
The truck. The beer bottle.
A nice kiss or two. Ambien.
Bryn. Bryn? Oh my God, did
I talk to Bryn? Did I ask him
to score some H for me, or
was that only a dream? No.
Not a dream. We're supposed
to meet up tomorrow. What
the fuck have I done? I pull

myself from bed. As soon as I
stand, the room somersaults.
I barely make it to the bathroom
on time and as I empty bile
into the toilet, stink sweating
and skull beating pain, a trill
of excitement trembles through
my veins. I'm going to see
Bryn again! And visit the Lady.
I just have to fake my way
through this day first.

A Couple of Days Before Christmas

Gives me the perfect excuse
to do two things—go shopping
alone, and take money out of
my bank account. Do I feel
guilty? Yeah, a little. But I'll
be careful with the H, no needles
or pipes, just a whiff now and then,
when the crazy shit takes over.

Mom drops me at the mall
midmorning, promises to pick
me up in three hours. As I watch
her drive away, regret plucks.
Still, I go inside, and the moment
I see Bryn, smiling exactly the way
he did the first day we met, every
last bit of guilt vanishes. He doesn't
wait for me to reach him, but rushes
straight toward me and for one
ridiculous instant, I'm scared.

But his hug is friendly. Loving.
*Wow. You look great. So happy
you called. I never thought
I'd see you again. Hey, I've got
the stuff. Let's take a drive.*
When I start to protest, he kisses
me silent. *We can't do this here.
Just a quick stop at the beach?*

How can I say no?

A Poem by Joan Streit

How Can I Say No

To my child—tell her
she can't come home,
she doesn't belong
here—my flesh and

blood

daughter? When you
give your full measure
of love to the Lord, it

isn't

permissible to sidestep
his laws, no matter what
your heart whispers. Eden has

always

been willful, and when she met
her punishments with stonewall
stares, I wondered if she was

thicker

than most. Spare the rod,
spoil the child, as God would
have. That's how I was raised,
and I knew no better way

than

that to bring my girls up right.
Some might think I could have
been kinder, a cool drink of

water

to soothe their thirsting souls.
I say it takes a scalding tap
to scrub sin away.

Eden
Forgiveness

Is the most precious thing
in the world. God's forgiveness
tends to be expected by believers.
Taken for granted, really.
I knew God had forgiven me

the moment I heard him speak
through the priest who'd heard
of this place and sent me here.
A Bible story is embedded in
my brain: A woman, caught

in the act of adultery, was brought
before Jesus by the Pharisees,
who told him Moses would have
had her stoned to death. What
would he do? This was a test,

of course, but rather than interfere
with their laws, Jesus said, *He that
is without sin among you, let him
first cast a stone at her.* Instead,
they left, one by one, leaving her

there alone with Jesus, who told
her he did not condemn her, only
she was to *go and sin no more.*
I never feared God's condemnation.
It was Andrew's that terrified me.

I Told Him Everything

I've had a long time to think
about a partial confession.
But keeping secrets from Andrew
would be the same as lying
to him, and that I can never do.

Some of what I said stung.
A powerful hurt reflected in
his eyes. He listened without
comment until the very end,
hanging his head once in a while.

But I didn't stop until every
ugly truth gurgled out, bubbles
in a cauldron, and I really thought
he'd tell me, "Sorry for your trouble.
Been nice knowing you." But no.

> Instead, he kneeled in front
> of me, laid his chin on my knees,
> and I understood his pain was
> for himself. *Oh, Eden. If I'd had*
> *any idea your mother was capable*
>
> *of such cruelty, I would've risked*
> *prison and taken you away*
> *in a heartbeat. Now all I can do*
> *is try and make it up to you.*
> *Can you ever forgive me?*

He Asked Me

To forgive him. I was stunned.
Still am. His heart is huge, and
he swears it belongs to me forever,
no matter what. We just have to
figure out where we go from here.

The notarized, signed emancipation
papers arrived. We filed them
right away and got a court date
after the first of the year. Now the
hearing notice has to be served

on my parents. Shouldn't be hard.
Papa—no, Pastor Streit—is well
known in Boise. I haven't heard
back from Marlene about Elko
County. Sarah warned me that

the wheels of bureaucracy turn
slowly, but tomorrow is Christmas.
I can't imagine spending it locked
up at Tears of Zion. Oh, and Eve
must be so cold! Those rooms

were like ovens in the summer.
They must be like freezers when snow's
on the ground. Thinking about
it makes me so angry! I wish
there was something I could do.

I Never Would Have Imagined

Spending Christmas at a place
like Walk Straight, either. Much
like Thanksgiving, most of the girls
don't have wonderful holiday
memories, but I do have a few.

With Papa being a pastor,
Christmas took on even deeper
meaning, and we did it in style
when I was little. Not that we had
a lot of gifts. My parents didn't

believe in them. *This is Jesus's
birthday, not yours,* Mama told
us. Still, we always had a lovely
tree, and the carols filled me
with happiness. The presents

we did receive were usually
clothes, and something new
to wear was a rare thing. Right
now, I'd love a sweater or pair
of jeans that no one else wore first.

There will be a Christmas party
here, with excellent food and
communion. But one day, I will
celebrate the holidays with Andrew,
in a home of our own. What a dream!

Another Tradition

My family adhered to—
because as pastor, Papa
pretty much had to—was
Christmas Eve church
services. I asked Sarah

for permission to attend
a local service tonight,
and not only did she agree,
but she also said it was okay
for Andrew to come along.

He's been at a nearby motel
for several days, but will
have to go back to Boise soon,
to start the new semester.
He picks me up in a rented

> car—a small sedan, very unlike
> anything he drives back home.
> *It's not much to look at,* he
> apologizes, *but it's comfortable.*
> *Where to, beautiful lady?*

"I thought it would be proper
to say thank you to the priest
at Guardian Angel Cathedral.
He's the one who helped me.
I don't know much about

Catholic protocol, though,
so you'll have to help me
out." I give him directions
and he starts the car, after
a Christmas Eve kiss.

> *I haven't been to Mass in*
> *a very long time, you know.*
> *But I'm grateful to the priest*
> *who helped you, and I'm happy*
> *to thank him personally.*

It's about a fifteen-minute
drive, plenty of time to talk.
Andrew's been thinking,
he says, and he wants me
to consider something carefully.

> *I know your emancipation*
> *is underway. But I don't want*
> *us to be apart for another year.*
> *I looked into transferring*
> *to the university here, but*
>
> *the logistics are a nightmare.*
> *Besides, my mom still needs*
> *my help at the ranch, and to tell*
> *you the truth, I can't imagine*
> *living in this city. I'd do it for you.*

> But I'm wondering if there
> isn't a better way. We've been
> driving along Charleston Blvd,
> and make a right turn down
> the strip. I haven't been anywhere

near this part of the city since
I moved into Walk Straight,
and my discomfort grows as we
approach the big casinos. My voice
is thick when I ask, "Like what?"

> Please don't think I'm crazy,
> because I've thought and thought
> about this, especially as it regards
> your sister. What if we approach
> your parents directly? Sarah's right.

> It's possible they don't realize
> exactly what's going on at Tears
> of Zion. Your mother is a harpy,
> for sure, but that doesn't mean
> she can't be reasoned with.

"You can't be serious! When she
was here, she wouldn't even talk
to me except to tell me, yet again,
how I'm damned to eternal hell.
She doesn't know what reason is."

The Cathedral

Is only a block off the strip,
behind the Encore. Andrew
pulls into the parking lot
a few minutes before the four p.m.
Mass is scheduled to begin.

    I start to open the car door,
    but he stops me. *Wait. I want*
    to give you your Christmas
    present before we go inside.
    He reaches into his jacket

    pocket. *Sorry I didn't wrap*
    it, but I figured you wouldn't
    care. Out comes his closed fist,
    which he opens slowly. Centered
    in his palm is a gold ring with

    three square diamonds, two
    small stones flanking a larger
    one in the middle. *It's my mom's,*
    but she wants you to have it.
    Will you marry me, Eden?

"I . . . uh . . ." The air is being
sucked from the car. Either that,
or I've forgotten how to breathe.
"Are . . . are you sure?" He erases
the space between us, kisses me

gently. *I'm one hundred percent
positive. There is no one in the world
but you for me. We're young, I know.
But if our love has survived the past
eight months, eight years or eighty*

*can't possibly destroy it. I want you
to be my wife, and I want us to live
together out in the country, far, far
away from this city and its memories.
You don't belong here any more*

*than I do. You can have a career
if you want one. In fact, I'll help you
through college. Or you can stay
home and raise a bunch of kids.
Or colts. Or puppies. So . . . ?*

I can't comprehend how we'll work
it out, but I know we've got to try.
The idea of him leaving me behind
scares me more than the thought
of facing my mother. "Yes. Yes!"

This kiss leaves me panting,
probably not the right way to go
to church. I take a deep breath.
"Let's go inside or we'll be late.
I've got something to thank God for."

A Catholic Mass

Is like no church I've ever
experienced. Compared
to Papa's boisterous call
to stand up, confess, and
speak in tongues, the priest's

soft liturgical repetition
is soothing, the music—
both traditional carols and
melodies familiar to most
parishioners, but not me—

more lullaby than praise
song. Christmas trees and
tall poinsettias surround
the altar, sentries guarding
Baby Jesus, who smiles

at us all from his crèche.
My left hand wriggles into
Andrew's right, which plays
with his mother's ring,
circling that telltale finger.

I haven't really spoken to
God very much in the time
since I left Tears of Zion.
I talk to him now, in my heart.
"Forgive me for losing faith

in you. Forgive me for
blaming you for the actions
of people who hurt me in
your name. Forgive the things
I've done and help me to walk

forward in your light. Give
me the strength I need to fight
for love and Eve's safety.
Thank you for speaking to
Andrew's heart and bringing

him back into my life. I will
never take him for granted,
will always cherish and honor
him. Please guide my way
in the future. In your name."

Amen. Around me, others
are chanting an entreaty for
peace, and an overwhelming
sense of serenity washes over
me. This is how God should

feel. Not like a punishment.
Not like something to fear.
I don't want to live afraid
anymore. Not of God. Not
of Tears of Zion. Not of Mama.

Andrew Is Right

The only way to move past
the things that scare me most
is to confront them head-on.
I won't have to do it alone.
Not with Andrew at my side.

As everyone bows their heads
for the benediction, it strikes
me that the things I've regretted
have been the wrong ones—things
beyond my ability to control

then, or change now. If I could
wish for anything, it would be
to go back and be just a regular
high school kid again. I swear
I'd find a way to have more fun.

Join clubs. Go to dances. Maybe
try out for musicals or sing in
the choir. Of course, I'd have to
convince my parents, but since
this is all fantasy, anyway, I can

make them be open to everything,
including Andrew. Because he'd
have to be there, too. Okay, that
kind of wish can't come true.
But Andrew is here with me now.

Post-Mass

I seek out Father Gregory,
whose expression says
I look familiar, but he's not
sure why. I could pretend
we met under different

circumstances, but that
would negate the reason
I'm here. "Hello, Father.
I'm not sure you remember,
but you helped me find

my way into a safe haven,
and I wanted to thank you
for that." Recognition flickers
in his eyes and, looking at
Andrew, a hint of surprise.

> *You are most welcome.*
> *It's good to see how well*
> *you're doing. Our heavenly*
> *father is merciful, yes?*
> *Merry Christmas to you.*

"He is, indeed, Father, and
Merry Christmas to you as
well." We shake hands all
around, and Andrew and I
are on our way, blessed.

The Plan

Is for Andrew to take me out
to a nice dinner. I had no idea
it would be to celebrate our
engagement. Can this really
be happening? He reserved

a table at Hugo's Cellar, a cool
old mafia-themed steakhouse on
Fremont, well away from the strip.
On the way in, the hostess hands
me a rose. (Every lady gets one,

but still I feel special.) We
Idahoans are skeptical about
seafood, but all about the beef.
Andrew and I both order steaks
and are waiting for our tableside

salad to appear before I even try
to talk. "Andrew, I've been thinking. . . ."
He looks concerned, so I hurry,
"Don't worry. I haven't changed
my mind. In fact, what I want

to say is, you're right. I don't know
if the direct route will turn out
to be the best route, but I do
believe it's the only way to deal
with Mama, and not only her,

but Samuel Ruenhaven, too.
I want to go to Elko and talk
to the district attorney. But I
should confront my parents first.
Boise is my home—our home.

I won't be afraid to walk down
the street or bump into people
I happen to know. If you don't care
about ugly gossip, how can I?
As for my family, I don't need

a relationship, except with Eve.
The support of your mom and
sister is more than enough. We'll
have to work out some logistics.
But I'm sure Sarah will help us."

Andrew sneaks his hand under
the table, rests it on my knee.
Not long ago, I would've flinched.
*You're a brave girl, Eden, but you
don't have to do this alone. I love you.*

"I know. And I love you, too."
Our waiter interrupts, wheeling
a salad cart to the table. It's the start
of an excellent meal, capping off
a memorable Christmas Eve.

A Poem by Cody Bennett

A Memorable Christmas Eve Eve

Never thought about
the holidays with regard
to hospitals and patients.
I always assumed a shopping
mall was the only place to see

                                   Santa

and sit on his lap for a pic.
Who knew the Jolly Old Elf
straps on his gear,
hops in his sleigh, and

                                   comes

calling on the bedridden,
wheelchair jockeys, and
caregivers who draw short
straws, condemning them

                                   to

spend their holiday
emptying bedpans and
collection bags, inserting
catheters, and going to

                                   town

on overcooked turkey,
soggy stuffing, weepy
cranberry sauce, and some
pretty damn good pumpkin pie?

Cody
Santa Did Come to Call

On us patients here at Mojave Palms Rehab
Hospital. He dropped by yesterday, Christmas
Eve Eve. Guess that's the best he could do

during this busy holiday season. Hey, not
complaining. The dude brought gifts—
comfy plaid flannel pajamas and matching

robes, the key word being "matching." This
morning, we were a matched set of patients.
Last night, we had an okay not-quite-Christmas

dinner, with Santa carving the turkey, which
was dry, and in need of gravy. Yeah, so the food
here isn't exactly like Mom's home cooking.

It might be marginally better than at the last
hospital, but that's a narrow margin. Still, I like
it here. My roommate, Craig, is pretty cool.

He's a T4 complete, much further into his rehab
than I, and quite the cheerleader. He got to go
home for Christmas, and without his rather large

presence, the room feels empty. He's given me
all kinds of advice, and actual interaction with
someone who's worked through the initial stages

of mobility grief and come out swinging has been
a blessing. As for the staff, they've been great.
The caregivers are kind. Well, except for the PTs,

who give the requisite amount of physical therapist
crap. They're drill sergeants, forcing us to be the best
we can be with our limited skills. I've only been here

a week, with one day off to detour muscle strain,
but I already feel stronger. Mandy is, in fact, hot,
and she's not above flaunting her assets (just a small

tease) to encourage correct behaviors like on-time
arrival for scheduled workouts and giving one
hundred and ten percent every time we meet.

Right now, the work is all about balance, core and
upper-body strength. One day at a time, one skill set
at a time. But this place has the latest, greatest

equipment, and before I leave here, I'll be on
my feet again. Not without help. Not without
braces or crutches or a walker. But I will stand

upright, and once that happens, losing those aids
will be totally up to me. I'll never be what I was,
but come to think of it, that Cody wasn't such

a great guy anyway. What I've lost physically
to injury I've gained in strength of will. At least
on good days, and not every day is one of those.

404

Last Night

My brain vacationed in Dreamland.
At first it is a nice place to be. I am
home for Christmas, and Jack is there,

too, and we are drinking eggnog in front
of the fireplace. Christmas stockings,
embroidered with our names, hang from

the mantel, which is a little strange,
because our fireplace is gas and doesn't
have a mantel, but you know how dreams

go. Now Mom turns on her personal
iTunes Christmas playlist, which is
traditional carols jazzed up by a trio

of greats—Frank Sinatra, Elvis, and
John Lennon, backed by Mötley Crüe—
and yeah, absolutely that's weird, but

dreams often are. From weird to
completely whacked, for no real
reason Cory starts shouting at Jack,

> *Why the fuck didn't you tell me*
> *you're dead? Dead people drink*
> *eggnog. You're totally messed up.*

> That makes Jack laugh like a crazy
> man. *Well duh. Dead is shorthand*
> *for messed up. You'll know all about*

that soon enough. You're halfway
to hell already. In fact, I'll take you
back there with me right now.

Jack reaches out with a rotting
zombie hand and shuffles forward
in slo-mo, singing "So This Is

Christmas" in decent harmony
with John Lennon. Cory screams
and the next thing we know, he throws

his ankle monitor bracelet at Jack
and goes running out the door.
"Come back, Cory!" I yell, and

I'm on my feet, running after him,
trying to catch him before the cops
do. The little shit is fast, but I'm

faster. I always have been. Cory
could never beat me in a footrace
and I'm starting to catch up, when *BAM* . . .

My legs worked fine in my dream,
but when I woke up and tried to jump
out of bed, they didn't remember how.

Bad Start to the Day

And it hasn't improved since. Fall
out of bed before breakfast, your appetite
vanishes along with the nightmare.

PT on an empty stomach might work
fine as a weight-loss gimmick, but
halfway through rolling forward and

back over a medicine ball, gravity
trumps form. Abuse your body
long enough, despite lack of feeling,

pain takes center stage. Hard to get,
unless the experience belongs to you.
It belongs to me, and I still don't get it.

So when Mom and Ronnie both show
up midafternoon to visit, I'm not
in the best of moods. At least now

I don't have to be prone and pissed off.
I'd rather be in my chair for Mom's news,
which her scowl tells me isn't good.

> Ronnie asks if she should leave, but
> Mom says, *No. You're practically
> family, aren't you? You might as well*
>
> *hear this. Cory had a huge meltdown
> last night. He found out about the house,
> so he went on a tear and started smashing*

> furniture against the walls, screaming,
> "They want our house? How will they
> like it now?" He actually threw a chair
>
> at the sliding glass door. Luckily, it
> didn't break. It would be hugely expensive
> to replace. I called a handyman about
>
> patching the holes and repainting. His
> estimate is eight hundred dollars.
> If I could, I'd make Cory do it, but . . .

"What the hell is wrong with him?
That kid needs serious help.
He hasn't been drinking, has he?"

> Mom shakes her head. *There's no*
> *alcohol in the cupboards, except maybe*
> *in cold medicine or something.*
>
> *Actually, I never thought about that.*
> *No, I think he's just scared, Cody.*
> *But he won't even talk about it.*

I'm frustrated. She needs me at home,
at least as long as we have one,
but I can't even get in and out of

the doors in my chair. "Tell Cory
either he comes here to see me or I'm
coming to him, one way or another."

408

I'll do my best to convince him,
but I don't think he'll visit. I'd better
get home before he burns it down.

I watch her go, hunched over as if
she's sixty instead of forty-two.
When I'm positive she's out of earshot,

I tell Ronnie, "Every time I see her
she looks older. I don't know what I
can do to help her. I'm not even sure

which one of us is the most responsible.
Probably me, but maybe not. She has
to deal with Cory the most, and what

he did last night . . . How could he?"
Ronnie looks every bit as confused
as I feel, and almost afraid to say

anything. Finally, she hugs me. *I'm*
so, so sorry. Your mom's definitely
been through a lot. But she's strong.

"Staying strong takes a toll, doesn't
it? First Cory. Then Jack. Then me.
And now, the house. It fucking sucks."

She's quiet for a minute, but now
she asks, *Why didn't you mention*
there was a problem with your house?

"Ah, you know. It wasn't like I was
trying to hide it from you or anything.
It just didn't seem like something

you needed to worry about. You've
done enough stressing over me
without tossing that into the mix."

>Cody, I love you. Even if things
>were one hundred percent okay,
>I'd worry about you, just because.
>
>So, why don't you tell me what's up
>with your house? Other than
>the newly decorated walls, that is.

I give her the lowdown. "If not
for Cory's intensive supervision
program, we'd probably be on our

way back to Kansas by now. Uncle
Vern said we could stay with him
for a while. Scared the crap out of me.

But if Mom has to sell on a short sale,
she won't have money to invest, and
her income won't qualify her for a loan.

So we'd be renting, and in this city
pretty sure whatever she could afford
wouldn't be in the best neighborhood."

410

I'm Actually Very Sure

About that. Mom's done some
scouting, without much success.
And as far as anything accessible,

just, no. "Don't suppose we could
crowdsource enough money for
a house suitable for the disabled,

could we? Yeah, probably a long shot."
I rotate my chair until I'm facing
Ronnie straight on, knees touching

knees. Today she's wearing bright
green contacts and her eyes remind
me of emeralds. "You are incredible,

know that? Hey, think you could flirt
a little with Cory and maybe convince
him to visit me for Christmas?"

> She smiles. *Persuasion is my middle*
> *name. I'll stop by your house on*
> *my way home. But first, let's make out.*

Ronnie takes control, and ten
seconds into this very hot kiss,
my day begins to improve.

When she lifts my hands to
the luscious, full rounds of her
breasts, encourages me to explore

411

the suede skin beneath her sweater,
the bad of this day sizzles away
like water dripped on a hot skillet.

If it wasn't for the float of voices
somewhere beyond the door,
I'd be tempted to see how far

my messed-up body would let me
take her, and just how far it might
follow. I rest my forehead against

the taut muscles of her abdomen.
"I have no clue why you're still
here, after the god-awful shit

I've done, and I'm pretty sure
you'll get sick of me eventually,
but I'm damn sure going to cherish

every single minute together with
you. By the way, you smell amazing."
She wears her perfume like she wears

her hair—in gentle wisps. The thought
initiates a rush of pleasure, static.
Ronnie lowers her hand and though

> I can't feel it, I believe her when
> she whispers, *Look what woke up.*
> *Is that what's called muscle memory?*

Tomorrow Is Christmas

And that is the best gift I can imagine—
the knowledge that I might actually
be able to give Ronnie pleasure, and not

just with my hands and mouth, but
the way an intact man does, and maybe
even come myself. "Thank you, baby."

> *Baby,* she purrs. *I like that. But what*
> *are you thanking me for?* Those
> gemstone eyes lock onto mine.

"For keeping my hope alive. Seriously,
Ronnie, without you, I would have
given up already. You make me want

to get better. I want to be strong for you.
Will you come see me tomorrow?
It's Christmas, so if you can't, it's okay."

> *Baby,* she repeats, redirecting the word.
> *Would I miss spending Christmas with*
> *you? Anyway, don't you want your present?*

We agree that I do, of course I do,
and she kisses me goodbye, flits
from the room, a beautiful hummingbird.

A Poem by Ginger Cordell
Brielle Kisses Me Goodbye

And though our hearts
say this isn't forever,
our brains insist that's
a misrepresentation, as

          time

will keep shuffling
forward, wearing us on
its shoulders. Our love

          is

young, and perhaps
that's good, because
well-seasoned connection
would sever more

          painfully,

scar deeper. We promise
to keep in touch, knowing
our separate journeys
make it unlikely, that the

          impatient

erosion of affection
is hurried with distance.

Ginger
Saying Goodbye Sucks

I'm not sure which was harder,
kissing Brielle goodbye, promising
it wasn't the end of us, but knowing
it probably was; or finally, completely

giving up on the hope of Alex and
me together again and happy.
There's a lesson here, and that is
I have to find happiness inside

myself before I try to partner again.
But knowing there's a lesson and
learning it are two different things.
Right now I am torn between the need

to leave and the desire to stay where
I've come to feel safe for the first
time in my life, and where seedling
love took root in my heart, though

I didn't believe it was possible.
It isn't fair. But then, I should
be used to that by now, shouldn't
I? Does life ever get fair, though?

These thoughts tumble around in
my head as Gram steers her new used
minivan onto Interstate 15 South.
We'll be home in less than three

hours, as long as the vehicle
cooperates. "Thank you for coming
to get me. I never thought I'd
make it home for Christmas."

> *Christmas Eve, she corrects.*
> *The kids are so excited to see*
> *you. They even made you some*
> *special presents. Can't say what!*

I'd forgotten how cheerful
she always is, or at least pretends
to be. "Gram, I'm so sorry for all
the worry I put you through,

and for not being there to help
when you needed me. I never told
you what happened, but meant
to, and then I got sucked into—"

> *We don't have to talk about it*
> *now. Or ever, if you don't want*
> *to. I know you wouldn't have*
> *run off like that without a reason.*

"No, I wouldn't have. But I do want
to talk about it. It's important to me
that you know." I tell her everything,
start to finish, going back all the way

to Walt, the first of my so-called
mother's men who paid to have
a little fun with her daughter or,
as Iris put it, "to make me a real

girl" by ripping me apart. I don't
try to remember all the others
I've invested so much effort into
trying to forget. I just tell Gram

Walt wasn't the only one, finishing
the bulk of my confession with
the man who forced my hand that
day, convinced me running away

was my only option. "Also, so you
know, not that it matters I guess,
Alex and I did strip for money
in Vegas, but I never let a man

touch me, and I probably never
will in the future." I keep the part
about sleeping with girls to myself
for the time being. What I just shared

is more than enough. She gives
it some time to sink in, and I keep
my mouth shut while she does,
staring out the window at desert.

It isn't a beautiful landscape,
and it won't improve by the time
we reach Barstow. Someday I'll live
in the forest or near the ocean, or

maybe find a place where I can have
both. Northern California or Maine.
West Coast or East, makes no difference,
as long as there are trees and water.

> Finally, Gram takes a deep breath,
> releases it in a low whistle. *I never
> even suspected anything like that,
> Ginger. Why didn't you tell me?*

"I'm not sure," I admit. "I was
hurt. Embarrassed. Scared. But
mostly I was pissed at Iris. I couldn't
stand to look at her. Couldn't take

a chance on her doing something
like that again, and she would have.
I'll never forgive her. I hate her."
My voice has risen in volume and

pitch, building toward a wail before
total breakdown. "I'm s-sor-ry." It
escapes as huge sobs. "But I don't care
that she's dying. Is that wrong?"

Gram Stays Silent

For a very, very long time.
Is she angry? Disappointed?
Have I managed to smother
every hint of good cheer?

    Finally, she opens her mouth.
    I'm going to tell you something
    I haven't talked about in many
    years. I never thought it was

    proper to share this, but now
    I think you should know. I told
    you Iris's childhood was no walk
    in the park. Military brats never

    have it easy, but what happened
    to her at Fort Irwin was beyond
    terrible. She falls quiet again,
    gathering her thoughts. *I believed*

    the neighborhood was safe, and
    I let her outside to ride her bike
    all the time. Turned out I was naive.
    Not every soldier is a good guy,

    and one evening as she rode home
    one of the not-good ones got hold
    of her. She was only seven. That
    man raped her, almost killed her,

and would have, except Mark—your
grandfather—heard Iris screaming.
He beat that bastard within an inch
of his life, but the damage to your

mother was already irreversible.
I will forever carry a heap of guilt.
It's why I've continued to support
her, and even apologized for her

behavior, despite the awful choices
she's made, including how she earns
a living. Now I'm not claiming
the incident in any way pardons

the things she allowed done to you,
but it does explain, to some extent,
why she went the direction she did.
I can't tell you it's best to forgive her,

but what I can say with certainty is
holding on to resentment won't make
you any happier, and banking hatred
inside will eat your soul alive.

No! I don't want there to be a reason
for what she did. I want to hate her.
Forgive her? I've never forgiven anyone.
I have no clue what the word even means.

Sobering

That's what it is,
like having a bucket
of ice water splashed
into my face, and as

chilling. I have never
offered forgiveness
to a single living person.
Or to a dead one, either.

Even after his death,
I never pardoned my father
for deserting Mary Ann
and me, leaving us at

the mercy of Iris's whims.
Instead, I've choked back
a giant grudge, held it in.
Pointless, really. As for

people still breathing,
the men whose scars
I'll always wear aren't
worthy of clemency.

But Gram is totally right.
Stowing hatred for them
does nothing but deny me
any chance at happiness.

The problem, of course,
is how to free myself of
the rage, welded into
the iron jaws of memory.

And then, there's Alex.
In some ways, she hurt
me more than the others
because I gifted her with

trust, something I don't
own much of. And while
she claimed to love me,
slowly, slowly, she excised

me from her life, declared
my devotion dependency.
Unnecessary, when in my
eyes it was affirmation that

I could, in fact, experience
such depth of emotion.
That wound still bleeds.
Will forgiveness suture it?

Finally, Iris. Mother. Traitor.
How do I reach beyond my own
pain, tap into hers, and find
a measure of sympathy?

Gram's Stooped Stucco House

Has never looked so welcoming,
and that's before we go inside,
where my family is waiting.
Gram pulls the minivan into

> the driveway. *Welcome home,*
> *Ginger. It hasn't changed much,*
> *I'm afraid. Maybe one day I'll*
> *hit the lotto and we can remodel.*

I like the sound of "we," and yet,
a sudden attack of nerves makes
me hesitate. The kids have always
looked up to me, and I am so not

a role model. Doesn't matter.
The front door opens, and out
spills the pack of my siblings,
running toward me, to a rousing

> chorus: *Ginger! Ginger! Ginger!*
> *Missed you. Where you been?*
> *Wait till you see the Christmas tree!*
> *Wait till you see your presents!*

Now four pairs of arms wrap
around me—all except Mary Ann,
who stands back slightly, observing.
"Okay, okay, let me look at you.

Wow. I can't believe how big
you all are!" I barely recognize
them. How can so little time apart
make such a difference, or did I

somehow forget the way they
looked before? No, they've changed.
Honey and Pepper have grown
their hair to below their shoulders.

Porter is two inches taller at least,
and his cheeks have lost baby fat.
Sandy looks more boy than toddler
now, and that has everything to do

with the scars the accident left on
his face. Mary Ann has changed
the most. Not only does she look
older, but she also seems more . . .

worldly, I guess. Is it her makeup,
something she never wore before
I left here? Or is it something
else? Something more sinister?

Whatever it is, I wade through
the kids clamoring at my feet, go
straight to her side and open my
arms, inviting her hug. "Hey."

She rewards my effort with
a reluctant embrace, pulls back
immediately. Everything is not
okay, but I refuse to believe

the worst until I hear it from
her mouth. "We've got a lot
to talk about, yeah? I know
I've got plenty to tell you."

> She nods, and her shoulders
> relax a notch or two. *Just so
> you know, I'm glad you're home,
> but I'm still mad at you for leaving.*

"I don't blame you," I say, but
she's already walking away.
Honey and Pepper scramble
inside behind her, followed by

> Gram and Porter, who carries
> my small suitcase. Sandy slides
> his little hand into mine, tugs gently.
> *Hey, Ginguh. Where ya been?*

I reach down, scoop him up—
he's not too big for me to manage
that yet. "That's a very long story.
Think I'll save it for another day."

A Poem by Seth Parnell
Another Day

We always believe
we'll have another day
to make things right,
but the concept of future

                                                reconciliation

is a pencil sketch.
Erasable by circumstances
beyond our power to foresee,
and what remains

                                                isn't

predictable. The longer
you wait, the wider
the rift becomes,
and it isn't

                                                always

possible to manage
the crossing before
continental drift carries
you too far apart. It's

                                                a

sad fact of life
that distance weakens
bonds, and reconnection
is simply not a

                                                given.

Seth
Finding a Christmas Eve Flight

On such short notice was a nightmare.
I finally managed to book one into

Evansville, but the layover in Detroit
is impossible, and the price tag was

out of sight. Still, I'm going, and
I'm scared as hell, and not just because

I've only ever flown one other time—
when I left Louisville with Carl—and

the weather looks to be an ugly mess
of blizzarding snow. No, I'm terrified

that Dad will turn me away, even as
weak as I hear he is, tell me he can't

bear to look at me, his blood-born
abomination. It's almost enough

to make me forget the whole idea,
stay here where I feel safe, though

that right there is a ridiculous notion.
Look at me. "That right there." "Notion."

I'm thinking in Indiana vernacular,
something I've tried to culture away

for close to a year now, ever since
I first hooked up with Loren back

in Louisville, escaping field work
for cultivation of a whole different

kind. Loren. Wonder what he's up
to now. Preaching? Partnered?

Partnered and preaching? Funny,
though they look nothing alike,

Micah's soft-spoken determination
reminds me of Loren. Both, in fact,

are a bit too determined to succeed
in their chosen careers, no matter

what it takes, even if that means
love taking a backseat to their dreams.

Even if that means me, unfortunately,
taking a backseat to their dreams.

I think I can still convince Micah
to move in with me, but not until

I return from this trip. This sad, lonely
journey to say a final goodbye to Dad.

When I Called

Aunt Kate, she gave it to me straight.
Despite decades of hard work, all that

sausage and gravy was not good for
Dad's heart. By the time he actually

decided something was wrong and
went in to see a doctor, hard-core

       measures were necessary. *They sent*
       him by ambulance straight to St. Mary's

       in Evansville, she told me. *They performed*
       a quadruple bypass, but apparently there

       was also extensive damage to the heart
       itself. He was terribly sick already, and

       has had complications. He's in intensive
       care and the prognosis isn't good. Try

       your best to get here right away. Sorry
       to do this to you at Christmastime.

She never asked where I've been,
or what happened to make me go.

Dad must have told her something,
but it was not part of the discussion.

I suppose at some point it needs to
be. I won't hide who I am anymore.

Micah drops me off at the airport,
and I kiss him goodbye in full view

of a throng of Christmas Eve travelers.
"I wish you could come with me.

Hey, maybe you could fly out next
week. I've got enough cash for a ticket,

and I'd love for you to see where I
come from. Even if it is covered in snow."

> He smiles wistfully. *Maybe one day.*
> *But I have to work next week. Besides,*
>
> *if I go back there, it won't be in winter.*
> *I had the chance to relocate in the Midwest,*
>
> *but this California boy hates deep-freeze*
> *cold. Why do you think I moved to Vegas?*

I shrug. "So you could find a cute
boy, fall in love, and settle down?"

> *You sound like Mom. Hey, better go.*
> *Those cabbies are giving me dirty looks.*

One More

Long kiss goodbye, dirty looks
from cabbies be damned. One

more promise to see him in
a few days. One more plea for

him to consider sharing a place
when I get back. One very large

stab of pain when he drives off
without looking back, just a small

wave over his shoulder. I wander
over to curbside check-in, get in line,

and suddenly it hits me that I could
go home and never return to Vegas.

Would Micah even miss me?
Would he ask me to return?

Someone behind me taps my
shoulder. *Line's moving, dude.*

"Sorry," I mutter, shuffling
forward and digging in my pocket

for my wallet and ID. As I approach
the counter, I notice the sign:

TIPS APPRECIATED. The baggage
guy is an older man, grizzled and slightly

bent, but he lifts my duffel easily,
assures me it will reach my flight in

plenty of time, and when I slip him
a ten, his eyes go wide. "Merry Christmas."

Kind is as kind does, my mom used to say,
and that seems to be the case because

when I make a few missteps at security,
the TSA people calmly remind me

to remove *everything* from my pockets.
I reach the correct gate in plenty of

time, only to find my flight's delayed
due to the Midwest weather. While

I wait I should charge my phone,
and that reminds me I need to make

a couple of calls—one to YouCenter
to let them know I won't be in, and

the other to Pippa. "Hey. I'm heading
home for a couple of days. You okay?"

Never better, she jokes. *But are you
really going back to Indiana?*

"As long as the weather gods allow
it. My dad's in the hospital." I omit

the deathbed part, but Pippa intuits
it anyway. *Oh, wow. Sorry. The Grim*

*Reaper does love the holidays. Seth?
I was thinking about community.*

*It's the next best thing to family,
isn't it? Will you help me find mine?*

"I'll do the best I can. Meanwhile,
you heal up and get out of there."

*And find a cheap plastic surgeon.
Can't go around looking like this.*

"You'll always be beautiful, Pippa.
Oh. Just called my flight. See you soon."

*Hey. One thing before you go. Try
to forgive your dad. Easy to say,*

*hard to do, I know. But if you don't,
you'll beat yourself up forever. Be safe.*

"You, too. Have a happy Christmas."
Who the hell made her so wise?

433

Squished into a Middle Seat

At the very back of the plane, not
much to do for three and a half hours,

I entertain myself with my laptop
for a while, but after the drink service

and two Jack Daniel's, I put it away
and sink into an alcohol-enhanced stupor.

I close my eyes, wishing back-row
seats reclined and wondering if

someone might be joining the Mile
High Club in the lavatory behind me,

or if people ever pay random strangers
for the experience. I will myself to nap.

Floating. Floating. Someone taps
my arm and I straighten, ready to let

my seatmate out to go to the bathroom.
Except he's sleeping, and the seat on

the aisle is empty. So why does it seem
occupied? I extend my hand into

the space, and for just a second, I feel
him there. "Dad?" The barest hint

of fingertips brush my cheek
before vanishing, and I know.

He's Gone

He didn't wait for me. Was that by
design, or did he try to hang on?

"No." It's not even a whisper. "Why?"
Why did you leave without saying

goodbye? Except, you did, didn't you?
Does this mean you've forgiven me?

"I forgive you, too." It's important
I say those words out loud, to steep

them in meaning. The man beside me
stirs, and I swallow the sound of my tears.

Maybe I'm wrong. Maybe it was only
a by-product of my buzz. Yeah, that's it.

So why do I shiver at the skin pluck
of goose bumps? I close my eyes again,

am vaguely aware when the aisle seat
refills with a flesh-and-blood human.

Window-seat man begins to snore.
I want another drink. But now the captain

informs us we're on our final descent
into Detroit, where the temperature

is five degrees Fahrenheit, under
a light snowfall. The flight attendant

adds an apology for our late start,
reminds us many connections have

also been delayed. Mine was hours
away and even if the Evansville

flight is on time, I'll have to wait
at least an hour to board it, which

proves to be the case. When we touch
down, out come the cell phones. That

includes mine. The expected message
from Aunt Kate has not yet appeared,

so I text her first. DAD DIDN'T MAKE IT.
The forty-one rows in front of me

deplane first, and I am most of the way
to my connecting gate before the bell

      on my phone sounds, signaling her
      response: *I'M SO SORRY, SETH. HIS*

      PASSING WAS PEACEFUL. BUT HOW
      DID YOU KNOW? How did I know, indeed?

If I tell her, she'll think I'm crazy.
"Gay" is probably bad enough.

One Word

Keeps surfacing on the ninety-
minute flight to Evansville: lost.

So many things lost to me, and
much too soon. My mother, claimed

by cancer before I could ever even
try to make her understand the "me"

of me. My identity, through the early
years of my childhood, not because

I couldn't see it, but because of what
was expected of me. My faith, stolen

by one who claimed to stand fast
representing it. One deviated priest,

and my God was taken from me.
And Dad, who deserted this world

in favor of the next where, he believed,
the love of his life awaits him in

eternity. But where lies the key
to heaven's gate? In dogma or ancient

scripture? Or might it be found within
the creeds of love and forgiveness?

A Poem by Whitney Lang

Deserting This World

Would be easy. The Lady
would make it a gentle ride.
So why has it taken me this
long to recognize that fact?
What's the point of

fighting

to hold on to solid
footing, when slipping
toward darkness
requires almost no
effort and the struggle

to live

a routine existence
is an uphill battle?
Anyway, how can "average"
be a goal for someone
like me, who is

tempted

by the extraordinary
and drawn toward
the unexpected?
It must be better

to die

a quick death
than to stare at the clock,
as the hours drag you toward
the very same inevitable
conclusion.

Whitney
What Have I Done?

After everything I managed
to live through—barely—before,
eking out a slender escape
from the hands of death, knotted
around my throat, how can
I invite the demon king
back into my life?

I. Am. An. Addict.
There is zero doubt of that,
and not only am I addicted to
the sensuous dance with the poppy,
but I am one hundred percent hooked
on the son of a bitch sleeping
beside me. Why did I call Bryn?

In less than five minutes,
he convinced me to leave
the relative safety of the mall
and take a drive to the beach,
despite the fact I understood
there was treachery in his motive.
I'd asked for the heroin,
that wasn't his fault, and he didn't
need to twist my arm to make me
take a whiff. Oh, I wanted to visit
the Lady, and she was everything
I remembered. One tiny taste,
every drop of fear melted like candle
wax tongued by flame.

Then Bryn kissed me. Things
are a little hazy this morning,
but I think I asked him to.
I haven't wanted a man near
me in a very long time,
but Bryn is the man who taught
me what it means to be a woman
(if not a lady), and his practiced
touch rekindled the passion
I'd truly believed died in Vegas.

He laid me back on a pillow
of sand, and though it was cool,
the billowing heat of my body
warmed it soon enough. I closed
my eyes, and didn't move,
just let him take me all the way
there, listening to the serenade
of surf beneath the steady,
building beat of my heart.

And when he said he loved me,
I stupidly confessed, "Oh God,
I love you, too." And that was all
I needed for him to convince me
to leave Santa Cruz behind again.

He is a masterful player.
And I have been played.
And I know I've been played.
And I invited the game.

The Question Is

Do I really want to keep playing,
knowing this game allows no
winners? I slip out from under
the covers, tiptoe into the little
bathroom, sit on the cracked
toilet seat, pee into the rust-stained
porcelain bowl. The experience
carries me straight back to Vegas,
a place I vowed never to return to.

We're halfway there now, in
a seedy motel, all Bryn could find
off the freeway, two nights
before Christmas. Or maybe all
he could afford. I go to the sink
to wash my hands and can't avoid
looking at the girl in the mirror.

> She stares back at me with mascara-
> stained eyes, still holding vestiges
> of the H inside them, and she insists,
> *You're better than this. He says*
> *he won't lock you back in his stable,*
> *that when you were taken from him*
> *he realized that you were the only*
> *girl he loved. But you know it's a lie.*

She's right. He lies, and the Lady
is a liar, too, but last night, held
in her arms, I finally felt right.

It Would Be So Easy

To go back into the other
room for that little plastic
bag of powdered courage.

Snort myself brave.
Chase the dragon, and
smoke myself fearless.
Send Bryn into a drug-
store for clean needles.
Shoot myself heroic.
How many heroes require
such encouragement
to face their enemies,
conquer them—or not?

> *Dope or no, you'll never*
> *be a hero,* says Girl-in-
> the-Mirror, *and your past*
> *is the enemy. Tomorrow*
> *embraces hope. Yesterday*
> *holds despair. It's not too*
> *late to turn back around.*

"Shut up," I tell her, then
turn the shower faucet
as hot as I can get it, do
my best to steam away
the lingering tendrils of H,
and scrub the scent
of Bryn from my skin.

No Clean Clothes

I put on yesterday's, then
reach into my purse, past
the plastic bag, to find my
hairbrush. On its way out,
it bumps my cell, which
I've tried to avoid, knowing
there'll be messages from Mom.

I go ahead and check them
as I wrangle the snarls from
my hair. As expected,
she's left quite a few.

> *I'M HERE TO PICK YOU UP.*
> *WHERE ARE YOU?*
> *WHITNEY? I'M HERE.*
> *WHERE ARE YOU?*
> *WHITNEY, ARE YOU OKAY?*
> *WHERE ARE YOU?*
> *WHITNEY?*
> *WHERE ARE YOU?*

There are voice mails, too,
including one from Dad:
Whitney, your mother called.
She's worried sick. Where are you?
There's even one from James.
Hey, Whitney. I was hoping
to see you today. Where are you?

Good question.
Where the fuck am I?

All Sense

Of feeling right dissolves
completely. James. Damn.
I might have had an actual
shot at something like a normal
relationship. That's gone now.

> Bryn stirs in bed, rolls
> over and into awareness.
> It takes him a minute to
> realize where he is and who
> he's with. *Whitney. Right.*
> *Morning, babe.* He smiles,
> lifts back the covers.
> *How about a little lovin'?*

Once upon a time, I would
have been tempted. Instead,
I'm sort of creeped out, and
shake my head. "Not right
now. I already showered."

> *Hey, that's okay. I've got*
> *nothing against a clean*
> *woman, although raunchy*
> *is usually better.* He laughs
> at his own stupid joke,
> very much resembling a hyena.

I've a made a huge mistake.
But how do I rectify that?

The Direct Approach

Is the only way. "Hey, Bryn.
I've been thinking. As much
as I've missed you, I can't go
back to Vegas. I really don't
want to be in the life again
and I know that's where I'll
end up. I'm so, so sorry, but
will you please take me home?"

> All signs of humor vanish
> from his face. He sits up,
> swings his feet over the side
> of the bed to the floor. *Home?*
> *I do hope you're kidding, bitch.*
> His voice drips menace like
> venom. *Surely you wouldn't*
> *have asked me to drive all*
> *the way to Santa Cruz just to*
> *deliver some dope, would you?*

Every nerve in my body
jumps to attention. This
is a royal fuckup. "I . . .
uh . . . okay, listen. You
don't have to take me back.
I'll call my parents to come
pick me up or I'll take a bus
or something. Look. I was
in a bad place, and you came
to mind, and I just wanted
to hear your voice, and—"

*And you called and begged
me to come to you.* He stands,
starts toward me. *Because
you can't forget how good
I was to you, and you know
you'll never find anyone else
who'll love you the way I do.*

I watch his approach, half
hypnotized by his confident
motion, not to mention
the way he can make me
believe that he really does
love me. But now that he's
close enough to look into
his eyes, the predator rises,
and I understand that I'm
in major trouble unless I
play this hand well. "I know
you love me, Bryn, and I
love you, too. I always will."

I take a small backward
step, and Bryn counters,
reaching out for me. "Stop."

*Stop? Oh, I can't stop now,
pretty Whitney. You're mine,
and that means I can do whatever
I please with you, whore.*

He Lunges at Me

I manage to sidestep, but
he's between me and the door,
no way out but past him.
"Please, Bryn. I won't bother
you again." I try to circle
him, but he lunges for me
again. This time he catches

> hold of my shirt, jerks and
> I am in his grasp. *I'll never
> let you go again. The first
> thing I'm going to do is fuck
> you dirty. I actually hate clean.*

He pushes me facedown
on the bed, ignoring my weak
plea to leave me alone. Just
as he starts to rip at my clothes,
there's pounding on the door.

> *What the fuck? Who is it?*
> Bryn yells, then he hisses
> at me, *Keep your mouth shut
> or I'll kick your ass, hear?*

> > *Police. Open the door.*

"Help me!" I scream, ready
for Bryn's blows. Unbelievably,
he chooses defeat, backs away,
and I have, once again, been rescued.

I'll Never Forget

This Christmas Eve—the one
I spend in custody of the Kern
County Sheriff's Office
waiting for my parents to come
pick me up. Bryn was arrested,
charged with rape and kidnapping
with the intent of trafficking
a child under the age of seventeen.

With all the crazy commotion,
I managed to sneak the heroin
out of my purse and toss it
under a car in the parking lot
without being spotted. I swear
I will never touch that shit
again. This time I'll work
the programs, choose a sponsor,
quit relying on substances
to see me through tough times.

Probably. I hope. I have to.

The cops are nice. After all,
it's Christmas Eve and I'm a heisted
teenager who was on her way
to market. I don't confess
that I called the alleged broker,
invited his advances, though
surely my mom and dad suspect
that's the way it went down.
Neither do I ask how they found me.

My Parents Pick Me Up

The two, together, as if they
actually need each other to lean on.
So weird. After wading through
the paperwork, it's late afternoon
by the time we start the four-hour
drive home. The first sixty or
so miles are mostly silent. Finally,
I say, "I know you're pissed, and
I don't blame you. I'm really, truly
sorry. Guess I'm not fixed yet, but
I want to be, and I need your help."

> Now comes the barrage:
> *Who is he? Where did you meet*
> *him? When?* And most of all, *Why?*

I answer them fairly honestly,
right up until the last one
because I don't know why.
"I was really scared I'd never
see you again. I tried to get
away, but he was too strong.
Please, Mom. Please, Dad.
I want to get well, I want
to be normal, or something
close to it. I swear I'll work
hard to get there. But I can't
do it without your support."
Down drops the curtain
of silence again. We all
have some thinking to do.

449

A Poem by Eden Streit
I Don't Know Why

God smiled on me,
and sent him my way,
this uncomplicated
gentle man whose

        love

threads my veins, pulses
within my heart, and
fortifies me, sustenance
for my hungry soul. Hope

        flickers

within me, when not so
very long ago I was lost,
wandering the shadows,

        a

weary traveler on a winding
track to nowhere.
But then, like the Magi,
I caught sight of a

        star

to guide my way out
of the wintry desert,
toward meadows green
with spring, and planted

        in

them, countless possibilities.
The sun rose within me,
light blossoming from

        the darkness.

Eden

The Sun Rises

On this Christmas morning,
and the spirit of the day blooms
inside of me. I'm up at first light,
and waiting for Andrew, who
will pick me up at seven for

the very long drive—nine hours,
with luck—to Boise. I didn't want
to wait, once determination set
in. That and the message I truly
believe God delivered through

Andrew. I have to go home. Today.
With the proper paperwork already
in place, I'm safe enough from
my parents' grasp to risk an in-person
dialogue. I don't belong to them

anymore. When I called Sarah last
night to let her know I'm leaving
Walk Straight, she counseled me
to return, at least long enough to
appear in court on my scheduled date.

I promised I would, and asked
for sanctioned leave from my job
here until I can make it back.
A deal is a deal, and Andrew says
he can live with whatever it takes

to move us one step closer to
spending the rest of our lives
together. I glance down at my
left hand, as I've done dozens
of times in the few hours since

Andrew gave me his mother's
ring. The diamonds glimmer in
the muted early light. Can there
be a luckier girl in the whole
universe? Lucky. The word

makes me think about the girls
here, safely off the streets
this Christmas. A wave of sadness
splashes into me, for Shayleece,
forever sleeping in the ground,

and for the walking dead who
must spend today in backseats
and alleys and cheap motels,
servicing customers. If I could
help them, I would. Wait . . .

Maybe I can't do much to help
them now, but with the right
focus, I can one day. And with
sudden clarity I understand
what God is calling me to do.

Andrew Is Right on Time

It being Christmas, the girls
are allowed to sleep in, and
few are stirring as I pick up
my small bag and slip out
the door. He greets me with

> the sweetest kiss and his eyes
> shine with love when he says,
> *Merry Christmas, my lady.*
> *Ready to go?* Since I'm seated
> shotgun and belted in, the answer

should be obvious, but I agree,
"Ready as I'll ever be." I suffer
a bit of déjà vu riding in his
Tundra. It starts to fade several
miles in, but I expect it to resurface

in full force as we get closer to
Boise. The highway is mostly
deserted, and we make excellent
time, stopping only to eat and use
the restroom. We listen to music

and talk about the scenery, or lack
of it, and I tell Andrew that I've
decided to go into social work,
without mentioning the God factor.
That's between me and him.

At one point, Andrew starts
to look a little road weary.
"I wish I could help you
drive, but I don't know how.
Promise you'll teach me?"

>He smiles. *I think you're old
enough, and out on the ranch
is the perfect place to learn.
Dad taught me to drive his
pickup when I was eleven.*

>*Speaking of the ranch, Mom
and Mariah are expecting us
to stop by for dinner before
we go to your parents' house.
Hope that's okay with you.*

"I'll need fortification, and
I can't think of a better place
to find it. Thank you for sharing
your family with me. I wish
I had presents for them."

>*Don't worry. I did a little Vegas
souvenir shopping. Fuzzy dice
for Mariah, who will probably burn
them, and for Mom, a photo of Elvis,
signed by the King himself, they said.*

454

That Makes Me Laugh

But when we get to the ranch,
I discover he wasn't kidding.
I'm pretty sure Elvis's signature
is a fake, especially since Andrew
tells me the picture only cost

five dollars. We bump up the long
dirt driveway, and now the déjà vu
slams into me like a semi. This
time of year, there's no alfalfa
to smell. The fields are winter-

bare and shimmer beneath a thin
layer of ice. But the memory of
that afternoon carries the green
scent with it, and nerves attack
in the same way—what will happen

next? I remember the feeling—
like standing at the very edge
of a cliff, the wind in my face—
knowing Andrew and I were about
to make love, each of us gifting

the other with our virginity.
I carried the beauty of that with
me through all the ugliness that
soon followed, and it's entrenched
in me now. "I love you, Andrew."

The words slip out so easily
and his reply comes as quickly.
*And I love you. But what was
that for?* He puts the Tundra
into park in front of the house.

"Nothing. Everything. Just
thinking about the last time
I was here. It's all I thought
about at Tears of Zion, and it's
the only reason I'm halfway sane."

Before he can respond, the front
door opens, and out bounds
a bluetick hound. "You're right.
She's not a puppy anymore."
Sheila sniffs around the truck,

looking for Andrew, who jumps
out to scratch her head hello.
When I exit the cab, her attention
shifts to me, and she comes over,
tail stump wagging recognition.

Now Andrew's mom and Mariah
materialize on the porch, signaling
to come inside, out of the cold.
Andrew takes my hand, and Sheila
leads the way into my soon-to-be home.

The Sense of Family

Is almost overwhelming,
everyone yammering happily
and simply expecting I will
join in because they accept
me as one of them already.

The house is as I remember
it—hardwood and leather,
refurbished antiques—only
prettified with the season's
decorations, including a tree

that touches the ceiling. We
gather in the kitchen, basking
in the oven's warmth, not to
mention its perfumes—prime
rib, sweet potatoes, and apple

   pie. Andrew's mom comes
   over, lifts my left hand. *I knew*
   it would fit you, don't ask me
   how. It looks beautiful, too.
   I'm so happy for you and Andrew.

"I love it. Thank you. And thank
you for encouraging Andrew's faith
in me. I promise to make you proud
of me." Somehow, I believe her
when she says I already have.

I assume Andrew has told
everyone why I'm here, so I
don't go into it. In fact, I try
hard to avoid thinking about it
mid-celebration. Dinner is even

better than last night's five-star
Vegas experience, and that much
I do relate, along with the details
of my coming emancipation.
"My counselor is looking into

transferring jurisdiction to Idaho.
The requirements are similar—
school, the ability to support myself,
a place to live. I've got those in Vegas.
What I don't have there is Andrew."

> *Between the three of us, we've*
> *got plenty of connections here,*
> says Andrew's mom, who now
> insists I call her Victoria. *We'll*
> *work it out. Andrew needs you.*

> *She's right,* agrees Andrew.
> *I absolutely need you here*
> *close to me.* He takes my hand,
> infusing me with his strength.
> Good. I'm going to need it.

There Is Discussion

About whether to wait until
tomorrow to go to my parents',
but by the time we finish our
pie, I feel bolstered by the love
I've absorbed for the past three

hours. "Hopefully they'll have
a little Christmas spirit left
and will let me come in," I tell
Andrew on the way over.
He parks on the street in front

of the house that will never be
my home again, but when he starts
to get out, I stop him. "I know they
won't let *you* in. Last thing you
need is a trespassing charge."

> *Are you sure you want to do*
> *this alone?* There are lights on
> inside, and movement beyond
> the windows, and it would be
> easy, in this moment, to change

my mind. But then I think about
Eve, alone in the cold on this
Christmas night, and I discover
my courage again. "Just don't go
anywhere, in case I come running."

I Toss a Prayer

Toward heaven as I approach
the door, ring the bell. The weight
of the footsteps tells me Mama
will answer, and she does. "Hello,
Mama. Merry Christmas."

> She startles. *What are you doing*
> *here?* Then she notices Andrew's
> truck beneath the streetlight. *Of*
> *course. I should have guessed.*
> Papa moves into place behind her.

"May I come inside for a few
minutes, Mama? When I saw you
in Las Vegas, you never gave me
the chance to tell you about Tears
of Zion. There's stuff you should know."

> She starts to say no, but Papa
> rests his hand on her shoulder.
> *It's Christmas, Joan. Show some*
> *compassion. Maybe what she has*
> *to say is important.* Papa as the voice

of reason? Maybe Somebody's
whispering into his ear. For
whatever reason, my parents
step back, let me inside, where
it's even more sterile than I recall.

460

I start the conversation as if
they're totally ignorant of Samuel
Ruenhaven's tactics. "I'm not sure
how much of this you're aware of,
but . . ." I tell them everything,

watching their expressions change
from haughty to something like
horrified. I wait for Mama to call
me a liar. Instead, she shakes
her head slowly, disbelieving.

> *No. Samuel wouldn't approve*
> *of such things. He's a man of God.*
> *I've known him for years, or I'd*
> *never have sent you girls to him.*
> *You're wrong. You must be.*

"Mama. I was there." I let that
sink in. "And now Eve's there."
I start to tell her I'm planning to
talk to the Elko DA, but change
my mind. One call from Mama

to Tears of Zion, the place might
fold up and vanish into oblivion.
"Will you help me get her out
of there? Please?" They can't
possibly say no. Can they?

A Poem by Cody Bennett
Can't Say No

To my angel.
I'd give her the universe
if it was in my power,
and it would be

nothing

compared to what
she's given me.
Whenever she's close
she makes me feel

like

I can accomplish
anything, all she has
to do is offer a word
of encouragement.
The thought of losing

her

sears hotter than
phantom bolts of pain,
those unappreciated
interruptions

in

almost every one of
my days. But she swears
she'll stay, and that someday we'll travel

the world

together, damn
the disability, and she
makes me believe it's true.

Cody
I Wonder How Many People

Take Christmas for granted.
Family. Friends. Decorations.
Gifts. Food. A little alcohol.

Always in the past I figured
there would be another Christmas.
Maybe even a better Christmas

than the one I was celebrating.
Mom was central to every holiday
gathering, and for most of my life,

my brother was there, too. In recent
memory, Jack looms large, singing
carols in his brilliant baritone,

and cracking ridiculous jokes that
never failed to make us laugh.
If someone would have told me last

year that Jack wouldn't be here today,
or that Cory would be fresh out of
lockup, while Mom toiled her butt

off at a miserable job just to make
ends meet, I would've called him a liar.
And if he'd insisted I'd soon gamble

463

away most of our money, then
try to earn it back by turning
tricks, often with men, I would

have spit in his face. And if he
somehow could have convinced
me the choices I'd make would

result in my becoming a T12
incomplete paraplegic, and
wheelchair-bound for the rest

of my life, I would've spiked
my eggnog with a lethal dose
of strychnine and happily taken

that long, dark walk into eternity
before having to witness any
of that, let alone accept the facts

of my future. Yet, here I am, alive
if not exactly kicking, and holding
my own in a staring match with

tomorrow. So, yeah, it's Christmas.
And if I can't have my legs back,
all I really want for it is Ronnie.

I Did Not Expect Her Early

Christmas is a day for family,
and I told her I'd be grateful
for any time she could spare.

She'll be here after dinner.
Mom shows up right before,
and she brings me a present.

Cory shuffles into the room,
eyes on the ground, and I know
he must be struggling with more

than the hospital stink. No, he
can't quite bring himself to look
at me. Fuck that. Get used to it.

"Cory! Dude! Jesus, you look like
shit. But I don't care. Come over
here and give me a hug, man."

I'm chilling in bed, on top of
the blankets because they keep
the temp hovering well over seventy

and I'm dressed to go to dinner.
As I use my hands to help my legs
swing over the bed, Cory chances

a glance, wincing as he watches
my well-rehearsed protocol. "What?
It took work to figure this out.

Now, if you don't come give me
a hug, I swear I'll flop out of bed,
onto the floor and crawl over to you."

> *No! Holy shit. I don't want to*
> *see that.* He looks ready to bolt.
> Instead, he takes a deep breath,

forces himself to cross the room.
His hug, however, is lukewarm.
"Hope you're not worried about

hurting me. In case you haven't
noticed, I'm almost bulletproof.
In fact, I'm immune to anything

except a real bullet." It's lame,
and Cory doesn't find it funny.
He backs away like I'm on fire.

> *Shut the fuck up. How can*
> *you joke about being so messed*
> *up?* He looks over at our mom

for support, but she just shrugs.
"Hey, Mom, can you let us talk
privately for a couple of minutes?"

I wait for her to clear the door
before I jump all over my little
brother. "Listen. What happened

to me sucks. But I'm mostly to blame
for the hand I was dealt, and now
I have no choice but to play it.

Actually, that's wrong. I could choose
to lie here feeling sorry for myself,
and I've done a fair amount of that already,

but it won't help Mom dig out of this
mess. She needs me, and she needs
you, so grow the fuck up now."

   He bristles, pulls himself straight
   and tall as he's able. But what comes
   out of his mouth is, *I'm scared.*

"*You're* scared? I'm scared, dude,
and pissed, too. I want to fuck
my girlfriend. I want to go skating.

Hell, I just want to stand up and
walk but that won't happen without
commitment. Will you help me try?"

   His expression morphs to horrified.
   Me? Now? Don't you need, like,
   crutches or something? That busts

me up. "No. In the future. Like maybe
after dinner? I'm kidding, Cory. I just
want to be able to count on you."

467

He Agrees

But it's hardly a foregone conclusion.
Still, it's a step (so to speak) in
the right direction. He and Mom walk

me to the dining room. "Sure you
won't stay? I hear it's turkey potpie,
and probably good. Cook's a genius."

      Mom shakes her head. *I promised*
      Cory we'd go to Red Lobster.
      Saved up two paychecks, even.

            Cory responds to my "really?"
            look. *Hey, they don't serve seafood*
            in jail, you know, except for some

            fried supposed-to-be-shrimp.
            So many times I got a craving
            for that damn Ultimate Feast.

      It's the only thing he wanted for
      Christmas. But don't worry. He
      got socks and underwear, too.

That makes us all laugh. Mom,
being a practical woman, always
put such necessities under the tree

so there were more gifts to unwrap
than the few toys she could afford.
I guess some things never change.

The Potpie Rocks

The leftover turkey finally got
the gravy it needed. The company
is fine, but I find myself wishing

I was at Red Lobster with Mom
and Cory. How long it will take her
to feel comfortable including me?

Oh, well. After dinner, some guys
are playing cards and invite me to join
them. I decline gently. Not only do

I need to leave any form of gambling
deep in my wake, but my girl will
be here any time, and nothing

is as important as being with her.
I wheel back to my room, anxious
to share time with her tonight.

It's a short wait, and she's a vision,
in a short red skirt and white angora
sweater. "Mm. You look yummy."

> I expect her to go gooey. Instead,
> she's all business, and excited.
> *We'll get to the kissing and stuff*
>
> *in a minute. But first, don't you*
> *want your present? Oh, almost*
> *forgot. Merry Christmas, Cody.*

Her Hands Are Empty

"Merry Christmas to you, but
I don't see any presents. Wait.
Are they under your clothes?"

> *Stop. No. Listen. You've never*
> *really asked about my parents.*
> *Like, who my dad is or anything.*

Hm. I guess I haven't. "Is he a serial
killer or president or a lion tamer?"
Oops. She's irritated. "Sorry. I'll shut up."

> *Good. You should. My father happens*
> *to be the CEO of a big gaming tech*
> *company. He also deals in investment*
>
> *properties, and has purchased quite*
> *a few short sales. I asked if he'd be*
> *interested in buying your mom's house*
>
> *and renting it back to her. He said*
> *he'd look into it, and as you know,*
> *I can be very persuasive.* She winks.

"You're serious." She is a bottomless
well of surprises. Emotions—relief,
joy, disbelief, and most of all, love—

upwell inside me. How can I possibly
be this lucky? I reach for her, thinking
Santa Claus must be real after all.

A Poem by Ginger Cordell
Santa Must Be Real

That's what my little
brother said when he saw
the tree this Christmas

morning.

How did Gram manage
it? Two presents for each
of us, not extravagant,
but for the love they came
wrapped in. The memory
of little Sandy's face

brings

joy, hours later.
I've forgotten the concept
of finding happiness
in little things. Coming
home makes everything

new

and I never want to leave,
though I know one day
I'll have to find a more
positive way out into
the bigger world, enticed by

possibilities.

Ginger
Home

The concept is still foreign,
though Gram's is the closest
I've come to a place I can always
return to. One thing's for sure.

I'll never go back to Las Vegas,
not even for "fun" because, though
most Sin City tourists either
don't know, or don't care, Vegas

fun is carried on the backs of people
who clean toilets or sweep streets
or turn tricks, not to get rich, but to
squeeze some semblance of living

from the fight to exist. Only CEOs
and pimps prosper, and sometimes
they are one and the same. No,
people go to Vegas in search

of dreams, but rarely notice
the living, breathing nightmares
right under their noses. Unless,
of course, that's what their dreams

consist of. It hurts to think about
the girls I've left behind there—Alex,
who'll probably never leave. And
Brielle, who'll move on without me.

Hard to Leave Love Behind

But there's plenty here,
surrounding me like a force
field. The kids love in the way
children do, with pure devotion.

When they asked where
I've been, I detoured around
everything prior to House
of Hope, and told them

I've been living with some
girls who were in need of
help, which was one hundred
percent accurate. I failed

to mention the fact that
I was one of those girls,
or exactly what kind of
help we needed. Only

Mary Ann is old enough
to understand there were
words to be read between
the lines. Before, I would

have believed she was too
young to hear my story.
But now I see the importance
of telling her everything,

so she'll understand what's
at stake within the realm
of choices—those we make,
and those others try to take

from us, especially as young
women. I want her to be
informed, so she can make
smart decisions. I also want

her to be afraid, or at least
cautious. There are predators
everywhere, and sometimes
they look totally harmless.

And there are people who
offer up prey to feed those
carnivores—people like
Miranda's brother, Ricardo,

who traded in his sister on
his dope debt. People like our
mother, who I'm struggling
to find compassion for.

When I got home yesterday,
my prodigal return caused
way too much commotion
to even consider attempting

some sort of conversation
with Iris. She was in the living
room, sitting in the old recliner,
specter-pale and quivering

as she watched an old black-
and-white holiday movie on TV.
She squinted at me when I came
in, managed a little wave,

and I acknowledged that with
a curt nod before taking my stuff
into the bedroom I'll share again
with the girls. Nothing has changed

while I was gone except the art,
hung with Scotch tape, proof
of Honey's and Pepper's slight
improvement as watercolorists.

The kids swirled around me,
then jumped on the beds,
chattering like monkeys, and
the noise and sharp motion

was almost too much. I flopped
down anyway, absorbing
their energy, and tried to remember
being that young, if I ever was.

Yesterday's Homecoming

Is something I'll always remember.
Dinner was Gram's enchiladas,
and afterward the kids brought out
their surprises—tie-dyed T-shirts,

one short-sleeved, in orange, yellow,
and red, the other long, in turquoise
and purple. "Wow! These are amazing,"
I gushed, and though I'd never in a million

years pick them out in a store, I'll wear
them and make them look good.
Then we watched *A Christmas Story*
and *Elf* on TV, until Gram finally said

enough and insisted the young ones go
to bed or Santa wouldn't come. Iris sat
in the same chair, droopy-eyed, sharing
space but not the experience, and I couldn't

help but steal glances. She is dying.
I've never been this close to death.
I can feel it, hovering near, waiting
to tap her on the shoulder. She'll

survive this Christmas Day, probably
even see the New Year, but not
a lot of it. She deserves pity.
But is she worthy of forgiveness?

The Kids Are All in the Kitchen

Baking and decorating Christmas
cookies with Gram. Iris is in her
usual place, quietly drinking wine.
I sit on the corner of the sofa

closest to her, and she looks at
me with inquisitive eyes. *Glad
you came home. We missed you
around here. 'Specially Mary Ann.*

*An' now I can't work, would
be good for you to. Your gram
could use some help paying
the bills. Lots of bills. Too many.*

How much do I say? Is now
even the right time? Screw it.
"Do you know why I left, Iris?"
Something changes in her eyes,

which seem to shroud black.
I think I know, she snarls. *What
do you want from me? An apology?*
At least she doesn't deny it. *Because . . .*

Now the dark veil lifts and tears
trickle. *Goddamn it, I'm sorry.
So fucking sorry. I'm a crap mother
and always have been, and now*

it's too late to fix it. I really wish
I could, but I can't take any of it
back, and I'm just so goddamn sorry.
I wasted my life. I could've been

somebody. But here's the thing. . . .
She wipes the snot dripping from
her nose with the back of her hand.
You can still be somebody. I won't

be here to see it, and that makes
me sad. Listen to me, Ginger girl.
The past will influence your future,
but it doesn't have to destroy it.

Holy shit. Iris as philosopher?
I hand her a box of tissues, refill
her glass from the bottle on the end
table. "Merry Christmas, Iris. I need

a cookie." I don't know if that was
enough to help me forgive her. Maybe,
with time, and that's more than I could
have said only five minutes ago.

A Poem by Seth Parnell
With Time

He'll forgive me,
that's what I kept telling
myself, repeating it in
my head like a mantra. With

                time

he'll come to accept
me for who I am,
the way I was born,
how the good Lord
exactly created me. Dad

                was

only forty-eight, not old
enough for his heart
to fail in such spectacular
fashion. This event was

                not

in my game plan. How
on God's good green earth
could he just up and die

                on

me? Why couldn't
he hold on a couple more
hours? I was almost there,
Dad, and we could have said

                our

goodbyes. My Christmas
dinner: a heaping plate
of sadness with a giant bowl
of regret on the

                side.

Seth
Empty

The fields are empty. Dad managed
to harvest the corn before he got sick.

Aunt Kate says it was a good crop
this year, and that gives me a lick

of pride. Lick. Yeah. I figure I'll go
ahead and indulge the Indiana farm

boy in me by de-culturing his voice
for a while. It's damn cold today,

Christmas Day, but I'm walking
the Parnell land in a big old down

jacket, stocking cap, and winter-weight
gloves, all of them Dad's. I inhale

the scent of him clinging to his clothes,
exhale streams of warm breath into

the snow-frosted air. Our hunting
hound, Ralph, stays close by my side.

Aunt Kate brought him to her place
when Dad went into the hospital,

and when we got there last night,
Ralph practically knocked me over,

he was so happy to see me. I reach
down and stroke his head now.

"At least someone around here missed
me. What are we going to do with you

when I go back to Vegas?" It won't
be for a while. The funeral is set

for next week, and then there's legal
stuff to deal with. Dad didn't have

a whole lot, just the farm and equipment,
a decent Ford truck, and a small bank

account. Aunt Kate says she hasn't seen
Dad's will, but she's sure he left everything

to me. Ralph and I circle around to
the barn. Dad kept a few chickens

and they're all inside, along with
Matilda and Jane, the goats who manage

weed control. Aunt Kate's been feeding
them, but she lives in town, fifteen minutes

away, so I told her I'd care for the critters
while I'm here. I toss hay to the goats

and scratch to the chickens, just like
when I was a kid. Nostalgia hits hard,

carried in the perfume of oats and seed,
motor oil and manure; and in the cluck

of hens and the munching of the nannies
and the creak of old rafters in the wind.

It presses me down to the ground, where
I sit, surrounded by ghosts. "Why?"

It escapes, a wail of mourning. "How
could you die and leave me without

a friendly word between us? Damn
you, Dad!" Ralph creeps over, lays

his head in my lap, telling me I'm not
totally alone, here in the barn, here on

my farm, here where I worked and played
and hid from myself. Here at home.

All the fear and rage I've kept bottled
inside spills out of me now in a flood

of tears. "Why, Ralph? Why did I wait
so long to come home? I could have

made him listen. Could have made him
change his mind, and now I'll never

get the chance. I should have tried
harder!" I give myself permission

to cry for a good, long time. Once
I'm mostly finished, I get to my feet.

"Come on, Ralph, let's go." He follows
me to the house, and that is empty,

too. Not of furnishings—those are all
here, exactly the way they were the day

Dad sent me away. I'm slightly gratified
to see he didn't change my room.

There are dishes in the sink. I wash them,
put them away in their proper place in

the cupboard. After Mom died, Dad and I
made sure to keep her kitchen organized

the way she liked it, in her honor. I pay
tribute in the same way now, neatening

the house and making Dad's bed,
which I've never seen tousled before.

Dirty Dishes and an Unmade Bed

Dad must have been feeling really
bad to leave the place like this.

And what will I do with it now?
I click the heat lower. I'll be back

later, but I'm supposed to share
Christmas dinner with Aunt Kate

and the clan. I load Ralph into Dad's
Ford, drive slowly along the vacant

road, the route to town so familiar
I can drive it with my eyes closed,

as Dad used to say. Damn. I miss it,
and I also miss the family gathered

at Aunt Kate's—cousins and in-laws,
and little kids, laughing and arguing

and jostling around. Everyone seems
welcoming, either because they don't

know or care I'm gay, or maybe they
just feel sorry for me. Doesn't matter.

They suck me right into the midst
of them, and today that is necessary.

In Honor of Dad

Aunt Kate chose to roast a huge prime
rib. It was his absolute favorite. She's even

fixed it just the way he liked, with a rock
salt and cracked peppercorn coating. As it

finishes, filling the house with its heavenly
scent, the men find a game to watch while

the women play a rousing game of euchre
and the kids entertain themselves. When Kate

goes to check the meat's progress, I follow
her into the oven warmth and quiet.

"Can I help with anything?" I ask, watching
her set the roasting pan on the granite

        countertop. *I think I've got things under*
        control, thanks. She turns toward me,

        grinning. *You know, considering how much*
        you always liked to cook with your dad,

        I kind of thought you might wind up a chef
        in some fancy restaurant or something.

"I've actually been considering culinary
school. But now . . ." I think about the farm—

about the sparring emotions coming home
initiated. Home. I'm here. But can I stay?

"Aunt Kate? Did Dad tell you why I left?
I mean, did he tell you . . . about me?"

She inserts a digital thermometer into
the heart of the prime rib. *About you?*

Not sure if she's distracted or acting
coy. But I have to know. "Did Dad tell

you he kicked me out because I quote-
unquote chose the path to damnation?"

I thought I was cried out, but I was wrong.
The room sways slightly. "Did he tell you

he wouldn't talk to me or let me come
home until I decided I'm not . . . not . . ."

Gay? She turns to face me. *No, Seth.*
Bud didn't tell me. He was a private

man and held everything close. But I
knew. I've known for a very long time.

I want to talk more, but now we hear
a volley of rapid-fire questions beyond

the door: *How's that meat coming?*
Are we going to eat soon? Should

someone set the table? Did Kate
make eggnog? Hey. Where did Seth go?

I'll finish the conversation with
a question of my own. "If you can

accept me, why couldn't Dad?
Now we'll never get the chance—"

Oh, there you are! Uncle Dan comes
looking for us. *Everything okay?*

Just fine, says Aunt Kate. *The meat's*
resting for ten, then I'll ask you to carve.

Sure thing. Smells mighty fine. I'll go
let everyone know it's almost time.

Kate waits till he's gone. *Try not to fret.*
I've got something for you later. Now, here.

She hands me a platter of baked potatoes,
and I carry them to the dining room table.

I don't care if I look like I've been crying.
A dead dad at Christmas gives me the right.

After Dinner

Aunt Kate pulls me down the hall,
into her room. She lifts an envelope

       off her dresser. I picked up Bud's stuff
       from the hospital, and this was in it.

       I'm not sure when he found the time
       or energy. I'll leave you alone with it.

It's a note to me from Dad, written
in a shaky hand, barely legible.

Dear Seth, I wish I could say this face-to-face,
but I don't think I'm gonna make it. I wouldn't

mind dying so much except for a couple of things.
One is the farm. Without you there, I'm scared

of what will become of it. I don't want it to fall
into bad hands. See to it that doesn't happen.

The other is you, son. I'm a stubborn fool, and
I let my pride get in the way of loving you without

conditions, as God would have me do. Please forgive
me, and I pray the Lord forgives me, too. Just know,

despite the harsh words, I never stopped loving you,
though it took this to see it. I promise, if God allows,

I'll always stay close to you. All my worldly
possessions belong to you now, including this:

It's the Recipe for Venison Sausage

Guess Dad approves of my culinary
ambitions. I reread the note ten or twelve

times, etching his words into my heart.
I need time to think. I call for Ralph,

bid adieu to the family. Snowflakes dance
in the headlights as we maneuver the icy

road to the farm. Home. Suddenly, I understand
I can't go back to Vegas. Not sure I'm cut

out to be a full-time farmer. But maybe
I can hire outside help, keep the old place

in good hands. I still want to go to school,
but I bet I can find a good program in

Louisville and commute. Memories, good
and bad, linger in that city, but that's where

I first found my community, and I can always
tap into that there. Community leads me to

Pippa, who I adore, and Micah, whom I love.
Neither belongs in rural Indiana, but maybe

I can convince them to give Louisville a try.
If not, I'll weather the loss and move on.

A Poem by Whitney Lang
Move On

I want to. I really do want
to turn my back on yesterday,
leapfrog today, into

                    tomorrow,

but how is that possible,
tethered by fear? People keep
asking what I'm frightened
of. The real question

                 is

what doesn't trouble me?
I'm scared I can't escape
the legacy of turning tricks,
that too much filth and

                 too

little affection will forever
define my relationships.
I'm afraid I've deviated so

                 far

from decency that I'll never
again deserve respect,
let alone a full measure
of love, and keep pushing it

                 away.

I'm terrified that faces
will float from the past,
into the present, and there
will be no place to hide.

Whitney
Top to Bottom

Left to right, the Lang family
totally defines dysfunction. I mean,
after everything that happened
yesterday, the sun rises and everyone
pretends it's just another Christmas.

Mom wanted to drive me straight
back to rehab, but I managed to persuade
her to bring me home, and let me mend
my mind via outpatient therapy.
I built a strong three-pronged argument.
One: I need to rely on my family
to follow through with treatment.
Two: Inpatient care costs a whole
lot more. And three: They'd be closed
for Christmas anyway.

Okay, the last one is weak, but
the other two swayed her, or maybe
it was her feeling guilty about Kyra
unwrapping presents while I was locked
away. So home we came, and with a stop
for dinner, we arrived before Santa.
Lang tradition dictates no presents go
under the tree until Christmas Eve,
which made sense when Kyra and
I were little. Not so much after
we knew what was what, but Mom
has always insisted on it anyway.

So this morning we wake up,
grab coffee, and collect ourselves
at the tree, where someone-not-Santa
has deposited presents sometime
between midnight and dawn.
Quaint tradition, but it put a strange
slant to the big picture. Whatever.
I'll just try to embrace the weirdness.

I don't have presents for anyone,
and truthfully, I am surprised to
find gifts for me. As usual, Mom
gives Kyra and me clothes. She loves
to shop, and building our wardrobes
gives her pleasure. I don't think she realizes
how much weight I've lost. She's bought
me last year's size six, and everything
from jeans to sweaters will be baggy.
That's fine. I'm not into "tight" at
the moment, and won't be for a while.

From Dad, an iPad for each of us,
and a Mac Air for Mom. He's all
about Apple, from his phone to
his computer, and probably gets
volume discounts. Kyra gives me
a purse. Coach, of course, maroon
leather, and way too big. It will
swallow the few things I carry.

492

After the Whole Gifting Thing

The four of us, yes, including Dad,
go to work on dinner. I can't
remember *ever* doing something
as family-wholesome as that.
Mom assigns jobs. Kyra, of course,
is responsible for the plum pudding.
Dad volunteers to do the pumpkin
pie, which only scares me a little.
And, no surprise, I get to do
the gingerbread while Mom takes
charge of everything else.

The kitchen feels claustrophobic,
and a few seconds of panic set
in. But when I try to explain,
rather than let me get some fresh
air, Mom is adamant that I stay.

> *Sit at the table and take deep*
> *breaths. We're doing this as*
> *a cohesive unit. I realize that's*
> *new for us all, but I can't see*
> *another way to keep us together,*
> *and I refuse to let us fall apart.*

I have no idea what's gotten into
her, except maybe it has everything
to do with almost losing me, not
once, but twice. Turns out, she had
GPS tracking installed on my phone.
Just in case. And that proved provident.

That Information

Was passed down on our trip
home last night, when I asked
how the cops knew where to find me.

> You didn't think we'd take
> a chance on you disappearing
> again, did you? Mom asked.

> You do realize technology
> makes tracking people relatively
> easy these days? interjected Dad.

So then they gave me the lowdown
on GPS tracking, and made it very
clear that if they are paying my cell phone
bill, I can expect they will know
where I am anytime they need to.

But there's more to this story,
the surprising plot twist if this were
a novel. Mom shared this part on the way
home, too. I haven't as yet approached
Kyra, asked about motive. I'll wait until
her plum pudding is steaming.

Who knew that's how you make plum
pudding? Who knew the absolute best
plum pudding begins a year in advance?
She only started a couple of days ago,
so tonight's will be decent. Then, I bet,
she'll go straight to work on next
Christmas's, and it will be perfect.

Of Course It Will

Because Kyra will make damn
sure to improve. That's my sister.
As this part of the story goes,
she was putting together the fruits,
spices, and cognac that went into
her plum pudding when Mom
dropped me off at the mall,
where Bryn lay in waiting
like the predator he is.

She was missing an ingredient
and wanted to call Mom to pick
it up, but her phone was dead,
and she'd left her charger back
at school, so she went into my
room to look for mine.

I guess I'd dropped Bryn's business
card on the floor the night I found
it in my pocket. Kyra discovered
it, and something about the Perfect
Poses Photography logo sparked.
When Mom couldn't find me at
the mall, it clicked into place and
was an important piece of the puzzle
when Mom reported me missing.

With the pudding steaming nicely,
she excuses herself and goes into
the other room. I follow. "Kyra?
Can I talk to you for a minute?"

She flops on the sofa, signals
for me to join her. *Guess so.*

"Why did you show Mom Bryn's
card? You didn't have to, and I'd
be back in Vegas, out of your hair."

She squints, and her forehead
creases. *What? Like I wouldn't
show it to her? Whitney, you piss
me off regularly, and there are
things about you I don't get at
all. This last little "adventure,"
for instance. Just . . . why? You've
got so much potential. Why are
you so intent on throwing it away?*

"I . . . I don't know. I guess
I never thought anyone cared."

*We all care! Look, just because
none of us is the huggy-kissy type
doesn't mean we don't love you.
Do you really believe I'd rather
you were back in Las Vegas?*

I can only respond with a shrug.

Kyra is quiet for a moment.
*Looks like we've got to work
on some relationship building.*

It's an Acknowledgment

And it's a start. I'm thinking long
and hard about the roles I've played
within my failed relationships.
My family has been fractured
for a while. The support I've received
lately is the most I've had from Mom
and Dad since I was a little kid,
before their partnership ruptured.
That they're trying to repair it now
is largely because of me, so maybe
I can be a catalyst for good there.
Or maybe they'll fail at it again.

Kyra? When we were little, I looked
up to her, but she outshone me in
every way, and after a while it got
old taking the backseat to her well-
earned accomplishments. I chose
silent resentment in favor of expressing
my feelings, and that was a mistake.

Lucas was never a real relationship
at all. I clung to the idea that he cared
about me, though he was nothing but
all out for himself. Good riddance.

And now, James: If there's the slimmest
chance for us, it will be rooted in honesty.
I want to try if he does. I need someone
wonderful in my life, and guess what.
He's calling me right this minute.

A Poem by Eden Streit
Someone Wonderful

Is in love with me.
He's my light, my warmth,
my bread and water.
How did I make it
through even one day

                    without

him? Someone wonderful
promises to spend the rest
of his days by my side.
People will say we're too
young to experience undying

                    love

that time will agree.
But the bond between
our hearts is steel, unbreakable,
and with proper care, won't rust.
One day he and I will explore

                    the world

hand in hand, and maybe
little hands will join ours.
Someone wonderful
gives me hope for the future
and without him my life

                    is colorless.

Eden
Mama and Papa Listen

To my Tears of Zion exposé.
I'm not sure they really believe
me, but at least they don't send
me away. They haven't as yet
agreed to remove Eve from

Ruenhaven's grasp. What else
can I say to convince them
she's in evil hands? "May I ask
you something? What did Father
tell you about how I left?"

       As always, it's Mama who
       answers. *He said, like your sister's*
       namesake, you listened to
       the serpent. That you seduced
       that man, who was weak of spirit.

"No. He seduced me, with food
and soap. And I wasn't the first
girl he'd coerced in that way.
When you're starving, you'll do
anything for a piece of fruit.

Eve is hungry right now, Mama.
I don't know if Jerome is back,
or if there are others like him,
but whatever she did, this is not
a proper punishment for it."

She jumps on the defensive.
What she did *was emulate* you.
You ought to be ashamed of
yourself for encouraging her
immodest behavior. Just look

at you now, in fact. I knew
you'd figure a way to get back
together with that person
out there. Why . . . why . . .
It's a regular abomination.

It's no wonder you ended up
on the streets in that hideous
city. It was God's chastisement.
You can't circumvent his laws
and expect anything less.

Slapped down. I remember
this feeling so well, like I
could never deserve God's
mercy. I look her straight in
the eye. "Return to the scriptures,

Mama. 'If we confess our sins,
he is faithful and just to forgive
us our sins, and to cleanse us
from all unrighteousness.' God
has forgiven me. Why can't you?"

Tough Question

One she's having a hard time
answering. While she thinks
about it, I go to the door,
wave to Andrew for him to
join me. Might as well get

        to the meat of things. When
        Mama starts to sputter, Papa
        actually quiets her. Curiosity?
        Guilt? Some tiny hint of love?
        Leave her be. She deserves to
        have her say, and so does the boy.

As Andrew speeds up the walk,
no doubt worried that I'm knee-
deep in trouble, it occurs to me
that Papa rarely dared to disagree
with Mama in the past. Has he

grown tired of her domineering
attitude? Has my command of
scripture swayed him? Does he
hear the truth of my words?
Does he, maybe, miss having

his children in his household,
and sincerely regret he didn't
stand up for us sooner? I'd like
to think all of the above hold true.
I'd like to believe my papa loves me.

Whoa

Sobering thought, because
it doesn't include Mama. Would
I like to believe my mama loves
me, too? On some deep personal
level, I really don't care anymore.

      Andrew crosses the threshold,
      and as he does, I vow my children
      will never doubt their mother's
      love. *Are you okay?* he asks,
      concern obvious in his voice.

"Absolutely. I just don't want
to break our news to them without
you beside me." I twine my fingers
into his, squeeze hard, and tug
him toward the living room.

Mama's hackles rise noticeably,
and I try to lower them first.
"Do you know what thought
just crossed my mind, Mama?
That I don't believe you love me,

and to be honest, I wonder if you
ever did. I think you're afraid
of love, and that makes me sad.
Because love is *of* God, not in
spite of him. And you're wrong.

My love for Andrew is not
an abomination. It's real, and
beautiful, and so, of God. Look . . ."
I extend my left hand. "Despite
all that's happened, and Andrew

knows everything, he wants to
marry me. Yes, we're young, but
you were only a couple of years
older when you married Papa.
I wish . . ." A giant knot forms

in my throat, and I can't finish,
so Andrew tries. *I know it's hard
for you to believe this, but when
I first met Eden, I'd never been
in love before. And do you know*

*what made me love her almost
immediately? First, her incredible
spirit, which could only be born
of God. And second, her respect
for Creation, which had to come*

*from you. I'm sorry ego came
into play last year—both mine
and yours. Mine, because yes,
I wanted her to love me. And
yours, for much the same reason.*

Double Whoa

Forward momentum at full
throttle, I do my best to swallow
the lump in my throat. "Without
your permission, we can't get
married until I turn eighteen,

despite the emancipation.
It's only a year, and we don't
mind a long engagement, but
I don't want to spend it in Las
Vegas. Andrew and I plan to

live here in Boise. This is our
home. I hope we can maintain
a civil relationship with you, and
I'd very much like to stay in close
contact with Eve. I really wish

you can find room in your hearts
for me, but if not, I'll work through
it. Either way, please, please find
room there for Eve. She deserves
parents who will show her love."

Mama sits, speechless, eyes cast
toward the floor. Papa looks a bit
shell-shocked. "Come on, Andrew,
we should go. Merry Christmas,
Mama. Merry Christmas, Papa."

It's a Picture-Perfect Christmas Night

Crisp and clear, with myriad
stars sequinning the black velvet
sky. I beam a silent thank-you
in that direction. I'm not sure
how much we accomplished,

> but it could have gone worse,
> and as we left Papa said,
> *You've given us a lot to think
> about.* At least one of them
> heard us. I hope we used all

the right words. Andrew slides
his arm around my shoulders,
snugs me tightly against him
as we walk to the Tundra.
"I'll still need to go to Elko."

> *I figured as much. I'm on semester
> break for another week. We'll go
> in a day or two. Everything will
> be okay, Eden. I promise. Hey,
> have I told you lately I love you?*

"Andrew, you just told my parents
you love me." We stop beneath
a streetlight, where anyone can see.
And this time when he kisses me,
I know without a doubt I'm home.

Author's Note

I first became interested in the subject of Domestic Minor Sex Trafficking (DMST) when I came across the statistic that the average age of young women introduced into prostitution is twelve. This was in 2007, just as the widespread problem of child sex trafficking was becoming news. I spent the next year researching and writing *Tricks*, which introduces five teen characters from different parts of the country, all of whom, for very different reasons, end up turning tricks in Las Vegas.

All five lived on in the minds of readers, and eventually a sequel was called for, as the characters' fates were still undecided at the end of the book. While *Traffick* provides those answers, it also introduces readers to other DMST victims, some of whom become survivors, and others who don't. All these characters are inspired by very real people, living very real lives as DMST victims. We have become much more aware of the problem in the last decade, and awareness is the beginning of change.

With new federal guidelines in place, the penalties for DMST pandering have greatly increased. Trafficking children under the age of fourteen now carries a mandatory life sentence in many states, including Nevada. However, DMST will continue as long as there is a market. Education is paramount, as is intervention by law enforcement and great organizations like Children of the Night, GEMS: Girls Educational and Mentoring Services, and other rescue services. Help is available.

You can find a service provider in your area by calling the National Human Trafficking and Smuggling Center at 888-373-7888.

Or, report suspected child prostitution activity to the National Center for Missing & Exploited Children at 800-THE-LOST or cybertipline.com.

According to the National Human Trafficking and Smuggling Center:

- Human trafficking is the exploitation of a person for the purposes of forced labor or commercial sex, regardless of citizenship or nationality. Despite the connotation of the word, "trafficking" doesn't always indicate movement between cities.
- Sex trafficking is when a commercial sex act is induced by force, fraud, or coercion, or whenever the person induced to perform such an act has not attained eighteen years of age.
- Trafficking happens to US citizens, within the borders of this country, and in every state.
- The average age of a child introduced to DMST is twelve.
- Daily in the United States between 150,000 and 300,000 children under eighteen are trafficked.
- Up to 30 percent of DMST victims are boys, including straight, gay, and transgendered youth.
- More than 70 percent of homeless youth living on the streets turn tricks to survive.
- Victims of DMST don't always self-identify as victims. Often they believe they don't deserve a better life, or that their pimps truly love them and this is a small price to pay for that love.

How can you live your life if it has been based on lies?

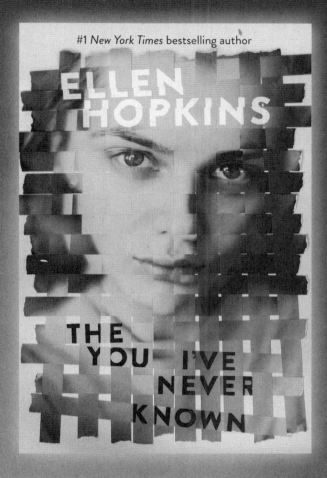

Read on for a sneak peek at Ellen Hopkins's riveting newest novel, written in both verse and prose.

To Begin

Oh, to be given the gifts
of the chameleon!

Not only the ability
to match the vital facade
to circumstance at will,

but also the capacity
to see in two directions
simultaneously.

Left. Right.
Forward. Backward.

How much gentler
our time on this planet,
and how much more

certain of our place
in the world we would be,
drawing comfort

like water from the wells
of our homes.

Ariel

Home

Four letters,
one silent.
A single syllable
pregnant with meaning.

Home is more
than a leak-free roof
and insulated walls
that keep you warm
when the winter wind screams
and cool when summer
stomps all over you.

Home is a clearing
in the forest,
a safe place to run
when the trees shutter
all light and the crunch
of leaves in deepening darkness
drills fear into your heart.

Home is someone
or two who accepts you
for the person you believe
you are, and if that happens
to change, embraces the person
you ultimately find yourself to be.

I Can't Remember

Every place
Dad and I have
called home. When
I was real little, the two
of us sometimes lived in
our car. Those memories
are in motion. Always moving.

I don't think
I minded it so much
then, though mixed in
with happy recollections
are snippets of intense fear.
I didn't dare ask why one stretch
of sky wasn't good enough to settle

under. My dad
likes to say he came
into this world infected
with wanderlust. He claims
I'm lucky, that at one day till
I turn seventeen I've seen way
more places than most folks see

in an entire
lifetime. I'm sure
he's right on the most
basic level, and while I
can't dig up snapshots of
North Dakota, West Virginia, or
Nebraska, how could I ever forget

watching Old
Faithful spouting
way up into the bold
amethyst Yellowstone sky,
or the granddaddy alligator
ambling along beside our car
on a stretch of Everglade roadway?

I've inhaled
heavenly sweet
plumeria perfume,
dodging pedicab traffic
in the craziness of Waikiki.
I've picnicked in the shadows
of redwoods older than the rumored

son of God;
nudged up against
the edge of the Grand
Canyon as a pair of eagles
played tag in the warm air
currents; seen Atlantic whales
spy-hop; bodysurfed in the Pacific;

and picked spring-
inspired Death Valley
wildflowers. I've listened
to Niagara Falls percussion,
the haunting song of courting
loons. So I guess my dad is right.
I'm luckier than a whole lot of people.

Yeah, On Paper

All that sounds pretty damn
awesome. But here's the deal.
I'd trade every bit of it to touch
down somewhere Dad didn't insist

we leave as soon as we arrived.
I truly don't think I'm greedy.
All I want is a real home, with
a backyard and a bedroom

I can fix up any way I choose,
the chance to make a friend
or two, and invite them to spend
the night. Not so much to ask, is it?

Well, I guess you'd have to query Dad.
I know he only wants what's best
for me, but somehow he's never
cared about my soul-deep longing

for roots. *Home is where the two
of us are,* was a favorite saying, and,
*The sky is the best roof there is. Except
when it's leaking.* The rain reference

cracked me up when I was real young.
But after a time or twenty, stranded
in our car while it poured because
we had nowhere else dry to stay,

my sense of humor failed me.
Then he'd teach me a new card
game or let me win at the ones
I already knew. He could be nice

like that. But as I aged beyond
the adorable little girl stage,
the desire for "place" growing,
he grew tired of my whining.

> That's what he called it. *Quit*
> *your goddamn whining,* he'd say.
> *You remind me of your mother. Why*
> *don't you run off and leave me, too?*

> *Who'd look out for you then, Miss*
> *Nothing's Ever Good Enough?*
> *No one, that's who! Not one person*
> *on this planet cares about you.*

> *No one but Daddy, who loves you*
> *more than anything in the whole wide*
> *world, and would lay down his life*
> *for you. You remember that, hear me?*

I heard those words too often,
in any number of combinations.
Almost always they came floating
in a fog of alcohol and tobacco.

Once in a While

But not often, those words
came punctuated by a jab
to my arm or the shake
of my shoulders or a whack
against the back of my head.
I learned not to cry.

> *Soldier up,* he'd say. *Soldiers*
> *don't cry. They swallow pain.*
> *Keep blubbering, I'll give you*
> *something to bawl about.*

He would, too. Afterward
always came his idea
of an apology—a piece of gum
or a handful of peanuts or,
if he felt really bad, he might
spring for a Popsicle.
Never a spoken, "I'm sorry."

> Closest he ever came was,
> *I'm raising you the way*
> *I was raised. I didn't turn*
> *out so bad, and neither will you.*

Then he'd open the dog-eared
atlas and we'd choose our next
point of interest to explore.
Together. Just the two of us.
That's all either of us needed.

He always made that crystal
clear. Of course, he managed
to find plenty of female
companionship whenever
the desire struck.

It took me years
to understand the reasons
for those relationships
and how selfish
his motives were.

I've read about men
who use their cute dogs
to bait women
into hooking up.
Dad used me.

The result was temporary
housing, a shot at education,
though I changed schools
more often than most military
kids do. All that moving, though
Dad was out of the army.

At least we slept
in actual beds
and used bathrooms
that didn't have stalls.
But still, I always knew
those houses would never
be home.

tricks

Also by Ellen Hopkins

Crank

Burned

Impulse

Glass

Identical

Fallout

Perfect

Tilt

Smoke

Rumble

Traffick

The You I've Never Known

People Kill People

tricks

Ellen Hopkins

Margaret K. McElderry Books
NEW YORK LONDON TORONTO SYDNEY NEW DELHI

MARGARET K. McELDERRY BOOKS

An imprint of Simon & Schuster Children's Publishing Division

1230 Avenue of the Americas, New York, New York 10020

This book is a work of fiction. Any references to historical events, real people,
or real places are used fictitiously. Other names, characters, places, and events are
products of the author's imagination, and any resemblance to actual events or places
or persons, living or dead, is entirely coincidental.

Text copyright © 2009 by Ellen Hopkins

Cover design and illustration by Sammy Yuen Jr.

All rights reserved, including the right of reproduction in whole or in part in any form.

MARGARET K. McELDERRY BOOKS is a trademark of Simon & Schuster, Inc.

For information about special discounts for bulk purchases, please contact
Simon & Schuster Special Sales at 1-866-506-1949 or business@simonandschuster.com.

The Simon & Schuster Speakers Bureau can bring authors to your live event.

For more information or to book an event, contact the Simon & Schuster Speakers Bureau
at 1-866-248-3049 or visit our website at www.simonspeakers.com.

Also available in a Margaret K. McElderry Books hardcover edition

Book edited by Emma D. Dryden

Book design by Sammy Yuen Jr.

The text for this book was set in Trade Gothic Condensed 18.

Manufactured in the United States of America

This Margaret K. McElderry Books paperback edition January 2017

10   9

The Library of Congress has cataloged the hardcover edition as follows:

Hopkins, Ellen.

Tricks / Ellen Hopkins.

p. cm.

Summary: Five troubled teenagers fall into prostitution
as they search for freedom, safety, community, family, and love.

ISBN 978-1-4169-5007-3 (hc)

ISBN 978-1-4169-9642-2 (eBook)

[1. Novels in verse. 2. Family problems—Fiction.

3. Emotional problems—Fiction. 4. Prostitution—Fiction.] I. Title.

PZ7.5.H67Tr 2009

[Fic]—dc22

2009020297

ISBN 978-1-4814-9824-1 (trade pbk)

This book is dedicated to the fine members of law enforcement, social work, and the judiciary who truly care about young people forced to walk the streets in search of simple sustenance. With a major nod to Randy Sutton of the Las Vegas P.D., Judge William Voy, and Children of the Night.

Special thanks must also go to three amazing friends, exceptional writers Susan Hart Lindquist, Jim Averbeck, and Suzanne Morgan Williams, who push me to reach ever deeper for the very best stories I'm capable of writing. This book is better because of them. And my life is better because they are in it.

tricks

A Poem by Eden Streit
Eyes Tell Stories

But do they know how
to craft fiction? Do
they know how to spin

lies?

His eyes swear forever,
flatter with vows of only
me. But are they empty

promises?

I stare into his eyes, as
into a crystal ball, but
I cannot find forever,

only

movies of yesterday,
a sketchbook of today,
dreams of a shared

tomorrow.

His eyes whisper secrets.
But are they truths or fairy tales?
I wonder if even he

knows.

Eden
Some People

Never find the right kind of love.
You know, the kind that steals

your breath away, like diving into snowmelt.
The kind that jolts your heart,

sets it beating apace, an anxious
hiccuping of hummingbird wings.

The kind that makes every terrible
minute apart feel like hours. Days.

Some people flit from one possibility
to the next, never experiencing the incredible

connection of two people, rocked by destiny.
Never knowing what it means to love

someone else more than themselves.
More than life itself, or the promise

of something better, beyond this world.
More, even (forgive me!) than God.

Lucky me. I found the right kind
of love. With the wrong person.

Not Wrong for Me

No, not at all. Andrew is pretty much
perfect. Not gorgeous, not in a male

model kind of way, but he is really cute,
with crazy hair that sometimes hides

his eyes, dark chocolate eyes that hold
laughter, even when he's deadly serious.

He's not a hunk, but toned, and tall enough
to effortlessly tuck me under his arms,

arms that are gentle but strong from honest
ranch work, arms that make me feel

safe when they gather me in. It's the only
time I really feel wanted, and the absolute

best part of any day is when I manage
to steal cherished time with Andrew.

No, he's not even a little wrong for me
except maybe—maybe!—in the eyes

of God. But much, much worse than that,
he's completely wrong for my parents.

See, My Papa

Is a hellfire-and-brimstone-preaching
Assembly of God minister, and Mama

is his not-nearly-as-sweet-as-she-seems
right-hand woman, and by almighty God,

their daughters (that's me, Eden, and my
little sister, Eve—yeah, no pressure at all)

will toe the Pentecostal line. Sometimes
Eve and I even pretend to talk in tongues,

just to keep them believing we're heaven-
bound, despite the fact that we go to public school

(Mama's too lazy to homeschool) and come
face-to-face with the unsaved every day.

But anyway, my father and mother
maintain certain expectations when

it comes to their daughters' all-too-human
future plans and desires.

>   Papa: *Our daughters will find
>   husbands within their faith.*
>
>   Mama: *Our daughters will not
>   date until they're ready to marry.*

You Get My Dilemma

I'm definitely not ready to marry,
so I can't risk letting them know

I'm already dating, let alone dating
a guy who isn't born-again, and even

worse, doesn't believe he needs to be.
Andrew is spiritual, yes. But religious?

   Religion is for followers, he told
   me once. *Followers and puppets.*

   At my stricken look, he became not
   quite apologetic. *Sorry. But I don't*

   need some money-grubbing preacher
   defining my relationship with God.

At the time, I was only half in love
with Andrew and thought I needed

definitions. "What, exactly, *is* your
relationship with our Heavenly Father?"

   He gently touched my cheek, smiled.
   First off, I don't think God is a guy.

   Some Old Testament—writing fart
   made that up to keep his old lady

                    in line. He paused, then added, *Why*
                    would God need a pecker, anyway?

Yes, he enjoyed the horrified look
on my face. More laughter settled

into those amazing eyes, creasing
them at the corners. So sexy!

                    Anyway, I relate to God in a very
                    personal way. Don't need anyone

                    to tell me how to do it better. I see
                    His hand everywhere—in red sunrises

                    and orange sunsets; in rain, falling
                    on thirsty fields; in how a newborn

                    lamb finds his mama in the herd. I thank
                    God for these things. And for you.

After that, I was a lot more than
halfway in love with Andrew.

The Funny Thing Is

We actually met at a revival, where nearly
everyone was babbling in tongues,

or getting a healthy dose of Holy Spirit
healing. Andrew's sister, Mariah, had

forsaken her Roman Catholic roots
in favor of born-again believing and had

dragged her brother along that night,
hoping he'd find salvation. Instead

he found me, sitting in the very back
row, half grinning at the goings-on.

      He slid into an empty seat beside me.
      So . . . , he whispered. *Come here often?*

I hadn't noticed him come in, and when
I turned to respond, my voice caught

in my throat. Andrew was the best-looking
guy to ever sit next to me,

let alone actually say something to me.
In fact, I didn't know they came that cute

in Idaho. A good ten seconds passed before
I realized he had asked a question.

"I . . . uh . . . well, yes, in fact I come here
fairly regularly. See the short guy up there?"

I pointed toward Papa, who kept the crowd
chanting and praying while the visiting evangelist

busily laid on his hands. "He's the regular
preacher and happens to be my father."

Andrew's jaw fell. He looked back and
forth, Papa to me. *You're kidding, right?*

His consternation surprised me. "No,
not kidding. Why would you think so?"

He measured me again. *It's just . . . you look
so normal, and this . . .* He shook his head.

I leaned closer to him, and for the first
time inhaled his characteristic scent—

clean and somehow green, like the alfalfa
fields I later learned he helps work for cash.

I dropped my voice very low. "Promise not
to tell, but I know just what you mean."

8

It Was a Defining Moment

For me, who had never dared confess
that I have questioned church dogma

for quite some time, mostly because I am
highly aware of hypocrisy and notice

it all too often among my father's flock.
I mean, how can you claim to walk

in the light of the Lord when you're
cheating on your husband or stealing

from your best friend/business partner?
Okay, I'm something of a cynic.

But there was more that evening—instant
connection, to a guy who on the surface

was very different from me. And yet,
we both knew instinctively that we needed

something from each other. Some people might
call it chemistry—two parts hydrogen,

one part oxygen, voilà! You've got water.
A steady trickle, building to a cascade.

If Andrew

Was the poser type, things would
probably be easier. I mean, if he could

pretend to accept the Lord into his heart,
on my father's strictest of terms, maybe

we could be seen together in public—not
really dating, of course. Not without a ring.

But Andrew is the most honest person
I've ever met, and deadly honest that night.

> *Did you* have *to come to this thing?*
> *It seems kind of, um . . . theatrical.*

We had slipped out the back door,
when everyone's attention turned to

some unbelievable miracle at the front
of the church. I smiled. "Theatrical.

That sums it up pretty well, I guess.
You probably couldn't see it in back, but . . ."

I glanced around dramatically, whispered,
"Brother Bradley even wears makeup!"

> Andrew laughed warmly. *So why do*
> *you come, then? Pure entertainment?*

I shrugged. "Certain expectations are
attached to the 'pastor's daughter' job

description. Easier just to meet them, or
at least pretend they don't bother you."

It was early November, and the night wore
a chill. I shivered at the nip in the air,

or at the sudden magnetic pull I felt toward
this perfect stranger. Without a second

thought, Andrew took off his leather
jacket, eased it around my shoulders.

Cool tonight, he observed. *All
the signs point to a hard winter.*

He was standing very close to me.
I sank into that earthy green aura, looked

up into his eyes. "You don't believe in
miracles, but you do believe in signs?"

His eyes didn't stray an inch. *Who
says I don't believe in miracles?*

They happen every day. And I think
we both knew that one just might have.

It Was Unfamiliar Turf

I mean, of course I'd thought guys were cute
before, and the truth is, I'd even kissed

a few. But they'd all been "kiss and run,"
and none had come sprinting back for seconds.

Probably because most of the guys here
at Boise High know who my father is.

But Andrew went to Borah High, clear
across town, and he graduated last year.

He's a freshman at Boise State, where his mom
teaches feminist theory. Yes, she and his rancher

dad make an odd couple. Love is like that.
Guess where his progressive theories came from.

That makes him nineteen, all the more reason
we have to keep our relationship discreet.

In Idaho, age of consent is eighteen,
and my parents wouldn't even think

twice about locking him up for statutory.
That horrible thought has crossed my mind

more than once in the four months since
Andrew decided to take a chance on me.

Four Months

Of him coming to church with Mariah,
both of us patiently wading through Papa's

sermons, then waiting for post-services coffee
hours to slip separately out the side doors, into

the thick stand of riverside trees for a walk.
Conversation. After a while, we held hands

as we ducked in between the old cottonwoods,
grown skeletal with autumn. We joked about

how soon we'd have to bring our own leaves
for cover. And then one day Andrew stopped.

He pleated me into his arms, burrowed his face
in my hair, inhaled. *Smells like rain,* he said.

My heart quickstepped. He wanted to kiss
me. That scared me. What if I wasn't good?

His lips brushed my forehead, the pulse
in my right temple. *Will I burn if I kiss you?*

I was scared, but not of burning, and I wanted
that kiss more than anything I'd ever wanted

in my life. "Probably. And I'll burn with you.
But it will be worth it." I closed my eyes.

It was cold that morning, maybe thirty
degrees. But Andrew's lips were feverish

against mine. It was the kiss in the dream
you never want to wake up from—sultry,

fueled by desire, and yet somehow innocent,
because brand-new, budding love was the heart

of our passion. Andrew lifted me gently
in his sinewy arms, spun me in small circles,

lips still welded to mine. I'd never known
such joy, and it all flowed from Andrew.

And when we finally stopped, I knew
my life had irrevocably changed.

Day by Day

I've grown to love him more and more.
Now, though I haven't dared confess

it yet, I'm forever and ever in love with
him. After I tell him (if I ever find the nerve),

I'll have to hide it from everyone. Boise,
Idaho, isn't very big. Word gets around.

Can't even tell Eve. She's awful about
keeping secrets. Good thing she goes to

middle school, where she isn't privy
to what happens here at Boise High.

I'm sixteen, a junior. A year and a half,
and I'll be free to do whatever I please.

For now, I'm sneaking off to spend
a few precious minutes with Andrew.

I duck out the exit, run down the steps,
hoping I don't trip. Last thing I need

is an emergency room visit when I'm
supposed to be in study hall. Around one

corner. Two. And there's his Tundra across
the street, idling at the curb. He spots me

and even from here, I can see his face
light up. Glance left. No one I know.

Right. Ditto. No familiar faces or cars.
I don't even wait for the corner,

but jaywalk midblock at a furious
pace, practically dive through the door

and across the seat, barely saying hello
before kissing Andrew like I might

never see him again. Maybe that's because
always, in the back of my mind, I realize

that's a distinct possibility, if we're ever
discovered kissing like this. One other

thought branded into my brain is that maybe
kissing like this will bring God's almighty wrath

crashing down all around us. I swear, God,
it's not just about the delicious electricity

coursing through my veins. It's all about love.
And you are the source of that, right? Amen.

A Poem by Seth Parnell
Possibilities

As a child, I was wary,
often felt cornered.
To escape, I regularly
stashed myself

                   in the closet,

comforted by curtains
of cotton. Silk. Velour.
Avoided wool, which
encouraged my

                   itching

the ever-present rashes
on my arms, legs. My skin
reacted to secrets, lies,
and taunts by wanting

                   to break out.

Now I hide behind
a wall of silence, bricked
in by the crushing
desire to confess,

                   but afraid of

my family's reaction.
Fearful I don't have
the strength to survive

                   the fallout.

Seth
As Far Back

As I can remember,
  I have known that
  I was different. I think
  I was maybe five
when I decided that.

I was the little boy
  who liked art projects
  and ant farm tending
  better than riding bikes
or playing army rangers.

Not easy, coming from
  a long line of farmers and
  factory workers. Dad's big
  dream for his only son has
always been tool and die.

My dream is liberal arts,
  a New Agey university.
  Berkeley, maybe. Or,
  even better, San Francisco.
But that won't happen.

Not with Mom Gone

She was the one who
    supported my escape
    plan. *You reach for your*
    dreams, she said. *Factory*
work is killing us all.

Factory work may
    have jump-started it,
    but it was cancer that
    took my mom, one year
and three months ago.

At least she didn't
    have to find out about
    me. She loved me, sure,
    with all her heart. Wanted
me to be happy, with all her

heart. But when it came to
    sex, she was all Catholic
    in her thinking. Sex was
    for making babies, and only
after marriage. I'll never forget

what she said when my cousin
  Liz got pregnant. She was just
  sixteen and her boyfriend hauled
  his butt out of town, all the way
to an army base in Georgia.

  Mom got off the phone with
    Aunt Josie, clucking like a hen.
    Who would have believed
    our pretty little Liz would
  grow up to be such a whore?

  I thought that was harsh,
    and told her so. She said,
    flat out, *Getting pregnant*
    without getting married first
  makes her a whore in God's eyes.

I knew better than to argue
        with Mom, but if she felt
        that strongly about unmarried
        sex, no way could I ever let
her know about me, suffer

the disgrace that would have
        followed. Beyond Mom,
        Indiana's holier-than-thou
        conservatives hate "fags" almost
as much as those freaks in Kansas

do—the ones who picket dead
        soldiers' funerals, claiming
        their fate was God's way of
        getting back at gays. How in
the hell are the two things related?

And Anyway

If God were inclined
        to punish someone
        just for being the way
        he created them, it would
be punishment enough

to insert that innocent
        soul inside the womb
        of a native Indianan.
        These cornfields and
gravel roads are no place

for someone like me.
        Considering almost every
        guy I ever knew growing up
        is a total jock, with no plans
for the future but farming

or assembly-line work,
        it sure isn't easy to fit in
        at school, even without
        overtly jumping out of
that frigging closet.

I can't even tell Dad,
        though I've come very
        close a couple of times,
        in response to his totally
cliché homophobic views:

> *Bible says God made*
> *Adam and Eve, not Adam*
> *and Steve, and no damn*
> *bleeding-heart liberal*
> *gonna tell me different.*

Most definitely not *this*
  bleeding-heart liberal.
  Of course, Dad has no clue
  that's what I am. Or have
become. Because of *who*

I am, all the way inside,
  the biggest part of me,
  the part I need to hide.
  Wonder what he'd say
if I told him the first person

to recognize what I am
  was a priest. Father Howard
  knew. Took advantage, too.
  Maybe I'll confess it all
to Dad someday. But not

while he's still grieving
  over Mom. I am too.
  And if I lost my dad
  because of any of this, I really
don't know what I'd do.

So I Keep the Real Seth

Mostly hidden away.
It is spring, a time of hope,
locked in the rich loam
we till and plant. Corn.
Maize. The main ingredient

in American ethanol,
the fuel of the future, and
so it fuels our dreams. It's
a cold March day, but the sun
threatens to thaw me,

like it has started to thaw
the ground. The big John
Deere has little trouble
tugging the tiller, turning
the soil, readying it for seed.

I don't mind this work.
There's something satisfying
about the submission, dirt
to churning blades. Submission,
yes, and almost as ancient

as the submission of one
beast, throat up to another.
One human, facedown
to another. And always,
always another, hungering.

Hunger

Drives the beast, human
      or otherwise, and it is
      the essence of humanity.
      Hunger for food. Power.
Sex. All tangled together.

It was hunger that made
      me post a personal ad
      on the Internet. Hunger
      for something I knew
I could never taste here.

Hunger that put me on
      the freeway to Louisville,
      far away enough to promise
      secrecy unattainable at home.
Hunger that gave me

the courage to knock on
      a stranger's door. Looking
      back, I realize the danger.
      But then I felt invincible.
Or maybe just starved.

I'd Dated Girls, of Course

Trying to convince
    myself the attraction
    toward guys I'd always felt
    was just a passing thing.
Satan, luring me with

the promise of a penis.
    I'd even fallen for a female.
    Janet Winkler was dream-girl
    pretty and sweeter than
just-turned apple cider.

But love and sexual desire
    don't always go hand in hand.
    Luckily, Janet wasn't looking
    to get laid, which worked out
just fine. After a while,

though, I figured *I* should
    be looking to get laid, like
    every other guy my age. So
    why did the thought of sex
with Janet—who I believed

I loved, even—not turn
    me on one bit? Worse, why
    did the idea of sex with her
    Neanderthal jock big brother
turn me on so completely?

Not that Leon Winkler
        is particularly special.
        Not good-looking. Definitely
        not the brightest bulb in the
socket. What he does have

going on is a fullback's
        physique. Pure muscle.
        (That includes inside his
        two-inch-thick skull.) I'd catch
myself watching his butt,

thinking it was perfect.
        Something not exactly
        hetero about that. Weird
        thing was, that didn't
bother me. Well, except for

the idea someone might
        notice how my eyes often
        fell toward the rhythm
        of his exit. I never once
lusted for Janet like that.

I tried to let her down
        easy. Gave her the ol'
        "It's not you, it's me"
        routine. But breaking up
is never an easy thing.

Not Easy for Janet

Who never saw it coming.
　　　　When I told her, she looked
　　　　as if she'd been run over
　　　　by a bulldozer. *But you*
told me you love me.

"I do love you," I said.
　　　　"But things are, well . . .
　　　　confusing right now. You
　　　　know my mom is sick. . . ."
Can't believe I used

her cancer as an excuse
　　　　to try and smooth things
　　　　over. And it worked, to
　　　　a point, anyway. At least
it gave Janet something

　　　　to hold on to. *I know, Seth.*
　　　　　　But don't you think you
　　　　　　need someone to . . . ?
　　　　The denial in my eyes
spoke clearly. She tried

another tactic, sliding
　　　　her arms around my neck,
　　　　seeking to comfort me. Then
　　　　she kissed me, and it was
a different kind of kiss

than any we'd shared
before. Swollen with desire.
Demanding. Lips still locked
to mine, she murmured, *What
if I give you this . . . ?*

Her hand found my own,
urged it along her body's
contours, all the way to
the place between her legs,
the one I had never asked for.

To be honest, I thought
about doing it. What if it
cured my confusion after all?
In the heat of the moment,
I even got hard, especially

when Janet touched me,
dropped onto her knees,
lowered my zipper, started
to do what I never suspected
she knew how to do. Yes . . .

No! Shouldn't . . . How . . . ?
The haze in my brain
cleared instantly, and I pushed
her away. "No. I can't,"
was all I could say.

All Janet Could Say

Before she stalked off
        was, *Up yours! What are*
        you, anyway? Gay? Not
        really expecting a response,
she pivoted sharply, went

in search of moral support.
        So she never heard me say,
        way under my breath, "Maybe
        I *am* gay." It was time, maybe
past, to find out for sure.

But not in Perry County,
        Indiana, where if you're
        not related to someone,
        you know someone who
is. All fact here is rooted

in gossip, and gossip can
        prove deadly. Like last year,
        little Billy Caldwell told Nate
        Fisher that he saw Nate's mom
kissing some guy out back

of a tavern. Total lie, but
        that didn't help Nate's mom
        when Nate's dad went looking
        for her, with a loaded shotgun.
Caught up to her after Mass.

Sunday morning, and when
      he was done, that church
      parking lot looked like a street
      in Baghdad. After, Billy felt
kind of bad. But he blamed

Nate's dad one hundred percent.
      Not Nate, who took out
      his grief on Billy's hunting
      dog. That hound isn't much
good for hunting now, not

with an eye missing. Since
      I'd really like to hang on
      to both of my eyes and all
      of my limbs, I figured I'd
better find my true self

somewhere other than Perry
      County. Best way I could
      think of was through the
      "be anyone you choose to be"
possibilities of online dating.

Granted, One Possibility

Was hooking up with a creep—
　　　a pervert, looking to spread
　　　some incurable disease to some
　　　poor, horny idiot. I met more
than one pervert, but I never

let them do me. Nope, horny
　　　or not, I wasn't an idiot. No
　　　homosexual yokel, anxious
　　　enough to get laid to let any
guy who swung the correct

direction into my jeans.
　　　I wanted my first real sex
　　　to be with the right guy. Someone
　　　experienced enough to teach
me, but not humiliate me.

Someone good-looking.
　　　Young. Educated. A good
　　　talker, yes, but a good listener,
　　　too. Someone maybe even
hoping to fall in love.

Incredibly

Unimaginably, Loren turned
       out to be all those things,
       and I found him in Louisville!
       He opened my eyes to a wider
world, introduced me to the

avant-garde—performance art,
       nude theater, alternative
       lit. He gave me a taste
       for caviar, pâté, excellent
California cabernet. After

years of fried chicken and
       Pabst Blue Ribbon, such
       adjustments could only be
       born of love. Truthfully,
love was unexpected. I've

said it before, and I'll repeat,
       I didn't fall out of the tree
       yesterday. But that first day,
       when Loren opened his door,
I took one look and fell

flat on my face. Figuratively,
       of course. I barely stumbled
       as I crossed the threshold—
       into his apartment, and into
the certainty of who I am.

A Poem by Whitney Lang
Stumbling

I only have one question,
scraping the inside of me.
Answer it, and I will

stumble

back into her shadow.
Shut my mouth, never
ask again. I've tried to
ignore it, but it won't go

away.

It haunts my dreams,
chases me through
every single day, and I

don't

have the strength to
turn around. Face it
down. So please tell me
and I swear I'll never

ask

again. It's in your
power to make it go
away. And all you have
to do is tell me

why

you love her more.

Whitney
Living in Someone's Shadow

Totally blows. Don't get
me wrong. I love my sister.
Just not as much as my mother
loves her. Doesn't matter how

hard I try, I can never quite
measure up to Kyra. I'm pretty.
She's beautiful. I'm smart.
She's a genius. I can sing

a tolerable alto. She'll solo,
lead soprano, at the Met.
Mom's own failed dreams
resurrected in Kyra.

And speaking of dreams,
mine are small. *Shortsighted,*
Mom calls them. Interior
design, maybe. Or fashion.

Kyra, however, is majoring
in International Relations.
I don't get it. What does
she want to be? A spy?

I thought things would get
better when she went off
to Vassar. Two thousand,
three hundred and fifty-six

miles away from Santa Cruz,
the pretentious California beach
town where we live. But no
amount of miles can make

her shadow disappear. It's
only longer, stretched across
the continent. Her on one side.
Me stuck fast on the other.

It's Not So Bad

When my dad's home. He's an
investment banker in the fine
old city of San Francisco.
Too far to commute every day,

so he keeps an apartment there
four nights a week, comes home
for regular three-day weekends.
Used to be regular, anyway.

My dad's my hero, and when
he's home he makes Mom stay
off my ass. I don't say words
like "ass" when he's around.

Don't want him to think I'm
a "foul-mouthed bitch," as my
mom enjoys calling me. Wonder
where I got the mouth from.

Anyway, Daddy loves me,
and if he happens to play
favorites, the dice usually roll
my way. Probably just making

up for Mom. But hey, that's
okay. One out of two ain't bad.
I just hate when they argue.
Because it's usually about me.

More and More Lately

It seems like Mom makes
a point of staying gone when
Daddy's home. She golfs. Plays
tennis. Spends hours at the gym.

Sometimes she visits a friend
in Monterey. I assume a female
friend, but wouldn't put it past Mom
to have a thing going on the side.

Pretty sure she doesn't have a bi
side, but whatever floats her lead-
bottomed boat, as long as it means
she's hanging out anywhere but here.

I love when it's just Daddy and me.
Usually it's here in SC, but once
in a while, I'll go into the city,
spend the weekend with him there.

San Francisco has to be the most
beautiful place in the world, with
its stunning old homes, stacked
like Legos on its incredibly steep

hills. There are museums. Galleries.
The symphony and the ballet.
Daddy has taught me to appreciate
all of these things, and not give

a sideways glance at SF's uglier
underbelly. Homeless people.
Panhandlers. Drug dealers, pimps,
and Tenderloin freaks, often only

a street or two removed from
the thriving business district
and the vibrant waterfront tourist
traffic. A city of enigmas.

I like enigmas. I mean, face
it. Semi-absent father. Absent-
for-the-moment sister. Totally
absent mother, not a whole lot

of affection, but plenty of time
all on my own, I'm a walking,
talking poster child for early
promiscuity. Aren't I?

Well, Not Exactly

See, between the longtime local
hype about AIDS and a real-time
example of how rotten young
mothering can make a person

(Mom was only nineteen when she
had Kyra; I followed a little over three
years later), not to mention how truly
disgusting venereal diseases

look in those movies they show
you in school, I have not been
in a hurry to let just any guy
pluck the rosebud. True love first,

I've always said, and that has
been enough to keep me a virgin.
Up until now. I mean, technically
I'm still a virgin at fifteen.

But I'm also in love, and I'm pretty
sure Lucas loves me, too. We've been
skin-on-skin. I just haven't let him
talk me into "all the way in."

That's Liable to Change

Any time. I've been holding out,
wanting to be certain that he loves
me for more than my bod. But how
can you really know that?

We've been together almost
a year. He's a senior at Kirby,
the same private college prep school
that prepped Kyra for Vassar.

She was valedictorian, of course.
I take AP classes at Empire. Less
pressure. Less having to live up
to valedictorian expectations.

Lucas and I met at a Kirby honor
choir performance last spring. Kyra
sang two solos. Lucas stood in the back
row, mostly faking the words. Once

in a while he actually belted out a few
in a deep, mellow bass. I couldn't
help but stare. And not at Kyra.
Lucas stole my attention completely.

I mean, he's freaking beautiful.
His hair falls, a lush gold cascade,
well past his shoulders. It frames
the steep angles of his face perfectly.

His eyes are green, but almost
clear, like cool emerald pools.
You want to dive deep down
into them and swim awhile.

That first night, after the sheet
music was all stored away,
I went looking for Kyra and cookies,
not necessarily in that order.

I found her, talking with Lucas.
And for not even close to the first
time in my life, the little green
monster sank its fangs into me.

Kyra wasn't interested in Lucas.
Her taste in men runs toward PhD
candidates (total geeks). But I
wasn't sure Lucas knew that.

So I took dead aim at making
darn sure he did, pushing straight
in between them. "Hey, sis," I said,
"Mom is looking for you."

That Was Mostly a Lie

But it worked. Kyra kisses
Mom's butt almost as much
as Mom kisses hers. She took
off with a simple, *Excuse me.*

I turned to Lucas. "Good
performance. You've got
a great voice. . . ." Better
eyes, but I didn't go there.

His smile revealed major bucks
in dental work. *Yeah. At least
when I can remember the words.
So . . . you're Kyra's little sister?*

The "little" made me wince.
Of course, I was only fourteen
at the time. Kyra's eighteenth
birthday was sneaking up.

Whatever. I had to play nice.
"That's me. Kyra's little sister.
But you can call me Whitney
if you want. It's shorter."

Something about the tone
of my voice tipped him off.
Ooh. Struck a nerve, huh?
Well, little sis, no worries.

He gave a long, assessing look.
You measure up okay. Besides . . .
He lowered his voice. *Just between*
you and me, your sister's a bitch.

O-M-G! No one, and I mean *no*
one, had ever told me that before.
I studied his face, trying to find
a hint of insincerity. Couldn't.

Something sparked between us.
Maybe it was as simple as him
thinking my sister was a bitch.
Sharing my opinion. Something

others rarely do. And not only
sharing it, but not being afraid to
voice such an unpopular sentiment.
"Just between you and me, I agree."

Okay, Very Likely

He saw how much I needed
to hear that, and maybe he figured
it might be a way into my panties,
and maybe it will lead to that eventually.

Maybe even soon. I'm not really sure
how or why I've held out this long,
except that protecting my virginity
is one thing I can accomplish

all on my own. Won't give it away
too cheaply. Not even to Lucas,
whose touch simply electrifies me.
That night, as the reception broke up

and we started toward our families,
our hands touched. The energy
was pure magic. He felt it too,
turned back to me immediately.

His smile was lupine. Ravenous.
I needed to get to know this guy,
and so when he said, *Uh . . . don't*
suppose you'd give me your number?

I recited it once. Repeated it.
Asked him to repeat it to me,
a feat that he managed easily.
He remembered it too.

It Kind of Surprised Me

When he called a couple of days
later. Not sure why. I guess it's
because I always set myself up
for disappointment. Not that time.

> *Hey*, he said, *it's Lucas, from
> Kirby*. . . . Like I wouldn't have
> remembered! *I was thinking about
> a day trip to Big Sur. Interested?*

Like I wouldn't have been!
But I didn't want him to know
my temp had just flared well over
one-oh-one. "Uh, maybe. When?"

> *I don't suppose you could, like,
> ditch school tomorrow?* At
> my long pause, he laughed. *Okay.
> How about Saturday, then?*

That gave me two whole days
to make up a believable excuse.
No way would Mom let me go
to Big Sur with a guy I just met.

Okay, she wouldn't have let me
go with any guy. Not that I cared.
Getting away with stuff was a well-
loved hobby. And even if it wasn't,

I would have done just about
anything to spend the day with
someone who made me feel
important. Pretty, maybe. Alive.

Believe it or not, my mom made
it easy. *I'm playing golf with Cyn
tomorrow,* she told me on Friday.
And we're doing dinner afterward.

You'll be okay here alone, right?
She barely even heard my ramble
about going over to Trish's for
he day. *Great. I'll be home late.*

Just like that, my Saturday had
opened up. And, very much like
my wandering mother, I was oh-
so-ready to go out and play.

We Played That Saturday

Lucas's silver Eclipse Spyder
seemed to maneuver those
Highway 1 curves all by itself.
Good thing, considering how

buzzed we got. Okay, it wasn't
the first time I'd smoked weed,
but I'd rarely smoked myself
so close to outer space before.

      Finally Lucas pulled well off
      the road, parked. *C'mon.*
      I want to show you something.
      He took my hand, led me along

      a narrow trail to a steep rock
      wall. No way could you climb
      up from the front, but around back,
      little ledges allowed access to the top.

Despite the residual morning mist,
the view of the crest-and-crash
Pacific literally stole my breath
away. "Insane," I managed.

We sat, lost in our buzz and the roar
of the sea, and when he slipped
his arm around my shoulder, it
felt right. No, better than right.

It felt necessary. He wanted
to kiss me, I knew that. And
I wanted to let him, but I was
afraid I'd look like an idiot.

I'd only ever kissed two other
guys, in an eighth-grade game
of Truth or Dare. Not real kisses.
Not even real practice kisses.

Still, when he touched my face,
it rotated easily toward his. And
when our eyes locked, I dove into
those emerald pools and our first

kiss was an effortless float.
All the love I'd ever thirsted
for swelled, symphonic. Finally,
too soon, he pulled away. *Wow.*

A Man of Few Words

Most definitely, but I didn't
need words then. I needed
another kiss, which he gave
me, and another. And another.

Without asking for more. Even
though by the end of that make-out
session, my body was saying, "Please,
more." And it has many times since.

A few days ago Daddy was in the city,
and Mom was off at some fashion
show. I asked Lucas to come over.
We were making out hot and heavy.

He started to unbutton my blouse.
I let him. And when he unzipped
my jeans, I helped him help me
out of them. Snared by the heat

of his kiss, I barely noticed when
he slipped out of his own Levis.
Skin urgent against skin, only
panties and boxers between us,

I was ready to shed that final thin
barrier, allow him access to the most
private part of me, when familiar faces
floated past the window. Not-quite busted!

A Poem by Ginger Cordell
Faces

I wear many faces,
some way too old
to fit the girl glued
to the back of them.

I

keep my faces in a box,
stashed inside of me.
It's murky in there,
overcast with feelings I

don't

allow anyone to see.
Not that anyone cares
enough to go looking.
No one wants to

know

what bothers me. Too
hung up on their own
problems. Sometimes
I think I have to see

the real

Ginger, so I open
the box, search inside.
But no matter how hard
I look, I can't find

me.

Ginger
SOP

Standard operating procedure.
       Iris is yelling again. At the phone.
At the guy on the other end.

At what he's done to her world—
       her totally messed-up, totally self-
centered piece of the universe.

Wish she would just shut the fuck
       up. Hang up. Forget Hal or Bill
or Joe or Frank or whatever this

one's name is. I can't remember
       them all. Only a couple of names,
a face or two. A few other body

parts I'll never be able to forget.
       All because of Iris's "womanly
needs." That's what she calls

her overinflated sex drive. Why
       can't she stop thinking about
herself and act like a mom?

She could start by letting us call
        her Mom. But, no, she insists on
Iris. Says it makes her feel pretty.

Not sure she was ever really
        pretty, but if she was, too
many babies and too much

hard living has sucked her dry.
        Too much, too many. That
describes Iris pretty damn well.

Too much booze. Too many
        smokes. Way too many
pills. Speed. Downers.

Everything in between. Any-
        thing to shut off and shut
up what's left of her brain.

A Door Slams

Guess she's done on the phone.
      Done with another Mr. Wrong.
Thirty seconds, she'll be in here,

crying. Wanting me to say, "Don't
      cry, Iris. Everything will be okay."
And, you know, maybe it will.

"Okay" is all in how you look at
      things. Compared to some bum
on the street, or some starving

kid in Africa, we're okay, living
      with our grandma, who manages
to feed Iris and us six kids.

Six kids, five different fathers.
      Only Maryann and I share one,
not that we know one damn thing

about him, except he's an army
        lifer who gave us his face (neither
of us takes after our mother) and his

last name. Guess Iris actually
        married him. Wonder if she
ever officially unmarried him.

Yes, no, or maybe so, the other
        kids—Porter, Honey, Pepper,
and Sandy—all have different

fathers, but share the same last
        name. Belcher, just like Gram's.
Our first names come courtesy

of Iris's infatuation with ancient
        black-and-white TV reruns. Ginger
and Mary Ann were characters on

Gilligan's Island. Porter and
        Sandy were on a show about
a dolphin named Flipper. Pepper

was *Police Woman*, and Honey
        West was a private investigator,
cop, or other woman-in-danger.

Anyway, we've been at Gram's
        place in California for seven months,
eating every day, sleeping warm.

But I don't know how long it will
        last. Iris gets along with her mother
about how she gets along with her men.

Thirty Seconds Is Up

Iris doesn't bother to knock.
        She slaps against the door,
pushes her way into the room

that I share with Mary Ann, Honey,
        and Pepper. Four girls, two
beds. Luckily, only I'm here now.

        Iris tosses herself across my bed,
                lands facedown against rumpled
        blankets. *Bastard! Why are they all*

such bastards? She sobs, and her
        body shakes like she's got the DTs.
Like she'd ever suffer through detox.

I should feel sorry for her, I guess.
        But I don't. I can't. She makes
me sick. Maybe because I know

I could turn out just like her. No way
        to dig myself out of this grave for
the living. No way I've found yet.

I try to dig up a little sympathy.
        "He wasn't such a great guy
anyway, Iris." He was nasty.

But she doesn't think so. *No one's*
            p-perf-fect. I thought we
      were doing just f-f-fine.

Anger punches me suddenly,
            hard, little blows to the gut.
"Maybe he found out how you

make your . . . uh . . . living.
            Not many guys will put up
with someone who screws

other guys for money. And if
            they do, then all they're after
is free booze and an easy lay."

      She jerks upright, grabs me
            by the shoulders, shakes till
      my teeth rattle. *You little bitch.*

      How dare you talk to me like
            that? You know anything
      I do to get by, I do for you.

"You"

Meaning her collective offspring.
       I look into her eyes and find only
honesty there. She means every

word, hasn't even the slightest
       clue how full of shit she totally
is. I don't care. She should know.

"Some people wait tables or work
       in grocery stores, Iris. Hustling
BJs is lazy work." All on your knees.

Emotions cycle through her eyes
       like a color wheel. She wants
to hit me. Wants to hug me.

       Her hands, still attached to my
              shoulders, tremble. *I'm sorry.*
I just don't know anything else.

       Finally her hands fall away.
              I thought maybe things would
change with Greg. Get better.

What planet does she live on?
       "Get real! What guy wants
a woman like . . . like you?"

Smacked Down

That's how she looks, but I don't
        feel bad about it. She wants me
to mother her. Well, what mother

with half a pair of balls wouldn't say
        the same thing? (Not counting
my mother!) And I've got a full pair.

        I swear I can see smoke billowing
            from her ears. *Who made you so
stinking mean?* She spits the *s*'s.

What a fucking stupid question!
        Isn't she expecting my answer?
"Who do you fricking think?"

            She wants to say more, but at this
                exact moment, Gram comes
            into the room, carrying an armful

            of detergenty-smelling laundry.
                Her head swivels toward us.
            Uh. Am I interrupting something?

Iris shakes her head. *Nothing
        important. I need a smoke.*
She rolls off the bed. *And a beer.*

I Must Look

As pissed as I feel. Without
     a word, Gram lays the folded
clothes on the other bed.

She turns toward me slowly,
     and for maybe the hundredth
time, I wonder what has carved

such deep wrinkles into her face.
     She's only, like, fifty-three
or so, and I'm pretty sure that,

        unlike Iris, Gram used to be
          a knockout. *You okay?*
        Her voice is pillow soft.

My eyes sting suddenly. It
     should be Iris—Mom—
asking if I'm okay. "No."

        Gram comes over, sits on
          the edge of the bed. Up
        close, her face looks like

        earthquake-splintered stone.
          Worn, but not worn out.
        I wish I could change things

for you. And for her, too.
        Her childhood was no
walk in the park either. Not

easy, being an army brat. And
        touching down in Barstow
wasn't exactly a reward for years

spent hauling around the U.S.
        Then, when her dad got killed . . .
well, she went starved dog wild.

Between Fort Irwin, Edwards,
        and the Marine Corps bases,
there were plenty of men willing

to be stand-ins for her fallen
        father. Only it wasn't exactly
daughterly love they were after.

Guess That Explains

How she got knocked up
      with me when she was
only sixteen. Just my age.

And maybe it explains why
      she never outgrew teendom.
Still, "Why are you taking her

side? She pisses you off too.
      Not like we can't hear you
yell at each other, you know."

          Gram nods. *I know. I'm sorry.*
               It's not such a big place.
          Barely enough room to fit

          you all in. But we'll get by.
               Yes, I get mad at Iris. She can
          be downright infuriating. Always

          was a selfish girl. Never one
               to think about others, or try
          to spare their feelings. Not

          mother material, not at all. Not
               fair to any of you to pop you
          out, then leave you to mostly fend

for yourselves. Even coyotes and
　　　　　jackals do better by their pups.
All I'm asking is for her to get

a job. Something legit. Pay taxes,
　　　　　stop whoring arou—She skids
to a stop, has said too much.

"It's okay. I know what she does.
　　　　Hate what she does. She'll never
stop. Not for you. Not for any of us."

In the Next Room

Sandy starts up a fuss. Short
           nap. He'll be a little turdcake
tonight. Gram and I move at

the same time. Iris will let him
           squish around in his wet Pull-Up
until someone else changes it. I stop

Gram with a touch of my hand.
           "I'll get him. You do enough."
I kiss her cheek gently before

sliding off the bed, onto the chipped
           linoleum floor. Nothing special
about Gram's house. Except Gram.

           One second, she says, giving me
                      a fierce hug. *I know things haven't*
           been easy for you kids. A regular

           parade of Iris's men, most of 'em
                      bad ones, in and out of your lives.
           Not even knowing your daddies.

           Moving around, cycling through
                      homes. No homes at all sometimes.
           And not because the army was giving

anyone orders. I wish I'd known
         sooner, but Iris didn't talk to me
at all for years. Anger just eats

a person up inside, and I swear
         that girl was born angry. Anyway,
that ain't no here nor there.

But now you know where I live.
         Whatever happens, I want you
to remember this is always your home.

Love, unlike any I've ever known,
         floods through me. I kiss Gram's
cheek. "I will." I want to say more,

but I'm afraid if I do I'll jinx
         myself, and the other kids too.
Speaking of them, there's Sandy

again, crying like he's dying.
         "Better go!" I dash toward
the door, and as I leave, I can

         hear Gram's quiet, *Tsk-tsk.*
                  Then she whispers, *Too bad Iris*
         can't be more like her daughter.

I Don't Think

She meant me to hear it.
        But I did, and I flush,
blood warm with pleasure.

That was probably the nicest
        thing anyone has ever said
about me, if not to me directly.

I start toward the small bedroom
        that used to belong to Iris when
she was in high school. I hate

going in there, because I know
        it's where she got preggers
with me. Same bed, even. No,

I'm not guessing. One night,
        after a beer or two too many,
Iris felt the warped need to share

the whole story—how Private First
        Class Kenneth Cordell sneaked
in through the window, not once,

but enough times to make damn
        sure and knock up one Iris Ann
Belcher. Thanks so much, Daddy.

A Poem by Cody Bennett
Not Damn Sure

Where my real daddy ran
to, if he settled down in some
Podunk town or if he fell flat
off the face of the earth.

No clue

who he is or why Mom
slept with him seventeen
years ago, give or take.
Maybe it was rape.

No lie.

Mom is pretty much
a prude. A nice prude.
and all things considered,
a really great mom.

No complaints

about her or how we
live. Yeah, I've got
a stepdad, but he's pretty
damn good to us.

No reason

to turn all emo over not
knowing my real—scratch
that—I mean biological
father. Why would I want to?

No worries.

Cody
After Wichita

Vegas is a strange, strange city.
I mean, everything in Wichita is
ebony and ivory. Everyone knows
where everyone else stands on things
like immigration (electrify the wall)
or global warming (greenhouse . . . huh?).

But in Vegas, no one knows
one damn thing about their next-
door neighbor, even. We moved
here almost two years ago, and
the only reason I know anyone
on the block is because of school.

Even there, unless you really
push hard, you don't make
friends, and if you do, they're
liable to move away before long.
They say Vegas is a transient
city. Whole lot of truth in that.

People come. People go. Not
like Wichita, where people
mostly stay. Guess I miss
some things about Kansas.
But worrying over it won't help
anyone. Especially not me.

I Go with the Flow

Don't make waves, don't
buck the current. I clean my
room, play nice with my little
brother. Maintain a solid 3.0
GPA. Might even go on to
college. Meanwhile, I work

part time at GameStop to pay
for gas and insurance. My hair
is trimmed, my clothes are neat,
and I never wear all black,
except to funerals. You probably
wouldn't notice me walking

down the street, unless you
happen to be attracted to
"average." It's not such a bad
thing to be. When you fly
well below the radar, you get
away with a hell of a lot.

Of Course

My mom would forgive me
just about anything. Always
trying to make up for the absent
father thing. Not sure why.
My stepfather, Jack, is really
pretty cool. To her. To me.

He's an aircraft mechanic,
working a civil service job
at Nellis AFB. Mom met him
at Boeing in Wichita. She was
a receptionist there. It wasn't
exactly love at first sight, at least

not for her. She called him
"persistent." He called himself
"bit by the love bug." Okay,
that's corny, but hey, that's Jack.
I've gotten used to corny. Typical
Jack joke: *A rope orders a drink,*

> *but the bartender says, "We don't*
> *serve ropes here." The rope goes*
> *outside, ties himself up, unravels*
> *one end, goes back inside. Bartender*
> *says, "Hey, aren't you that rope?"*
> *Rope shakes his head. "Frayed knot."*

Get It?

You know, "frayed knot,"
meaning "'fraid not." Corny
as hell, like I said. But also kind
of funny. Anyway, it's easy
enough to put up with corny when
it's from-the-heart honest.

Jack is honest as a mare-sniffing
stud, which is why he gets along
with Mom. She can't stand when
people lie. Can't blame her, so I try
not to do much out-and-out lying.
"Omitting" is something else.

I do my fair share of omitting.
Despite Mom's ongoing request
to know where I'm going, who
I'll be with, and when I'll be home,
she rarely questions the bare-bones
details I usually provide.

I suppose that might change if
I ever fall into serious trouble.
But so far I've done a whole
lot of weekend partying without
getting busted, addicted, or dead.
Smarter than the average stoner.

Tonight Being Saturday Night

I plan on a little fun before
going home. First I have to
finish my shift. One hour and
counting, the door buzzer
signals a customer. Hope he
knows exactly what he wants.

Oops. I mean she, and not just
any "she," but Veronica Carino.
I haven't seen her around much
lately. Not since I broke up
with Alyssa, her best friend.
"Hey, Ronnie. What's up?"

She barely glances my way
as she starts a counterclockwise
circumnavigation. Wii. Xbox.
PlayStation. Doesn't she know
what system she has? "Can I help
you find what you're looking for?"

      Finally she reaches the counter,
      leans across, inflating the scoop
      of her tank top. *Thanks, but I think*
      I found it. She wets her lips with
      the tip of her tongue, pouts full on.
      How come you haven't called me?

Is This a Trick?

Something she and Alyssa cooked
up to make me look like a jerk?
Ronnie Carino has never even
batted her pretty green eyes at
me before. Let alone given me
an up-close view of those tasty-looking

tits. Something twitches
behind my zipper. Glad I'm
standing behind the counter.
"Uh . . . called you? Guess
I figured since 'Lyss and I broke
up, you'd probably be mad at me."

> Ronnie takes a deep breath,
> rounding the mounds I can't
> quit staring at. Then she exhales
> in a big sigh. *Why would I be mad
> at you? You and 'Lyssa weren't
> good for each other. Oil and H_2O . . .*

True enough. We argued over
everything, from music to sports.
Only one thing was really good
between us. . . . That twitch again.
"So, are you saying you want to go
out with me?" The direct approach

usually cuts straight through
the bullshit, but it can backfire.
I half expect her to laugh and tell
me I'm out of my mind. Instead
she smiles a total come-on. *Yeah.
Why? Does that surprise you?*

Can't she see the shock in my
eyes? I feel like I touched a hot
wire. "Kinda, I guess." I watch
her inhale. Exhale. Ah, why not?
One reason comes immediately
to mind. "What about Alyssa?"

    *She'll get totally pissed off. But
    after she thinks about it, she'll be
    okay . . . or maybe she won't. . . .*
    Ronnie dips even lower, giving
    me a quick nipple shot before
    drawing back and straightening.

    *Right now, I don't care what
    'Lyss thinks. Do you?* She waits
    for me to answer. The thought
    crosses my mind again that this
    could all be a setup. Still, I shake
    my head. *Great. How 'bout tonight?*

I Watch Ronnie Leave

Wondering what the hell just
went down. Thinking with my
dick. That's for sure. So what
is Ronnie thinking with? That
makes the dick in question
think even harder. Thank God

when the door opens next, it's
a bunch of kids. Keeping an eye
on them will help me forget
about what might happen tonight.
Ronnie and I are going to Frozen75,
the only underage club in Vegas.

I guess she's on some special list
so we won't have to wait in line
to get in. No booze inside, but
whatever. I just want to watch her
dance. We can keep the refreshments
in my car. And as for dessert . . .

Stop that! One of the kids comes
over, whining about Pokémon
Purple, and why don't we have
it, when it's right in front of his
grubby, little face. "Hang on a
sec and I'll get it for you." Brat.

The Rest of the Hour

Creeps by. *Tick-tick . . . tick.*
I'm actually happy when people
come in, asking dopey questions.
At least it keeps me from looking
at the freaking clock every ten
seconds. Why am I so anxious?

Well, yeah, there is the idea
that I just might hook up with
one very hot girl. I have to admit
I have thought about boinking
her more than once, while
taking solo care of a hard-on.

Oh yeah, the big M. I probably
do it more than I should, and
Ronnie is definite boner bait,
at least when I'm left to my
own imagination instead of
Internet porn. Viva la webcams!

Good thing Mom and Jack
aren't too nosy when it comes
to my personal web-browsing
history. One very good example
of "omission." If they asked, would
I out-and-out lie? Who wouldn't?

Now, at Least

I won't have to lie about where
I'm going tonight. I can omit
confessing the fun stuff, should
any of it actually happen. Finally
I get to clock out. Need to shower
off the customers' germs, put on

clean clothes. Girls love clean.
I'm good with giving it to them.
It's warm for late March, but then
it never gets really cool in Vegas.
The dry desert air is peppered
with exhaust and city noise.

It's a short ride home, radio
screaming, and I'm singing
to myself as I park, head up
the walk to the front door. Life
is good, and I can't help but smile
as I go inside. Mom and Jack

are in the kitchen. Even from
here, the tone of Mom's voice
makes me know something's
up. I close the distance quietly.
Wait and see what the doctor says.
Could be lots of things besides . . .

Doctor?

Is someone hurt? Sick? What?
I push through the door. "Lots
of things besides what?" My eyes
whip back and forth between them.
Both their faces are the color of old
paper. Almost, but not quite, white.

> Jack recovers first. *Not important,*
> *son. I've just been having some*
> *problems with indigestion. Went*
> *in for tests. Could be an ulcer.*
> *Or maybe just your mother's*
> *cookin'. Nothing to worry about.*

Then why is Mom wearing
worry in two long horizontal
lines across her forehead and
two short vertical creases just
above her nose? She's easier
to read than a comic book.

Right Now

I don't really want to read her,
at least not all the way to the last
page. So I'm relieved when she
reaches deep down for some humor.
*You want to blame my cooking?
Then take me out to dinner.*

The garage door slams and in
marches Cory. He's thirteen,
a skater, and thinks he's tough.
I let him maintain the fantasy.
Cory may be pushing six feet
tall, but he's a little kid inside.

We all clam up immediately,
something Cory totally misses
as he launches a verbal upchuck.
*I can't believe it! They outlawed
boards at the park. Something
about liability. Damn it to hell!*

Mom sucks in her breath, and Jack
jumps up from his chair. *What
did you say, young man? You
apologize to your mother right
this minute!* His face is bright
red. But he doesn't look sick.

Cory does not apologize. He stomps
into the living room, muttering
a long string of very bad curse
words. *Hmph . . . mother . . . sucker . . .
hmph . . . have to if . . .* Hey, did he
say something about me?

Jack trails him, and Mom and
I follow. We are just in time to
see Jack grab Cory by the collar.
He spins him around until they're
face-to-face. *This is still my house,
young man. Now you apologize.*

There is something mean in
Cory's eyes, something I don't
remember seeing before. But Jack
is in charge. Cory lowers his glare
to the floor. *Sorry. Now let me go.*
He tempers his tone. *Please.*

It's Almost Seven

By the time I pick up Ronnie,
who claims the front seat like
she owns "shotgun." Damn,
the girl is fine, in a short denim
skirt and skimpy lavender tank
top. Oh, Ronnie and her tanks.

> *Wave nice to my mommy,* she
> says, turning to do the same.
> Then she yells out the window,
> *Don't worry, Mom. We won't
> stay out too late. Cross my heart.*
> Now, a mean whisper. *Let's go!*

She doesn't have to ask twice.
Last thing I need is her mom
smelling the bud in my pocket.
I aim for the freeway. "You look
great." Compliments are good ice-
breakers. Ronnie is the ice queen.

> But tonight she seems almost
> thawed. Not quite warm, but
> not completely bitchy. She sniffs
> the air. *Smells like you brought
> the party.* We've never gotten high
> together. First time for everything.

By the Time

We reach Frozen75, we've def
gotten high together. This guy
I work with scores really good
bud, and he's not above dealing
a little to me. "So what do you
think about the smoke?"

The ice queen has defrosted all
the way to room temp. She laughs.
It's awesome. Then she reaches
over, touches my leg. *Tonight
will be fun. Thanks for taking me.*
Her hand strokes my thigh gently.

Which raises my heart rate,
which raises several questions.
Why me? Why now? Why go out
of her way for tonight? But one
of those questions will do for now.
"I . . . I have to ask. Why me?"

Out of the corner of my eye
(I don't dare look away from
the road), I can see her shake
her head. *You really don't know,
do you? Cody, I've been in love
with you for a very long time.*

A Poem by Eden Streit

Being in Love

Means hard questions.
Will I? Won't I? Should
I? Could I? Yes? No?

You?

Me? There is no me
without you. Is there
a you without

me?

And if we're truly one,
how will I breathe when
circumstance pries us

apart?

You are my oxygen, my
sustenance, the blood
inside my veins. When

we

touch, you are my skin,
hold all my joy inside
of you. When you go, I

wither.

Eden
Saturday Evening

Papa is officiating a wedding. Mama,
of course, went along. Few enough

excuses to get all dressed up around here.
Eve put on her Sunday best and went too.

The bride has a really cute little brother,
just about a year older than Eve.

The groom has a nice-looking brother
too, but I'm not the least bit interested.

I've got someone I'd much rather see,
so I begged off. Told them I didn't

feel very well. God is going to strike me
down for sure if I keep lying this way.

But I've got at least three hours
to spend with Andrew. There's a park

right down the street from our house.
It's a short walk on a cool night,

but by the time I reach Andrew's truck,
I'm hot all over. From the inside out.

No One Around

I slip into the Tundra unobserved.
As the interior light goes dark,

I move into Andrew's arms, accept
his gentle kiss. But we don't dare

stay here. "Let's go for a drive. Can't
believe how much I've missed you."

He grins and puts the truck in gear.
It's only been four days, you know.

I slide my hand into the warmth of his.
"And all I could think about was you."

True. Too true. In class. PE. The library.
At home. Bible study. The dinner table.

Faces. Whiteboards. Gym mats. Smudged
together. Bells. Laughter. Curses. Blurred

into white noise. Locker room armpits. Floor wax.
Gourmet cafeteria. Marker ink. All smeared

into senseless potpourri. Four days, the only
clear picture, Andrew's face. The only sound

I wanted to hear, his soft *hello*. The only scent
my nose kept sniffing for, alfalfa green.

We Drive into the Foothills

Andrew knows this area well. He turns
up a dirt road, slick with spring melt ice.

Unlikely we'll run into anyone back here.
Certainly not any old spy from Papa's church.

    Andrew parks. *Pretty tonight. Looks*
    like you could reach out and touch

    the stars. Come on. He tugs me into
    the chill March air, lifts me into the bed

    of his truck. There's a double sleeping bag
    there. We climb inside, and he slides his arm

    around my shoulder, pulls my head against
    his chest. *Nice.* He sighs. *Very, very nice.*

Suddenly we're kissing, beneath an ocean
of distant suns. Can't believe it's me here,

in this amazing place, with this amazing guy.
I want him to hold me forever, never let go.

I feel like I'm in a movie. Unrehearsed words
tumble out of my mouth. "I love you."

There

Said it. Didn't really mean to, but now
I've gone and done it. I tense, waiting

> for his response. It's swift. *Oh God,*
> *Eden, I love you, too. How did I ever*

> *live without you? It's like I was missing*
> *a huge part of me. The best part of me.*

> *Until I found you. I want . . . I want . . .*
> He loses his words. He never does that.

I kiss his temples. Close his eyes with
kisses. "What? What do you want?"

> His eyes stay closed. I stare up into the night
> as he says, *I want to be with you always,*

> *to share forever with you. I want to give*
> *you more than I have to give now—security,*

> *a comfortable life.* He pauses. Considers.
> Decides to finish. *I want to take from you*

> *what I've no right to take. Not now. Not yet.*
> *But that doesn't make me want it less. . . .*

I Get What He Means

And as much as I would like to chalk
it up to him being a guy, truth is I want

it too. At least I think I do, and only when
I'm this close to Andrew. When I am, God

forgive me, I want to know what it means
to give myself to him so completely. Want

to feel what it's like when it's absolutely
right. Not that I've felt it when it's wrong,

or felt "it" at all. But I don't want my heart
to feel wrong about my body feeling good.

I have no doubt it will feel incredible with Andrew.
"I want to too. But I'm scared. I've never . . ."

> *I know. I know you haven't, and I know*
> *you're scared. I'm scared too. You might*
>
> *not believe this, but I've never either.* He
> stops. Smiles. *Don't tell anyone, okay?*
>
> *When you're ready, when you trust me*
> *enough, I want you to be my first. My only.*

I So Want to Be

His first. His only. I so want him to be
mine. "I promise to be your first.

"Your only. If we just had a little more
time, I would be those things tonight. . . ."

> *No. Not tonight. Not in the cold, hard bed*
> *of a pickup truck. When we do it, it will*
>
> *be in a warm feather bed, with soft quilts*
> *and pillows you fall into. I want it*
>
> *to be perfect. And if we don't get it right*
> *the first time . . .* He lets me finish.

"Practice makes perfect?" We laugh
together. Easy. Meant to be. And I know

the first time someone makes love to me,
it *will* be perfect. Because it will be Andrew.

We Should Head Back

But I can't. Not quite yet. I need some
answers that will prove he means what

he says. "So why did you wait? And how
did you know the right person was me?"

> *I know all guys are supposed to be sluts
> or something. But sex with just anyone*

> *never did seem exactly right to me.
> Maybe it's my Catholic upbringing,*

> *or hell, who knows? Maybe I need Viagra
> already.* He laughs. *Nah, that can't be*

> *the problem. When I'm with you, I don't
> need a pill to want to make love to you.*

He always says the right things.
Maybe he should be a politician.

> *As for you, I suspected you might be
> the right person the first night we met.*

> *You were so sure of yourself, your beliefs,
> and you didn't let me sway you. I loved*

> *your self-confidence, your obvious loyalty.
> Your solid sense of right and wrong.*

Okay, so maybe he's not exactly politician
material. "When did you know for sure?"

The first time I kissed you. One kiss,
I was totally hooked. Addicted to you.

I could never love anyone the way I love
you. I'd follow you across the universe.

I look up at the sky, brimming stars
and the rise of a waning moon.

"The universe is a big place. If I was lost
up there, how would you ever find me?"

He gathers me in, kisses me gently.
Don't you know? We're connected

by an invisible chain. It's very long, very
light. But also very strong. It can't rust.

Can't break. And the only thing that can
sever it is if you ever stop loving me.

We Drive Back into Town

Back to the park, which is deserted.
Dark, but for a single streetlight

at the far end. Andrew parks away
from it and I slide across the seat, into

his arms. One last kiss. Or two. I don't
want to stop. Don't want to go home.

"I'll never stop loving you," I whisper.
"And I want to make love with you soon."

My body aches with wanting that very
thing. "Maybe we should run away."

> *If I thought that was the right thing*
> *to do, I wouldn't hesitate one minute.*
>
> *But it's not. You'd never forgive yourself,*
> *and that would mean never forgiving me.*
>
> *Once you turn eighteen, once I graduate,*
> *we can go anywhere. I'll get a job. You can*
>
> *go to school. Or stay home and let me take*
> *care of you. Whatever makes you happy.*
>
> He kisses me one last time. *As long as*
> *we're together, everything will be all right.*

I Walk Home Slowly

Trying to soak up the things Andrew
said tonight. Sponge them up, absorb

them through my skin, into my flesh, so
they'll always live inside of me. I know

Andrew and I were meant to be together.
How can I prove it to my parents? How

can I make them understand that love
this real, this deep, must come from God?

I look up again at the night sky, but here,
city lights take center stage, mute

the celestial backdrop. I don't belong
here, in the city. Don't belong in my

parents' cold house. I'm a stray, called
to another place. A wild place, where

rules and expectations don't dare intrude.
A warm place, safe in Andrew's arms.

The House Is Quiet

They're still not home, and that's great
by me. I don't need questions. Don't want

to make up excuses. Have no patience
for a sister-to-sister chat session.

The clock says nine thirty, but it seems
much later. I go into my room, trade

jeans for a soft flannel nightgown,
lie on my bed in the dark, listening

to silence. Something happened tonight.
Something wonderful. Terrifying.

An awakening. This must be how Eve
(the original) felt after taking a bite

of forbidden fruit. Every nerve on fire,
every fiber of flesh alive with desire.

If Andrew was here, beside me on my
not-exactly-a-feather bed, I would give

him my virginity, give it gladly, without
a second thought. It belongs to him.

I close my eyes, return to the foothills,
to the back of the Tundra, to a double

sleeping bag. I slip inside, into the warm
envelope of goose down. And Andrew.

His voice fills my head. *I want to
take from you what I've no right to. . . .*

Oh, Andrew. I want that too. Tonight.
Right now. My body is begging to learn

what your body wants to teach it. Need
blisters up, and with it, a way to teach

myself some of what I'm dying to know.
Abstinence programs encourage it.

Mama not only discourages it, but swears
it put Mary Magdalene on the highway

to degradation. What Mama forgets is that Mary
Magdalene was the forgiveness poster child.

My Hand, Disguised

As Andrew's hand, moves lightly
down my neck, over collarbone,

breastbone. Goose bumps rise in
unusual places, and my body tingles

in a completely foreign way. Because
of Andrew. But he's not here. I pretend

he is and let "his" hands explore the rounds
of my breasts, move in tighter and tighter

orbits, and now fingers circle the hard
center nubs, raised like it's cold in here.

It's not. I'm burning up. Delirious with
raw need. My hand wants to slide lower,

to a place I know nothing about except
what they call it in books. And suddenly

it comes to me how completely inept
I'll be when Andrew and I finally

share that warm feather bed, with comfy
quilts and pillows we can fall into.

I Turn on the Light

Go to the computer, try to avoid
looking at the Calvary screen saver.

Jesus, hanging on the cross, staring
down at his poor crying mother.

Mama downloaded that, no doubt
specifically to deter the kind of

Internet exploration I have in mind.
I just have to be very careful not to surf

to the wrong kind of website. A touch
of the mouse, Golgotha dissolves

into the ether and voilà, up pops
Windows. Double-click on Explorer.

Here it comes, ready to take me where
I need to go. But where is that, exactly?

Might as well get straight to the point.
I type in, "losing your virginity."

When I Hear

The door open, the sounds of return,
I hurry to turn off the computer

before Eve catches me, breathlessly
reading stories about other girls' first

times. Some wonderful, some awful.
Some taken by force, some given

away. Some total disappointments.
Some more than they expected.

What none of them had, at least I'm
pretty sure they didn't, was Andrew.

I rush into bed, pick up a book on
the nightstand, pretend I'm reading.

      Eve breezes into the room, sighing.
      I love weddings. You should have come.

Her goofy grin says a lot. "So . . .
Zach asked you to dance or what?"

      Mama wouldn't let me. But he asked.
      She looks at me. *How did you know?*

"I'm a good guesser." And I'm guessing
she never once thought about losing it.

A Poem by Seth Parnell
Losing It

Some days I think
I'm losing my mind.
What seems so

               clear

most of the time
becomes a big question
mark. Am I really

               the way

I perceive myself, or
is the person others see
the truth of me? I wait

               for

answers, but inside
I know I have to go out
and find them. And

               answers,

like knowledge, are
not always where we
look first for them.

Seth
Worked My Farmer Butt Off

All day. Can't believe
    my dad wants to give
    me grief over going out.
    What's a Saturday
night for, anyway?

        I think you should stay
            home tonight, he says.
            Hard to get up Sunday
            morning when you're
        out late the night before.

We're at the dinner table,
    finishing off big ol' plates
    of venison sausage, biscuits,
    and mushroom gravy. A mediocre
rendition of Mom's recipe.

        Dad seconds my opinion.
            Not as good as your
            mother's, I know. I don't
            have her magic touch.
        But I do the best I can.

He does. If he left it to
        me, we'd eat nothing
        but bologna and cheese,
        with the odd pizza thrown
in for a little variety.

I save my more gourmet
        palate for when I go out
        with Loren. Not that Dad
        would understand the draw
anyway. Caviar? Fish bait,

right? And pâté? Glorified
        liverwurst. Still, in some
        circles, venison sausage
        is probably considered
quite the taste sensation.

"Dinner's great, Dad. I bet
        some of those hoity-toity
        big-city chefs would kill
        for this recipe." Probably
not. But Dad's face lights.

                Think so? Well, I wouldn't
                want 'em to kill anyone,
                but I wouldn't mind
                selling the secret formula
        for big bucks, you know?

Other Than Large Male Deer

Big bucks are something
      I'm pretty sure Dad
      gave up on having a long
      time ago, if he ever really
cared about such a thing.

I glance toward a photo
      of Mom and Dad, taken
      on their twentieth anniversary,
      before we knew she was sick.
They look content. In love,

despite years of worry,
      debt, and loss. Through
      years of struggling to make
      ends meet, they had each
other. And that was plenty.

Dad wears his age less
      gracefully now. Factory
      work and farming, a one-
      two punch. Add loneliness . . .
Guilt swells. But I have plans.

Plans

For an evening with Loren.
    Plans that require getting
    out of the house. Plans
    I would rather not outline
in detail. I hate lying to Dad,

but I can't see a way around
    it. "Tell you what. I'll do
    a little research. See if I can
    find a five-star chef with a
hankering for deer meat.

Meanwhile, I'm gonna run
    into town. Billy Clayborn's
    band is playing at Bristow
    Tavern. Thought I'd take
a listen. Maybe I'll get lucky. . . ."

I leave it hanging. Dad
    has never asked, but
    surely he's wondered
    if, at almost eighteen,
I've ever once gotten lucky.

        The comment sinks in
            like a hog in mud—
            slow but sure. Finally
            he says, *Okay then. Just
        don't stay out real late.*

I Know

He wants me to go to Mass
     with him in the morning.
     How can he go through
     the motions? I've heard
him talking to himself.

He blames God for taking
     Mom early, taking her
     first. Yet come Sunday
     morning, he's on his knees,
genuflecting. Bowing down.

Maybe he's searching.
     For Mom. For proof
     that there's something
     beyond this soil. This
earth. Maybe it's a way

to keep on belonging.
     Whatever it is, I sweeten
     the deal, mostly because
     I plan to stay out pretty late.
Scratch that. Real late.

"How about if I go
     to Mass on my way
     to Bristow? That way,
     if I do get lucky, I'll
already be absolved."

Dad Laughs Softly

Shakes his head, but says,
Okay. I guess you're old
enough to make your
own decisions about
stuff like religion and . . .

He can't bring himself
to finish. But Catholic
or not, I'm sure he wants
his son to have "normal"
sexual desires. Wonder

if he suspects otherwise.
I'm relatively sure he knows
I have no plans to fulfill my
Mass obligation tonight
or any night. I've pretty

much given up on the idea
of salvation. Catholicism
and homosexuality only
go hand in hand in the
highest church circles.

Not Much Doubt

I'm damned anyway,
        so I swing the old Chevy
        toward the freeway, Louisville,
        and Loren. My heart pumps
wildly in anticipation.

I turn up the radio, change
        the station from country to
        alternative. My Chemical
        Romance fades and the DJ
segues into a Muse rocker.

Before I met Loren, I'd never
        heard of either group. Now
        the Dixie Chicks and Rascal
        Flatts have taken a backseat
to music more relevant to me.

Muse, in fact, was playing
        the first day I let Loren
        show me what love can
        be when two people give
themselves completely

to each other. It was our
        fourth date. Up until then,
        we'd only talked. Kissed
        a little. Touched even less,
and only with our clothes on.

Loren was patient about
the rest. *I'm not looking
for an easy lay,* he said.
*If I wanted that, I'd
pick someone up in a bar.*

He could without even
trying. He's beautiful.
I'm happy he doesn't do
gay bars. "So what are
you looking for, then?"

*A friend. A partner who
I can trust. Sex that
is more than mutual
masturbation. Sex that
is an outpouring of love.*

Up Until

Our fourth time together,
        individual masturbation
        was the bulk of my sexual
        experience. There were
a few short chapters of "touch

me here, I'll touch you there"
        in my very slim book of
        adolescent sexual escapades,
        but nothing more. I had no
idea what to do beyond that.

When I slipped into my
        fantasies, I always had
        sex with men. But that
        day, overwhelmed as I
was with desire for Loren,

I was scared. Nothing
        had ever scared me so
        much, not even knowing
        my mom was going to die.
Does every person feel

like that their first time?
        Like what if they do it
        wrong? Or worse, what
        if they do it poorly—so
horribly their partner laughs?

Loren Didn't Laugh

There proved to be nothing
    to laugh about. Unexpectedly,
    it all came very easily.
    Like, yes, that was exactly
how it was meant to be—

me, taking control. Before we
    started, I had no clear idea
    about our roles. Who's on
    top and who's not means
nothing when you aren't

completely positive
    that you belong in either
    position. But that night,
    one kiss and need struck
with enough force to erase

all doubt, all hesitation.
    I didn't wait for Loren to
    say it was okay, didn't ask
    him to show me what to do.
Pure animal instinct led me

just where I wanted to go.
It wasn't tender. Wasn't
pretty. It was a raw, naked
joining, energized from years
of dreaming about what it

could be like, or should be
like. I gave, he took, and
when it was over, like Adam,
I shook at the forbidden
taste of new awareness.

Afterward, with his head
nested gently against my
chest, Loren whispered,
Are you sure you've
never done that before?

"Never." My voice floated
up from a deep haze of
contentment. "But I want
to do it again." It was a long
few minutes before I could.

Since That Day

I've grown more and
      more confident in
      the part I'm supposed
      to play. Loren is older.
More experienced. Wiser,

in many ways. He is also
      softer. Passive. Anxious
      to please me, let me have
      my way. He has become
my favorite teacher ever.

I can barely make it through
      each week, pretending to
      be the same old Seth at home,
      when a short drive will
allow the new, improved Seth

to come out and play. I am
      torn, wanting to keep
      my dad satisfied, when
      I know Loren is waiting
to satisfy me. One day soon

I'll have to decide which
      Seth I can live without.
      Until then, Improved Seth will
      have to escape when he can.
And he's escaped tonight.

By the Time

I knock on Loren's door,
      treading a maelstrom
      of love and lust, I have
      almost made up my mind
to leave Dad and home in

my wake and move to
      Louisville before
      I graduate in June.
      I know it's not long,
but I'm sick of pretending.

Loren opens the door.
      I don't wait for his greeting
      before pushing inside and
      yanking him tight up against
me. "God, I've missed you!"

      He stiffens, and I finally
      take a good look at
      the worry sculpted in
      his face. *I missed you,*
too. *Come on. Sit down.*

Something is definitely
      wrong. I follow him
      to the couch, afraid
      to ask what it is. What
kind of bad news do I have

to hear now? He couldn't be
 sick, could he? No. Too young.
 Too healthy. Unless . . . No!
 Stop it. Just ask. I search
his eyes. "What's wrong?"

 Nothing. He takes my hand.
  I mean, nothing major.
  Relax, Seth. It's just . . . He
 reaches toward the coffee
table, picks up a letter.

 I got this today. He cradles
  the paper protectively, like
  he doesn't want me to know
  what's there. *You know I go to*
 school at Louisville Seminary. . . .

Uh-huh. Louisville Presbyterian
 Theological Seminary. Studying
 marriage and family therapy.
 I nod my head, but I'm
totally confused. "Yes. So?"

 A requirement for my BA
  is three months of "field
  study." They're sending
  me to a congregation in
 New York for the summer.

Something Thick

But tasteless rises up my
      throat, into my mouth.
      I break out in a panicky
      sweat. "Congregation?
You mean, like a priest?"

      He manages a thin smile.
         More like a minister, but
         yes. That is my calling.
         But you knew that.
      He rests a hand on my knee.

"I don't know. I guess . . ."
      Guess? What else would
      a seminarian have planned?
      But what about me? Us?
"What does that mean for us?"

      Time apart. You can't
         come with me. I'll be
         living at the church. He lets
         that sink in. *Don't worry*
      now. I don't leave until May.

Don't worry? He hacked
      me off at the knees.
      But it's only temporary.
      "You're coming back, right?"
The silence screams.

A Poem by Whitney Lang
Scream

*I whisper and you close
your eyes. I speak and
you turn away. If I
scream, will you finally*

hear

*me beg you to hold me
close to you, promise
you'll never let go? Do*

my tears

*upset you? Can you
see them fall on fallow
ground—the soil
of your heart?*

Fear

*is a better friend than
you, who feels nothing,
beneath the weight of*

my pain.

Whitney
I Despise Shopping

But it's Paige's idea of heaven,
so we're going to Capitola Mall.
Mom hangs out with Paige's mom
and *encourages* our friendship.

She wouldn't, if she knew anything
at all about Paige other than that her mom
plays a mean game of tennis. But she
doesn't, so we're on our way to the mall.

> *Did you go out with Lucas last
> night?* Paige broke up with her last
> boyfriend a few months ago and dates
> vicariously through me. Voyeuristic ho!

I don't mind entertaining her—or
making her jealous, either. "Actually,
we spent most of the day together.
We hung out down at the Boardwalk."

> *Uh-huh. And what else?* Voyeuristic
> enough to want details beyond
> arcade games and carnival rides.
> *Have you two done the dirty yet?*

I swear, she's panting. I could
make her day—her month, even—
by inventing something juicy. But
where would that leave what's left

of my reputation? Do I care? Jeez.
My reputation might just improve
if people believed I was having
regular sex with someone

as delicious as Lucas. One thing
for sure. Whatever I tell Paige
will most definitely get around.
She's not very good at secrets.

Maybe I'll just keep her guessing.
I attempt an air of mystery. "C'mon,
Paige. You wouldn't want me
to screw and tell, would you?"

We Both Know

She would, and we both know
the way I've circumvented
her question means I'm still
a virgin. Technically, anyway.

It's the "technically" part that
has now piqued her interest.
*Okay, then. How far have you
gone? I want every single detail.*

Ah, what the hell? "We almost
did last week. In fact, we were
just about naked. . . ." I tell her
the story about not quite getting

busted, right there on my living
room couch. "You've never seen
two people get dressed so fast.
I didn't even have time to put on

my bra. Good thing Daddy dropped
his keys. Gave me time to hide it
under the cushion. Things had to
look pretty suspicious, though."

Paige giggles. *Oh, yeah. Messy
hair and smeared makeup.
Been there, done that. But what
about yesterday? Did you . . . ?*

"Nah. Everything but. Wrong
time of the month and all." Now
that was a big slice of truth. I don't
usually talk about my periods.

But Paige wants even more.
Did you, like, use your mouth?
Her eyes light up. Is she waiting
for a (ha!) blow-by-blow description?

"Why? Need instructions? 'Cause
you can get tips on the Web, you know."
I am something of an expert there,
because I checked 'em out myself.

She laughs. *Nah. That's okay.
I think I've got it figured out.
Just wondering if you have.
Anyway, it's not rocket science.*

Now I have to laugh. "Except the part
where it goes off like a rocket."
We both bust up, and now she knows
I've got it figured out too.

Capitola Mall

Isn't huge, but it's big enough.
And, it being Sunday, it's pretty
crowded. I don't mind crowds.
People watching is a fun pastime.

Paige cruises the parking lot slowly,
waiting for someone to vacate
a spot close to an entrance. "There's
probably room in the garage."

> *Probably. But you never know*
> *what kind of weirdo might be*
> *lurking in a parking garage.*
> *Mom says it's safer out here.*

Is there more than one kind
of weirdo? Okay, I can't let
that one slip past. "How many
kinds of weirdos are there?"

> She doesn't laugh. *Lots. And*
> *the worst are the ones you*
> *don't suspect. They're the ones*
> *you invite inside your front door.*

Inside the Mall

I can't help but go on a weirdo
watch. Paige is right. Potential
freaks loiter everywhere, and
they come in all shapes, sizes,

genders, and ages. "Hey, Paige.
Check that out." I point to a boy,
maybe six, staring, drop-jawed,
through the window of Victoria's

Secret. "Future weirdo, for sure."
We crack up, but when we're well
down the aisle I glance back over
my shoulder. He's still there.

> Paige doesn't notice, could
> care less anyway. *Let's go*
> *to the Gap. I need some jeans.*
> Her focus shift is immediate, intense.

> Mind on her goal, she picks
> up her pace. So much for people
> watching. Faces, bodies, and packages
> blur. Motion sickness threatens.

Finally, Gap in sight, she slows
a little. Enough for me to notice
a really cute guy sitting outside
the door, waiting for someone,

at least that's my guess. As we
approach, he notices us, too, and
the smile he gives me could melt
an entire iceberg in two seconds flat.

Weirdo? Maybe. I mean, he's at least
ten years older than me, and he's def
taken an interest. Do weirdos come
this hot? My guess is no, but I'm not

here to pick up a guy (yeah, Lucas,
remember him?), especially one who
could be my—what? Big brother?
Wow, it might be cool to have a big

brother hot enough to be a rock star.
No, wait. All my friends would want
me to introduce them. Then they
wouldn't be my friends any more,

because they'd be doing it with my
brother. Scratch all that. Don't want
a hot brother, or any brother at all.
Don't even want my sister, and why

the heck am I thinking all this,
anyway, just because some pervert
guy sitting outside the Gap might
or might not have checked me out?

Warped

But who's warped, him or me?
Okay, I'm pretty sure I know
the answer. Pretty sure I've gone
from appreciating some nice-looking

(hot) older guy to imagining
I have some fictional brother who
is doing unmentionable things with
my best friends. I steal a covert glance

at Paige, who is def not noticing
the guy (who is def not my brother)
at all, let alone having sex with him.
I need food. Haven't eaten today.

As Paige and I go inside, I can feel
not-brother's eyes crawling all over
my back. I nudge Paige. "Psst. Did
you see that cute guy checking us out?"

> *What guy?* She turns, and I follow
> her eyes, only to find his eyes
> locked on me. *Well, he's def*
> *checking you out. Talk about*
>
> *robbing the cradle, or wanting to.*
> *Like, totally tasteless. C'mon. There's*
> *a pair of skinny jeans with my*
> *name on them right over there.*

Someone Should Tell

Paige that "skinny jeans" are
most def not her best friend.
She and I are the same age,
and about the same height.

But she's got a lot more
curves. In a way, I envy that.
Paige looks more like a woman.
I, on the other hand, look like a girl.

Skinny jeans work better for girls.
Still, Paige manages to pour
herself into a pair. *Do they
make my butt look big?*

Well, duh. But I'm not
about to say so. Friends
don't tell friends they look
fat. Or even curvy. "Nah."

*Cool. So what are you waiting
for? Try some on. Check it out:
Thirty percent off.* She stands,
hands punctuating well-defined hips.

Debate is useless. I slip into
a pair and have to admit they
look pretty good. Oh, why not?
What's a trip to the mall for?

Shopping with Paige

Reminds me of that TV show:
TLC's *What Not to Wear.*
Paige has spent big bucks, and
what does she have to show for it?

A couple of pairs of too-tight
jeans, three blouses guaranteed
to show too much tummy and/or
cleavage, and a pair of hot pink

sneakers with soles as thick
as six hundred-page novels.
Now we're leaving Claire's,
where I'm pretty sure Paige

took advantage of a five-finger
discount. Not that she can't afford
a cheap pair of earrings. But ripping
them off gives her a total rush.

Hurry up, she urges, glancing
nervously over her shoulder
as we hustle toward the food
court. Talk about obvious!

Still, by the time yummy scents
of fat-laden foods entice our noses,
we see no sign of security on our
tail. Way to "borrow," Paige.

What do you want to eat? asks
Paige, sniffing the air. *Subway?
Pizza? Hey, you know what sounds
delish? A hot dog on a stick.*

The built-in joke is just too good to
pass up! "Damn, girl. You really *do*
need a boyfriend, you know?" We both
snort into gut-busting, pee-your-pants

laughter. "Oh . . . my . . . God!"
I stutter. "I have so got to pee."
I turn, ready to run. And who's
sitting at a table nearby, grinning

like an orangutan—a very hot
orangutan? The guy. The cute
not-my-brother weirdo. And he's checking
me out again. Is he, like, stalking me?

I Still Have to Pee

But before I do, I have to say
something to the hot monkey.
Ooh. That was a very bad thought.
Wonder how hot his monkey is.

Okay. Way worse thought.
What's up with me? "That guy
is over there, staring," I tell
Paige. "Let's go talk to him."

She pulls her eyes away from
the Hot Dog on a Stick sign.
What? Hey. No. That's stupid.
He might get the wrong idea.

Or exactly the right idea. "Yeah,
maybe. But don't you want to
know where he's coming from?"
I don't wait for her to answer.

I pull myself up very tall, take
dead aim at my stalker. Behind
me comes the sound of Paige,
scrambling to catch up. *Wait.*

Almost to his table, my courage
dissolves and I think seriously
about turning around, grabbing
Paige, and hauling buns out of there.

Too Late

The guy looks up, and the warmth
of his smile melts all thoughts of
running. *Hello.* One word out of his
killer mouth, I think I'm lost.

"Oh. Hey." Now what do I say?
"I . . . uh . . . just wondered if you
were looking at anything special."
Totally brilliant. Set myself up.

But he knows just what to say.
*Well, actually, yes. I was looking
at you, wasn't I? You're quite
special. But then, you know that.*

Is he saying I'm stuck-up?
Beside me, Paige chokes on
a half laugh. Guess that's what
she thinks he was saying.

He studies my face with amazing
eyes, the blue of robin eggs. *You are,
in fact, the most special young
woman I've seen in a long time.*

He so *is* a stalker. But a stalker
who knows how to make a girl feel . . .
uh . . . special. "I'm sorry, but
I don't get it. What do you want?"

> His grin widens. *Now that's*
> *a loaded question. I* want *more*
> *than you'll probably give me.*
> *But I'll settle for your name.*

Paige elbows me and clears
her throat, like I don't have
enough sense not to give my name
to a stranger. A totally luscious,

completely random, too-old-
for-me-to-even-consider-him,
somehow hypnotic stranger.
I find myself saying, "Whitney."

> *Whitney,* he repeats, nodding.
> *The name fits you. Well, Whitney,*
> *pleased to meet you. I'm Bryn.*
> *Care to sit down for a few?*

This Is Insane

For some stupid reason,
I really, really do want to
sit down with him for a few.
What is the big attraction?

It's not like a guy has never
put the moves on me before.
And I'm pretty sure that's what
this is, even though he's smooth.

> But Paige isn't taking the bait.
> *We were going to get something*
> *to eat, remember? And I thought*
> *you had to go*—She catches herself.

Fact is, I do have to go. Now.
"I'd like to sit, Bryn, but Pai—
uh . . . my friend is hungry.
Maybe another time?"

> His smile slips a little. But
> he says, *Of course.* Then he
> reaches into his pocket. *Here's*
> *my card. Call me sometime.*

A Poem by Ginger Cordell
Reach

They say you should
reach for the stars,
and I'd like to, but

                     my arms

are much too short.
They say to reach
out for hope, but I

                     don't

understand what hope
is. They say to reach for
goals, but I don't

                     know

how to define mine,
and so I won't listen.
But if you only tell me

                     how to

love you, I'll reach
into the depth of me
and find a way to

                     hold you.

Ginger
School Sucks

Don't even know why I try.
        We've moved around so
much, I've always been behind.

I'm not going to graduate without
        a hella lot of summer school
or something. And I don't plan to

spend summer vacation locked up
        in Barstow High, trying to figure
out algebra. Who needs it, anyway?

Not like I'm going to college. I'll be
        happy waitressing. Minimum
wage and tips isn't such a bad life.

Would be nice to settle into a town.
        (Not that Barstow's the one—it's
not!) Have a nice, steady job. A friend

or two. Maybe even fall in love,
        if there is such a thing, and if
I can ever get past . . . Anyway,

we've never stayed in one place
        long enough for me to make friends.
All I've had to hang with are sisters.

Actually, I've Kind of Connected

To one girl, Alex. She's in my
   creative writing class, and
she's totally goth. Black clothes,

black fingernails. Heavy black
   eyeliner, which somehow
makes her seem innocent,

like a little girl, trying too hard
   to look all grown up. There's
something about that—something

about her—that is really
   attractive to me. More than
once since I've gotten to know

her, I have thought about
   what it might be like to hold
her. I've even fantasized about

kissing her. It's major weird
   and kind of messed up, I guess.
I've never kissed anyone,

guy or girl. Been kissed,
   but it was never my idea,
and I hated it. Hated them.

I want to know what a real
          kiss is like. But why I keep
thinking about doing it with

Alex is a mystery. She has
          never even halfway come on
to me. That's cool. Who needs

complications? It's good
          enough to have a friend.
And anyway, I'm guessing

it isn't easy for her to get
          close to people. She has
had a tough life, maybe

tougher than mine. Her mom's
          doing hard time for armed
robbery, and she lives with her

loser stepdad, who's a bartender
          at some sleazy club out on
Old Highway 58. Wonder if

I should try to set him up
          with Iris. A pair of low-life
druggies. The perfect couple.

Alex and I

Are hanging out downtown,
        scoping out people, scoping
us out. I take a deep drag off

a bummed Kool, cough like a
        dweeb on the exhale. "Does
your stepdad have a girlfriend?"

                Alex keeps watching people
                      walk by. She rarely looks you
                in the eye. *Nah. No one special,*

                not since Lydia boogied on
                      down the road. Guess he has
                fuck buddies, though. Why?

"I dunno. It just came to me
        that maybe he and my mom
should hook up or something."

                She doesn't miss a beat.
                      You kidding? You don't
                like your mom or what?

I laugh. "Not much, actually.
        But she's easier to deal with
when she's got a man in her life."

> *Really? Seems to me life is a lot*
> > *easier without getting attached*
> *to someone. Too complicated.*

"God, do you know my mom?
> But she thinks having a guy
around makes her important."

> Alex snorts. *How old is she,*
> > *anyway? Sounds like she*
> *still plays with Barbies.*

"I doubt she ever played with
> Barbies. Just a shitload of
Kens." And Sams. And Bills.

But, as much as I think Alex
> is pretty okay, I'm not about
to share too much information

about Iris and how she brings in
> cash. Besides, maybe Iris would
stop tricking for the right guy.

Maybe if the right guy came along,
> we could live a nice, normal
life. However that's defined.

I Guess Nothing Says

Moms have to be good
        people, though. I mean,
look at Britney Spears. She

might not be a complete
        whore, but she's not
exactly a shining example

of motherhood. And, just
        down the block, a woman
in baggy sweats yanks her

                little girl along, yelling,
                        Hurry the hell up, would
                you? The kid's bawling.

And then there's Alex's
        mom. Busted for robbing
a liquor store with a gun.

All for another fix. A few
        hours of finding a way to
forget everything. Alex included.

I hope I'm never a mom. But
        if I am, I'll make damn
sure my kids look up to me.

Speaking of Kids

I really ought to get home.
        Gram has a hair appointment
this afternoon, so unless Iris

suddenly figured out motherhood,
        Mary Ann is the only one there to
take care of the little kids until I get

home. "Better go," I tell Alex.
        "Time to play mom. How
'bout a smoke for the road?"

        She grimaces. *At least my winner*
        mother had the sense to get fixed.
        You're gonna pay me back, right?

Pay her . . . oh, for the cigs.
        "Yeah, sure. I can 'borrow'
some from Iri—uh, my mom."

Not sure why I don't want
        Alex to know I call her Iris.
Yeah, it makes her seem like

less of a mom, but Alex knows
        she's not much of a mom anyway.
Anyone with eyes could guess it.

I Walk Up the Street

Slowly, sucking nicotine into
        my lungs. Tastes like crap,
and I know if I don't stop it will

kill me. But it satisfies some
        deep call. And what the hell?
I don't want to live too damn long.

Suddenly an ambulance screams
        by. Fear punches my gut. Without
a doubt, I know exactly where

it's headed. I throw the lit Kool
        into the gutter, start to run,
choking on yellowish smoke.

I round the corner and sure as day,
        the square red truck is in front
of Gram's, warning lights spinning.

Beside it, a police cruiser blocks
        most of the street, and another
is parked farther up the road, routing

traffic away. Shit, shit, shit! I run
        faster, barely able to breathe.
Fricking cigarettes! I skid to a stop,

try to take in what I see. Two
　　　　paramedics kneel next to Sandy.
His little body lies in the street,

unmoving. "Is he okay?" I scream,
　　　　trying to push closer, only to be
stopped by a young police officer.

　　　　*Give them some room. The little
　　　　　　boy is breathing. That's all
　　　　we know. Are you the mother?*

"No. I'm his sister. But I—I—"
　　　　What else is there to say right
now? "Wha-what happened?"

　　　　Hit and run. His radio scratches
　　　　　　some unintelligible information.
　　　　Hang on. I've got to take this call.

　　　　*Your, uh, sister over there saw
　　　　　　the whole thing. Why don't you
　　　　talk to her? But stay right here.*

Like I would go somewhere?
　　　　Damn me. Why wasn't I here?
Must be what he's thinking too.

Mary Ann Stands Sobbing

On the sidewalk, eyes wide
    with fear. "What happened?"
I struggle to keep my voice gentle.

    He—I—Sandy was kicking
        a ball on the lawn. Pepper
    and Honey started to fight, and . . .

    when I tried to stop them, I guess
        the ball rolled into the street
    and Sandy ran after it and . . .

    I guess a motorcycle came down
        the street and ran over him and
    just kept going and . . . and . . . I

    was right there and I didn't mean—
        Oh my God, I'm so sorry. . . . Oh
    my God, I'm so sorry. . . .

I grab her shoulders, shake hard.
    "Stop it. It's not your fault. Go
take care of the kids. They're scared."

They all stand huddled together
    on the doorstep. Mary Ann goes
over to them as another ambulance

arrives. Two ambulances for one
　　　　person? Talk about overki—
Don't dare finish the thought.

Two new paramedics open the back
　　　　doors of their ambulance, remove
a gurney and a backboard.

Together, the four prepare Sandy
　　　　for a ride to the hospital. I can't
do anything but watch them

lift his still motionless form, tubes
　　　　running into his arm and an
oxygen mask over his face, onto

the wheeled stretcher. As they load
　　　　him into the waiting ambulance,
Officer Lemoore comes over to me.

　　　　Your brother has internal injuries.
　　　　　　They'll need someone to give
　　　　permission for treatment. Where

　　　　are your parents? Can you call
　　　　　　them and tell them to come
　　　　to Emergency right away?

I Tug My Eyes

Away from the ambulance,
        finally really look at the
policeman in front of me.

He must be straight out of
        the academy, not too many
years older than me. He's

good-looking, in a straight sort of
        way, with topaz gold eyes.
Eyes brimming sympathy.

"I—I'll try to get hold of my
        mom. But it will probably be
my grandmother. Is that okay?"

        He hesitates. The information
            sinks in. *Your mother would
        be best. She has custody, right?*

I nod. "But she's not always,
        uh . . ." How can I say this?
"Easy to track down."

I see. Well, do the best you can.
If we need to, we can get a court
order, but that takes time. And . . .

He shakes his head, and his
meaning is very clear: There
might not be a whole lot of time.

Guilt churns. I want to heave.
"Can't I go in the ambulance?
If he wakes up, he'll be scared."

He won't wake up. He's sedated.
Besides, you need to find your
mom. And someone needs to take

care of your brother and sisters.
He gestures toward the crew.
You're the oldest. It's up to you.

I Am the Oldest

It was up to me to make sure
      something like this never
happened. But no, I needed to

hang out downtown, smoking
      with Alex. If Sandy doesn't
pull through, I'll make sure a hit

      and run happens. To me. The cop
          follows me to the front door.
      I need to ask you a few questions,

      he says to Mary Ann, moving her
          off to one side. *Tell me again*
      what happened. Can you describe . . .

I push the other kids inside.
      "I need to get hold of Gram.
Go watch TV. And don't fight."

I try to call Iris first. Her cell
      goes straight to voice mail. Big
surprise. Gram left the beauty parlor

number next to the phone. No
      surprise there, either. She's
good about communication.

Hands Shaking

I dial the number, ask to speak
        to Vivian Belcher. "Gram?"
I force my voice calm, hope

she'll respond in the same way.
        "You have to go to Emergency
right away. There was an accident. . . ."

I don't tell her everything. Don't
        have to. Enough for her to know
Sandy's life hangs by a sliver.

I poke my head into the living
        room. Porter lies on the sofa,
absorbed in Hannah Montana.

Pepper and Honey sit on the floor,
        holding each other in silent
acceptance of one another, and

maybe of the small part they,
        too, played in the afternoon's
drama. I go to tell Officer Lemoore

that I got hold of Gram. He's finished
        with Mary Ann, whose face is white
as smoke. "Let's go inside," I say.

A Poem by Cody Bennett
Smoke

You stand in front of me,
pretending to be solid,
but you are nothing
more than smoke and

         mirrors.

You said you'd never
leave, that you would
care for us forever.
But now you claim you

         cannot

stay, that you've been
called away. When you
go, who will I turn to
when it all crashes down?

         Tell

me who. Then tell me
how I can believe in
anyone again, if all your
promises have been

         lies.

Cody
Nothing's Static

If I've learned anything at
all in sixteen years, it's that
things change. What you feel
bad about one day can turn
around like that. Same goes
for the things you care about.

Three weeks ago, I kind of liked
spending time at home, goofing
off online or picking at my guitar,
or just watching TV. But now
everything feels strained
at the Bennett house. Not

really like home at all. Everyone
is strung tight. On edge.
Concerned about the future.
Something to do with Jack's
digestive system. Whatever
it is, neither he nor Mom

wants to talk about it. Silence,
thick with apprehension, hangs
over the place like a shroud.
No more dinner table banter.
No more cheerful ribbing.
No more stupid jokes.

Three Weeks Ago

I didn't have a girlfriend.
Not being partnered up
wasn't so damn bad, not
that I totally mind having
the hottest girl in my crowd
acting like she can't get

enough of me. It's just kind
of complicated because, as
I suspected, Alyssa is not
very happy about Ronnie
jumping my bones, jumping
'Lyssa's ship in the process.

The first time 'Lyssa saw us
together, I thought she'd shit
on the spot. We were sitting
together (okay, like glued
together, front to front, Ronnie
in my lap) on the grass at

school. 'Lyssa came hauling
around the corner, headed
somewhere in a hurry. But
when she saw us, she braked
and did a double take. *Just
what do you think you're doing?*

I'm not sure if she was talking
to Ronnie or me, but Ronnie
jumped right down her throat.
*What does it look like we're
doing, Alyssa? Having tea?*
Then she laughed. Too hard.

'Lyssa puffed out her cheeks
and her face turned red—the rotten
red of an overripe tomato. Her
hands clenched. Unclenched.
I thought we were dog meat. But
all she said was, *That's fucked up.*

Oil and water or not, Alyssa
was the first girl I ever had
real feelings for. And now
her feelings were shredded.
I felt like shit. Still do. But
not enough to tell Ronnie to

take a hike. She's freaking
beautiful, with black coffee
eyes, shiny dark hair, and legs
that go up to there. Slipping
in between them is like making
love to warm milk and honey.

We Had Sex

The very first night we went
out together, although I didn't
think it was going to happen,
what with her brother being
a bouncer (okay, security guard)
at Frozen75, something she

neglected to tell me until we
slithered up to the front of
the line. Pissed off a bunch
of people, for sure. But, just
like any club, I guess, they
have an Invited Guest line.

And if your brother's a bouncer,
you're invited. Especially if he's
a bouncer the size of a VW
Beetle. Vince Carino plays
linebacker for the UNLV Rebels,
a decent university team,

usually the second best in the state.
Never mind there are only two,
and the one from that cowtown
up north, Reno, generally comes
out on top. Not always, though,
and when Vegas wins, it's party time.

Then Again

It's pretty much always party
time in Las Vegas. They don't
call it Sin City for nothing.
Ronnie and I partied down
that first night for sure. And
we've been partying ever since.

See, Vince is not only okay with
his sister and me being together.
He encourages it. Says she needs
a guy in her life to keep her in
line. Not that I'd ever try *that*
with Ronnie. I'm a pacifist.

Vince is not. But he is a partier.
Drinks like no serious athlete
should, not that I think he's
especially serious. What I think
is, he likes knocking people down—
smashing them into the ground.

Glad he seems to like me. Booze
isn't his only bad habit, though.
Pot. Pills. Crack. Probably other
stuff, but that's all I've seen. And
that's plenty. I so do *not* want to
know too much about Vince Carino.

Vince and I Have Shared

A bottle or two, a fistful of doobs,
pipes and pipes and pipes. Tonight,
we'll pass around all three at his
regular Friday poker game. Not sure
how I reached the heart of his inner
circle so quickly. Suppose it could

be because I'm usually the one
supplying the weed. Anyway,
I know zip about poker, but it
sounds like a hell of a lot more
fun than staying home, listening
to Jack cough and Mom sigh.

Before I go, I guess I should
brush up on the rules a little.
Punch a few words into my
search engine and I come up
with . . . whoa. Way too much
information. Let's start with

the basic what hand beats what?
One pair, two pair, three of a kind.
Easy enough to remember. Straight.
Flush. Full house. Four of a kind.
Straight flush. Royal flush. Together,
do those equal a hetero queen's toilet?

Damn It, Jack

You've cursed me! *You're*
the one who's supposed to
be coming up with corny jokes.
I'm supposed to laugh at them,
whether or not they're funny.
Now I need to check up on you.

He's in the living room, adrift on
anonymous painkillers. The TV
is blaring, and his eyes are aimed
at it, but vacant. Dread shoots through
my body on a wave of adrenaline.
"Hey, Jack. How's it going?"

> He jumps a little. *Huh? Oh.*
> *Hey, Cody. What's up, son?*
> His speech is slurred, just
> barely coherent. Fucking
> meds. *Where's your mom?*
> *Is she home from work yet?*

Damn. For a minute, I really
thought he might be dead. But
why would I think that? He's
only got indigestion. Jeez, man.
Talk about jumpy. Freaking
crack is famous for that.

But I've got to admit I like
the way it makes every nerve
come alive. Just like Ronnie
said it would. She's got a tidy
little habit. I have to be careful
not to let my own toking get

so out of hand. I swear I never
had a clue she had made friends
with the pipe. Best thing about
it is what a little horndog she turns
into when she's smoking. Boo
frigging yah! Whatever I want.

Jack Coughs

Pulling my mind away from
Ronnie's superior body, back
into the present, toward the sofa.
I go sit next to Jack. Boy, is his
face pale. "Mom's not home
yet. Can I bring you something?"

He turns toward me, eyes wet
with tears. (Tears?) *No, Cody,*
I'm okay. Where are you off
to tonight anyway? Got a hot date?
Before I can answer, a door slams.
Must be Cory. He's the only one

who comes into the house like
that. Sure enough, he stomps
into the room, grinning like a goat.
Damn, even from here he smells
like a brewery. *Hey! What's up?*
Why you look sho—so serious?

Jack takes it in. Turns to me.
He's messed up, huh? I could
say no, and Jack might even go
for it. But Cory's way too young
to start down this ol' road. I nod.
You been drinking, Cory boy?

Cory's face flushes, from beer
and defiance. *So what? Cody
drinks all the time. You never
sh—say nothing to him!* Fingers
knotting and unknotting, he
waits for someone's next move.

If he's expecting me to deny
it, he's drunker than he looks.
I don't want the situation to
get out of hand. I'll try humor.
"'Never say nothing' is a double
negative. What you said means—"

Suddenly Cory wobbles.
Weaves. Drops face-first to
the floor. *Holy shit,* says Jack,
trying to get up, and wobbling
almost as bad as Cory before
he took his literal nosedive.

I nudge Jack back down on
the overstuffed cushion. "No
worries. Other than a lump or
two, I'm guessing he'll be fine
once he sleeps it off. I'll get him
to bed." Like when he was little.

I Pick Him Up

Off the floor, haul him to his
room, thinking about when we
were younger, before Jack came
along. I took my big-brother job
seriously then, and often helped
Mom feed him, bathe him, put

him to bed. Déjà vu! Except this
time he smells like cheap brew.
Thirteen! How did he even get
hold of the stuff? Ripped it off,
no doubt. But from where? Or
who? Damn it all, Cory! I tuck

a light blanket around him, go
to check on Jack. He's snoring,
pushed down into a painkiller
pit. I pull up the foot of the La-Z-
Boy, cover him with Mom's
favorite afghan. She'll be home

soon. Think I'll make my escape
now. Things could get ugly—or
at least complicated—when everyone wakes up and accusations get
kicked back and forth. I don't want
to play explanation dodgeball.

It's a Short Drive

To Vince's apartment, not far
from the UNLV campus. But since
it's Friday evening, just past six,
the freeway looks like a boulder
field. I opt for surface streets,
which aren't a whole lot better.

Which gives me way too much
time to think about what's going
on with Cory. I've been watching
the anger build up inside him, and
I know it's because things feel
fragile in our once rock solid home.

I wasn't much older than he is
the first time I sucked a few down.
But I drank those Coronas for fun.
I think Cory wanted to swallow his
fear and it took a couple too many
brews to make that happen.

Ah, here we go. Magenta Springs.
Why does that remind me of blood?
It's a pretty nice place, at least from
the outside. I park in a visitor's space
behind a tall stucco wall. My beater
car is probably safe. What about me?

The Game Hasn't Started Yet

Four or five guys are drinking.
Smoking. Snorting something
off the glass-topped coffee table.
They barely notice me join the party,
and that makes me a little nervous.
Vince is setting up the card table.

> He, at least, sees me come in. *Hey.*
> *Help me out here. You brought*
> *some of that good green, didn't you?*
> As I suspected, the key to my invite.
> When I nod, he surprises me. *Cool.*
> *I'll throw some extra chips your way.*

When he actually does, I'm even
more surprised. Six of us belly up
to the table, and I light a big fat one.
I buy in for fifty, and he slides me
sixty in chips. The dope is worth
more, but I didn't expect anything,

so I figure I'm ahead. "Thanks."
The poker-for-beginners rules
said to watch the other players,
learn how they "tell." In other
words, read their body language.
Three might as well tell for real.

You can see what they've got in
their eyes. But Vince and some guy
called Fly (pretty sure I don't want
to know why) are damn good at bluffing.
I keep my bets low. One pair ain't going
to beat much, and that's all I'm dealt

for several hands. I bluff a couple of
times, to make 'em think I know
the game. Down thirty, the deal goes
to Fly. I turn my cards over one at
a time. Ten. Eight. Ten. One pair.
Here we go again. King. Ten.

Holy crap. I swallow the rush. Can't
tell 'em I've got three of a kind. Ante up.
Don't bet too much. Ask for two cards
without smiling. One dude folds.
Another bets five. Vince calls, raises
ten. I flip one card. It's a three. Fuck.

Bet comes to me as I flip the last card.
Ten. Four of a kind? Calm. Stay calm.
I raise Vince twenty. Fly folds. Vince
looks into my eyes, but I give nothing
away. He calls, shows two pairs.
I win! For once in my life, I win!

I Leave Vince's

Two hundred dollars richer.
I'm walking on water, oh yeah,
and the rush is effing amazing.
Only one thing could make
this night better. I dial Ronnie's
number. "Hey. It's me. You

up for some fun?" I knew her
answer before I asked the question,
and she doesn't live far. When
I get there, it's too late to knock
on the door, so I go to her window.
It's the only one with a light in it.

My head is Tilt-A-Whirling with
substance abuse, but more because
of finishing off the evening as
a winner. I won at poker. And I'm
about to win at something even
better. Ronnie comes to the glass,

opens it, lets me inside. Her room
smells of roses, and she has nothing
on but a thigh-length shirt. She puts
a finger to her lips, but there's no
need for words once we fall together
into her bed. Night slips away.

A Poem by Eden Streit
Once

I thought fairy tales were
lies or worse, promises
spoken, yet meant to be
broken. Intent is all.

           Why

do grown-ups feel
the need to make up
a story, only to later
confess that it was a

           lie?

Why look for a prince
when frogs are much
more common? Why
reach for a dream

           when

you're at ease within
your nightmares? Why
scramble to disguise
what your personal

           truth is

when reality not only
hurts less in the long
run, but is most often

           the easier path?

Eden
Spring Break

And for once, it actually feels like spring
in Idaho. For most of my life, spring break

was called Easter vacation. Daddy about had
a meltdown when the school board caved

in and changed it. *What's this country
coming to when the Spring Bunny delivers*

spring eggs to children? As if he ever gave
two cents about bunnies and egg hunts. Not

in *his* church. Not on the holiest day of the year,
and Easter Sunday remains that for Christians

near and far. For the family of Pastor Streit,
it is even more, because at Papa's church,

it's an all-out celebration of the Resurrection,
and, dressed up in our Easter bonnets, we sit

front and center. I've never really minded
that before. But today, I'd much rather hang out

in back, pretending not to notice the good-looking
reformed Catholic sitting nearby.

Papa Has Noticed

Andrew, of course. No way would he miss
a possible convert wandering into his hallowed

sanctuary. Once or twice he's made the effort
to engage Andrew in conversation and Andrew,

bless his heart, does his best to respond
positively. No dunking yet (and Papa is quite

likely the reincarnation of John the Baptist
himself!), but he is cordial almost to the point

of brownnosing. Almost. And speaking of
nosing, Mama's ever-observant gaze is harder

to avoid. She must have seen something,
because two Sundays ago, she went fishing:

> *That McCarran boy is a fine-looking
> young man, don't you think, Eden?*

If Papa is John the Baptist (again), Mama
is the Inquisition incarnate. I tried not

to gulp, struggled to meet her eye. "Who?
Him?" I pretended to study his face

for the first time. "Well, now that you mention
it . . ." Then I almost blew it, almost smiled.

My mouth twitched. Mama pounced,
all lioness to my poor little gazelle.

> *Appearances can be deceptive.* Her hand
> settled on my shoulder. *Why, if I had tumbled*

> *for every handsome boy who looked my way,*
> *I shudder to think where I might be today!*

I bit hard on my lip, excused myself
to go to the bathroom, barely making it

through the door before shuddering
myself—with uncontainable laughter.

Needless to Say

Andrew and I have been completely
discreet at church since then. And today,

no way to flirt even a little, it's going to be
really tough. But you know, just seeing

Andrew at all makes any day special.
He's already there, with his sister

and mother, when we arrive. Mariah
smiles and waves. She is four years

older than Andrew, but the two are tight.
So tight, in fact, that he has confessed

our secret to her. So tight that, despite a little
righteous worry, she has chosen not only

>to keep quiet about our relationship, but
>also to nurture it. She comes over now.

>*Happy Easter,* she says to Papa before stroking
>Mama. *Lovely dress. That color is wonderful*

>*on you!* She takes my arm. *May I borrow Eden?*
>*I'd like to introduce her to my mother.*

>*Andrew and I are hoping to get her to church*
>*more than two or three times a year.*

If Mama is surprised that Mariah
and I are acquainted, she hides it well.

Of course. Eden, you know where
to find us. See you in a few minutes.

Mariah steers me toward love. Andrew wears
it like skin, so obvious it makes me blush.

His mother's face, so like his, lights as she
takes my hand in hers. Her voice is soft,

and still she forces it low. *Hello, Eden. I hope*
you don't mind that I tagged along today,

but I simply had to meet you. She draws me
a little bit away from anyone likely to overhear.

Then she looks me in the eye. *I've never*
seen Andrew so happy. Thank you for that.

My reply comes easily. "There is no
one like Andrew. Thank *you* for *that.*"

Old Mrs. Beatty

Launches a spirited "Old Rugged Cross"
on the aging organ, and I must fall back

into the role of perfect preacher's daughter.
I take my expected place in front, but find

every opportunity to glance behind me,
even as I hear the well-known story

of a love greater than any human love
could ever be. So sayeth Papa. Again.

Three rows back sits the greatest love
I'll ever know, and my heart promises

that our love was sparked, as all love is,
by God's love. So why—WHY—is it wrong?

Rephrase. Why—WHY—does my own
family think it's wrong when his doesn't?

Three rows back sits the one true love
of my life, surrounded by his own

family's love. A family that accepts me
for who I am, to him. A family I long to

be part of. And if that means leaving
my family behind, maybe I have to go.

As Soon as the Thought

Crosses my mind, I backtrack. Can't
go. Not yet. He's not ready for me.

And I am only sixteen. Sixteen.
Immersed in the Easter story. Thinking

about loving Andrew, about giving him
the ultimate gift—my virginity. This week.

Not that he knows it. But it's spring break.
Lots of girls give it away on spring break, right?

So it's normal. And, despite sitting in the front
row while my papa preaches about resurrection—

including ways to avoid it—I want to be normal.
Not "normal" as defined by abnormal people.

My people. My parents. I never considered
them (and so never considered me) abnormal

until I met Andrew. But it's completely clear
now. And the best way I can think of to become

completely normal is by becoming a woman.
All I need is the opportunity. Eve, help me.

Ironically

It is Eve (not the original) who sets it up.
See, my sister has asthma. Talking major.

And like I said, it is spring, also in a major
way. We had snow over the winter, an early

melt. Rain to follow. And that means wild
flowers. Early bloom of sage. Beautiful.

Obnoxious to someone who can't tolerate
pollen. Especially someone young. Someone

like Eve. It is Tuesday. Spring break. Eve
wakes, wheezing. Papa is off somewhere,

leaving Mama to rush my little sister
to Emergency. She calls just before noon.

> *They want to keep her for observation.*
> *I have to stay with her. You'll be okay?*

"I'm fine, Mama. You do what you need
to. If I'm not here, I'll be at the library.

I have to research a history paper." Guilt
wants to well as I hang up. I force it

back down, call Andrew, knowing
it's wrong. Wondering if I'm damned.

In the Back of My Mind

I'm thinking he'll take me to a hotel, all the while
stressing about how we'll get away with it.

Spies, remember? But when he picks me up,
we head out of town, and it occurs to me

that I never confessed what I had in mind
for the afternoon. "Where are we going?"

He pulls me very close to him, right
up against his very warm body. *Home.*

My parents went to Elko for a few days.
Not exactly a world-class destination,

but for them it's a second honeymoon.
You and I will go to Hawaii, okay?

He always says the right thing. "Okay.
But I'm allergic to pineapple." I'm not,

at least, not that I know for sure. But
they say humor steadies the nerves.

Nervous?

Let's see. Why wouldn't I be? My mom
and sister are at the ER, which is the only

reason I'm here. What if Mama calls and
I'm not home? Will she buy the library thing?

And what if something is really wrong
with Eve? Should I be *there*? Or here?

Andrew's parents are likely a few hundred
miles away. But are they really? And are

they discussing the likelihood of what is
going on *here*? Are they talking about me?

And even if they're not, and everything else
is on the up-and-up, am I seriously considering

doing that stuff I read on the Net the other
night? I answered all those "Are you really

ready" questions and came away with
a definite "Yes." But am I really, really?

Andrew answers the question for me,
though I'm sure he has no idea that's what

he's doing. *I can't wait to show you the ranch.
Someday it will be your home too.* No hint

of hesitation. He's not only saying his home
is mine, he's telling me his life is mine.

We turn down a long gravel driveway,
the smell of spring sharp through the windows.

Cattle graze in one field, horses in another.
I know nothing about either animal except

what I've seen on TV. But that will change
with time. Time with Andrew. One day,

not far in the future, we'll have plenty of time
together. Something powerful rises up inside me.

Home

Andrew parks the Tundra and we are home.
A bluetick pup lifts her head from the porch,

and when she sees Andrew, sprints to greet
him, tail stub wagging. I know how she feels.

Andrew bends to scratch her behind an ear.
Here now, little Sheila. Say hello to my Eden.

And now she is my puppy too. She licks
my hand, telling me so, and I cannot believe

that any of this is real. Where is my familiar
home? Where is Boise? I never want to return

to either. I slide my arms up around Andrew's
neck. "I love you. More than anything in

this world." And, for a swift-passing moment,
the thought crosses my mind that I love him

more than anything in *any* world. Torn, always
torn, I throw out a silent entreaty to whatever

might exist beyond this world: "If love like this
is wrong, Lord, go ahead and damn me."

I Feel Zero

Trepidation as Andrew takes my hand,
encourages me through the front door.

I hold my breath, not sure why. I feel
like a bride on her wedding night, despite

the nag inside my head who insists:
Not married. Not right. Not married . . .

"Shut up!" I will her, silently. Because,
despite the lack of white gown and cake,

dripping frosting flowers, I know what will
happen soon means Andrew and I are forever

one. Sheila, puppy of honor, follows us
inside. She's probably not nearly as impressed

as I am. The decor is simple. Real. Wood.
Leather. Antiques, refinished, as if the people

who own them care about their history.
And, of course, they do. "Oh, Andrew.

It's all so perfect. I love it!" And I do.
"But not nearly as much as I love you."

We're kissing. We've never kissed exactly
like this, because we've never felt this easy

with each other. No one here. No one
to see. Only Andrew and me.

(Sheila doesn't care. Doesn't count,
because she only wants what Andrew

and I do. Love.) We could talk, I guess.
But there's nothing, really, to say beyond

I love you, and we've already said that.
Andrew stops kissing me, and his eyes

ask what he's afraid to, and my eyes answer
in the same way, so he takes my hand, leads

me down the hall to the bedroom that I would
have picked as his without analyzing. It has

a big feather bed, with massive quilts and
pillows I have to fall into. With Andrew.

I Thought It Would Be

So easy. That loving him as much as I do would
conquer any hint of fear. But when he kisses

me, I'm shaking, and there are tears
in my eyes. *We don't have to,* he whispers.

"I know. I want to. I'm just . . ." Unsure.
I'm completely unsure about my body.

What if he hates it? But now he touches
me. His hands are tentative, and I remember

that this is new for him, too. *Is this
okay?* he asks. *Tell me what you like.*

He kisses me as he picks me up, lays
me gently on the bed. A slow, mutual

exploration begins. As we learn together,
the fear falls away, and sheer exhilaration—

like standing on the very edge of a cliff,
with the wind in your face—replaces it.

He likes my body, and I love his, and there
are only a few seconds of pain, before waves

of pleasure. Wave after swelling wave of
everything right. Wave after wave of love.

A Poem by Seth Parnell
Nothing's Right

Not when you know
someone you love
must leave too soon.

The thought of

losing a friend stings.
The pain of losing
a parent revisits you.
The insanity of

losing someone

who has become
your very heart slices
you right in two.

You can't

eat. Can't sleep. Can't
concentrate on simple
things. All you do
is wonder how you'll

live without

the necessary beat
inside your chest.
The weight of dread

takes your breath away.

Seth
Three Weeks

Until Loren leaves me.
    One month until my life
    falls into limbo. I never
    knew limbo was meant
to be experienced on earth.

I'm halfway there already.
    I fake my way through
    every day, eating, drinking,
    staring off into the classroom
void, with finals fast approaching.

I don't care about school,
    about getting into some
    highbrow university.
    Don't care about the price
of seed or serious lack of rain.

Will I care about any of
        that when he's gone?
        Maybe it will be easier,
        not sneaking off to see
him every stinking chance

I get. Not trying with
        every ounce of what's
        inside me to make him
        damn well remember
me every minute he's away.

I'd Be Lying

If I said things haven't changed
        between us already. It's like
        we've erected a tall wall
        of silence, and neither of us
will break down and be first

to try and scale the stupid
        thing. We used to talk for
        hours, discuss issues, confess
        latent secrets. We used to
have fun. Used to go out.

Now when he opens the door,
        I don't even say hello, just
        push my way through,
        barely close it behind me
before pulling him off down

the hall to the bedroom.
        We have changed there,
        too. Especially me. I take
        control from the start,
don't ask, only demand.

I want to hurt him, like
        he will hurt me when he
        goes off to minister. I only
        have one way to do that.
And I'm doing it now.

He Accepts

Every jolt of punishment
      without a word or even
      a sigh. When I can't give
      any more, when the act
is finished, I stand back,

      waiting. Expecting anger.
         Tears. Anything but his
         soft, *Don't you know how*
         sorry I am that I have
to go? *I love you, Seth.*

And the tears that finally
      come are mine. "Jesus,
      Loren. Why did I have to
      meet you at all? What do
I do when you leave?

"Go back to school, back to
      farming? Back to the old
      me, who was never me
      at all?" I look at him, find
his eyes, but no answers.

He comes over to me,
  slides his arms up
  around my neck, kisses
  the kind of kiss that makes
me want more. A lot more.

Just when I think I'm ready
  for more, he stops me.
  Let's clean up and go out
  for a while. I'm starving.
How about some Italian?

As I start to say no, my
  belly rumbles a good one.
  I haven't eaten a darn thing
  since morning Cheerios.
"Sure, why the hell not?"

Probably a good idea
  to get out of this place
  before I start to cry again.
  Sometimes, top crust
or not, I feel like a total girl.

Despite That

And despite being an hour
    from home, I don't want
    to look like a girl when
    Loren and I go out, not
even in this neighborhood,

where many of the people
    I see could easily be identified
    as "gay." Not even knowing
    most everyone here *is* gay.
Who knows who might be

cruising this place for
    a date or just for kicks?
    Hetero couples wander
    the sidewalks. Looking
for a threesome? Or just

to be somewhere safe, where
    one half of the couple won't
    ask the other, *What the* HELL
    are you looking at? Somewhere
safe? Is there such a place?

Loren Leads the Way

Weaving us in and out
        of the Bohemians
        crowding the sidewalk.
        It's nice to be out with
him. But it also makes me

sad. We used to do this
        more when we first got
        together. Restaurants.
        Theater. Long walks,
talking about life in general.

Then it all became about
        sex. More sex. Better
        sex. Unusual sex. Like
        most couples, I guess.
Is that what I'm really

afraid of losing? Not
        connection or affection,
        not the growth caused
        by absorbing love? If
so, what have I become?

I Can't Help

But think about that as
          Pietro escorts us to
          our favorite table, one
          we haven't asked for in
too many weeks, a fact he

                reminds us of. *Why have*
                    you stayed away so
                    long, misters? I was
                    beginning to think you
              maybe got bad fish last time.

          Loren always orders the
              fresh fish. He responds,
              Now you know we've never
              gotten so much as a single
          bad mouthful here, Pietro.

              The broad Italian smiles.
                Well then, we have on
                the menu fresh sea bass
                tonight. . . . He goes on to
              describe the specials in detail.

I'll stick with my usual
          mushroom raviolis.
          I lost Pietro after sea bass,
          wondering if, without Loren,
I'll ever eat here again.

I Guess I Might

If I ever happen to come
        to Louisville again, once
        Loren's gone. The food
        is delicious. If the place
was in a different part of

town, I might even bring
        Dad along, see if he could
        interest Pietro in his supersecret
        recipe for venison
sausage, biscuits, and gravy.

        The thought makes me smile,
            and that makes Loren smile
            too. *What?* he says, the corners
            of his mouth still curled in
        that oh-so-familiar way.

It's hard to put him and Dad
        in the same place, even if
        that place is inside my head.
        "Nothing." Under the table,
Loren's hand finds my thigh.

        So, he says, *I thought*
            we might go out for
            a little while after we
            finish dessert. There's
        a club not far from here. . . .

His touch is doing strange
        things to me. At least, they
        feel awfully strange in a
        restaurant. "A club? You
mean . . . ? You're not serious."

      Completely serious. Tonight
        they even let underage guys
        inside, as long as they have
        a sponsor. I figured I could
      sponsor you. How about it?

Right now, my body wants
        him to do more than "sponsor"
        me. But I have to admit, I'm
        a little curious. "I thought
you didn't like gay bars."

      I don't. Not alone. But I'm
        not alone tonight, am I?
        He spies Pietro, bringing
        our tiramisu, and his hand
      falls away. Leaves me cold.

Cold Becomes Clammy

As Loren and I make our
　　　way past Mr. ID Checker
　　　at the door to Fringe. He
　　　looks at Loren's license,
nods, barely glances at mine.

I shake my head. "What was
　　　that? He didn't give a damn
　　　about how old I am. And just
　　　why do you have to show ID
to prove you're underage?"

　　　Loren grins. *You're supposed*
　　　　　to be eighteen to get in.
　　　　　But you're right, he doesn't
　　　　　really care. Kentucky
　　is notoriously lax on

　　such things. It hasn't been
　　　　all that long since they
　　　　raised the drinking age
　　　　to twenty-one, and they
　　don't very often bust bars

　　for serving to minors.
　　　　Still, I wouldn't stand
　　　　right in front of the guy,
　　　　sipping bourbon. He
　　might decide to get nasty.

191

Fringe

Is a lot different than I
     thought it would be.
     I expected sleazy, but it
     borders on upscale, all dark
wood and brass and suede.

It's not that late, as bar
     scenes go, so the place
     isn't too crowded. Still,
     maybe fifty or sixty guys
are drinking, laughing,

and hitting on other guys,
     if they're not coupled up
     already. Loren and I find
     cushy chairs in the back,
and he goes to order drinks.

I use the opportunity to
     check out the river of faces.
     Many are average. You
     wouldn't look twice at
them on the street. A few

you wouldn't want to look
     at. Okay, they're not very
     attractive, and when they
     openly stare at me, it
creeps me out completely.

There are also some beautiful
            men here. Most of them are
            younger, yet a fair number
            gravitate toward much older
guys. I don't think it's all about

love. I watch a decent-looking
            middle-aged man, sandy
            haired and very well dressed,
            head off to the men's room.
Within three minutes, his young

companion flirts obnoxiously.
            Glad he didn't pick me to flirt
            with. When the older guy
            returns, he is not pleased.
He slams his fist on the table,

grabs his designer overcoat,
            and stomps toward the door,
            followed by the younger guy.
            If I beat up a table, would
Loren follow me out the door?

Would He Decide to Stay

If I tried coercion instead
        of a simple plea? What if
        I threatened his family?
        Like I could, considering
I don't know who—or where—

they are. He's never shared
        that information with me, nor
        told me where he went to school,
        or how (or if) he outed himself.
That's a lot not to tell me.

He returns now with two
        sugar-rimmed glasses,
        filled with amber liquid
        and some sort of green
leaves. *Mint juleps,* he says.

Froufrou drinks? I take a big
        swallow, fight to not choke.
        "H-holy crap. What's in
        these things?" Whatever
it is burns going down.

        He can't help but laugh.
           Bourbon. A little sugar
           syrup, some mint leaves,
           but other than that,
        bourbon. Sip, don't gulp.

I'm Doing a Fair Job

Of sipping, not gulping,
> when one of the most
> incredible-looking men I've ever seen
> shakes his butt by. My mouth
must have dropped open,

> because Loren turns to see
> > what I'm staring at. *My, my.*
> > *He* is *a fine work of art, isn't*
> > *he?* We watch the guy cozy
> up to a what might be less

than affectionately termed
> "old faggot." Within five
> seconds, the ancient dude is
> buying the fine work of art
a drink. "What's up with that?"

> *Oh hon, haven't you ever*
> > *heard the term "sugar*
> > *daddy"? Lots of young*
> > *guys go looking for easy*
> *drinks, easy meals, maybe*

> *even a place to stay. When*
> > *you look like him*—he
> > points toward Pretty Boy,
> > then he turns and his eyes
> scan my face—*or you,*

it isn't hard at all to find
           someone who'll take
           care of you. Sometimes
           they'll set you up in your
own place, or move you

into theirs. Sometimes
           you live like a movie
           star, even. The price
           tag is regular sex.
He waits for my reaction.

"Regular sex, with someone
           like that?" I take a deep
           drink of minty bourbon,
           actually enjoy the burn.
"I could never do that!"

Loren shakes his head.
           Never say never, dear.
           You might be surprised at
           what you can do, should
circumstances dictate.

A Poem by Whitney Lang
Circumstances

Create our conception,
how we live, what kind
of person we manage

                                                              to grow

into. Another day,
a different hour, take
a left and not a

                                                              right,

you'd wind up a whole
different being. Knowing
if that would be better

                                                              requires

a realm of experience
only decades can build.
Roses? Lilies? Moonlight?

                                                              Sunlight?

Which do I prefer? Ask
me again in thirty
or forty years.

Whitney
The Best Thing

About my mom being such
a bitch is not worrying
about trying to make her
proud of me. Smoke it

up, drink it up, and if
I happen to get caught,
well, wouldn't it just slay
her if the news got around?

Kyra, too. Oh, she'd pretend
that her concern was all
about me, rather than her
precious reputation,

but that would be total
toad crap. "Total toad
crap." TTC. Hey, I like
that. TTC, my new spew.

Kyra's Home

From Vassar. Normal
college geeks go to places
like Florida or Mexico
for spring break. Not Kyra.

She comes home to spend
time with Mom, who actually
rescheduled a tennis game
to take her into the city.

I sooooo need some new
clothes, Kyra fished.
The styles back east are
sooooo not me, you know?

Like jeans aren't the same
beyond the Mississippi.
Like you can't find angora
in Manhattan! TTC, for sure.

Mom swallowed the bait.
We'll run up to Sacramento
Street. There's a new boutique
I've been dying to check out.

Then maybe Daddy can take
time to have lunch with us. New
York seafood can't possibly
compare to San Francisco's.

Sounds fun, said Kyra. *Give*
Daddy a call and see if he can
make it. I'll go take a shower.
Unless you want it first. . . .

Directed at me. "No, no.
Go ahead. I'm not planning
on going anywhere special
today, just hanging out here."

Mom just shook her head, but
Kyra sputtered, *You're not*
coming? But you have to! It will
be so much more fun with you.

Like they really wanted me
to come. Talk about TTC!
"No, you guys go. I don't feel
so great today, anyway."

Kyra might have argued
more, but Mom decided,
You should stay home then.
Last thing I need is a bug.

Last Thing

Any of us needs is Mom
with a bug. She's bitchy
enough totally healthy.
Weird, but I can't remember

the last time she was sick.
Too freaking mean, I guess.
She probably scares the bugs
away. Anyway, Kyra and

she continued their mutual
butt-kiss fest all the way out
the door. I have to admit
I half wanted to change

my mind and go with them.
If I believed they really
wanted my company, I just
might have. Instead, knowing

I'll have the place to myself
most of the day, I called Lucas
as soon as the door slammed
behind Butt Kissers One and Two.

After the Last Fiasco

Lucas was just a bit hesitant.
Are you sure*? Man, last time*
was a way close call. I definitely
don't need that kind of trouble.

What a wuss! But that's not
what I said. What I said was,
"They won't be home until
three at the absolute earliest.

Come over right now. Please?"
Then I made my voice all
breathy, hoping that was sexy.
"I really, really need to see you."

Need to see him, to melt like candle
wax against his heat. Need his heat.
Any heat. Need to feel warmed,
wanted. For a change.

But I didn't say any of that,
either. No use letting him know
I'm needy. Anyway, it worked.
He should be here any minute.

I Did Shower

Even borrowed some of Kyra's
way expensive ginger-scented
shampoo and lotion. No wonder
she always smells so good!

The last time I went to the mall
with Paige, one of the few
investments I made was in
a sapphire blue satin nightshirt

with matching bikini panties.
Good thing my cute stalker,
Bryn, didn't see me buy
this outfit. He would have

followed me home for sure.
I still have his card in my purse.
Not sure what for. Anyway,
all dressed down in sapphire

satin, damp hair, and smooth
skin perfumed with ginger,
I feel sexier than I ever have
before. Could I really *be* sexy?

Lucas Makes Me Wait

Almost two hours. It's closing
in on noon by the time he decides
to grace me with his presence.
I've chewed three fingernails

clear down to the quick,
yanked several strands of hair
out of my head. Not great
ways to deal with nerves,

and I know it when I'm doing
them, but can't seem to stop
myself, especially just sitting
in limbo next to the window.

By the time his Eclipse streaks
into view, I'm totally in need
of fake nails and my scalp
pulses pain. And I'm pissed.

But when I open the door,
see Lucas standing there, in
all his tanned hotness, anger
morphs back into neediness.

> He checks me out, gives a low
> whistle. *You should dress like
> that more often. Nylons and heels,
> you'd be just about perfect.*

The pout that pops up is not
manufactured. "What do you
mean, 'just about'? Not the right
thing to say to someone you

kept waiting for two hours."
I let him in anyway, and he
rewards me with one of his
luscious kisses. Def perfect.

Too soon, he pulls away.
*Sorry I'm late. But I wanted
to pick up a little something
to make the afternoon interesting.*

He reaches into his jacket
pocket, pulls out a small metal
can. Inside is a miniature baggie,
a razor blade, and a short length

of drinking straw. *All we need
is something to chop this up on.
Something glass, like a mirror
or maybe a picture.*

I'm not sure what's in the bag,
let alone if I want to try it.
So why do I jump to my feet
to go find something glass?

What's in the Baggie

Is a half-dollar-sized chunk
of something yellowish white.
It sparkles in the sunlight.
Lucas slices off a thin section

>and tells me, *Cocaine, clean
>as you can find anywhere.
>My brother knows the importer.
>Wait until you try it.*

I don't want to admit the idea
scares me. Weed is one thing.
Cocaine is another. I've seen
it waste people. Seen it waste

entire families, in fact, when
one parent or the other (or both)
invests everything they have
into staying buzzed on coke.

>Lucas keeps chopping, but my
>silence alerts him. *You've done
>coke before, right? No? Oh,
>baby, you're gonna love it.*

>*You're totally gonna fly.
>Don't worry.* He grins like
>a leprechaun. *You're safe
>flying with me. Mostly, anyway.*

I Watch Lucas

Suck two long, thin, sparkly
yellowish lines up his nose.
Then he hands the picture to me.
Not too hard or you'll sneeze.

I inhale gently, one line up
the right nostril, the other
up the left. Immediately,
both sides of my nose go

cold and numb. Now, just like
that, my heart is racing and
the hairs on my arms rise,
sending little chills throughout

my entire body. OMG. No
wonder people like this drug.
I look at Lucas, who's watching
me carefully. "More, please."

He laughs. *Careful now.
A little of this goes a long
way.* But he indulges me,
and himself, with two more.

Every nerve jumps to attention.
I can't feel my mouth or nose,
but other parts of my body
are begging to be touched.

Lucas indulges them, too,
with his hands and his mouth.
I love how he kisses, love how
his fingers move over my body.

Everything is hard. Everything
is warm. No, cold. No, warm.
I've never felt so alive. Never
felt so in love. I glance at the clock.

Not even one. We have plenty
of time. But I don't want to
do it here on the couch. "Let's
go to my bedroom, okay?"

I Don't Have to Ask Twice

Lucas scoops me up into
his toned arms, carries me
down the hall, like a groom
clutching his bride. The thought

makes me blush, and I have
no clue why. I rest my head
against his chest for the entire
ten-second journey. Then

he lays me gently on the bed,
unbuttons my shirt, peels
back the blue satin, stares
at what he has uncovered.

I am totally exposed, totally
flying high, and yet I do, in
fact, feel safe with Lucas,
even as he lowers himself

over me. Every ounce of me
wants what he's about to do,
and yet for just an instant,
regret stings and I say, "Wait."

> He pauses. *What? You
> don't want me to stop,
> do you? Because I don't
> think I can. I need you. See?*

He lowers my hand to feel
his need, and my heart screams,
"Hurry!" Still, my brain whispers,
"You can never take this back."

I look up into Lucas's eyes.
"I don't want you to stop.
But please don't go too fast.
I'm afraid . . ." Afraid it will

       hurt. Afraid it will change me.
       Afraid . . . afraid . . . the word
       thumps in time with my heartbeat,
       even as Lucas soothes, *I'll go easy*.

And he does. And I'm ready.
And it does feel good, despite
the pain, because it also hurts.
And then, it's just over.

Still Buzzed

And yet also drained, we lie
together for a while. I don't
know if it was good for Lucas
or not. I want to ask, but I don't

want to ask because if I do and
he says no, it will leave a scar.
I don't even know if it was good
for me, because I'm not sure

what "good sex" is. Your first time
probably isn't so good, right?
Because I didn't exactly feel
fireworks. Maybe I was too

numb. Doesn't matter. What's
done is done, and I love Lucas
even more now because he is
my first. My ear rests against

his chest. I listen to the promise
of his heart, and suddenly
my mouth is moving and what
spills from it is, "I love you."

I Wait for Him

To tell me he loves me, too.
After several seconds, I notice
I've been holding my breath.
I grab air as he rolls out of bed.

> *It's getting late. Don't want*
> *to get busted.* He stands, looks
> down, at himself and the bed.
> But not at me. Why won't he

> look at me? *We'd better clean*
> *up. And you might want*
> *to wash your sheets. You're*
> *not on your period, are you?*

"No, not for . . ." Now I notice
how the front of him is splashed
red, and the crimson stain
flowering on my bed. My face

burns. "It's not my period."
How could he not know that
the first time can make a girl bleed?
Or did he maybe not believe . . . ?

A Poem by Ginger Cordell
Bleed

Open a vein, feel
the rush, exodus,

delicious.

Don't be afraid,
there's no pain
in the letting,

delectable.

Watch the red
flow, let it go,

drip,

make it slow,

drip.

If you've done
it right, you won't
wake from the night's
indescribably peaceful

dream.

Ginger
You Would Think

The possibility of losing
        a child would be a wake-up
call. Not for Iris. No way.

Sandy is still in a coma,
        wandering around some-
where deep inside his brain.

The doctors don't know
        if he's going to make it.
They say we should pray.

Gram's done a whole lot
        of praying. She's the one
who sits by his side, day

after day. Iris says it's too
        hard to see her little boy
that way. She's only been

to the hospital two or three
        times. Makes Gram mad.
Makes me mad too. Iris

doesn't give two squirts
        who she pisses off. All
she cares about is herself.

It's Been a Month

A month of worry, of guilt,
        of my having to play the role
of "Mom" even more, because

Gram isn't there to help
        me do it. A month of
Mary Ann, withdrawing

into a silent, blank-eyed
        world where accidents
don't happen, especially

not on her watch. I try to
        help, but she isn't ready
to quit blaming herself.

A month of mounting bills—
        doctor bills, ambulance bills,
hospital bills—that Gram

        is determined somehow
                to pay. *Where there's a will,
        there has to be a way.*

        A month of Iris diving
                deeper and deeper into
        bottomless bottles of numb.

She Has a New Boyfriend

A big-boned truck-driving
        son of a bitch, with eyes
like a crow's—black, dead.

I've seen eyes like those
        before, on another of
Iris's badass lays, one

I can't forget. I do my best
        never to think of him, what
he did. Try never to remember

that place in my childhood,
        but sometimes it pops into
view despite all my efforts

to keep it hidden. I was almost
        ten, and we lived in Pahrump,
the butthole of Nevada. Iris

worked at a cathouse, making
        money her usual way, only
without walking the streets.

Walt was a miner, and though
        he was a regular paying
customer at Mimi's, he had

an appetite for younger
          meat. Iris was younger then
too, but even at twenty-six,

she was way too old for Walt.
          Still, he paid for her, then he
followed her home. She let

him move in for a while.
          I remember his sour sweat,
coming in after working backhoe.

I remember how he touched
          Iris, and how she didn't
care that her kids could see.

          I remember his Marlboro breath
                    falling all down around me when
          he said, *Let me show you something.*

On Another Day

It wouldn't have happened,
     couldn't have happened.
Too many witnesses around.

But for some odd reason,
     that particular afternoon,
Iris had taken the other kids

     to play in the park. *You stay
          and start dinner*, she said.
     We won't be gone very long.

I didn't mind. I was too old
     for swings, and I've always
liked spending time by myself.

But it wasn't more than ten
     minutes before Walt came
through the door. He didn't

     ask where Iris was, or why
          the house was so quiet.
     He didn't say one word.

I opened a can of refried
     beans, spooned them into
a pot. I had no real reason

to be afraid. So why did my
		hands shake? I kept my back
to him but could feel his eyes,

		carving into me. Finally,
			he started toward the living
		room. *Bring me a beer, sweets.*

		I dug one from the fridge.
			But he wasn't on the couch,
		as expected. *Back here,* he called

from Iris's room. He was already
		out of his jeans. I didn't know
much then, but I knew there was

something very wrong about
		that. Still, I took him the beer,
holding my breath against his

		stench. He grabbed my hand,
			jerked me hard against him.
		Let me show you something.

I tried to run, but he was faster.
		Tried to fight. He was stronger.
Tried to scream. He choked my cries.

When He Finished

(Thank God it didn't take long),
        he rolled off me with a grunt.
  Reached for his beer. Slammed it.

Ripped and pried, swallowed
      up by the shame of what that
meant, I crawled into the bathroom

to scrub away the evidence.
      Not that I'd dare tell anyone.
Not when he followed me,

           stood in the doorway, watching
                me, finally said, *Tell a soul,
          I'll do your sister, too.* He knew

that was a bigger threat than
      saying he'd hurt Iris or some
other TV kind of shit. Because

I knew he *would* come back
      for Mary Ann. She was only
eight. If he did this to her, she'd

die for sure. It had almost
      killed me. I'll probably
always link sex with pain.

All That Comes Back

Like a sucker punch, mirrored
            now in Harry's corpse-cold
eyes, moving all over my body—

climbing up, shimmying back
            down. I hate them. Hate him,
because he's no different from Walt.

            Iris doesn't notice, or maybe
                        doesn't mind. She's always
            saying, *You be nice to Harry.*

            We want to keep him happy.
                        She's bold about bringing
            Harry around, bold because

Gram is mostly at the hospital.
            Her path has only crossed
Harry's a couple of times,

and when that happens, their
            dislike for each other hangs
thick in the air like smog.

Iris pretends that it doesn't.
            Iris is good at pretending.
She breathes make-believe.

Not Sure

If Harry is tuned in to
       how Iris earns her booze
and pill money. Don't think

so, though. She has always
       tried to keep pleasure and
business in two different boxes.

Ugh. Bad double meaning
       there. A sick sort of laugh
escapes and Iris, who is at

       this very moment sitting
              across the room from me,
       asks, *What's so funny?*

Which makes me bust up
       even more. All I can do
is snort, "Nuh . . . nothing."

              Harry, who is sitting next
                     to Iris, slurping a Keystone,
              butts in. *Then why the hell*

are you laughing? Those crow
eyes take even bolder liberties
with my body, and there's

something in his voice—
something far beyond mean.
Something approaching

sadistic. *People don't just up
and laugh for no damn
reason, do they, little girl?*

Anger firecrackers. I want
to yell. Instead I keep my
voice very low. "I don't know

who in the fuck you think
you are, but you're nothing
to me. I don't answer to you."

Fists knotting, Harry jumps
to his feet. Iris reacts by
jumping to hers. *W-wait,*

baby. No need to get mad.
The words puff from her
mouth. *She's just a dumb kid.*

A Nuclear Bomb

Goes off inside my skull—
        a white-hot mushroom
cloud of rage. "Yeah, well,

at least I'm not a whore! Wait.
        'Whore' is too good a word
for you and what you do.

'Hooker' works much better."
        I hesitate just long enough to
gain some satisfaction from

the look on Iris's face. Then
        I escape out the front door
before the shit smacks the fan.

It's May, and Mojave heat
        practically knocks me off
my feet, but I run. Run from

Iris, from her crow. He'd pick
        my bones clean, and I know it.
Run from Gram's house, not

home without her in it. Run
        from shadow into overbearing
sunlight. Run toward town.

I wish I could keep running.
       Farther. Forever. Wish
nothing could turn me back.

I run all the way to Alex's house.
       By the time I get there, sweat
streams from every pore, washing

       away hurt and anger. Luckily,
           when I pound on the door,
       it is Alex who answers. *Hey.*

       She steps back, and I fall into
           cool darkness. It's like diving
       deep. *What happened?* she asks.

We are alone in the place,
       and that is good, because
for some stupid reason, I tell

her the entire story, including
       the stuff about Walt. Words
keep spilling out of my mouth

as if a faucet broke. When I
       finally stop, I'm crying.
And Alex is holding me.

No One Has Ever

Held me like this before,
        strong but kind. Gentle,
even. Fact is, I'm surprised

I'm letting her hold me.
        My MO is to withdraw.
But this feels good, and that

makes me cry harder. What
        have I missed? "I'm sorry.
You didn't need to hear all that."

        Alex brushes the hair from my
            forehead, mindless of sweat.
        It's okay. I understand. Men

        are dogs for the most part.
            Scratch that. Dogs are kind
        of cute, and they only come on

        strong when the bitch is
            in heat. She goes quiet,
        lets me finish feeling sorry

for myself. Finally I go quiet
        too. I look up, wanting to
thank her. She smiles. Kisses me.

It's a Soft Kiss

On the mouth, sensual,
  and it's exactly the way
I imagined it might be.

Her lips are smoothed
  by a sheen of raspberry
ice, and they make no demands

beyond this sweet three
  seconds of connection.
Iris's men dissolve, salt

  in rainwater. There is no
   more, no "let's have sex,"
  which leaves me both content

  and confused. *I think you*
   need a drink, she says.
  As she goes into the kitchen,

a new fantasy springs
  to life. "Have you ever
thought about running

away?" I call after her.
  She returns with a couple
of Cokes, spiked heavily

with what I think is rum.
      All the time. No one would
even miss me. What about you?

"I'd go right now, but who
      would take care of the kids?
And anyway, where would I go?"

We sip our drinks in silence.
      The afternoon slips by, hazy
with alcohol. Finally I glance

at the clock. Almost six. I don't
      want to go, but someone has to
make dinner. When I get home,

      Iris is on the phone. She turns,
         smiling. *Sandy will be okay.*
      They'll release him in a few days.

A Poem by Cody Bennett
Release

I'm not the religious
type. Mom goes to church
but I mostly ignore it.

                                      Not sure

if there is a God or why
some all-powerful being
would give half a damn

                                      about

the likes of me. Lately,
though, I've tossed out
a prayer or two, thrown
them like fastballs at

                                      heaven,

if there is such a thing.
I'm afraid they only
bounced back to

                                      Earth, or

spun out into space,
unheard. Either way,
guess I'll give it another
try. Why not? What the

                                      hell

have I got to lose?

Cody
Falling Apart

That's how everything feels,
like it's dissolving one molecule
at a time. I'm scared. Damn it,
I hate to admit it, but my gut churns
night and day. I can barely eat.
Only booze goes down and stays.

Mom is at church right now.
Church, of all places! We haven't
been regular churchgoers since
we left Wichita. Now she's not only
religious. Apparently she's Catholic,
and asking for intervention. Praying

for a miracle. Some sort of Hail Mary
sign that Jack will make it home
again, happy, healthy, and maybe
a little wiser about indigestion and
what that can mean. That persistent
bellyache? Turned out Tums

weren't going to fix it. No wonder
I can't eat. Too much information
about what causes stomach cancer
and what happens when it metastasizes,
infiltrating blood and cells to infect
the esophagus, pancreas, and who

knows what else. It's just about
enough to make me choose a liquid
diet. Water. Bottled. (Tap water can
be carcinogenic.) V8 (low sodium—
salt is a factor in stomach cancer)
for your veggies. A little bouillon

(takes care of the protein requirement,
right?) watered down with vodka.
And for dessert, stiff megashots
of gin. Hey, someone besides Cory
should drink it. He's developed
a tidy habit and isn't real good

at hiding it. But Mom and Jack
can't turn him around. They barely
notice him. Or me. More important
shit on their minds. Like praying
for miracles. Like staying alive
just one more fucking day.

So Cory Drinks

Way too much. Pickling his brain,
and much too young to end up relish.
But how can I say anything when I
drink? And more. I smoke. Snort.
Pop pills. Anything to keep from
thinking about death, come knocking.

When Cory and I finish off Jack's
dwindling booze stash, scoring more
won't be a problem. Vinnie will happily
buy. At least as long as I keep bringing
bud to the Friday night games.
I've become a regular, and I've learned

to play poker, not that I always
win. Not even. I've dropped a dime
or two. But the rush that comes
when I do win is worth every penny
down the drain. Gambling is like
snorting cocaine. Up. Down. Up.

And, despite knowing you have to
crash sometime, all you can think
about when you're doing it is the high.
I've dropped two hun in a single night.
That sucked. But once I won almost six.
Oh, yeah! Put me clear through the roof.

A New Rush

I've just tapped into is online
gaming. Roulette. Blackjack.
Poker. More. I've learned how
to play games I never even knew
existed. It's fun. Really fun. In
fact, it's a total, amazing rush,

and you don't even have to leave
home to get it. All you need
is a computer and a way to deposit
some cash in your own Internet
casino account. And hey, I've got
a bank card. Not a whole lot in my

personal checking, but that's about
to change. All I need is one big win.
And what's really insane is the casino
gives you a cash bonus to sign up. I put
in five hundred; they threw in three.
I'm ahead already. Well, was ahead.

I've gone through the bonus and a little
more. But that's the nature of gambling.
Win some. Lose some. Just have to
stay on top of things. Walk if it isn't
your night. Tonight I'm almost even.
All I need is one hand, the right hand. . . .

Shit!

Okay, that wasn't the right hand.
At least I only had twenty riding.
Maybe I should switch to roulette.
My brain isn't working so well right
now. Not sharp enough for poker.
Roll the ball, watch it go round

     and round. Come on, twenty-seven!
     Just as the traitorous ball drops
     into thirty-four, my cell phone rings.
     My face flushes hot, like a little kid
     caught dipping his fingers in the frosting.
     But it's just Ronnie. *Hey. What's up?*

"Uh . . . not much. What's up with
you?" She wants me to come get her,
and as she waits for my response,
I can picture her face, all pouty
with impatience. Pretty face. Better
body, all sleek and tan and . . .

Ah, what the hell? I'm not making
much progress here tonight. "Sure,
babe. Give me a few." Why not?
Would be good to get out of the house,
and boning Ronnie is the one thing that
can take my mind off everything else.

First Things First

Just one more spin of the ball.
Come on, twenty-seven, come on,
twenty-seven. Sixteen? Shit!
Stop. Ronnie's waiting, something
she's not real damn good at.
Besides, Lady Luck doesn't seem

to have joined me tonight. Bitch.
One more. Ten on twenty-seven.
Odds are better if you play the same
number. Yeah, I know I could play
columns or colors, but what's the fun
of winning even money or two to one

when thirty-five to one puts you over
the top? Come on . . . Twenty-seven!
Fuck yeah! There it is! Maybe you
just gotta call ol' Lady Luck names.
Three-fifty in the bank and I'm going
after the finest little piece of pie

in Vegas. In a minute. I'm playing
on casino bucks now, and I'm on
a roll. Think I'll try a hand or two
of blackjack. Another swallow
of gin to keep the courage flowing.
Oh yeah, it's definitely this boy's night.

Damn Lucky Dealer

So much for three of the three-fifty
I won earlier. Blackjack
isn't my game tonight, that's for
sure. I need to learn the finer points,
like when to double down. Ah, hell.
The phone again. What time is it?

        Almost ten? Where did the last
        two hours go, and what does this
        do to my odds of getting laid?
        Ronnie's pissed, I'm guessing.
        She is. *I thought you were coming*
        over. I've got school tomorrow.

Quick! Make something up. "Sorry.
I . . . uh . . . Cory came in all messed
up. I had to help Mom get him to bed."
I'll probably burn for lies like that,
but I think it worked, so I sign off,
delete all incriminating history.

        The extra-long pause means she thinks
        I might be bullshitting her. But finally
        she gives in. What else can she do?
        She so wants me! *Come over anyway.*
        My parents are in bed. I'll sneak
        you in through the window.

Her House

Is fairly close to mine. Good
thing. Hanging out in my room,
I didn't notice how buzzed I was.
I'm definitely feeling it now,
though. It's hard to drive a straight
line. Thank God I can take side

streets. If I actually had to talk to
a cop, he'd haul my ass in, no
doubt. Gonna be hard enough trying
to say a few coherent words to
Ronnie. Even this late at night,
it's really warm—probably pushing

eighty. I drive with the windows
down, letting air movement fight
brain blur. Every street in Vegas
is well lit, and everywhere you
look at night, bursts of neon
color the obnoxious skyline.

I cruise slowly, tripping on a tall
turquoise tower, how it seems
to weave in and out of the breeze-ruffled
palm trees lining the street.
Suddenly, something—someone?—
dashes into the road right in front

of me. I punch the brakes, honk
the horn, barely manage to miss
the dimwad, who skids to a halt
on the far side of the street.
Then he turns back toward
my car. What? Who? Cory!

He rips around to the passenger
door, jerks it open, jumps inside.
Go! I shake my head, try to make
some sense of what just went down.
Did I almost run over my brother?
Fucking hurry up, okay?

The Tone of His Voice

Is enough to make me comply.
I punch the gas pedal, no tangible
clue why, almost overwhelmed
by the smell of cheap booze clinging
to my little brother. "What the hell
is going on, Cory?" As the question

sputters from my mouth, I get
a sickly feeling I don't want to hear
the answer. But hey, he's not exactly
dying to give me an answer. *Nothing.*
Not a goddamn thing. So why
are his hands shaking? And how

is it obvious, in the murky half-light
inside the car, that his face is
approximately the color of dirty cotton?
Whatever. He'll tell me when he feels
like it—or maybe he won't. I'm not
the type to pry. As I turn the corner,

I hear his small, tortured exhale as
he scrunches down in the seat. A patrol
car comes cruising up the block toward
us, spotlight sweeping sidewalks,
yards. Looking for Cory, no doubt.
What has the dumb shit done?

I Try Not to Think

About that as I fight a sudden
explosion of fear. I'm driving in
a straight line, under the limit, at
least the speed limit. As for blood
alcohol, there is a very good
possibility that I'm well over

the .08. And should this cop decide
to pull me over, just in case he
really ought to take a look (and hey,
apparently he should!), exactly
what charges might I have to face,
for no more reason than having

a certain passenger in my car?
Whatever Cory has done, I want
to wring the little prick's neck.
"What the hell did you do, Cory?"
My hands are slick with sweat
against the sticky steering wheel.

I keep glancing in my rearview
mirror, sure I'm minutes away
from a trip to juvie. But the cop
keeps driving up the block, likely
positive in his little pea brain that
whoever he's looking for is on foot.

Or maybe he's just too lazy
to worry about possibilities
(and viable possibilities at that),
driving by in the other direction.
Speaking of driving by, I just
motored on past Ronnie's.

The house was dark, except
for a light in a single window.
A bedroom window, where
I have no doubt a gorgeous,
well-built girl sits waiting to
do me, after she's finished

bitching me out completely.
Major butt kissing in order,
if I happen to actually make it
home without becoming a suspect
in a . . . what? What the fuck?
Suddenly my head is clear.

I turn another corner. Drive away
from home. Stay under the limit.
Find a deserted street, pull right up
against the sidewalk. "If you don't
tell me exactly what's going on, I'll
knock your bony ass to the curb."

His Answer

Is a couple minutes coming, like
he's considering making up a lie.
Finally his shoulders sag. It will
be the truth. *I kinda broke into
a house. They had an alarm.*
He doesn't look at me, just stares

out the window, into the night,
the same night I'm staring into.
"What do you mean, 'kinda'?
You can't 'kinda' break into
a house. You did or you didn't."
Jeez, I sound just like Jack, at

least just like Jack before . . .
Now I get to play dad to Cory,
not that it's a role I want, or
do very well. Still, I can't just
sit here and say okay to burglary.
Anyway, "Kinda or not . . . why?"

Zero hesitation. *Why the fuck
not? Jesus, Cody, do you live
on a different planet? We need
the stinking money! Jack's never
going back to work. You know that.
Don't you hear Mom jabbering*

about too many bills, not enough
insurance and such? What do you
think's gonna happen to her
when he kicks the freaking bucket?
What's gonna happen to . . . us?
He stutters. Breaks. Tries to buck

up. But suddenly, like fragile glass
stressed beyond redemption,
he simply shatters. *Fuck it!*
Cory's giant sobs fill the front
seat with booze-infused exhales.
He probably wants to cry like a man—

alone within his pain. This may
be the wrong thing to do. But as
I watch him, my own fear hiccups
to the surface. I pull my tough,
break-and-enter little brother
into my arms, and we cry together.

Headlights Turn the Corner

Flooding us with halogen blue
light. Cop? No, but it comes to
me that we probably look like
gay dudes making out or something.
Cory must think so too, because
he jerks like he's been shocked.

> *Sorry. That was totally lame.*
> *Let's go before we get arrested.*
> He withdraws across the seat, gaze
> again drawn to the neon-spiked
> night. Too bad Jack isn't here,
> ready with some witty remark

to make everything okay. Too
bad Jack isn't here, period. "No
worries. But don't ever do anything
like that again. Shit, Cory, if you
get busted, you'll just make things
worse. We'll be okay. I promise."

I start toward home, chewing on
how I could have promised such
an unlikely thing. Now I've got to
find a way to keep my word.
One way comes to mind. All
I need is a little investment capital.

A Poem by Eden Streit
Need

Need is a curious thing.
Until you plant the seed,
nurture it, encourage its

                                       awakening,

you're not even sure
it's there. But once it
germinates, nudges up,

                                       breaking ground,

you can no longer deny
it has always lain dormant
inside you. And now,

                                       blossoming

with every kiss, every
touch of his hand, this
new kind of need is

                                       growing,

sprouting shoots,
tendrils of desire
threading you,

                                       consuming you.

Eden
Six Months

Since Andrew and I first started seeing
each other. Almost a month since

we took our relationship all the way,
clear over the top, dropping me eye-deep

into a bottomless pit of obsession.
That's pretty much how it feels.

Like I'm in so deep I'll never climb out,
not that I want to. So okay. I'm obsessed.

Whether or not God will forgive me remains
to be seen. But I have absolutely no clue

how I could un-obsess myself if Andrew
ever decided he didn't want me in his life.

So far, though, Andrew seems every
bit as obsessed with me as I am with him.

We have learned a lot about each other.
How to touch. Where to kiss. When to let go.

Before this month, I didn't really believe
I was his first. But I was. Am. I have taught

him as much as he has taught me, all
through mutual experimentation. Mad

sex scientists, that's us. There have been
clumsy moments, yes. But they are rare. Few.

The worst was when it suddenly came to us
that, swept downstream by a flood of desire,

we hadn't used protection the first time.
But either I'm sterile or the timing was right,

because three days later I started my period.
We've been careful ever since. I wish

I could go on the pill, but I know for certain
if I showed my face at Planned Parenthood,

word would get back to my parents. A trip
to the pharmacy would yield the same result.

Meaning birth control—condoms, not the best,
but better than nothing—is up to Andrew.

With or Without Condoms

(Because after all, we don't have to have
sex *every* time we see each other, do we?)

I'm hoping to see Andrew today. Saturday,
so no school, and I'm done with my chores.

I've just got to come up with the right little
white lie. Or big black lie. Whatever.

Mama seems kind of suspicious lately.
I think what they say about being in love

is true—some inner glow becomes obvious
to everyone around you, even those

you most want to keep solidly in the dark.
"So, Mama. Shania and I are doing

an English project on *The Lord of
the Rings.* She invited me over to work

on it. Would that be okay?" Shania
is, like, my only friend. I've known

her since she moved here in second grade
and her family joined Papa's church.

Once in a while we do stuff together,
and the English project is for real.

If I really go over there before meeting
Andrew, it will be a big white lie.

Mom is busy paying bills. She barely
glances my way. That's good, because

when she says, *Um. Guess so,* I can
actually feel the love flicker ignite.

I hurry out the door before she changes
her mind. The day is warm and scented

with spring blooms. Shania is watering
the yard when I get there. "Hey, girl."

A fair amount of surprise fills her eyes.
Eden. What are you doing here?

"Mama let me escape for a while. Just
thought I'd drop by and say hi. Why?"

She shakes her head. *It's just that . . .
well, lately . . . I haven't seen you much.*

Guilt nibbles. "I know. I'm sorry. I guess
I've been kind of distracted." By Andrew.

Can't Tell Her That Part

Or can I? Should I? It would feel good
to confess something this special.

Shania saves me the trouble. *By your
boyfriend?* Does she know? Or is she

guessing? "I suppose you could call
him that." I'm not telling everything.

Really? A big grin crinkles her eyes.
So okay, she's guessing. Good thing.

But now that the cat has halfway escaped
from the bag, she wants to know all.

*Come inside and tell me more.
Who is he? Is he cute? How old*

is he? Does he go to our school?
She grills me all the way through

the front door. "Hang on a sec.
I'll tell you all about him. . . ."

Well, not all. "But first, I need to
make a call. Can I use your phone?"

An Hour Later

I say good-bye to Shania, who
is slightly wiser about Andrew.

I didn't tell her he happens to be the very
cute guy who sits in the back at church

most Sundays, or that he is picking me
up just down the block in a few minutes.

As I start walking, I can, in fact, see
the Tundra, patiently lurking curbside.

> The obsession thing quickens my pace,
> but behind me I hear Shania's *Bye.*

I turn to wave, and see curiosity has
drawn her all the way to the sidewalk.

But Andrew is parked facing away from
her. I hurry on past the Tundra, motion

discreetly for him to follow me around
the corner. Out of Shania's sight, I fling

open the door, slide across the seat, and kiss
Andrew like I haven't seen him in days.

Mostly because I haven't. Every filament
of me shimmers. "We have got to stop

meeting like this, you know." Then
I add, "Almost forgot. I love you."

He rewards me with that beautiful
smile. *And I love you. Where to?*

I shrug. "Anywhere. But not too far.
I should probably be home by four."

Gotcha. He starts the Tundra, and
as he pulls away from the curb,

a little white car slows its approach.
I can't help but notice the driver—

Shania's sister, Caitlyn. And she most
definitely notices me. Her expression

is an interesting mixture—one part
curiosity, one part disbelief, one

part . . . jealousy? Is this trouble? I know
I should probably have Andrew turn

straight around, drop me off near the house.
But he's so close. And he smells so good.

I need to be with him more than anything.
And if this is trouble, it already is.

A Quarter to Four

Andrew drops me off around the corner
from home. It has been an amazing

afternoon, filled with love and making love.
He kisses me. *See you soon. Very soon.*

Ten to four, I walk in the door. Mama
and Papa are sitting there, waiting for me.

Nine to four, I know I'm most definitely
in trouble. Likely the major kind. "Hi?"

Mama pounces first. *Where have you
been? And who have you been with?*

Then she assesses my semi-disheveled
state. *And what have you been doing?*

Guilt flushes my face, burns my ears.
But I'm going to play stupid anyway.

"I told you before I left I was going to
Shania's." Stop there. See what happens.

Papa shadows Mama as she stands, takes
a step in my direction, fists clenching.

*You know very well what I'm talking
about. You were with that McCarran boy.*

Five to Four

My life is over. At least the slender
wedge of it that holds happiness.

Denial is ridiculous. Still, the words
pop out of my mouth, "Says who?"

> I already know the answer. It is Papa
> who gives it. *Caitlyn Curry. Your mother*
>
> *called to ask you to pick up some butter*
> *on your way home. Caitlyn said you had*
>
> *already left. And that she saw you in*
> *a truck with the young man. Now I want*
>
> *to know why you were with him. And why*
> *you lied.* His face is redder than mine.

Deception impossible, defiance
flares. "I was with Andrew because

I'm in love with him. And why
I lied should be pretty damn obvious."

> At the very intentional curse word,
> Mama gasps. Papa pushes her behind
>
> him, advances. *You apologize to your*
> *mother this instant, you little trollop.*

Trollop? Who uses that word for real?
Laughter dribbles from my mouth.

And I stand my ground. "But I'm not
sorry, Papa. I'm tired of you and Mama

treating me like a little girl. I'm old enough
to fall in love. Why won't you let me?"

                Mama's turn. Her voice drips
                icicles. *I believe you're confusing*

                love and desire. Do you really think
                that man is in love with you? What

                he wants . . . Once again, her eyes travel
                over me, trying to look under my clothes

                to the sin she intuits beneath them.
                He wants your innocence. I will not

                let you succumb to temptation. She is
                past Papa, hands moving toward me.

                They fall. I don't dare try to defend
                myself. I've been here before. Tears

                sting my eyes. From the pain of her blows.
                And from the heartbreak tomorrow holds.

Heartbroken

Face bruised, eyes swollen almost
shut from crying, no way can I go

to church today. Mama would stay,
to keep an eye on me, but it happens

to be Mother's Day. All the ladies will
turn out in their best dresses, to be celebrated.

> *Don't you dare take one step out
> of this house,* Mama warns. *If you*
>
> *do, I'll know, I promise you that.
> I'll take care of Mr. McCarran, too.*

As soon as the car is out of sight,
I rush to the phone. Thank God

> Andrew is still home. *Hey. I was just
> heading out the door. Everything okay?*

The whole ugly tale comes gushing
out, and I can't believe I dare to beg,

"Hurry and come pick me up. Please!"
It may be a very long time before I get

to see him again. I need to see him today.
Right away. Even looking the way I do.

Twenty Minutes Later

I am in Andrew's arms, crying softly
against his chest. He lets me whimper

for a few minutes, then pushes me
gently away and says, *Look at me.*

Let me see what she did. His hands
are kind as they soothe the bruises,

trace the contours of my face. But
his eyes smolder, hot with anger.

*How could anyone do something
like that to their child?* he demands.

"It doesn't matter. All that matters
is how we can see each other now.

Without you, my life is meaningless.
Without you, I have nothing to live for."

*Don't say that! And don't mean that.
You have everything to live for. We'll*

figure something out. I promise. He
tugs me back into his arms. *I promise.*

I Want to Stay

Knotted to Andrew forever, warm
and safe, and loved. But he insists,

> I am home before my parents get
> back from church. *Don't give her*
>
> *a reason to hurt you. Please, Eden.*
> *It's my fault she did this to you.*

I start to argue, but he won't let me,
and he won't let me stay any longer.

> One last quick kiss and he urges, *Just go.*
> *If she catches you, who knows how long*
>
> *it will be before we can see each other*
> *again? I love you. Now go on.*

He's right, of course, and I hurry. But
when I turn the corner, I can see

our car in the driveway. My stomach
lurches, like I'm in an elevator and

the cable snaps. I fall to my knees
and vomit until there's nothing left

but cramps. I wobble to my feet,
up the sidewalk, and in the front door.

Mama Is Waiting

Sitting on a straight-backed chair,
facing the door. *You were with him*

just now, weren't you? She already
knows the answer. Why try to lie?

The truth is doubtless magnified by
the tear storm in my eyes. "Yes."

I expect the same chaotic anger
she threw at me yesterday. She stands,

and my muscles clench. But she stays
remarkably calm as she approaches.

I knew it when he didn't show up
at church today. I'm not sure why

it took me so long to realize what
the two of you were up to sitting

back there. . . . Her jaw goes tight,
and her left hand reaches for me.

I wince, but she simply slides her
arm around my shoulder, guides me

toward the kitchen. *We need to talk.*
I'll make some tea. She pushes me

into a chair. My stomach churns acid
as I watch her put two cups of water

into the microwave, reach for teabags
and sugar. Silence overwhelms the room

until she puts the steaming cups onto
the table. *Get the cream, please.*

I go to the refrigerator, take the cream
from its reserved spot on the top shelf.

Mama pours a little in each cup, hands
me the carton, which I return to its place.

Wordlessly she hands me a cup, takes
a sip of her own, gestures for me

to do the same. The tea is sickeningly
sweet, but I don't dare not drink it.

Finally she says, *There can only be one
explanation for such total disobedience.*

Head spinning, I wait for her to finish.
You are obviously possessed by demons.

A Poem by Seth Parnell
Demons

*I never believed
in demons or monsters
lurking under my bed.
But lately I've started to*

                                                   wonder

*if evil hasn't in fact
infiltrated this world,
slithering streets and
sidewalks, wearing*

                                                   what-

*ever disguise suits its
immediate purpose.
When a choirboy
is molested, is it by*

                                                 the devil

*in a priest costume?
Or does Satan play
a more clever game
to get what he*

                                                 wants?

*To win the contest,
accomplish his goals,
might the prince of hatred
mask himself as love?*

Seth
I Never Realized

What a bogus holiday Mother's
    Day is until I didn't have
    a mother anymore. No one
    to send flowers to. No one
to cook a special breakfast for.

The ironic thing is, my mom
    used to call Mother's Day
    a "Hallmark holiday." You
    know, something invented
to buy pricey greeting cards for.

    I know how much my men
        love me, she said more
        than once. *I sure don't need*
        a three-dollar card or candy
    to prove that there fact to me.

Regardless, Dad and I
    always sprang for some
    silly card, with glittery
    roses, spring greenery,
and flowery sentiment.

Maybe Hallmark should invent
        some new holidays, like Dead
        Mother's Day. They could tweak
        their old motto: *When you* still
care enough to send the very best.

Only where would you send it to?
        Better yet, how about Breaking
        Up Day? They could invent a new
        motto: *A cheerful good-bye when
you don't give a damn anymore.*

No Card

To ease the pain of Loren
      leaving today. Part of me
      doesn't want to see him.
      I'm not much good at
good-byes. But the bigger

part wants to hold him one
      last time. Wants to haul
      him off into the bedroom,
      make love to him, convince
him he can never go away.

Dread simmers in my gut.
      Approaching Loren's door,
      it works itself into a full boil.
      I reach for the bell, change
my mind, let myself in with

the spare key Loren gave me.
      "Hello?" Even as the word
      slips past my lips, I know
      he's not here. He rented
the apartment furnished.

Couch. Coffee table. Easy
      chair. Nothing missing.
      Nothing except Loren.
      His absence overwhelms
the room. "Loren?" I say it,

knowing it's useless, follow
      the silence into the bedroom.
      The closet and bureau drawers
      are empty. The only trace
of Loren is a hint of his cologne.

      That, and a note left on
            the bed, beside rumpled
            memories: *Dearest Seth,*
            I'm sorry to have left you
this way, but I couldn't say

good-bye face-to-face. Total
      coward, I know. Rent is paid
      through the end of the month.
      Go ahead and use the place
until then, if you want. I'll

write you once I'm settled, okay?
      I wish I could see you graduate.
      It's such a big day—the start
      of the rest of your life. Enjoy!
I love you very much. Loren.

I Haven't Cried

Since Mom died. I mean, after
       something like that, what's
       left to cry about, right?
       But I let myself cry now.
Loss is loss. Doesn't take

death to create it. My legs give
       way. I slide to the floor next
       to the bed, rest my head
       against the bare mattress.
I can smell him there, smell

us there. I reread the note.
       Phrases jump out at me:
       . . . see you graduate . . . rest
       of your life . . . love you . . .
Suddenly, certainly, it hits me.

Loren won't cheer for me
       when I get my diploma.
       He isn't including himself
       in the rest of my life. He
isn't coming back. Ever.

Why didn't I get that sooner?
　　　All the hurt I've been holding
　　　dissipates, like a ghost in sun-
　　　light. Something dark replaces
it—a black tidal wave of anger.

How could Loren dare say
　　　he loves me? You can't
　　　walk away from someone
　　　you love, leave them
drowning in your desertion.

If love has no more meaning
　　　than that, you can keep it.
　　　I don't want it now or ever
　　　again. Don't want to hear
the word or wear its scars.

I'll go back to the farm,
　　　to fields rich with hope.
　　　Go back to my books, prep
　　　for finals. I'll celebrate leaving
high school. And then what?

Suddenly I'm Thirsty

And not for water or soda.
        What's calling is a stiff
        shot of good ol' Kentucky
        bourbon. Maybe Loren
left a little behind. I go to

the kitchen, half-hopeful.
        But the cupboards, like
        the closet, are not only
        empty but spotless. That's
Loren, okay. OCD clean.

Hell, I need to get out of
        here anyway. I'll go down-
        town, find a way into Fringe.
        I remember Loren saying,
All you need is a sponsor.

So I'll go find a sponsor.
        Some old Viagra-stiff
        queen, hopeful that buying
        a drink means buying a lay.
They were thick as flies

last time Loren and I went
        to Fringe. And hey, if I find
        one, he can think whatever
        he likes. Wanting and getting
are two different things.

Sunday, Late Afternoon

The sidewalks aren't especially
        crowded. I don't want to look
        like I'm anxious for a date, so
        I hang out a half block from
Fringe, trying to find the balls

to go up to some strange, lone,
        obviously gay older dude
        and ask if he'd like to sponsor
        me past the familiar bouncer
at Fringe's front door. And what

will that guy think? And why
        do I care about that anyway?
        Just as I'm sure I should give
        up on this idea, an attractive
man, maybe fifty, gives me

exactly the right kind of smile—
        interested but also hesitant,
        as if he's not positive why
        I'm checking him out. Yes,
I think this one might just do.

The Smile

I return leaves zero room for
    misinterpretation. Where
    did I learn to be such
    a flirt? This is a whole new
side of the not-so-static me.

Wonder if it's business as
    usual for the guy, who
    on further inspection may
    be a few years beyond fifty.
Still, he's not bad-looking,

very well dressed. Familiar.
    I've seen him before. Here?
    I can barely make out his face. . . .
    Yes, here. Oh, I remember.
The guy who stormed off,

leaving the younger guy to
    follow him out the door.
    He's a regular, then. He'll
    know what I mean. I smile,
and he takes that in stride,

doesn't flinch or look away.
　　　　I'll take that as an invitation.
　　　　I walk right up to him,
　　　　hoping he likes the straightforward approach. "Hi. I'm Seth.

I was hoping to get into Fringe."
　　　　His eyes, an odd, almost clear
　　　　blue, travel my body, starting
　　　　around thigh level. Finally
they lock onto my own eyes.

　　　　Pleased to meet you, Seth.
　　　　　I'm Carl. And I happen
　　　　　to be heading there myself.
　　　　　I imagine you're in need
　　　of an escort. Care to join me?

Escort?

Seems to me I'm the one
        escorting him, at least in
        the classic sense of the word.
        I guess he's using it in place
of "sponsor." Sounds less

like Alcoholics Anonymous,
        but more like Rent-a-Guy.
        Whatever. I've got my
        ticket inside. "Thanks, Carl.
I appreciate the invitation."

I fall in a step or two behind
        him, note how well his pricey
        clothing fits his slender body.
        The security dude waves us
right through the door, not even

checking IDs. He recognizes
        both of us, and if he's surprised
        I'm with someone other than
        Loren, he hides it really well.
What I want now is whiskey.

Carl reads my mind, or maybe
　　　　it's written all over my face.
　　　　The first drink is on me.
　　　　What's your pleasure?
Kentucky permeates his accent.

"I'll have a mint julep, please."
　　　　In memory of Loren. Bastard!
　　　　I can't believe he'd leave
　　　　without saying good-bye.
One drink will not be enough.

Carl gives me a funny look
　　　　but goes to the bar and returns
　　　　with two frosty, mint-trimmed
　　　　glasses. He takes a long swallow.
Oh my, that is good, but not

for a novice drinker. Tell me
　　　　who introduced you to this
　　　　li'l libation. If it's a long
　　　　story, so much the better.
He settles back into his chair.

I sip my julep, fight the sudden
        blitz of memory. The second
        swallow is bigger. The minty
        burn clears my throat, trickles
down the esophagus, into my

rumbling belly. A little voice
        warns, "Could be trouble."
        I tell it to shut up, look at
        Carl to see if he might have
heard it. Or at least intuited it.

He wears a patient smile. Oh,
        yes. He asked for the story.
        I don't want to talk about
        Loren. But what the hell?
I'm drinking in his honor.

"I actually had my first one
            of these right here, with my . . ."
            The word sticks in my craw.
            A gulp of bourbon clears
it, raises a nice, warm buzz.

Suddenly I want to talk, and
            before I know it, I have
            vomited the whole tale,
            going all the way back
to Janet and how I lusted

after her football-player
            brother, forward past
            Mom and Dead Mother's
            Day, to Loren's promises.
Betrayal. Ultimate desertion.

Carl Listens

Without comment, except
    a nod every now and again.
    When I finally slow to a stop,
    he raises one finger, gets up
and goes to the bar. He comes

    back with two more drinks
        and a bowl of snack mix.
        Thought you could use both
        of these. He watches me dive
    into the pair before saying,

    One thing I've learned in one
        or two years on this planet
        is to put myself first. Love
        is a fine thing while it lasts,
    but rarely is it permanent.

    We don't know each other
        at all, but if I might offer
        a word of advice, gleaned
        from many relationships?
    He waits for a response,

    and when I offer a nod, he says,
        In lieu of love, lust will do nicely.
        Now why don't I buy us dinner?
        I start to say no, and he hurries
    to add, *No strings attached.*

Two Hours

Four courses of French cuisine
    and two bottles of wine later,
    my stomach is churning with rich food,
    my head buzzing with alcohol.
Carl and I exit the restaurant

and I look for my truck. Where
    did I leave the damn thing?
    "Uh, th-thanks s-sho much for
    a great evening. I have to go.
It's-sh a long drive home."

    Carl assesses my obvious
        condition. *I can't let you*
        behind the wheel like that.
        You can stay the night at my
    place. No worries. It's clean.

"Uh . . . I d-don't . . ." The words
    blur. I can't drive like this.
    "Okay." It's a short walk
    to Carl's tenth-floor apartment.
Once inside, I call Dad, make up

a lie about staying the night
    with some girl I met at a party.
    He sounds relieved, but whether
    that's because he can tell I'm drunk
or because of the "girl," I don't know.

That accomplished, I take
a long look around. The place
is beautifully decorated. Tall
windows overlook the city.
Someday I'll live like this.

I have to pee. Again Carl
reads my mind. *The guest
bathroom is right there. Oh,
you'll find new toothbrushes
in the medicine cabinet.*

Sounds like a plan. Between
garlic, shallots, whiskey,
and wine, my mouth could
use a good scrub. I take full
advantage of the guest bathroom.

When I come out, smelling
of mouthwash and expensive
lavender soap, Carl is in red silk
pajamas. He hands me a matching
pair. *Unless you sleep naked?*

His message is clear, in his words
and in his eyes. I have the choice—
leather sofa or feather mattress.
I remember how he said, *Lust
will do*, and follow him to his bed.

A Poem by Whitney Lang
Follow Me

That's what he said.
Follow me, and find
the meaning of love
in my bed.

                                                   I followed,

found sheets cold
as death. Neither of us
could warm them,
not me, not

                                                   him.

Not a maelstrom
of body heat so intense
it felt like fever. After,
we slept, chilled.

                                                 He tossed

and turned, lost
in some obnoxious
dream. And when we
woke, he ordered

                                                 me away.

Whitney
So Basically

Life sucks even more than it
did before. I mean, everything's
the same on the Mom and Kyra
front. Kyra went back to Vassar,

along with two suitcases stuffed
with trendy new boutique clothes.
Mom went back to tennis and
whatever else she does at her club.

Dad went back to the city, where
he seems to stay for longer and longer
periods. He and Mom barely speak,
even on those rare occasions when

they happen to be in the same room.
Nothing much new there. What's
new is no Lucas, and it has nothing
to do with his graduation, fast

approaching. He tells me he has to
study for finals, but we both know
that's bull. He'll ace them, like he
aces every test, stoned to the nth

degree or not. He's brilliant.
Beautiful. And def avoiding me.
Near as I can tell, it started right
after I gave him my virginity.

Since that day, he doesn't return
my phone calls, and if I happen to
catch him, he always has an excuse
for why he can't see me. Did I do

something wrong? He won't even
tell me that much. Only a couple
of weeks until school's out, plus
summer vacation. Then he's off

to college in San Diego. Not so far,
but far enough I won't see him often.
I want to share this time with him,
burn him into memory so I can

find him there when I need him. How
can he be so selfish as to take that
away from me? One thing for sure.
I'm going to find a way to ask him.

The Way Practically Falls

Into my lap. It's the Friday after
Mother's Day. (Still musing over
how my mom got mad because
I didn't give her a card. Some bullshit

sentimental tripe about what a great
mother she is? What's her doctor
prescribing, and can I get some?)
I'm sitting on the grass at lunch,

not eating as usual, when a shadow
falls over me, drawing my attention.
"What's up, Skylar?" She's never
been a friend. What does she want?

> *Not much*, she says. *Just wondering*
> *if you're going to the party tonight.*
> She stands, left hand perched on
> an all too obvious hipbone.

I may not eat much, but I bet
she throws up what she *does* eat.
Not that I care. "Party? What
party?" I haven't heard a thing.

> She smiles, and something in
> *how* she smiles activates my radar.
> *There's a party at Lucas's house.*
> *You* did *know about it, didn't you?*

Obviously, she's pretty sure I didn't.
But I can't possibly admit it to her.
"Oh. That party. Um, I haven't
decided if I'm going yet."

Really? Her smile grows wider.
*Does that mean you and Lucas
aren't a thing anymore?* She looks
like a coyote eyeing a jackrabbit.

Anger—and a fair bit of confusion—
throbs in my temples. What does she
know? "How is my relationship with
Lucas any of your business?"

Her eyes go marble cold. *Guess
it isn't, if there* is *a relationship.
I heard you two broke up is all.
If I made a mistake, I'm sorry.*

Off she goes, clearly knowing
something I don't. But what?
And how does she know it? Looks
like I'm going to a party tonight.

I Talk Paige

Into driving me. Mom's not home
when she picks me up, so I leave
a note: *Gone to a movie with Paige.*
More like a soap opera, probably.

I have no real idea what's going
to happen, but I've got a feeling
it may not be pretty. I've been
over and over Skylar's remarks,

and I can only conclude that Lucas
said something to somebody that
somehow got back around to Skylar.
Well, fine. If he's having a party,

makes sense he'll be there. And if
he's there, he won't be able to
ignore me. I'll see to that, though
I will try playing "nice" first.

I don't feel nice right now. I feel
angry. Ignored. About the same
way I feel around Mom and Kyra.
Suffering from "Nothing Syndrome."

Lucas Was Supposed to Be

The antidote to that illness.
Instead he has become another
symptom. What is wrong with
me? Why aren't I worth loving?

I say none of this to Paige, of course.
She's thrilled to be going to a party
with real, live guys and probable
substance abuse. Why spoil her fairy tale?

"Hang a left." We turn into Lucas's
neighborhood. Holy crud. This isn't
a party. This is a major sometime-
tonight-a-neighbor-will-call-the-cops

freaking bash. And he didn't
invite me? My earlier irritation
blossoms into full-bodied anger.
"Hurry up, would you?"

> *Where am I going to park?* whines
> Paige, cruising slowly past a mega-line
> of cars. *Looks like the whole
> darn town is here!* She turns

the corner and finally spies an empty
slot next to the curb. *Always good
to get a little exercise before getting
buzzed, right?* She giggles.

Usually I can handle Paige's goofball
laugh. But not tonight. Not right now.
Still, I'm not going to snap. I'll save
that for Lucas. Because suddenly,

without a doubt, I know I've been
dumped. But why? Why? A wave
of tears swells, hot and salty.
"Come on. I think I need a drink."

There's Plenty to Drink

People leak out of Lucas's house,
onto the porch and lawn. Some
I recognize. Others I don't, but
they all pretty much have one

thing in common—sixteen-ounce
red plastic party cups. "Let's go
find the alcohol." I don't wait
for Paige's response, just push

through the crowd, into the house.
I've only been here twice before,
and both times it was a lot emptier.
The alcohol seems to be in the kitchen,

at least that's where most of the noise
is. I work my way through the human
knot, stopping twice to take a hit
off lit blunts. By the time I reach

the kitchen, I've got a nice little
pot buzz going on, something to
mellow the fog of anger. At least
until I walk through the door.

to find Lucas, zipper to zipper
with Skylar. No. How can that
be? Oh! My! God! That whore
was effing taunting me!

Not Only That

But she wanted me to come tonight,
wanted me to see them together.
I played right into it too. Well,
if she wants me in her face,

I'm all the way there. I stomp right
up to them, push between them.
"Excuse the hell out of me!"
Directed at Lucas, who is totally

blown away by my being here,
and not just at the party, but right
here, pressed up against him.
"Thanks for the heads-up."

Directed over my shoulder at
Skylar, who backs out of my way,
grinning like Hannibal Lecter
in *Silence of the Lambs*.

Lucas gives me the stupidest
huh? look ever. "What?" I spit.
"Didn't expect me? Well, FYI, your—
your—friend, there, invited me."

Now he looks confused. *Friend—*
who—what—what do you want,
Whitney? He glances back and forth
between Skylar and me, unsure

of what I'll do next. I'll make it easy,
not that he deserves it. "All I want
is to talk to you. I think you owe
me at least that much, don't you?"

                Uh, yeah . . . sure . . . He dares turn
                toward Skylar, as if asking for her
                permission. He never treated me
                with such respect. Tears threaten.

No. Won't cry. I make my voice
hard. "I'm sure she doesn't mind,
do you, Skylar?" She shakes her head,
and I dismiss her. "Good. Lucas,

I'll meet you in your bedroom,
okay?" He exits the kitchen without
looking at either of us. I start to
follow, change my mind.

First I Pour

A hefty shot (okay, more like four)
of Cuervo Gold. No need to bother
with salt or limes, no worries
about tequila burn going down.

It feels good. Great. May make me sick
tomorrow, but it's stoking the courage
I'm in desperate need of. Another stiff
pour and I head for Lucas's bedroom,

feeling tequila heat creep back up
from my belly, all the way to my face.
My ears are ringing too. Hope I can
remember the way to his bedroom.

Both times I was here before, that's
exactly where we ended up. Nothing
major happened then, but now I wish
it would have. At least if it's over

between us, and it's def looking that
way. But why? I still don't get what
happened. All I did was finally say
okay. All I did was say, "I love you."

Lucas Is Sitting on the Bed

Wearing a completely unexpected
expression—pity. Can that be right?
What the hell? A deep swallow
of Cuervo sandpapers my throat.

I go over to Lucas, drop down on
my knees, rest my hands on his legs,
look up into his eyes, "Lucas, will
you please tell me what's going on?"

        He doesn't answer right away, and
        for some stupid reason, that makes
        me think there's hope for us. But
        when he finally speaks, his voice

        is ice. *When you first told me you*
        were a virgin, I didn't believe you.
        Not a lot of those around, you know?
        But when I figured out you were telling

        the truth, I totally wanted to pop your
        cherry. You were my first virgin, and
        you'll probably be my last. Because . . .
        sorry, but virgin sex really isn't very good.

I jerk my hands off his legs, wobble
to my feet. "F-fuck you! I c-c-can't
believe tha'sh all I meant to you." One
more gulp and I repeat, "Fuck you!"

I Stumble Out the Door

Go in search of Paige. I have to
get the hell out of here! My heart
knocks in my chest. My face is on
fire—with booze and embarrassment.

How could I have believed he loved
me? How could I have given my love
to such an asshole? "Paige?" Did I just
yell that? Everyone is staring. Maybe

that's because tears cascade down my
face, which is probably streaked black
with mascara. "Has anyone seen Paige?"
Someone points toward the living room,

where my dear friend Paige has hooked
up with some guy I sort of recognize
from school. They're making out like . . .
like they're really into each other.

She looks at me, clearly torn between
wanting to help me and preferring to stay
right where she is. "Never mind," I say.
"I'll find another ride home." On my

way to the front door, I pass Skylar,
staring at me with—fuck that!—pity.
"Hope you're not a virgin. Oh, wait.
Forgot who I'm talking to."

Now What?

I go outside, sit on the sidewalk, will
myself not to get sick. Can't call Mom
to pick me up, not here. Don't know if
I've got enough cash for a taxi home.

I reach into my purse, find my wallet.
When I open it, a business card falls
out. *Perfect Poses Photography.*
Wha . . . ? At the bottom is a name.

Bryn Dawson. Bryn? Oh yeah,
hot monkey, the guy from the mall.
I remember his face, the way his eyes
looked at me. Don't suppose he . . .

Nah, Friday night, he's out somewhere,
with some hot female orangutan.
So why does my hand reach
for my cell phone, and why do my

fingers dial his number? One ring . . .
This is stupid. And now he'll have my
number. Two rings . . . Hang up, stupid.
I can just imagine Paige, asking me

what the hey I'm thinking. Three rings . . .
See? He's so out with someone else.
And why would you think, even if he
wasn't, that he'd even remember you?

Must Be Fate

Because someone, I'm assuming him,
answers on the fourth ring. "Bryn?
This is Whitney. You probably don't
remember me, but we met at the mall

and you gave me your card. . . ."
Definitely must be fate, because he
does remember me. I break down
into an inebriated crying binge.

He'll hang up now for sure. But
when I tell him, "Sh-shorry to bug
you, but something bad just happened
and I really need a ride. . . ."

He barely hesitates before he answers,
*No problem, Whitney. Always happy
to help a damsel in distress. Give me
twenty minutes. And directions.*

A Poem by Ginger Cordell
Directions

Why doesn't life come
with them? "Go straight
until you hit sixteen, take a

                                       right,

then proceed slowly
until you're positive
it's okay to hang a

                                       left

toward where you belong."
I guess in someone else's world,
parents are road maps,
who tell you

                                 which way

is the correct direction
to travel. But without
a map, how

                                       do I

know the best route?
Without guidance,
how do I know
which way to

                                       go?

Ginger
School Totally Blew Today

First I got back my history final,
        with a big, fat D on top, despite
all the studying I did. I completely

effed up in that class, and to cop
        the credit, which is a requirement
for graduation, I'll have to do

summer school. Then our Nazi
        PE teacher started yelling at
the back of the pack running laps

        to *Move your lazy buns*. Damn,
                it's like over ninety out there in
        the sun. Still, I probably shouldn't

have yelled back, "Why don't you
        get *your* fat ass out here and run
with us? See how fast *you* can go."

The bitch wrote me up. Detention
        at least. Maybe suspension. To
top it all off, this guy I thought

I kind of liked called me an *emo*
        freak because I put blue streaks in
my hair. Yep. School definitely blew.

I Take My Time

Walking home, puffing on
          a bummed Kool. Don't
care much for menthols, but

I need nicotine to calm my
          nerves. Iris won't really
care if I get suspended. But

Gram will be *so disappointed*
          in me. She'll be spending
a lot more time at home once

they finally release Sandy,
          today or tomorrow. Guess
they have to do a couple more

tests to find out just how bad
          his brain damage is. Right now,
he's learning to talk all over again.

The house is quiet when I open
          the door, quiet except for the TV.
Where are the kids? Something's off.

I can feel it in my bones. "Iris?"
          No answer. But something—
someone?—moves, and suddenly

the TV goes silent. The hair on
　　　the back of my neck rises.
Little waves of panic churn in

my gut. Ridiculous, right? No
　　　murderer would be sitting
there watching TV. "Harry?"

　　　But the face that appears in
　　　　　the doorway doesn't belong
　　　to Harry. *You must be Ginger.*

　　　Iris has told me so much about
　　　　　you. Hey, I like your hair. Rad.
　　　The last word sounds weird,

　　　spoken by the guy, who is maybe
　　　　　forty-five and built like a bull.
　　　Did Iris dump Harry for this guy?

Not like it would be anything
　　　new. "Uh, right. Where is Iris,
anyway?" I need another cigarette.

　　　She and Harry took the kids
　　　　　for ice cream. Say, would
　　　you mind getting me a beer?

Déjà Vu Strikes

Lightning. Without a doubt
    I know I need to play my
cards just right. I want to yell,

"Get the fuck away from me."
    But every instinct screeches
for me to answer carefully.

"Uh, sure." I go to the fridge,
    reach in for a Keystone.
The guy is right behind me,

    beer breath hot on my neck.
        *Iris didn't lie. You really
are a knockout.* His arms wrap

around me, and his rough hands
    go straight to my boobs. I try
to knock them away but am no

    match for his strength. *You like
        it rough? 'Cause I'm just the guy
to give it that way. No extra charge.*

The words burn into my ear. "What?
    What the fuck did you say?" A sudden
burst of will pushes him back, away.

I turn to face him. He advances,
        a thin line of spit leaking from
his mouth to his chin. I stare at

        evil. *I said, no extra charge.*
                Already paid two hundred
        dollars for a good time with you.

        Might as well make it very good.
                He's on me, yanking my hair,
        pushing me to my knees. He flips

        me over. *You're even prettier*
                from behind, know that? I hear
        his zipper lower. It is the loudest

sound ever. "Don't," I try, but it
        sticks, pasted to disgust, lodged in
my throat. Useless to plead. Useless

        to fight. He yanks down my shorts
                in a single swift motion. He is on
        me. In me. Humiliating me in every

        possible way, right here on
                the kitchen floor. As promised,
        he is rough. Biting. Pounding.

Shredding. Ripping. "Please?"
　　　The word bounces off him, ping-pongs
weakly in my ears. Trying

to fight him only fuels him.
　　　For a fleeting second, I think
maybe someone will come

through the door to save me.
　　　And then, despite everything
that's happening to me, I laugh

　　　out loud. Save me? What did
　　　　　he say? *I already paid for
　　　a good time with you.* I've been

sold. And just who would
　　　sell me? The answer is all
too obvious: Iris. My mother.

And as he finishes, all sticky
　　　and stinking and revolting,
something else suddenly

becomes crystal clear. This day
　　　was exactly like that other day.
If this guy paid Iris, so did Walt.

When He's Gone

I use wet paper towels to clean
        the mess on the linoleum. Under
the sink, I find the Pine-Sol,

carry it to the shower. It stings,
        which means it's working.
I scrub my body over and over,

washing away all evidence of this
        afternoon. On TV, they want you
to call the cops. Tell. But what do

I say? "Hey. My mom took money
        to let some guy rape me." Who'd
believe that? I go to my room,

stuff clothes into my backpack.
        I'm gone. Where? No clue, but
this will never happen again. I feel

bad, leaving Gram to deal with Iris.
        But she's strong. And with Sandy
home, she'll be here, too. The others

will be safe. I'll write her a letter,
        tell her what she has to know so
she'll never let her guard down.

The Door Slams Behind Me

I stand on the step for a few
        seconds, confused about what
to do next. Can't pause long.

They'll be home soon. Not like
        ice cream takes forever. Only
longer than rape. Fuck! My eyes

burn, and not from the sun, sitting
        smack on the western hills. I stare
into it, and for one mega-brilliant

instant, all I can see is a stab
        of light. My feet start walking
toward it. Where else is there to go?

Throbbing with pain, inside
        and out, I find myself on Alex's
street. Should say good-bye.

She opens the door. *Damn,*
                man. You smell like toilet
        cleaner. What happened?

Alex lets me in and I sink
        into cool dark solace, repeat
the tale of Ginger, paid for.

I Love Alex

Love the way she lets me spew,
        contributing zero commentary,
until I'm obviously finished.

    When I am, what she says is,
        And I thought my *mother was*
    queen of the fucking wack jobs.

    So what are you going to do?
        She listens as I outline my
    non-plan for running away:

    Take off and see where I end up.
        Finally she shakes her head.
    Stupid idea. You can't just run

    off without some idea of where
        you're going and how you'll
    get there. The thing is, after we

    talked about it last time, I started
        thinking about the best way to
    leave this stinking shit hole.

Does that mean she wants to go
    too? "Really?" I hope she came
up with something good. "And . . . ?"

*Remember I told you about my
          dad's old girlfriend, Lydia?
Well, she lives in Henderson.*

*She told me to come visit any time.
          We'll stay with her until we can
find a way to get a place of our own.*

She has thought this through!
          A place of our own? Still . . . "Are
you sure you want to go too?"

*Hell yeah, girl. You can't go
          alone. Besides, there's nothing
for me here. Adventure calls!*

*I checked it out and the bus
          to Vegas costs thirty-five bucks.
No big deal, right? Any way*

*you could come up with maybe
          fifty? I've got a little stashed.
Enough for smokes and Cokes.*

Where could I get fifty bucks?
          The answer smacks me in the face.
She owes me a lot more than that.

I Leave My Stuff

Go on home. No cops, no alarms.
     No one missed me at all. Not
even Gram, who's fixing dinner.

In fact, everything seems so normal
     it almost makes me wonder if I
imagined what happened earlier.

I go over to Gram, give her
     a hug. "Something smells
good. We've sure missed your

cooking around here! Where
     is everybody? Is Sandy home?"
If he is, how can I possibly go?

     Gram keeps stirring her chili.
     *No. The tests they ran tired
the little guy out. They're keeping*

*him one more day, to be sure
     he'll be okay.* Worry weights her
sigh. *He'll be just fine, though.*

Guilt chews at me until a sudden
     whiff of Pine-Sol reminds me
why I'm here. "Where's Iris?"

Gram shakes her head. *She and*
her . . . her friend went out.
I doubt we'll see her tonight.

Perfect. She won't miss it until
morning, earliest. By then I'll be
all the way to Vegas. Now I need

a way back out of here. "Hey,
Gram. I was invited to spend
the night with my friend, Al—"

Probably should make up
a name. "Alicia. We're going to
study for finals. Is that okay?"

Sure thing, hon. I'm glad
you're finally making
some friends. Her smile

initiates a new round of guilt.
Especially considering that not
long after I'm gone, she'll find

out I already messed up on my
finals. Oh, well. By then she'll
have given up on me anyway.

The Kids

Are in the living room, watching
        the boob tube. They don't see
me slip down the hall, and that's best.

I go into Iris's room. Top dresser
        drawer, beneath her underwear—
yech!—there's a navy blue sock,

where she stashes her cash.
        I watched her do it once when
she was too drunk to realize

I was standing right there. Sure
        enough, it's here, stuffed with sex
money. I count out two hundred,

which doesn't include whatever
        Walt paid her. Screw it. I take
the whole wad—four hundred

sixty-nine dollars. In its place,
        I leave a note: *Not even close
to what you owe me. I hate you.*

"Bye, Gram," I call, eyes stinging.
        I ease out the door, into velvet
night, chasing a glimpse of freedom.

When I Come Through the Door

Alex is packed and waiting,
        rocking softly side to side
in a nerve-fueled rhythm.

Wow. I've never seen her
        look so worried. "Are you
sure you want to do this?"

      Her odd movement stills
            and she looks at me with
      shimmering eyes. *I've wanted*

      to run forever, but I was
            scared to run alone. I never
      told you the truth about Paul.

      he's not my stepdad. Mom
            and him never got married.
      When they sent her away,

      he let me stay with him,
            but only if I . . . you know.
      I have nothing here, or

      anywhere, except for what
            I have with you. Let's go
      before he gets home, okay?

The Half-Empty Bus

Idles, preparing for departure.
       The diesel fumes are strong,
but the seats are comfy. No one

cares about Alex and me
       in back, sipping rum from
a water bottle. Before long,

I feel zero fear. Zero pain.
       I flip up the armrest between
us, slip my hand into hers.

Heedless of any prying eyes,
       she kisses me, and I kiss back,
inhaling her intoxicating scent.

My heart dances. My body,
       abused so viciously just
hours ago, at last knows joy.

As the bus begins to roll,
       my lips spill words unspoken
until now. "I love you, Alex."

       I love you too. Now let's get
              the flying fuck out of here.
       Together we break free.

A Poem by Cody Bennett
Flying

Is that what it's like
when you die? Do you
slip out of your skin, go

                 soaring

up into a butterscotch
sky? Do you surf waves
of light? How far?

                 How high?

I hope that's what it's
like, but I'm afraid
it's a lot more like

                 falling

with no net to catch
you, and no way
of knowing

                 how hard

you will hit or where
you'll stop. Will you touch
down back on Earth, or

                 will you land

in the nightmare
you always feared
you'd never wake up from?

Cody
Funerals Suck

This isn't the first one I've had
to go to. There were a couple in
Wichita. But this is the first one
that mattered. Old people are
supposed to die. Jack wasn't old,
and he sure wasn't ready to die.

It's a blistering day, and we're
standing here graveside, dressed
all in black. Fuck you, Jack. How
could you leave us? You swore
you'd take care of us. And now
you're nothing but pickled flesh,

broken promises. Mom is a mess,
although she pretends she's okay
and looks steadier than Cory, who
is completely tattered. The two brace
each other, trying to stop shaking
as the minister drones on about

> *Going home to his heavenly father.*
> Funny, but none of us really thought
> much about heaven until the last
> few weeks. Is there such a place,
> and is Jack already there? Is there
> a chance in hell someday I'll join him?

If Funerals Suck

Wakes are worse. I don't even
know who half these people
are, laughing and drinking and
scarfing the food they brought
so Mom wouldn't have to worry
about cooking for a day or two.

They should just go and leave
the food. Better yet, run to
the grocery store and fill up
the fridge. It's almost empty.
The only thing emptier is my
chest—where my heart used to be.

    The doorbell rings. I open it
    to find Ronnie, a total knockout
    despite how ashen her face looks.
    Is all that pale meant for me?
    Hey, you. Her voice is soft. So
    is the hand that touches my cheek.

    How are you doing? Sorry
    I missed the service. I meant
    to come, but I overslept and . . .
    She shakes her head. *The truth*
    is, cemeteries scare me to death.
    The last word makes her flinch.

"Hey, it's okay. I'm not big on
them either." I take her hand,
pull her through the door. No
one else has even noticed her
presence. Good. "Let's go
to my room, okay?" I want

to hold her, want to make love
to her. Need to feel something
warm and alive. Need to fill
that empty space inside. I lead
her to my disheveled bedroom.
"Sorry it's so messy," I whisper,

pulling her into me. "God, you
smell good." Like baked apples.
Not like flowers. Don't want to
smell those. They remind me
of death. Ronnie rises on her tiptoes,
lifts her slick, honey-sweet lips

to meet mine. It's the sweetest
kiss ever, but it soon becomes
more. I lock the door, guide her
to my bed, and for maybe the very
first time, sex is more than getting
off. This time, sex feels like love.

For the First Time

I stop myself before Big Bang,
look down into Ronnie's violet blue
eyes. "I love you." And at this
moment, I do. And at the words,
surprise (or maybe disbelief)
contorts her pretty face. "What?"

Nothing. She smiles. *It's just . . .*
wow. She undulates seductively,
the rise and fall of her body like
salty waves beneath my own.
Another first, this time no faking
climbing higher and higher, until

she finishes with an amazing
gush and tears of satisfaction.
I love you, too, she exhales softly.
We lie, tangled together, unmoving,
unspeaking. And we both know
this is what sex should be.

All Awesome Things

Must come to an end, damn it
to hell. Ronnie and I are slipping
toward sleep, still intertwined,
when the doorknob rattles. *Cody?*
It's Cory. Good thing I locked it.
Are you in there? Can I come in?

Ronnie starts to scramble.
I hold her tight, put a finger
to my lips. "Shh." Then I say
toward the door, "Just a minute,
okay?" I've never had a girl
in here. He probably thinks

I'm taking care of business,
solo. I really don't want to let
Ronnie go. All the hurt will
come flooding back. But Cory
is waiting. I kiss Ronnie's face,
her neck, lick the shimmer

of sweat from the deep fold
between her breasts. She sighs,
and that makes me want more.
But Cory again bumps the door.
I rest my chin on her belly,
look into her eyes. "Thank you."

We Throw on Clothes

But dressed or undressed,
it's obvious what we've been
doing in here. When I open
the door, Cory is pretty much
amazed. *Oh. Uh . . . sorry. I, uh,
didn't know you . . .*

His face is the approximate
shade of an unripe plum.
Ronnie and I both have to
grin. "No problem, bro. Oh,
this is Ronnie. We've been
going out for a while now."

Cory has no patience for my
method of dealing with grief.
His voice, curt, slices the air.
*Yeah, well, people are starting
to leave. Mom's looking for you.*
He pivots sharply, leaves the room.

I start to apologize, but Ronnie
stops me, stroking my lips with
soft fingertips. *It's okay. He's
hurting. And your mom needs
you right now. I should go.* Her
kiss is a bittersweet good-bye.

One by One

Everyone leaves. Mom stands
at the door, looking worn. Torn.
Emptied. She has managed the day
so far without breaking down.
But now she dissolves. I go to her,
put my arm around her shoulder,

steer her to the sofa. "Sit down.
I'll get you a drink." Something
strong, to help her sleep. She hasn't
slept much since the day Jack up
and left us. Mom isn't much of
a drinker. I pour her three fingers.

She accepts the brandy without
protest. Sips it slowly, stares out
the window. Finally she says,
I never believed this day would
come. Some stupid part of me kept
insisting the doctors were wrong.

Oh God, I miss him so much already.
What am I going to do without him?
She swallows the last of her drink
in a giant gulp, throws her face
into her hands and sobs. I want to
help. But I have no answers.

I take her glass, go to refill it.
She deserves a good drunk, and
so do I. As I pour, Cory comes
in, checks out the brandy bottle
with covetous eyes. Oh, why not?
Mom won't care today. We sit

on opposite sides of our mother,
downing alcohol that cannot warm
the death chill infiltrating us, inside
and out. Soon the silence becomes
overwhelming, and Cory turns on
the TV. Doesn't matter what's on.

The three of us get drunk together,
semi-listening to the announcer
on *Sports Central*, droning on about
Jet Fuel, the unlikely winner of both
the Kentucky Derby and Preakness,
his even unlikelier odds of winning

the Belmont Stakes, and so the Triple
Crown. When Mom starts to nod
off, I help her to her feet, down
the hall to her room, gentle her onto
her bed. "I love you, Mom. Don't
worry. Everything will be all right."

Why Do I Keep Saying That?

Will everything be all right? How
the hell would I know? Fuck this!
Jack, if you weren't already dead,
I swear I'd . . . I'd . . . My legs
give and I don't fight, sinking
to the floor beside the bed Mom

and Jack shared for so many years.
She snores softly, and I hope she
isn't trapped in some disturbing
dream. I look around the room,
still so full of Jack. His clothes
drape the chair beside the window.

His shoes form a straight line just
inside the closet. The scent of Brut
deodorant lingers, as does a vague
hint of medicines, sweated despite
antiperspirant. Pictures of him and
Mom hang on the walls, and one of

my favorite family photos—camping
at Lake Mead—sits front and center
on the dresser, beside his belt and
wallet. Where are you now, Jack,
having left all this behind? Are you
whole? Is any of you left here?

Also on the Dresser

Is a stack of mail. From here,
I can see much of it is unopened.
I get up, go sort through it. Bills.
Power. Water. Trash. Mortgage.
Hospital. Doctor. American Express.
And there will be more coming.

Funeral home. Cemetery. Jesus!
Insurance won't take care of it all.
Neither will Jack's pension. I've got
a paycheck coming, but that barely
covers my own expenses. Stop!
Can't think about this now. Not today.

One day, at least, to mourn. One
day to try and forget about death.
Mom's totally gone. I need to get
high. Wacked. Out-of-my-brain
fried. No need for Mom to see
bills first thing when she wakes up.

I scoop everything off the dresser,
into an empty shoe box lying on
the floor. Jack wore new shoes
to his funeral. A big, fat joint is
calling my name. And after that,
I need to hear Ronnie's voice.

Bud and Booze

May not exactly cure what ails
ya, but partner 'em up and they'll
definitely make you forget it for
a while. I turn on my computer,
and the first thing that pops up
on my Yahoo page is news headlines.

And there, again, is Jet Fuel.
They're laying odds against him.
Which makes me wonder . . . Yeah,
oh yeah, there it is—an online Sportsbook
and yes, they are most definitely
taking bets on the Belmont, as well

as just about every professional
sporting event out there, from soccer
matches to major league baseball.
Why didn't I think of it before?
If there's one thing I know about,
it's baseball. Been a Kansas City

fan since I could spit, and the Royals
are looking good this year. I want
in on this action. First I need to set
up an account. Let's see. All I need
is a credit card and something to
prove I'm eighteen, which I won't be

for over a year. But where there's
a will—and I've definitely got
that—there's a way. It comes to me
suddenly that the way just walked
into my room in a shoe box, along
with a pile of bills. Jack's wallet

has three credit cards in it, along
with his driver's license. This may
be a gamble, but I'm betting they
won't be checking to see whether
or not Jack Bennett is dead or alive.
Not as long as the cards are good.

I sort through the stack, locate
the AmEx and two Visa bills,
check available credit. Damn right,
more than I thought. Cool. In less
than five minutes, I've got an
account set up and a hundred

smackeroos riding on tonight's
Royals game. When they win,
I'll pay the electric bill and buy
some groceries. Meanwhile,
I'll polish off this roach.
And I'll give Ronnie a call.

The Pot Buzz

Should make me feel better,
but all it does is combine
with the alcohol to make
loneliness hit like a freight
train. Mom's asleep, Cory's
out somewhere, doing who

knows what god-awful things.
Jack's dead. Dead. The word
repeats itself over and over.
Dead. Damn, man. Dead.
I need to hear Ronnie's
voice. She answers her phone

on the first ring. *I thought
you might call. Are you okay?*
She knows I'm not, but waits
for me to tell her so. *Do you
want me to come over? Vinnie's
here. He'll give me a ride.*

"Oh God, Ronnie, yes. I need
you." I do, and it feels awful
and wonderful, all smooshed
together. We'll make love, and
I'll forget about the Royals.
Forget about Jack. Forget . . . Dead.

Stinking Royals

Can't believe they lost last night,
and to the stupid Mariners to boot.
Oh, well. That means they have to
win today, so I'll lay down two
hundred. And while I'm at it, I'll
put fifty on St. Louis. Why shove

all my eggs into one flimsy carton?
Mom never even missed Jack's
wallet or the bills. She woke up,
fighting a hangover headache.
Me, being a hangover expert,
I convinced her to try a little hair

o' the dog. Cory didn't feel much
better. You'd think his tolerance
would be taller built by now.
The two of them are napping.
Good. I can't stand seeing so
much pain in two pairs of eyes.

Speaking of two pairs, just won
sixty bucks at poker. Almost made
up for the hundred I dropped
yesterday. My luck is coming
around. Just in time. Because
beyond major league baseball,

I'm planning on laying a major league
bundle on Jet Fuel. The odds on him
just keep growing longer and longer.
I'll wait a couple of days, see how
long they'll go. But right now,
a thousand-dollar bet on the win

could net almost twenty big ones.
Twenty thou would pay an awful
lot of bills. And now I need money
for my insurance. Between Jack
and Ronnie and spending a lot
of time in front of my computer,

I lost my job. Not that I care. Jobs
like GameStop are a dime a dozen.
And anyway, I've got bigger plans
than spending my days directing snot-
nosed kids to Pokémon Purple. High
finance is in my immediate future.

A Poem by Eden Streit
My Future

Is meaningless now,
flavorless as an icicle
melting, drip by

                                    drip

to puddle and freeze
again upon shadowed
ground. They say to

                                    drop

the pretense, as if
confessing my heart
was a game of charades.

                                    Tears

such as these could
only be born of soul-
ripping sorrow. They

                                    fall,

in relentless procession,
summer rain upon
parched playa,

                                    relentless.

Eden
Demon Possessed

Apparently, that's the real definition of falling
in love—Satan implanted some evil angel

inside me to steer me away from God's family.
And it isn't only Mama and Papa who think

so. Or claim to, in the name of the Almighty.
Almighty dollar, that is. Samuel Ruenhaven—

who *strongly prefers* being called Father—
graduated seminary the same time as Papa.

But Father's path led him to the stark sand
of northeastern Nevada, where he settled

a sizeable chunk of desert he dubbed Tears
of Zion. Oh, it's a very special place,

where Father and his "disciples" rehabilitate
incorrigible youth. Exorcise demons.

I've been here almost a month. Mama delivered
me personally, after slipping enough Lunesta

into my tea to knock me out for eleven hours.
When I finally woke up, we were bumping along

hundreds of miles from home. It will never
be "home" again for me. I hate it. Hate Mama

worse. When she saw me conscious that day,
head thumping from a narcotic hangover, almost

immediately she started in quoting Old Testament
scripture. That was the extent of our one-sided

"conversation." She never said another word
to me. I tuned her out, concentrated on trying

to connect psychically with Andrew, who
could have had no idea what happened to me.

I didn't know the details then myself. Couldn't
have guessed where we were headed. Even

when we pulled through the Tears of Zion gates,
I had no clue what was coming. I began to suspect

it wasn't good when Father waddled out to greet
Mama. She offered a hand, free of emotion,

and her plea was simple: *Do whatever
it takes to bring my daughter to her senses.*

Father's Methods

Are likewise uncomplicated. You can sum
them up in a single word: Deprivation.

No food for the first three days. Water only.
Flushing poisons, he claimed. *Cleansing*

body before examining soul. Since then,
an unvaried daily thousand-calorie diet—

oatmeal, thin soups, flat bread. Minimal sleep,
even now. *The subconscious is Satan's*

classroom. The worst thing is the isolation.
I rarely see anyone but Father and his disciples—

creepy guys who always dress in bleached white
jeans, matching T-shirts. And the sad, sick thing

is I'm almost glad to see them. I know that's
the point. But I don't know how to fight it.

I spend every day alone, silence squeezing
me until I think I'll go totally crazy. Insanity

might, in fact, be better. I'm supposed to be
reconsidering my choices. But all I do is pace

the perimeters of this featureless room, thinking
about Andrew. And how completely I love him.

Is He Thinking

About me? Wondering where I am?
Where is he? Home? Looking for me?

Or has Mama decided to have him arrested?
I have no answers. Can't process clearly.

My brain feels like day-old mush. Unstirred.
Undisturbed. Left for scavengers. And speaking

of bone pickers, the cloying scent of rabbit
brush precedes Jerome through the door.

As Father's believers go, Jerome is the least
offensive. Not that he's good-looking.

He's short, partly because he carries himself
as if his shoulders are weighted with iron.

What hair he has left is thin, reddish. It reminds
me of an alcoholic's morning eyes. His nose

is shaped like a toucan's bill, and the watery orbs
just above it look at me with a mixture

of sympathy and . . . lust? He places a tray
on the splintered table. *Eat hearty.*

"Right. Lukewarm oatmeal. Mmm." Unlike
some of the other disciples, Jerome allows

me a fair amount of sarcasm. *Lukewarm
is better than cold. And . . .* He glances around

the room, as if some voyeur stands in the corner,
watching. Then he takes something from the tray.

*Look what I brought you. Promise you
won't tell?* He holds out a napkin, unfolds

it slowly, revealing three beautiful strawberries.
First crop. Delicious. And just for you.

Their sweet red perfume permeates
the room's stale air. My mouth waters.

I start to reach for them, reconsider,
snatch my hand quickly away. "Why me?"

He creeps toward me, baiting, pallid
tongue circling his mouth suggestively.

Because I like you. He puts a berry
to my lips. *And because you're beautiful.*

Instinctively I suck the fruit onto my tongue,
crush it against the roof of my mouth, go weak

at the intense rush of pleasure. "Thank you." It
comes out a whisper. "I promise not to tell."

Jerome Isn't Quite Finished

He takes my hand, caresses it gently before
placing the other two berries on my palm.

If you're really good at keeping secrets . . .
His eyes bore into mine. Something feral

pacing there. *We could have a little fun.*
If you be good to me, I'll be really good

to you. Strawberries are just the beginning.
Cheese. Meat. Chocolate. Maybe even some

shampoo to use instead of that vile soap.
He touches my hair. *I bet it's pretty*

when it's clean. I bet it smells like rain.
Here now. What did I say? Don't cry.

A recollection clutches my throat,
chokes. It's Andrew's voice, surfacing

like a creature, dead and bloated,
from deep sea. Smells like rain.

Pain throbs. No, not pain, not even
agony. Something there is no word for.

Something I can't fight. Can't fight. Can't.
All I can think to do is say, "S-sorry."

My head spins. My legs go numb.
Jerome catches me as I collapse, and my tears

      soak into his bleached white shirt. *Okay,*
      baby, he soothes. *Go ahead and cry.*

I should jerk away, out of his arms, but
his gentle rock cradles my loneliness.

There is nurturing here, and it comes to me,
with a whoosh like sudden wind, that there just

might be a way out after all. And that way
could very well begin and end with Jerome.

So When He Kisses

The top of my head, I stay perfectly
still against him. And when his hands

begin a slow journey over the landscape
of my body, I grit my teeth. Do not

protest. Will not complain. Forgive
me, Andrew. Please understand.

It's my only way back to you. But
I won't give him everything.

I go as far as to let him open my blouse,
touch beneath my bra. Now he kisses

down my neck, to the skin he has just
exposed. Drawn tight up against him,

I feel him grown hard against my thigh.
Now it's he who shakes. Shivers

with hunger, and just like that, I am
in control. I push him away, but tenderly,

like a mother convincing the infant
at her breast that he's had enough.

I make my voice light. "That's all
you get for three strawberries."

He is pliable. Clay. He smiles, clearly into
the game this has unmistakably become.

*Fair enough. Father would probably miss
me now anyway. Just one question . . .*

He helps himself to a final taste.
What will you give me for ice cream?

I back away, closing buttons. Reach
down deep for the "inner whore"

Father claims all women harbor inside.
I smile. "Häagen-Dazs or store brand?"

The Door Locks

Behind Jerome, who promised
to *see what I can do* about Cherry

Garcia. Dirtied, I drop to the floor, tuck
my back into a corner, as if walls could

protect me. Lord, please forgive this
sin. What I've done. What I may do,

though I'm not exactly sure what that
might be. All I know is I have to escape

this place, run far, far away. From here.
From home. Toward what, I don't know,

except somehow, some way, that "what"
must bring me closer to Andrew. I'm tired.

Hungry. I glance at the bowl on the table,
oatmeal grown granite cold inside it.

I want pancakes. An omelet with sausage.
I want the key to this unbarred cell.

Jerome has perhaps offered it, if I will
only reach for it. I close my eyes. Think

of Mary Magdalene. What was her prison?
And how far did she go to get the key?

Some Biblical Scholars

Believe Magdalene wasn't really
a prostitute at all, but the woman

most loved by Jesus. A few even
think they might have been married.

Papa preaches that she was a whore,
reformed by the love of Christ. No sex

involved in the reformation. Mama echoes
this tale. But Mama thinks I'm a whore

too. A laugh bubbles up, bounces off
the barren walls. What incredible irony.

Sorry, Mama. Making love with Andrew
didn't make me a whore. But sending me

here might very well do exactly that.
I have nothing to lose. You've already

stolen everything important. Made me
an outcast. Tossed me into this wilderness

prison. And now the question becomes:
How far will *I* go to get the key?

To Know That

I need to find out what Father has in store
for me. We meet every afternoon except

on Sunday (no work on the Sabbath),
for "prayerful counseling." So far,

it's the only time I'm allowed out of my
room, into the sunlight, the sage-tainted air.

There are two long, low buildings, with
rows of doors just like mine. I'm not

the only one here. Once in a while, I see
other kids, working alone in the garden

or shoveling manure from the chicken
coops. Punishment? My guess is reward.

There are smaller cottages, too—staff
residences, I'm sure. A large house looms

in the distance. Father's, no doubt. Wonder
if there's a Mrs. Father. Probably not.

The chapel is large, with rows of chairs,
so I imagine there are Sunday services

that I'm still not holy enough to attend.
Don't know if there are classrooms

somewhere, or if any of us juvenile
delinquents are allowed schooling

other than what's taught in the Bible.
It's the only book I have in my room,

and I have to admit with no TV or other
distractions, I've read more Old Testament

here than ever before. Today as I walk,
escorted, to the chapel, the compound

looks deserted. How many of us are there,
biding our time in solitary, entertaining

ourselves with Leviticus? Do those further
on their way toward rehabilitation interact?

How many will actually be rehabilitated?
What exactly does that mean, and how is it

accomplished? How does someone leave
this place? No harm in asking, is there?

A Dozen Questions

Fill my head as I enter the chapel.
Father's office is tucked in back

of the altar. He is working at his
computer but turns and stands

as we enter. *Welcome, Eden. Brother
Stephen, you may leave us.* He motions

for me to sit before launching into
a long-winded entreaty to the Lord

to deliver wisdom. To me, obviously.
Father already knows everything.

I keep that to myself, of course.
In fact, I say nothing as he "counsels"

me on how I might return to the Path
Toward Salvation. Finally he finishes

and actually gives me the opening I need.
Do you have any questions for me?

I pretend thoughtfulness for a second.
"I've had lots and lots of time to think,

and I really believe you've opened
my eyes to my sinful ways. I was just

wondering what I have to do to prove
that to you so I can go back home."

He smiles. But it is a cheetah's smile.
Do you really believe I'm so foolish?

I find no hint of contrition in you.
What I see before me is a liar. Still,

you're not stupid. So you must understand
that your behavior reflects on your parents.

They don't want you to come home, do
not want your tarnish on their sterling

community standing, or for you to influence
your sister to repeat your mistakes.

You will be here for the foreseeable future.
Shall we decide to make the best of it?

Of course. I should have known. "Thank you,"
I say, meaning it. Because he just gave me

permission to do what it is I need to do. I am
completely resolute to leave this place. Soon.

A Poem by Seth Parnell
What I Need

Is something intangible,
and so, unattainable
because it is ever

           changing.

Neither can what I want
be defined. To someone
standing on the

           outside

perimeters of my life,
I might look one
hundred percent

           the same.

But if they had
the ability to split
me open, look deep

           inside,

they would know
the mask that
appears to be

           my face

is painted over
the real me, smoke
and mirrors,

           an illusion.

Seth
Graduation Came and Went

Whoopee. Finally free
 of educational necessity.
 No more pencils, no more
 books. No more Janet
Winkler's dirty looks.

I've got to stop drinking.
 But not right now. What
 else is there to do around
 here? Funny, but not so long
ago, I swore I'd be off to college.

Now I really don't care
 about moving on. What
 was I thinking? I'll never
 go on to school. What for?
My destiny was decided

for me by the circumstances
 of my birth. Hick boy from
 Indiana. What am I going to
 do? Turn into a rock star?
Or maybe run for president?

Yeah, I Know

The state of Indiana has
      produced one of each. But
      neither was gay. So hurray.
      It's farming for me. Oh well.
At least this little piece of

enlightenment has brought
      me closer to Dad. No more
      long afternoons in Kentucky,
      though I do sneak off and
meet Carl every now and again.

Not for love, but for lust.
      As older guys go, he's not
      so bad in the sack. And
      besides, he's incredibly
generous with the same

sort of perks I got from
      Loren. Gourmet dinners.
      Theater and concerts.
      Art house movies. Only
with Carl, the maître d's

know him by name, and sit
            us at view tables. He's got
            off-Broadway season tickets,
            not to mention box seats
at Churchill Downs. I'm not

a big gambler, and know
            squat about horse racing.
            But Carl knows enough
            for both of us. And it is
his money we wager.

Beyond any rush at the rare
            win, I love the atmosphere.
            Rich people, outfitted in
            elegance, sipping mint juleps
and inhaling the extravagant

potpourri of leather, grass
            hay, and Thoroughbred
            manure. It's a sensual
            experience, highlighted by
Carl's commanding presence.

He hasn't made me forget
            Loren, or soothed the sting
            of desertion, but he has made
            me realize that I don't have
to live my life in isolation.

Thinking of Loren

Makes me want liquor.
        Dad isn't much of a drinker,
        but there's usually beer
        in the fridge, and the afternoon
is hot for June. A cold brew

sounds pretty damn fine.
        I'm done tending garden
        for the day. Carrying gray
        water by the bucketful.
Looking up into the sharp

blue sky, no sign of rain.
        We can grow vegetables
        this way, but the corn looks
        mighty thirsty. We could lose
the whole crop, if God

doesn't cooperate. Weird,
        but not a hundred miles
        from here in Illinois, they're
        drowning under monstrous
thundershowers. Just goes

to show the randomness
        of the Almighty's hand.
        Hey, Ma, if you're up there,
        could you put in a good word
for the farm you left behind?

I Go into the Cool

Of the house. "Dad?" He has
        drawn the shades, flipped
        the small window air con on.
        The faux breeze it has raised
blows gently over the sweat

on my face. Aaaaah! Soap
        and water attack the grime
        on my hands, and now it's
        Miller time! I reach into
the fridge, find a frosty can,

        pop the top, take a long
            swallow. A voice falls
            over my shoulder like
            a shadow. *Who the hell*
are *you?* Iron hands—

Dad's hands—grab hold
        of my shoulders, spin
        me around to face him.
        The look in his eyes
is a blend of disbelief and

revulsion. He knows.
        But, "How?" He points
        to the kitchen table, to
        the envelope and pages
lying spread across it.

I gather Loren's letter, glance
        at the words, talking
        about his church, his new
        home, his congregation.
Talking about missing me,

wishing there was a way
        we could be together. It's not
        pornographic, but there is
        enough detail so Dad can
have no doubt what it means.

        I saw a New York postmark.
            Thought maybe it was from
            a college or something.
            My God, Seth. How could
        you? How long have you . . . ?

A vortex of emotions—anger,
        relief, fear—roil together,
        geyser from my mouth,
        "I've been gay—can you
even say the word gay?—

since I was born, Dad.
        This"—I wave the letter
        in front of his face—"is
        who I am. Who I've always
been. I can't change that."

I'd Give Anything

Not to cry. To prove, no
　　　matter my sexual lean,
　　　that I am every inch a man.
　　　But tears overflow my eyes,
stream down my face.

　　　The only good thing is,
　　　　　Dad's crying too. And
　　　　　he's definitely straight.
　　　　　But he says, *No, no, no.*
　　　You can't be . . . He can't

　　　say the word, after all.
　　　　　Thank God your mother
　　　　　didn't find out about this
　　　　　before she . . . It would
　　　have killed her. Sooner . . .

"No, Dad! How can you
　　　say that? Mom would
　　　have been all right with
　　　it. She loved me. Just like
I am. Even if I am gay."

　　　He goes silent. Shrinks
　　　　　somehow, like a corpse
　　　　　too long in the sun. *She*
　　　　　would not have accepted this.
　　　And neither can I. Not ever.

350

"Please, Dad." I reach out
for him but he recoils, as if
"gay" was something you
could catch. Time. It will take
time. That's all. "Please?"

He shakes his head. Hard.
*Homosexuality is a sin, an
abomination in the eyes of
God. Just the thought of you* . . .
His eyes go flat, drained

of love for me. Temporary,
right? *I kept hoping you'd
find the right girl, bring her
home. Get married. Have kids.
But not some—some man!*

*Not in my house. Not in my
face. Oh my God. What if
you have AIDS? Or some
other sick homo disease?*
He slows. Catches his breath.

Considers some moments
before he says, *You have
to go. Pack your stuff and get
the hell out of here.* He turns
his back to me. And I know

there is nothing I can say
        to make him change his
        mind. Still, I have to try.
        I swallow the mounting
hysteria. Keep my voice

low. "I'd say I was sorry,
        but I can't apologize for
        being who I am. I didn't ask
        to be gay. I was born this way,
and if you think it's been easy,

living a lie and knowing
        this day might come,
        you'd be wrong. I'm still
        the same person I was before
you found out. Still your s—"

His head starts moving back
        and forth before I can finish
        the word. "Okay, then. But
        where will I go? I have no job,
no money. How will I live?"

        Still facing away from me,
          he reaches for his wallet.
          Extracts two twenties. Tosses
          them to the floor. *Best I can do.*
        You'll figure something out.

Time

It will take time for him to
        accept this. Right? I *am* still
        his son. No way he can quit
        being my father. Quit loving
me. Not because of this. Right?

Loren's letter is still in my
        hand. I fold it carefully,
        slide it into my back pocket,
        along with the forty dollars
I retrieve from the linoleum.

My room is still my room.
        Isn't it? This has always been
        my haven. My sanctuary. How
        do I leave it, especially knowing
it may no longer be mine to

return to? Because I am who
        I am? I don't understand.
        Nothing is different. Not one
        damn thing, except there's
no reason to hide anymore.

I am not an abomination.
        In fact, I could easily argue
        that God wanted me this
        way. Dad will come around.
All it will take is time. Right?

Meanwhile, I've Been Banished

Damn you, Loren. This is
     all your fault, and you're
     not even around to give
     me a place to stay. I put
in a call to Carl. He's not

home, but I leave a brief
     message, asking if I can
     spend a day or two at his
     place. Hopefully he'll say
okay. Not sure what else to do.

On my way out of town,
     I stop by the cemetery.
     Might be a while before
     I can get back for a visit.
"Hey, Mom. How're things

Up There, anyway?" I kneel
     beside her grave, yank
     the weeds that have grown
     around her headstone. "Guess
you know what's going on

here. I'd appreciate it if you
     could maybe send a message
     Dad's way. A little intercession?
     You're not mad at me, are you?
I mean because of . . ." A fresh

storm of tears erupts.
      "You still love me, right?"
      A little breeze picks up
      suddenly, lifts my hair like
fingers. I'll take that as a sign.

I sit in the cool grass, as close
      to Mom as I can get, at least
      for now. I take Loren's letter
      from my pocket, begin to read,
dunking myself in loneliness.

            Dearest Seth, he begins. No
                  wonder Dad kept reading.
                  *Sorry I haven't written
                  sooner. You probably think
            I've forgotten you. Never!*

            Your touch, your taste,
                  *your scent, are etched
                  in my brain forever. . . .*
                  Why did he write these
            things to me now? Every

sentence brings the pain
      of missing him so alive.
      I read until the letter ends:
      *Our time together will always
remain a treasured memory.*

355

Ba-bump!

Not that I didn't already
       suspect his leaving meant
       he was dumping me for
       good. But to have it put
so succinctly, long distance,

is a two-fisted gut punch.
       And to have a Dear John
       letter be the one to bring
       me so completely down
is more like chopping me

in two, midsection. Why
       write at all? Just to make
       damn sure I knew that he
       was never coming back?
A low throb begins in my

temples, and my eyes glaze
       red with anger. That son
       of a bitch! If he were here,
       I'd rearrange his face.
Not that I'm one hundred

percent sure how you go
       about doing such a thing.
       It's a whole new, horrible
       thought for me. Hell, maybe
I'm a *real* man after all.

I Contemplate the Meaning

Of "real man" all the way
        to Louisville. I cruise
        slowly—I have nothing
        to hurry for—and by
the time I reach the city

limits, I've decided if
        being a real man means
        smashing someone
        in the face or turning
your back on a person

because of their sexuality,
        I'll just stay a girl. Guess
        my dad is a real man
        because he's decided
I'm not. Oh damn well.

I arrive at Carl's door,
        determined not to break
        down. But the minute
        I see his face, hear his
mellow-voiced welcome,

it all comes pouring from
        my mouth. What is it about
        Carl and confessions? He
        fixes strong drinks, listens
patiently. Finally he touches

my cheek gently. *I'm sorry.*
I never dared come out
to my parents. They both
went to their graves without
knowing. *I've regretted that.*

He thinks for a minute.
Finally he says, *I have so*
enjoyed your company.
You have been a balm for
this lonely old man. You may

stay for now, and I'd ask
you to stay longer, but
only yesterday I received
news that my company
has landed a big contract

in Las Vegas. I have to move
to Nevada as soon as I can
put it together on this end.
I'll be there at least a year,
maybe many more, with luck.

Vegas. Hot. Dry. Fifteen hundred
miles away, give or take. Forty
bucks won't cover a ticket. But
maybe I can convince Carl
I'm worth buying a ticket for.

A Poem by Whitney Lang
Worth

How much would you pay
to stay alive? I mean,
if you could somehow
get the money?

What

is your life worth?
Ten thousand? A mil?
How do you measure
something like that?

Is

your life more dear
than a homeless person's?
Or a mercenary's—who
kills innocents for money?

My life

might seem valuable
to a kidnapper or a life
insurance agent.
But what, really, is it

worth?

Whitney
Screw Lucas

Who needs the a-hole anyway?
I hope he and Skylar are totally
miserable together. And, no
doubt, they totally are. But

even if they're totally in love,
I am too, and with someone
so much better than Lucas
could ever pretend to be.

On a scale of one to ten, Lucas
might rate an eight point five.
Bryn is an eleven—classically
handsome, so smart it's almost

scary. Yes, he's a few years
older, but nothing wrong
with maturity. He knows what
he wants, where he's going.

And unlike Lucas, who is a
world-class bullshitter, Bryn, I know
in my heart, would never lie
to me. I trust him with my life.

That Night After Lucas's Party

Just as he promised, it took
twenty minutes (okay, maybe
twenty-five) for Bryn to collect
me, buzzed and brokenhearted.

While I waited, several people,
some of whom I've known
for years, walked on by me
without a word, despite

the steady rivulets of tears
ruining my makeup, streaking
my face. Too much drama,
I guess. And yet, here came

this complete stranger, in his
midnight blue BMW. He pulled
over, double-parked, came around
to open the passenger door for me.

> *Come on, sweetheart. Everything
> will be okay.* He settled me
> into the seat, buckled me in,
> as if I were a little child. *Where to?*

I shrugged. "I don't care,
as long as it's away from here."
Away from there. Away from
him. Away from friends,

not really friends at all,
if it meant you or some guy.
I stared out the window,
watching the procession

of streetlights, begging myself
not to get sick. "Thank you
for coming to get me. I didn't
know who else to call."

       Really? Already driving slowly,
       he took his foot completely off
       the gas pedal. *What about your*
       parents? Or, uh, your boyfriend?

I snorted. "My dad is hardly
ever home. And all my mom
cares about is my sister. And
as for my boyfriend . . ."

I wasn't sure how much to say.
But whatever. "That party was
at my *ex*-boyfriend's house."
There. Complete confession.

Well, not quite complete. Bryn
called me on the rest. *Ex, huh?*
Then why were you at his party?
Want to tell me what happened?

"Can we go somewhere and talk?
I know I shouldn't ask. I'm sure you
have better things to do." I could hardly
believe it when he said, *Not really.*

We Drove Down to the Beach

By the time we parked, got out,
and walked a little way, barefoot
in the cool, damp sand near the water's
edge, I had mostly sobered up.

I sat, combing the sand with my
toes, as I told him pretty much
everything about my pitiful life.
When I talked about Kyra and Mom,

> he kept nodding. Turns out he,
> his brother, and father have a similar
> relationship. *Like Dad, Shane is
> a high-priced criminal attorney.*

> *And me? Well, I'm just a lowly
> photographer. Never mind
> that I've shot most of the top
> modeling talent in this country.*

Which explained the company name
on his business card: *Perfect Poses.*
"So what are you doing in Santa
Cruz? Why not L.A. or New York?"

> He exhaled deeply. *My dad lives
> in Los Angeles. But my mom
> hated the city. She lived here . . .
> until she died a few weeks ago.*

"Oh wow. I'm so sorry. I hope
I didn't . . ." I couldn't finish.
I had sure stuck my big ol'
foot in my even bigger mouth.

*No. It's okay. I came here
to help settle the estate. She left
her house to me. So I really don't
know many people here yet.*

Which explained why he wasn't
busy that night. In need of a subject
change, I moved on to Lucas. "Not
everyone here is worth knowing. . . ."

I told the whole virgin thing. When
I finished, he responded with a hand,
placed gently on my knee. *What an
idiot. Does he not recognize*

*what a gift you gave him, what
an amazing opportunity you are?
You've lost not a thing, lovely
lady. You've lost not one thing.*

Okay, His Syntax

Can be a bit elevated. Overeducated,
maybe, like having a PhD in poetry,
which should come from the heart,
not from some cardboard rulebook.

But hey, nobody's perfect. And Bryn
comes just about as close as a guy
can come. Since that night, we've
seen each other almost every day.

It hasn't been that long—only
a couple of weeks. But day by
day, I tumble deeper and deeper
in love with him. Yeah, it was fast.

Can falling in love be too fast?
I don't think so, and neither
does Bryn. Best of all, he isn't
afraid to tell me he loves me.

The First Time He Told Me

Was the same time as our first
kiss. It was only a few days
after we started seeing each other.
He said he wanted to wait,

       thinking I wasn't quite ready for
      someone new. *I wanted you*
      to be sure. Rebound things can
      be incredible letdowns. So stop

      me if you don't want to hear
      this, okay? I don't know how you
      feel about love at first sight,
      but that day in the mall, I knew

      right away that you were unique,
      a girl who stood out in the crowd.
      And when I saw you sitting there
      on the curb, crying over someone

      who didn't deserve your broken
      heart, I wanted to make everything
      right again for you. I've never
      fallen for anyone so fast!

We were at our favorite beach
hideaway, listening to the symphony
of the waves as the sun set,
tangerine, on the horizon.

Bryn pulled me into his lap,
leaned his forehead against mine,
kissed me softly. *This is so odd
for me, Whitney. I've photographed*

*many beautiful girls. Had flings
with a few. But I never felt for any
of them what I already feel for you,
and we barely know each other.*

*You are more than a pretty face.
You are beautiful inside, and that
beauty radiates, shines like a star.
I know it's wrong—I am a few*

*years older than you—but you have
filled an empty place inside me.*
He turned to look me in the eye.
I love you, Whitney. I really do.

Then he kissed me, and though
I found hunger there, I also found
the love that he professed. And now
I experience that love every day.

We Haven't Made Love Yet

He says he wants me to be very,
very sure I want to, because
he treasures me for more than just
my body. I'm pretty sure I'm ready,

> but that isn't quite "very, very sure."
> Still, maybe today will be the day.
> Yes or no, first he's going to take
> some pics of me. *I want to show you*

> *just how beautiful you are,* he said.
> Then he took me shopping for what
> he wants me to wear—a long, flowing
> skirt and gauzy off-the-shoulder blouse.

> Both white. *A celebration of virginity,*
> was his explanation. *We'll send*
> *a couple to your old boyfriend.*
> He meant that last part too.

It's an incredible day—seventy
degrees, nonintrusive breeze.
Just enough to rile your hair,
carry scents of summer blossoms.

I feel pretty, all decked out in white,
with just enough makeup to enhance
my features, not make them obvious,
as per Bryn's request. Virginal.

We'll Do the Shoot

Where else? At the beach.
But down the coast, away
from town. As we S-curve
along serpentine Highway 101,

I can't help but think about
Lucas and our first time together.
Driving this same stretch of road.
Getting high. "You don't happen

to have any pot, do you?" Bryn
has never offered to get high
with me. Come to think of it,
we've never even discussed it.

He doesn't slow down. *Afraid not.*
I haven't smoked marijuana in years.
I do have some Valium, if you're
a little nervous. In there. He points

at the center console. Valium?
Why not? "I'm not exactly
nervous. But a good buzz never
hurt anyone, right?" I pop one,

wait for it to kick in, watching
the ocean's heave. By the time
we reach Bryn's chosen location,
I'm feeling pretty darn fine.

We walk down the deserted
beach until he finds a nice stretch
of undisturbed sand. *This will do.*
He unpacks his gear, then checks

me out, all up and down. *Take
off the bra and panties, okay?
We want a glimpse—a hint—
of what's under all that white.*

I do as instructed, allow Bryn
to position me exactly the way
he wants. He sits me, skirt tucked
provocatively between my bent

legs, and when he goes to move
my arms, his hand brushes against
the fabric covering my breasts.
My nipples go hard immediately.

Lovely, he says, assessing.
Exactly what I'm after. Then
he kisses me sweetly. *Exactly
what I'm after.* He makes me

feel like a real model—beautiful,
every man's desire. When he's
finished with his camera, he lays
me back on a thick blanket.

You are exceptionally lovely,
he says, brushing sand from
my hair. He settles beside me,
props himself on one elbow.

Bryn's free hand begins a slow
exploration of my body, over
the sheer fabric, tracing each
curve. *You don't mind, do you?*

Eyes closed to the lowering
sun, brain suspended on a Valium
cloud, I sigh, lift my head. "Kiss
me." He does, and then he lowers

his mouth to other, much more
intimate places. So this is making
love! Well, not quite. I want to know
the rest. "Make love to me."

You're sure? he asks, but there
can be no doubt I'm very, very
sure. Bryn guides me to a place
Lucas has no idea exists.

Okay, It's Kind of Disturbing

That, immediately after learning
the meaning of "orgasm," I think
of Lucas. Maybe it's because
I need to know, "Was that okay?"

      Oh, darling. Bryn kisses across
      my face. *That was more than*
      okay. That was extraordinary.
      With just a little practice,

      you will become perfection.
      And I so want to be . . .
      want to be your coach. But . . .
      He rolls away from me—déjà

vu of the most terrible kind.
I jerk upright, reach out for him.
"What? What did I do?" Oh my God,
he's not going to dump me too?

      Nothing, baby. He accepts my hand
      against his cheek. *It's just that*
      I got a call this morning, from
      an agency in Vegas. They want me

      to shoot a beauty pageant, plus
      some pre-event studio work. I'll be
      gone for several weeks. Oh, sunshine,
      I am sure going to miss you!

My Summer

Just grew a whole lot darker.
"Oh." It is barely audible, but
even if I could make words come
out, I wouldn't know what to say.

       He takes my hand, kisses
       my fingertips. *I probably*
       shouldn't have . . . you know.
       But I couldn't help myself.

       You looked like an angel.
       And now I want you more
       than ever. If only you could . . .
       He shakes his head. *Never mind.*

"What?" What he suggests
thrills me. Scares me. Tempts
me. And, finally, "I'm not sure
how I could pull it off."

       I know. I didn't really think
       you could. But it would be
       like a dream to spend every day
       with you. He pulls me to my feet,

       and we wander up the beach
       toward the car, his invitation
       echoing inside my head: *Come*
       with me. . . . Come with me.

Mom's Home

When Bryn drops me off. She takes
one look at me—how I'm dressed,
the state of my hair and makeup—
goes off on a rant. *Where in the hell*

have you been? And with whom?
I never gave you permission to go
anywhere. She catches her breath.
You do remember "permission"?

Suddenly she cares? "You do
remember that you actually have
to hang around the house long
enough to *give* permission?"

Rant becomes rave. *You shut*
the hell up. And you'd better
understand that you may not
leave this house for any reason.

I want to scream. But silence
is the better course of action.
"Whatever." I go to my room,
flop down on my bed. Where—

and why—did she find this sudden
case of maternal instinct? I consider
my next move carefully. Call Bryn.
"Okay. I'll go. Pick me up at ten."

A Poem by Ginger Cordell
Move Carefully

Who knows what lurks
beneath that beautiful
rock you want to turn

over?

I once thought
I wanted to live
on a mountain. But

how high

before the altitude
would take its toll?
Now I want to dive

under

deep water. But can
I hold my breath,
stand the pressure?

How low

can I go, and will
Fate keep the sharks
far away, or

will Destiny

in fact send some
hideous sea creature
to catch me in its jaws,

drag me down?

Ginger
They Call Vegas

Sin City, like calling it what it is
        somehow legitimizes the name.
Las Vegas *is* Sin City. Whole lot

of sinning going on, from fancy
        high-rise casino rooms to sleazy
well-off-the-strip motel dives.

People come here specifically
        to sin. But I wonder whether
it's really true that "what happens

in Vegas stays in Vegas."
        People stain themselves here.
I bet, no matter how hard they

scrub themselves after sinning,
        when they go home, a certain
amount of stain remains visible.

Then, I guess, it's up to the spouse
        or significant other to recognize
the meaning of that dark splotch

ghosting beneath the bleach.
        Most of 'em probably don't want
to look. Don't want to know.

The Reason

I know so damn much about
    the sinning is I have pretty well
been pushed into causing some

of it. As sin goes, at least so
    far, my own participation
has remained fairly mild.

See, when Alex and I first hit
    town, like a few weeks ago,
Lydia seemed okay with giving

        us a place to crash. Alex called
            her from the bus station. *Hey,*
        girl. You said to look you up if

        I ever made it to Vegas. Well,
            me and a friend just got here.
        Could you come pick us up?

It was early morning, and
    Lydia was not real happy
about having to pull herself

out of bed. We waited a couple
    of hours, sipping coffee, until
she finally showed, took us back

to her small tract house south
          of the city in a burb called
Henderson. She keeps her place

neat, with pretty flowers in trim
          beds, giving the impression
she wants to give—legitimate.

See, for a while Lydia worked
          as a stripper in a fairly nice
club near the Stratosphere.

          I made pretty good money.
                    Most of it went to the house,
          which took a big cut for keeping

          the girls safe. I did all the work,
                    they reaped sixty percent of
          the bennies. Hard to swallow.

So Lydia got smart, started her
          own business—Have Ur Cake
Escorts. Now she takes a cut from

          the girls (and guys) whose "dates"
                    she sets up. *I still strip for fun*
          once in a while. All on my own terms.

Her Neighbors

Are completely clueless
  about her means of support.
They think she's a showgirl.

The ultimate Vegas dream.
  Anyway, she let Alex and me
move into her spare bedroom.

    But not for free. *You can stay*
     for a week gratis. After that,
    I'd appreciate a little rent.

    She never asked why we were
     there, although she did mention
    Alex's dad. *How's he doing?*

  Alex shrugged. *Same ol',*
    you know? But if he happens
  to call, I don't want to talk to him.

Far as I know, he never did,
  and Lydia let the subject
drop. Alex and I looked for

under-the-table jobs, but they're
  hard to find, unless you're good
with pulling weeds for five

bucks an hour. A week came.
A week went by. Two. Plus
a couple of days. Finally Lydia

said something. *Okay, here's*
the deal. Both of you are pretty
girls. Great bods, with that fresh

look guys (especially old ones)
appreciate. You could make
boatloads taking off your clothes.

The clubs are careful about
underage girls, but work for
me, no one will check your IDs.

My first reaction was no way
would I ever let evil old pervs
see me naked. That's when Lydia

mentioned how much money
we could make. *Easily five*
hundred a night. And that's no

touching allowed. Bachelor
parties alone could make
the two of you very comfortable.

381

What She Forgot

To mention was that her cut
        for setting us up in the exotic
dancing business was one-third

the hourly rate. Tips are ours
        to earn and keep. And hey,
considering Lydia handles all

Have Ur Cake calls, screenings,
        and advertisement, she's
worth every penny. As per her

        well-advised counsel, Alex and I
                work exclusively as a team.
        Sooner or later, Lydia said,

        *you'll have to deal with a jerk
                who won't want to hear "no
        touching allowed," if you decide*

        *to stick to that. With two of you,
                you've got a fighting chance,
        or at the very least, a witness.*

So far, though we've had many
        requests for more, and a few
grumbles when we say no way,

the men have all honored
          the "look but don't touch"
rule. Our two-for-one fee

is three hundred an hour
          (a bargain!) plus tips for
straight dancing. Private

lap dances are twenty dollars
          per song. Girl-on-girl action
adds another hundred to the tab.

Besides Lydia, we give a cut
          to our regular taxi drivers,
who keep us off their meters.

They're cool and weren't hard
          to hook up with. Pretty much
everyone in Vegas is a scammer.

As for the actual stripping,
          Lydia gave us some pointers.
Turns out I'm a better dancer

than Alex. Her boobs are bigger,
          though, and really beautiful.
I swear I never knew I leaned

toward girls until I met Alex.
   Guess I never let myself lean any
way at all. Didn't dare get close

to anyone, male or female.
   But Alex and I are tight. I love
her heart. Her brains. Her body.

The men we perform for like
   when we dance with each other,
breast-to-breast or belly-to-ass,

tan skin against pale, ebony hair
   on blue-streaked blond, fingers
touching hidden places we won't

let "clients" touch. Powerful!
   That's how I feel, seeing how
helpless we make them. I so enjoy

reducing them to masturbation.
   It's like they are masturbating
for me, and I can control when

they come by how I move
   my body, what I let them see.
It's a game I win every time.

Another Few Weeks

We'll have saved enough
       to get our own place. Maybe
a nice little townhouse closer

to downtown, where most
       of the action is. Tonight
we've got a bachelor party.

Great gigs. Tips are good.
       And when there's a crowd
in the room, the dicks mostly

stay hidden. I'm standing
       by the window, keeping
watch for the cab, when Alex

       comes into the room, wearing
              a yummy short leather skirt.
       Just got a ten o'clock. We should

       be finished with the boys before
              nine. Younger guys tend to get
       started early. The best man booked

       us for seven, and they should all
              be well on their way to passing
       out before we even get there.

Which is why we collect our
          basic fee up front. Don't want
to get caught with our fingers

in some drunk guy's wallet.
          Of course, we do hope they
stay awake long enough to

reward our girl-girl routine.
          We knock on the condo door
at seven on the dot. The guy

                    who answers is pretty cute.
                              Hello, girls. Come right in.
                    Can I get you ladies something

                    to drink? We decline and he
                              escorts us inside, where a half
                    dozen guys are ogling cable porn.

          While I ask Best Man for cash
                    up front—six hundred, split
          seven ways—Alex flirts. *Okay,*

          boys, where's the groom? We
                    want to treat him right! Where did
          she learn that shtick? *Stripping*

for Dummies? Hah. Anyway,
      once the cash is safely tucked
away, Alex outlines the rules:

Absolutely no touching, or we
      leave immediately. One lap dance
is included, for the groom only.

If any of the rest of you are into
      that, it will cost extra. Tips are
encouraged! Any questions?

      One rat-looking dude pulls
         his eyes from the TV screen
      action. *How much for head?*

A couple other guys laugh
      nervously, but Alex has
it covered. *You'll have to ask*

your buddies. We don't do head,
      except on each other, and that
will cost an extra hundred.

No surprise that Ratman
      reaches into his pocket
for a Benjamin Franklin.

Seven Fifty, Minus Commission

Toward a place of our own,
      Alex and I bid adieu to groom,
Best Man, et al. Poor bride.

            We're giggling as we get into
                Leonard's cab. *What's so
            funny, girls? Care to share?*

            Alex hands over a fifty. *No
                offense, Len my dear, but
            men are just so disgusting.*

            *I mean, really. Would you dare
                beat off in front of your best
            friends?* We crack up again.

            Lenny looks into his rear-
                view mirror, grins. *Only if
            you two were dancing for us.*

It's a short drive to our next
      appointment, in a not very nice
part of town. Lenny promises

            to stay available, *Just in case
                you need a quick ride out
            of here. Be careful, okay?*

Hey, says Alex, *no worries.*
                 But if we don't call you in an
hour, it's okay to come looking.

She gives him a twenty for
            caring and off we go. Unlike
Best Man, this guy is a pug,

short, wrinkled, and bug-eyed.
            He doesn't talk as we handle
the business stuff, but he does

pay extra up front for a three-song
            lap dance. I glance at
Alex, who nods, meaning

she'll do it for him. She knows
            I never could. After a little
girl-on-girl rubbing, she goes

to take care of it. He sits
            very still in his chair, staring
as she strips free of her bra.

Suddenly his hands are all
            over her. "Hey. Cut it out.
Absolutely no touching allowed."

No good. Alex's eyes go just
          a little wild. *Okay, man, we're
out of here.* She tries, but

          the creep snakes his arms
                    around her waist, squeezes
          like a hungry boa constrictor.

          *All I want is a hand job. Give
                    it to me, I'll let you go. You,
          over there, play with yourself.*

          So much for control. Good
                    thing it doesn't take long. He
          finishes with a loud, *Aaaagh!*

He does let go of Alex, who
          wipes her hand on his shirt.
We grab our clothes, throw

ourselves out the door, mostly
          naked. Yank on what we can
at a dead run. Suddenly Alex

          starts to laugh. She holds up
                    a wad of bills. *Stupid shit
          just gave us a really big tip.*

Later, After Several Shots

Of whiskey (Lydia buys
         it for us, as long as we
drink it post-business only),

Alex and I go to bed.
         Fresh from the shower,
her skin is warm and apple-

         scented. I reach for her,
                  but she turns over, away
         from me. *Not now. I'm tired.*

Lately this happens more
         and more. When sex
is your job, it gets harder

and harder to let it be
         about love. "Please, Alex.
Can't I at least hold you?"

She sighs gently, backs up
         against me, into my arms.
Before long, she trumpets

Jim Beam—fueled snores.
         Wish I could laugh about
it. Wish she was really here.

A Poem by Cody Bennett
Might as Well Laugh

Crying is for babies,
little kids. Old people
who somehow can't

                          remember

the way to the toilet,
so have to rely on
Depends. Once,

                          when

I just couldn't hold
it anymore, I peed
my pants in the car.

                          Life

totally sucked until Jack
stopped and Mom got me
some clean ones. Cory

                          made

major fun of me for days!
Please, God, when I get
old, let me have enough

                          sense

to find my way to
the toilet!

Cody
So Lady Luck

Ain't no lady. She's a total bitch,
not to mention a tease. I mean
one minute she smiles, and dice
roll your way. Then she turns
right around and hands you snake
eyes. Three times in a fricking row.

Lately she hasn't even half-ass
grinned at me. Don't know what
it is, but I can't win an effing bet
to save my neck. Not even a little
one, and at the moment, I'm not
so sure I could even manage that.

The Belmont fucked me good.
I scraped together the thousand,
knew in my heart of hearts that
jerk-off Jet Fuel was gonna take
the Triple Crown, despite what
the so-called experts had to say.

That damn horse laid back just
a little from the start. I knew
the jockey was saving something
for the home stretch. Damn, my
heart got to thumping in my chest.
Thought it might give clean out,

especially when they turned
into that final straightaway,
and Jet Fuel found his stride.
I was jumping up and down.
Screaming, "Go, you sucka, go!"
He went. Finish line in sight,

he took the lead by a nose.
A neck. Then, from the back
of the pack, here came Girly
Girl, a stinking filly, no less.
I swear, once Jet Fuel took a look
at her ass, he was done racing.

Didn't place. Didn't show.
Hauled his butt across the line
in fourth. Girly Girl, a true long
shot, paid out forty to one. At
least the experts weren't right
about her, either. But Jet Fuel,

damn the nag, broke my bank
account. I should have known
to bet the filly. Girls always win,
always get their way. Except
when their boyfriends are
freaking penniless losers.

Saturday Is Ronnie's Birthday

I wish I could get her something
special, or at least take her out
to dinner somewhere really nice.
But I'm completely broke. Can't
lay my hands on a dime, thanks
to one too many bad bets. All

I need is one good wager to make
things right. But I don't have seed
money for even the smallest bet.
I suppose I could go stand on a street
corner, panhandle a buck or two.
        The sign could say: DADDY DIED.
        PLEASE HELP ME FEED MY FAMILY.

So far, we're still eating. But
Mom's bank account is definitely
dwindling. She's out right now,
looking for a job. I should be
doing that too, instead of combing
through Jack's clothing, hunting

spare bills, or at least change. One
little bet could make it all right.
Food. Bills. Insurance. Oh yeah,
and bud. I've pretty much had to go
cold turkey on that, and a good damn
buzz would make everything easier.

I've Scrounged

Four dollars, give or take, when
Mom comes slamming through
the garage door. Better exit her closet!
I tuck the cash into a pocket, head
toward the kitchen. She's at the sink,
faucet running, and over the top

of the water splash against stainless
steel, I can hear her crying. I don't
want to scare her, so I make a lot
of noise, stomping across the floor.
Her shoulders droop, so I know
she's heard me. "What's wrong?"

>She keeps her back toward me,
>keeps on scrubbing her hands.
>Only when I touch her does she
>speak. *I don't know what I was*
>*thinking. How can someone like*
>*me find work in Las Vegas?*

>*The only places that will hire*
>*a person my age are Wal-Mart*
>*and McDonald's, and even then*
>*I have to compete with young*
>*people. It's like once you turn*
>*fifty, you become disposable.*

I reach around her, turn off
the faucet. Then I spin her gently
around to face me. "You are not
disposable. Don't ever say that
again. Cory and I need you more
than ever. . . ." Especially Cory,

who needs an intact parent to turn
him around before there's no more
turning. But I can't say that. She's
got more than enough on her mind.
What I say, despite Mom's tears,
is, "Please try not to worry."

> *Don't worry? We're going to lose*
> *the house! The foreclosure notice*
> *will arrive any day. We'll be out on*
> *the street. . . .* Her body shudders,
> and she slumps into my arms.
> I carry her to the sofa. She's light

as weathered bones, and her skin
looks like old paper. "Mom? Mom!"
At my voice, she comes out of her trance.
> *I'm okay,* she mumbles. *Jack's pension*
> *will come through. We can always*
> *rent a little place. We'll be just fine.*

That Phrase Again

More and more, I'm starting
to believe we won't be "just
fine" after all. But I can't let
Mom know I feel that way.
"Yes, we will. You rest now."
She closes her eyes, and I sit

beside her for a few minutes,
holding her hand and brushing
obstinate wisps of hair back off
her face. Foreclosure. The word
has been in the news a lot lately,
especially here in Vegas. But

I had no idea it would ever
threaten us directly. Mom sinks
into troubled sleep. I have to do
something. But what? A job like
GameStop won't pay the mortgage.
Neither will Wal-Mart. So what?

Quick cash-shortage fixes
are plentiful in Vegas. Payday
loans won't work, since I'm
currently not getting paid.
Credit card advances are out,
considering every card in

the household is currently maxed.
(Thanks mostly to me.) One solution
remains. I go into my room, look
around. Not the computer. Not yet.
TV? Check. Stereo? Check.
And in the corner sits one more

dream I'll never attain anyway—
my guitar. I carry TV, tunes, and
instrument to my car, head toward
the far end of the strip, where pawnshops
are plentiful. I choose the one
that claims, "We Pay Top Dollar."

> The little puke behind the counter
> is not impressed by my twenty-
> inch flat panel television, nor
> my pricey Bose Wave Music
> System. *Fifty bucks for both.*
> Neither will he give me much

> for my amazing Martin guitar.
> *Forty.* But beggars have no
> power to negotiate. The dude
> thinks this stuff is hot, anyway.
> As I'm filling out the paperwork,
> he spies the ten-dollar gold piece

(a gift from Jack), hanging on
a gold rope chain (a gift from
Mom) around my neck. *You
interested in a loan against those?*
He eyes them covetously as
I run my fingers over the chain.

Fuck it. They're just things,
right? Still, I can picture Jack,
three Christmases ago, when
he handed me the little present,
wrapped in shiny purple foil.
He was so proud! I haven't

taken it off since that day.
But now I ask, "How much?"
The pissant wants to see them
closer, and after a quick inspection
offers one-fifty. "Two hundred,"
I counter, not expecting him

to say okay. But he does. I walk
out of Superduper Pawn not
quite three hundred dollars richer.
It weights my conscience heavily.
Now the question becomes,
what do I do with the money?

It Won't Cover

Even a quarter of the mortgage
payment. It might pay last month's
power bill, but that's about it.
I can't forget Ronnie's birthday.
Twenty will cover supermarket
flowers and a card. Wait.

My insurance is due. Can't let
that lapse, or the state of Nevada
will slap me with a hefty fine.
Shit. Shit. Shit. Three hundred
bucks is nothing! Maybe I should
turn around, go back for my stuff.

It's evening, thank God, a desert
breeze lifting to fight the almost
unbearable summer heat. As I go
to my car, the streetlights pop on.
They like to keep the sidewalks lit
here in Sin City, especially in

the seamier parts of town, where
crimes are nightly events. Some
are serious—robberies, gang
shootings. Others don't bother
me much. Prostitution, for instance.
A quick glance reveals five or six

working girls, a transgender and
a straight-up guy. Okay, maybe
not so straight. The driver of
the car that stops to make a deal
with him is definitely a dude.
Hey, whatever dings their dongs.

As for the girls, one is kind of
cute. She's young. Doesn't look
all used up, like the other ones.
Actually, the he/she might be
the prettiest one of all. Funny
what the right outfit and makeup

can do for a guy. The next car
to pull over, looking for tail,
chooses him/her. Wonder if
the guy knows for sure what kind
of tail lurks under those Frederick's
of Hollywood panties! Suuurprise!

Speaking of Frederick's, maybe
I'll forget about the flowers,
get Ronnie something pretty from
there. Something I can appreciate
too. Damn, now look what I've done.
I need Ronnie to ding *my* dong.

Frederick Has a Secret Too

And that is, his lingerie sure ain't
cheap. I dropped fifty without
even trying. Oh well. Ronnie will
be happy, and so will I. That leaves
me two forty, minus sales tax on
a red velvet panty/bra set and the price

of a power drink. Insurance. Gas,
at four bucks a gallon. Fuck it! I'm
broke again. Think, Cody, think.
Okay. If I fill the tank halfway,
I'll probably have twenty left for
a small bet somewhere. But where?

Sports haven't been real good to
me lately. Casino betting has always
been better. If I could parlay the twenty
into fifty, I could play poker at
Vince's tomorrow night. I always
walk away from there with serious

cash. Well, more often than not.
Now if I could just figure out a way
to score, I'd be sitting pretty, or at
least not quite so ugly. Wonder how
long the grace period is for my car
insurance. Better look into that.

First Things First

No need to worry about poker
if I don't have a stake, and twenty
won't cut it. Vince's games
have become so popular, he
made it a fifty-dollar buy-in.
I pump eight gallons into my tank,

head on home. I check the mail
on my way past the box. No
foreclosure notices, but plenty
of other bills, including American
Express and B of A Visa. I'll worry
about how to pay those another

day. Inside, Mom has moved
into her bedroom. The door
is closed, and behind it, it's coma
quiet. Cory's door is also closed.
I poke my head in, but he isn't
here. Didn't think he would be.

Not sure how he spends his time.
Pretty sure I don't want to know.
Even Mom doesn't really question
why he's out so late every night,
what time he makes it home.
What he's doing when he's gone.

I go into my room, turn on
the 'puter, navigate to one
of my favorite sites. The account
is empty. But I happen to have
one last card from Jack's wallet.
It's his ATM card, which draws

from Mom's bank account.
I've hesitated to use it because
I had no way to replace any cash
I took out of it. Now, a few bucks
in my pocket, I'll make a deposit
first thing in the morning.

A hundred should be plenty.
Ten-dollar blackjack bets are
pretty safe, and wins can add
up quickly. Hand number one:
draw. Nothing lost anyway.
Hand number two: I bust. Shit!

But I win the next two hands,
ka-ching, ka-ching. I knew
my luck would turn around
eventually. Ka-ching! So okay,
maybe a little larger bet. Let's go
twenty this time. Dealer holds

on sixteen. I've got fourteen. All
I need is seven or less. Come on!
No! Not nine! Damn, damn, damn.
It's okay. The Lady is still with me.
I can feel her, smiling. Big bet?
Small bet? Big bet? You bet!

I lay down thirty. It's my hand
and I know it. Deal to me: nineteen.
I hold. Hold my breath. Just as
the dealer draws twenty—fuck!—
the telephone rings. Who the hell
could it be, this time of night?

Caller ID

Informs me it's the "Las Vegas
Police Department." My throat
goes dry and my heart drops
into my gut. Cory! Little fucker
better not be dead. "H-hello?
Uh, no, this is his brother.

Hang on. I'll get my mother."
I start to call her, but she
materializes at my side, almost
as if she expected this call.
She takes the phone from my
hand, listens to Sergeant Givens

without saying more than a few
words. When she hangs up,
she looks at me with watery eyes,
shakes her head. *They arrested
Cory. He assaulted a woman
during a robbery attempt.*

A Poem by Eden Streit
Assaulted

By a glimpse of light,
I am reminded
how precious is

freedom.

Swallowed by darkness,
emptied of tears,
the song of the desert

calls

to me and I know
to find a way beyond
these plywood walls,

I must

become someone
I don't want to know.
I hope the real me will

follow.

And I pray the Lord
understands my reasons.
Forgives.

Eden
Escape from Tears of Zion

Does not come easy. Jerome is, in fact,
maneuverable, and the key to the lock.

He comes to me late at night, tells me
to do things I've never even imagined.

Things I should have saved for Andrew.
The first time will stay with me, a scar

on my heart. The door opened and though
I knew what that meant, I couldn't believe

that this supposed man of God would draw
back the sheet, pull up my shift and stand,

staring. *Forgive me*, he whispered, and
he meant that, even as he stripped,

lowered his ghostly white nakedness over
me. I swallowed the building scream.

Opened my legs. Wept as he plunged inside.
Choked on his Listerine-flavored tongue,

wielded like a weapon. His kiss was, in fact,
harder to accept. Sex is sex. A kiss means love.

After he left, I cried and cried, called into
the night, "Andrew, where are you?"

No answer came then. Or yet. The next
morning Jerome brought a hot biscuit,

with butter and honey. Nothing ever,
ever, has tasted so good. He came back

that night. Afterward, I cried and cried,
screamed into the night, "Andrew, save

me." But he didn't. Hasn't yet. The next
morning Jerome brought a perfect peach.

And so it has gone. I have my shampoo,
unscented so Father won't notice,

but at least my hair feels clean. Really
clean. I even got my Cherry Garcia.

Another small plus: Jerome always uses
a condom. That little detail has saved

more than a badly timed pregnancy.
It has probably saved my sanity.

Almost worse than the thought of having
his baby is the nightmare idea of his "leftovers."

After a Few Weeks

The straight sex has become routine.
Something I can shut myself off from.

       But now Jerome wants other things.
       Let me watch you touch yourself.

       Creepy things. *Did you know guys
       like to use vibrators too? Like this.*

       Downright disgusting things. *Your
       period? I like the taste of blood.*

How I wish I could say no. But even
if I thought he'd leave me alone,

saying yes is how I have convinced
him to make Father believe I am fit

for small freedoms. Like working
in the yard, pulling weeds and picking

vegetables. Out here, beyond the confines
of my room, I understand there is no way

to leave the place on foot. I can see
forever across the playa, and the road

is a straight, stretched wound. I can tell
cars are coming long before they arrive,

by dust mushrooms sprouting into the hot
blue Nevada sky. Hot? Working outside,

even midmorning, sweat pools in my armpits
and beads my skin, attracting bugs and dirt.

But anything is better than slow suffocation
in the tomb of my room. I observe people

come and go. Memorize schedules. Learn
where cars are parked, some left unlocked.

Ironically, Jerome is one of the worst
about leaving his keys under the floor mat.

I file that fact away. Plan A has gone awry.
Maybe it will come in handy with Plan B.

Plan A

Was to do whatever it took to get Jerome
to call Andrew, tell him where to find me.

But a major flaw in that strategy surfaced.
Oh, I have played on Jerome's sympathy.

Talked about home. Church. Papa. Told him
Mama is crazy, something he understands.

Jerome inherited his own "not rightness"
from the XX chromosome side of his family.

> *My mother used to lock my brother and me*
> *in the closet,* he told me. *Then she'd sit*
>
> *outside the door and listen. If she heard*
> *us praying to Jesus, she'd let us out.*

Even Mama isn't that bad. But our conversation
did reveal some mutual rocky ground. And keeping

him talking meant less time for other stuff.
Then yesterday I asked if he'd ever fallen in love.

> He blushed but said nothing for several
> seconds. Finally he confessed, *With you.*

Talk About Knocking

The squall out of my sails. In love with me?
Looks like loneliness works both ways

here at Tears of Zion. Jerome will not help
me reconnect with Andrew. Neither will he

leave my door unlocked so I can slip away
into the desert night (Plan B). Unless . . .

What would he do if I asked him to run
away with me? Does he *really* believe

he loves me? Would he desert Tears of Zion
and Father? Is this a job or true devotion?

Could I convince him? Could I make him
believe I'm in love with him, too? Could I

live with myself afterward? Could I ever
be forgiven for such painful deception?

> As I sit here, alone, questioning, phrases
> tumble into my head: *You'll be here*

> *for the foreseeable future. . . . Make*
> *the best of it. . . . Guys like vibrators too.*

Plan C begins to formulate. Yes, it's wrong.
But not as wrong as everything else.

Plan C

Means courting Jerome's affection,
pretending to enjoy his deviant sex.

Tonight that means letting him call me
"Mommy" as he sits on my lap and "nurses."

I stroke his hair as a mother would, dig deep
inside for the words, "Mommy loves you, Jerome."

That excites him, as I guessed it would.
I love you, too, Mommy. See how much?

Oh, Andrew. Even if you do find me, how
can you ever love me again after this?

I hold stubbornly to the dream that he will,
as Jerome turns his belly to "Mommy's."

Love or no, Jerome wants to punish Mommy.
The sex is rough, but it doesn't hurt nearly

as bad as the pretense. And it's even faster
than usual. When he finishes, I lay my head

on his knobby chest. "Too bad you have to go.
It would be nice to sleep together all night."

Jerome's chin lifts and falls against my hair.
Uh-huh. That surely would be nice.

I roll on top of him, look up into his eyes.
"What if we . . ." Soft kiss. "Never mind."

He shivers. Is much too easy. I feel
almost evil when he whispers, *What?*

I sit up, slide the naked place between my legs
over his skin. "We could leave. Together."

He shakes his head. His body stiffens.
No. I couldn't do that. It would be wrong.

"No more wrong than this." I lean forward,
cup my breasts, rub them over his face.

Confusion seeps into his eyes, and like it
or not, his muscles relax. All but one.

I rock back gently, invite him inside. "I'd be
all yours and take such good care of you."

The second time takes longer, but when
he's finally done, he says, *I'll think about it.*

After he leaves, I lie in an aura of hope.
Say a little prayer to Mary Magdalene.

Hope Begins to Fade

After two days. I haven't seen Jerome
even once. Did I scare him away?

I'm pretty sure he didn't say anything
to Father, who doesn't act strangely

at all during our regular sessions.
In fact, today he is almost friendly.

> *Brother Jerome tells me you've worked
> hard in the garden,* he says. *Is that right?*

What kind of game is this? Better play
along, whatever the rules. "Yes, Father."

> *Good. Hard work deserves a reward.
> Starting Sunday, you may attend*

> *the regular worship service. If that
> goes well, we can talk about school.*

Worship? School? No more isolation?
Is this some kind of a trick? Did Jerome

confess everything to Father after all?
I have no idea what to believe anymore.

One thing I know. It's wiser to say too
little than too much. "Thank you, Father."

Brother Stephen

Walks me back to my room. A girl,
a bit younger than me, rakes gravel

outside the chapel door. She looks up
as we pass and I smile at her, which only

makes her drop her eyes to the ground
again. But not before I see the fear

floating in them. Is she new here, then?
Or has she been here longer? Long enough,

perhaps, to know which is the greater
punishment—isolation or supervised

communion. The short exchange leaves
me uneasy. I wish I could talk to her.

   But that won't happen. Stephen herds
   me forward. *Hurry up, would you?*

"Why? Somewhere you have to be?"
A hard shove lets me know in no uncertain

terms that my sarcasm is not appreciated.
Except by what little is left of Eden.

Thank the Good Lord

The piece that remains is the one that can
find a streak of humor, however dark,

in almost anything. Otherwise, I would
have gone completely crackers by now.

Otherwise, *they* would have already won.
I'm not conceding yet, and I never will,

unless Andrew is out of my life forever.
Why did I think that? He's looking for me.

(Unless my parents had him locked up.)
Waiting for me. (Unless he believes

our separation was for the best.) Loving
me. (Unless he finds out what I've done.)

A wave of depression sweeps over me,
washes me into an icy black sea. I'm treading

       water, poorly, when the door opens.
       Why are you lying there in the dark?

It's Jerome. The smell of chicken broth
tells me he's brought my dinner.

He flips on the light, and I jump up to greet
him, kiss him on the cheek. "I'm so happy

to see you. Where have you been?
I thought for sure you were mad at me."

He sets down the tray. *Now, why would
you think a thing like that? I had a couple*

of days off is all. He reaches out, strokes
my hair. *So pretty. When we go, I'll buy*

*you shampoo that smells like roses.
You like the scent of roses, don't you?*

When we go? Chills charge through me.
"Of course, Jerome. Roses are my favorite."

*Good. I thought so. I have to go now,
but I'll be back later. We'll talk then.*

When He Returns

He outlines his plan. *We'll leave*
tomorrow night, when everyone's asleep.

By the time somebody misses you,
we'll be halfway to Salt Lake City.

Salt Lake City? Well, we can't go
back to Boise. Still, "Why go there?"

He shrugs. *My brother lives there.*
I can work for him under the table

until you turn eighteen. After that,
we're free to go wherever we want.

He has really thought this through.
So, "Why can't we leave tonight?"

No hurry, is there? I'm too tired
to drive very far tonight. Besides . . .

He lifts my arms, pulls my shift up
over my head. *I'm in need of your*

special brand of lovin'. Help me
out? He nudges me toward the bed.

As He Pokes

And pinches, I concentrate on ways
to *not* reach Salt Lake City. Afterward,

he takes me in his arms, like in some awful
romantic movie. Only in the movies,

the couple would really be in love, though
they might not know it yet. Despite everything

before, and what Jerome has hinted will come
soon, I have to fight not to resist him.

It's a losing battle. My body tenses.
He can't help but notice. *What's wrong?*

I drop my voice to a whisper. "Nothing.
It's just . . . I'm excited. And scared."

*Don't be scared. Everything will work
out fine. I promise.* He kisses me

and I draw from the deepest well of dark
deception to kiss him back like I mean it.

When the Door Closes

Behind him, I clean myself, as I do every
time he leaves, with soap and cold water

from the wash basin. The air in the room
is thick with heat and the smell of sweaty

sex, a smell I never knew existed until
just a few weeks ago. At first it made

me gag, but it has become something
I simply accept, because I have no other

choice. When all choice is taken from
you, life becomes a game of survival.

I lay the towel on the bed, lie on top
of it, so I don't have to touch the sheet.

Will I carry that habit with me if and when
I leave this place? Will Jerome really take

me out of here? What then? I have no
answers, but I do know I can't end up

in Salt Lake City. Wherever I go—Los
Angeles, maybe, or Reno or Las Vegas—

my only goal is to reconnect with Andrew.
And pray this nightmare ends with a red sunrise.

A Poem by Seth Parnell
Vegas

This city is a neon-
scaled hydra,
bellying across hot

          Mojave

sand. Cobra
heads, venomous, in
disguise pretend

          beauty,

lure you with hypnotic
eyes, copper
promises, and the

          bare

skin of gods intent
on mortal souls. Walk
cautiously, beware the

          brazen

slither of concrete
beneath your feet.
Do not listen to the

          arid

hiss of progress.

Seth
Before We Came

To Las Vegas, I had an inkling
        that Carl had money.
        But I had no idea exactly
        how much until he invited
me to relocate here with him.

Truth is, I didn't really
        expect him to agree
        to bring me along. In fact,
        I wasn't totally convinced
that I wanted to come.

The night my dad kicked
        me out, I was in turmoil.
        Where to go? What to do
        next? I had no clue. Carl
was my only solid ground,

and when he said he was
        moving, the earth quaked.
        The blood rushed away
        from my face. Carl reached
for me, as a father would.

Someone's Gay Father

I propped myself against
        him. "I don't know what
        to do. I can't go home. Have
        no home. No money. No job.
Sorry. Not your problem."

        He thought silently for what
            seemed a long while. Finally,
            he led me to the sofa, sat
            next to me. *I've never told
you about Simon,* he said.

*He lived with me until a few
            weeks before you and I met.
            He was what some call
            "kept." And I kept him.
It was a mutually beneficial ·*

*relationship. He enjoyed
            my hospitality. I enjoyed
            his company, and he looked
            good on my arm, at least
until he grew bored with it.*

A trophy—that's what the guy
        I first saw with Carl at
        Fringe was. Carl let the idea
        filter through my confusion.
I wasn't looking for another.

But if you would consider it,
        I'd think about taking you
        along. He kissed me, led
        me to bed. *Come on. Show*
me how much you want to go.

He asked me to do dark,
        obscene things. Things
        I'd never done before.
        And he wanted me to do
them without protection.

Feels better this way.
        And it's okay. I'm safe.
        I promise. You have to
        trust me. He was right.
I had no one else to trust.

A Few Days Later

I climbed on board a jet
     for the very first time. Sat
     in first class, where drinks
     are served before the plane's
wheels ever leave the tarmac.

Less than four hours later,
     we touched down sixteen
     hundred miles to the west,
     and a billion light-years
from everything I've ever

known. We disembarked
     the silver bird in Sin City,
     where trophy boyfriends
     are almost as common as
trophy wives. Carl likes me

on his arm. I'm not sure
     how I feel about being
     someone's prize, but it's
     better than being homeless,
that much I know. Neither

am I exactly sure how I feel
     about the world—at least
     my newest little corner of it—
     knowing I'm gay. I don't feel
judged. But I do feel exposed.

Culture Shock

Barely describes what
    it's like, coming from
    the wild land of Indiana to
    the wild life of Las Vegas.
This city defines insanity.

Not that I've traveled much,
    or at all really, but I can't
    imagine many other places
    so built on extravagance.
Or so reliant on human greed.

Casinos line the glitzy strip,
    masquerading as Venetian
    canals, Egyptian pyramids,
    Manhattan skyscrapers.
Their exteriors boast fountains,

pirate ships, giant lions with
    gaping mouth doorways,
    roller coasters. And almost
    everywhere you look—
billboards and signboards,

on taxicab roofs and
    giant-screen TVs on outdoor
    walls and indoor ceilings—
    you simply cannot escape
the sight of near-naked bodies.

Skin, Skin

Everywhere skin. Instead
     of Sin City, they should
     call this place Skin City.
     Female skin. Male skin.
Something-in-between skin.

They (meaning Skin City
     marketing geniuses)
     aren't choosy about gender,
     as long as the skin is flawless.
Bronze. Young. Beautiful.

I'm not griping. I like skin
     as much as the next guy.
     Maybe the real problem is,
     except for the first few days
here with Carl, I've pretty much

been left all alone to set up
     our luxury condominium
     in an upscale fringe suburb
     of the city. There's a lake
out here, and two golf courses.

All seem totally out of place
     in this hot-as-snot stretch
     of desert sand. One hundred
     twelve degrees in the shade?
Who says there isn't a hell?

If Vegas Is Hell

The devil himself probably
        lives here at Lake Las Vegas.
        He'd only settle for the best,
        right? Everything here is that,
from the boutique shopping

to the pristine marina, to
        manicured waterfront
        greens. It's beautiful, if hot.
        Perfect, with one small
blemish: Here, I'm not Seth.

I'm Seth, who's Carl's.
        Maybe that's not so bad.
        I don't know what to think
        anymore. Lots of people
would envy my life with Carl.

I eat well. Drink well. Dress
        well. And don't have to work
        for any of that, unless you
        count the sex. All I have to do
is keep the place picked up

(a housekeeper handles the real
        dirty stuff), keep myself fit
        (the workout facilities are
        excellent), and look pretty.
Hey, man. I'm a movie star!

One Big Problem

Is boredom. Back home
        I was never bored. Too
        much work to do. And
        when I was done, I could
go into town, hang out

with friends, play pool or
        dance or spread gossip.
        But here, I have no car,
        wouldn't know where to
drive it if I did. I can only

work out so much. Lying
        by the pool is a sure
        path to skin cancer. TV
        is a brain-sucking machine.
I need someone to talk to

when Carl is busy playing
        Mr. Real Estate Developer.
        So I've started spending too
        much time online, making
virtual friends. Fantasy

connections are better
        than no outside contact
        at all. I even found a chat
        room called Men Kept
by Men. My kind of room.

Sure, There Are Posers

Guys who only wish
        they were kept. And
        guys who wish someone
        would want to be kept
by them. Fishermen.

Then there are the guys
        who pretend they want
        to know all about you,
        and about five minutes
into the conversation,

they ask if you'll talk dirty
        to them, preferably on
        the phone. Masturbators.
        Every now and then, you
come across married guys

who want to meet for real,
        with or without their wives,
        usually the former. Cheap
        thrill seekers. I haven't
played in the flesh, but I don't

mind getting someone off
        telling dirty stories. There's
        a certain sick kind of power
        in that. I bet I've even
made a priest or two come.

Which Brings Me Back

To Father Howard. I guess
     the first time he gave me
     a hug, I was about twelve,
     and an altar boy, steeped
in Catholic tradition. I was

     preparing the altar for Mass
          when he called to me from
          the vestry. *Seth, come here*
          and help me a minute, please.
     It was a stifling summer

afternoon, and the loud
     hum of the air conditioner
     fought heavy rock music,
     streaming from the radio.
Father Howard was a twenty-

     first-century priest. *What do you*
          think of these colors? He held
          up some squares in turquoise
          hues. *I want to paint the office*
     and just can't seem to decide.

I went closer, studied
          the samples carefully.
          Finally I pointed to "Cool
          Caribbean." Father Howard
smiled. *I like that one too.*

Cool Caribbean it is, then.
          Thank you, Seth. As I turned
          to leave, his arms coiled
          around me. *You're very*
special to me, you know.

It was the first time a man
          had ever hugged me in such
          an intimate way. I liked it,
          twisted around to hug
him back. "Thanks, Father."

That was it. That time. I left,
          feeling very special. It never
          occurred to me that it might
          be wrong for a man of God
to embrace a boy in such a way.

435

Or Where

That first hug might lead.
     The next time we were
     alone together, Father Howard
     was bolder. His hug lasted
longer, and he massaged

     my shoulders. *You are such*
          a good-looking boy, he said.
          I bet the girls think so too.
          He paused, but when I didn't
     respond, he tried, *Other boys?*

My eyes went wide. I started
     to deny, but the adolescent
     tugs I'd felt had all been
     toward boys. I couldn't lie
to a priest. I stared at the floor.

     He tilted my chin, so I had
          to look in his eyes. *It's okay,*
          Seth. You're beautiful, just
          the way God made you.
     His lips, warm and soft,

brushed across my forehead.
     I was scared. Thrilled. Amazed
     at his acceptance of sin, born
     inside of me. Father Howard
left things there. That time.

The Next Time

Hugging segued to touching.
Not too much. But enough.
Later, there would be more
touching. Mutual touching.
But always gentle. Always

with deep affection. We never
had out-and-out (meaning in
and out) sex. And though I'd heard
about pedophile priests, for
some reason, I never thought

Father Howard might be one.
Not then, anyway. Not until
years later, when I read about
him losing his collar because
of another boy. In another town.

The picture became rainwater
clear. I wasn't special at all.
I was just one of the first
of many. I felt betrayed.
Used. White-hot pissed off.

But ultimately my emotions
cooled. Iced over. I could
have said no, and Father
Howard would have backed
off. But I didn't. And while

he most definitely took
            advantage of my youthful
            ignorance, he also made me
            believe that being drawn
to men didn't automatically

condemn me to hell. After
            Father Howard changed
            parishes, I moved on too—
            to girls in general and Janet
Winkler in particular. I'll always

feel bad about hurting her,
            but I can't be what I'm not.
            Bringing me back to what I am—
            gay, and being provided for
by someone I like but don't love.

Making Me

According to this guy Chad,
    a regular chatter in Men Kept
    by Men, *A whore, and not*
    a whole lot more. No worries,
mate. *I'm a whore too.*

Turns out Chad's keeper
    imported him all the way
    from Sydney, Down Under.
    But wherever he's from,
his assessment must be wrong.

Okay, I don't love Carl. But
    millions of people have lived
    together without being in love.
    I type, "How is this different
from a marriage of convenience?"

Chad's fingers are quick:
    Did you sign anything to
    make the arrangement legal?
    If your man drops dead,
what will happen to you?

Carl won't die any time soon.
    Right? I mean, he's not *that*
    old. Right? Okay. Valid point.
    One I should probably consider
sooner rather than later. Right?

A Poem by Whitney Lang
Sooner or Later

Someone

*you could not have
ever dreamed of
appears like a rainbow
bridging clouds, and*

steals

*your breath away.
Someone beautiful,
inside and out,
grabs hold of*

your

*hand, guides you
along a rarely traveled
road, to a place
where your broken*

heart

*can be mended, piece
by beating piece.
The cost, gratefully
afforded, is only*

your love.

Whitney
Free

That's what I am now. Free
of Mom, of Kyra's shadow.
Free of friction and the pain
of a shattered heart. I'm healed.

I'm also blown away by Vegas.
What a crazy city! I bet this
is what all those Saudi sheiks
wish their desert looked like.

Of course, on any given day,
there are probably a half-dozen
Middle Eastern moneybags
living it up here in Sin City.

This is where they come to get
away from Allah's watchful eye.
'Cause Vegas would scare the living
crap out of any deity worth his salt.

It's hot as hell and downright
filthy. Not like dusty dirty,
although when the wind blows
hard from the west, it's that, too.

Vegas is the kind of dirty every
mother worries about. What would
my mom say if she knew this is where
I ended up when I left that night?

Nothing, probably. I bet she's happy
I'm gone. One less irritation carving
wrinkles. Daddy must be worried
sick. It's been almost two months,

and I haven't let him know I'm okay.
Eventually I will. I'm more than
okay, actually. I'm great, because
I'm with Bryn, who loves me

more than anything. Who wants to
be with me always. Who needs me.
That's something all new—being
needed. Treasured. Protected.

> *I'll never let anyone hurt you,*
> Bryn promised. *You are my angel.*
> I've never been anyone's angel,
> either. Bryn has given me wings.

We're Staying

In a weekly motel—small, but mostly
clean and air-conditioned. And it's only
until Bryn has time to find us something
nicer. He's been working almost

every day, photographing wannabe
beauty pageant queens. I don't like
him ogling gorgeous girls for hours
at a time, but he comes home to me.

He photographs me, too. Lately,
the pics have all been naked.
*Such a beautiful body deserves
to be seen,* he says. *We could make*

*some extra money, too. To get
an even better place. More like
what you're used to. I want
only the very best for you.*

I don't mind posing without
clothes. Some of the finest art
ever was paintings of nudes.
Bryn makes me feel pretty,

and I like how that looks in photos.
At first it was kind of weird,
thinking about total strangers
seeing me that way, but it's not

so bad, really. And hey, maybe
Mom will come across one of them.
That would be awesome. Stupid cow
would probably be jealous.

> Bryn called a little while ago.
> *I'm on my way home, and I've*
> *got a little surprise for you.*
> *Hope you're up for some fun.*

Fun? Like what? He must have
gotten paid, which is good. I was
starting to worry a little about
how we were going to eat.

I guess inheriting his mom's house
was more about spending money
than making money, at least until
he can sell it. Not easy right now.

Because of the housing slump.
And because going back to Santa
Cruz would probably not be wise.
But he said we'd be fine, and we will.

Bryn Blows In

Like a breeze off the ocean,
lifting me with his presence.
Then his arms lift me for real,
spin me around and around.

> *Hey, baby.* He kisses me, infuses
> me with happiness. *What a day.*
> *Sorry I'm late.* The clock says
> it's eight eighteen. He *is* late.

> He carries me to the couch, sits
> me down. *Are you ready for my*
> *surprise? Two surprises, actually.*
> He reaches into a pocket for the first.

Guess it's not a dinner out.
Nope. Not even close. It's a dope-
sized plastic bag with some brown
substance inside. "What's that?"

> But I suspect his response:
> *Smack. One of the girls turned*
> *me on to a little. Thought*
> *you might like to share a taste.*

Heroin. I've never even thought
about trying it. "I don't know. . . .
That shit is scary as hell." Way
past meth, which is scary enough.

Bryn's Reaction

Is swift, completely unexpected.
*Oh, I see. You can do cocaine
with your other boyfriends, but
you won't try this for me?*

Holy Pete! He's never snapped
at me like that before. I've never
even heard him raise his voice.
My first instinct is to bark back,

but I don't want to fight with Bryn.
"I—I'm sorry. I just . . . didn't . . .
Uh . . ." Why am I apologizing?
"It's just, heroin is so addictive, and . . ."

He softens immediately. *No, hon.
Not if you only do a little, once
in a while. And the places it will
take you! I want to see you there.*

OMG. I can't believe I'm saying
okay to heroin. But I am. Except,
"No needles! No way will I shoot
up anything." I wait for his reaction.

*No problem. We'll just chase
the dragon, okay?* He means heated
tinfoil and a rolled-up bill to grab
the smoke, draw it up my nose.

I've seen people at parties do
meth the same way. Even before
Bryn creases the foil into a deep
V, my heart starts racing. Fear

is exhilarating, all on its own.
I watch him drop a pinhead of H
into the makeshift bowl, and goose
bumps cover my arms. I have no

idea what to expect when the smoke
lifts into the dollar bill "straw." Ugh.
It tastes like rotten ketchup. Bitter
and harsh in my throat. I start to choke.

> Bryn's warning is rough: *Don't
> you dare cough it out!* He checks
> out my eyes. Looking for pupil
> dilation, no doubt. It takes a while.

> *If you shoot up, you feel the effects
> instantaneously. Smoking it might
> take ten or fifteen minutes. Patience.
> Meanwhile, I have another surprise.*

It takes all of ten minutes before
I begin to feel kind of tingly. Euphoric.
Like everything in my life just fell
into place. The sensation is gentle,

not at all like the overwhelming
buzz I thought it would be. I can
handle this. What's all the hype
about, anyway? Bryn has finished

setting up the second surprise—
a webcam, hooked up to his
laptop. *I thought it would be fun
to put ourselves in the movies.*

America's Sexiest Home Videos.
Come here. Let's get nasty.
The tone of his voice lets me know
disagreeing is not an option.

But I don't want to disagree.
Every nerve in my body screams
to make love with Bryn, who responds
by taking "nasty" to a whole new level.

It is only afterward, floating
on a sensual fog, in an uneasy state
of half sleep, that it comes to me:
Bryn didn't join in the dragon chase.

A Week After

My first sweet-bitter taste of smack,
Bryn has talked me into indulging
again four or five times. I don't
want to get hooked, and I'm sure

I won't, as long as all I do is smoke
a little every now and again. I have to
admit I like the way it makes me
feel—like I'm on top of the world.

> Bryn never indulges. *I can't*
> *get it up if I do, and I want this*
> *to be all about you.* So why does
> he keep asking me to do things

> that seem mostly all about him?
> Things like performing dirty
> acts on pay-per-view webcam?
> *It won't be forever, I promise.*

> *Just long enough to save up*
> *some serious bank. I've got my*
> *eye on a really nice place. It's*
> *pricey, but you're so worth it.*

When I'm high, I don't mind.
But when I touch back down,
I start to worry. Is this the same
Bryn who valued my almost-virginity?

I Also Worry

About him spending more
and more time away from me.
Talking more and more about
"the girls," and I'm starting to

wonder if the girls he's talking
about are really pageant hopefuls.
If he's getting paid to photograph
models, he's not getting paid well.

Our money seems to come in spurts,
and some of that seems to be from
the webcam spurting going on.
He doesn't want me to work, though,

> except for private webcam spurting.
> *Some guys like to watch girls*
> *getting off all by themselves.*
> *Make it look good for the camera.*

I was never into touching myself,
but it isn't so bad, especially when
I'm high. Besides the occasional
H, Bryn supplies me with bud—

mediocre seeded Mexican—
and prescription downers. Not sure
where he gets them, and I really
don't care. As long as I'm buzzed,

the things he asks of me are easy
to do, and hey, anything's better
than wasting away in Santa Cruz.
God, if I were there, I'd be starting

my junior year of high school.
High school is so not me anymore.
Wonder what Paige is doing.
Wonder if she hooked up

with that guy after that night at
Lucas's party. Shit! Why did I have to
think about him? Wonder if he likes
it in San Diego. Wonder . . . stop

it. Fuck. Where the hell's my stash?
I locate it under the coffee table. Two
tokes of half-ass pot, a bigger question
hovers: Where the hell is Whitney?

It's Almost Midnight

When Bryn comes in. He's not
alone. The guy he's with is Latino,
I think. Olive-skinned. Dark-haired.
Okay-looking. Dressed well.

    Bryn comes over, kisses me.
    Hey, babe. This is my buddy,
    Oscar. He nods toward the stash
    box, sitting on the coffee table.

    Oscar's been very good to us,
    if you get my meaning. Now
    I want you to return the favor
    and be very, very nice to Oscar.

Very nice? Does he mean what
I think he means? Play hostess.
"Uh, nice to meet you, Oscar.
Can I get you something to drink?"

    Maybe after. Oscar comes over,
    touches my face. *You're right,*
    Bryn. She's very pretty. Tight
    little body, too. Yes, she'll do.

His hands slide over my front,
reach up under my blouse.
The skin of his fingers, seeking
my nipples, is calloused. Cold.

"No, wait. I can't. You're not
serious . . . Bryn?" He can't want
me to do this! I jerk away from
Oscar, turn to Bryn. Search his eyes.

> They are deadly serious, and so
> is Bryn when he says, *Yes, you
> can. And if you love me, you will.
> You* do *love me, don't you?*

"Of course I love you! But this
isn't . . ." Isn't right, is what I want
to say. But what *is* right, anymore?
Is this really what loving him means?

> Bryn's hands press down on
> my shoulders. *Do this for me,
> Whitney. Do this for us.* He kisses
> me. But it is the kiss of a stranger.

I Beg for a Buzz First

Pot won't do. It has to be
smack, and three long pulls
of the acrid smoke barely take
me to the place I need to be.

> Oscar watches. Waits impatiently
> for the H to kick in. *You should*
> *use a needle. Smoking the Lady*
> *is a waste of good dope.*

Fear-queasy, I stumble down
the hall, into the bedroom.
Oscar follows, shedding clothes.
His body is lean, muscular.

Another time, another place,
I might find him attractive,
but attraction is about choice.
I have no choice here but to

take off my own clothes, lie on
the bed, wait for him to come,
and do whatever it is he has paid
to do. I hate you, Bryn. I hate you.

Within Seconds

I hate Oscar, too. He breathes
beer, sweats onion, and there is no
love, no kindness, nothing but
greed to his sex. He grabs my wrists,

holds them over my head so I can't
move when he bites my neck,
and lower. I'll wear his teeth marks
for days. "Stop. You're hurting me."

> *You think that hurts? You ain't
> seen nothing yet.* His teeth close
> even harder and his hand squeezes
> my arms like a vise and now

his knees force my legs apart
and there is no pleasure to what
he does down there. Only pain.
Bruising pain. I give myself to

the morphine shroud, denying
the pounding between my thighs.
Something makes me look toward
the door. Bryn stands there, staring.

A Poem by Ginger Cordell
Staring

Into the midnight sky,
starlight defeated by
the scream of neon,

                                      truth

is hard to discern.
Does it sparkle?
Does it burn? If
a weightless moment

                                      transcends

the gravity of time,
what proof is there
of its existence?
Does it infuse

                                      every

tick of the clock,
each blink of an eye?
Which is harder to
bear—reality, or a

                                      lie?

Ginger
Our Own Place

Wasn't easy to come by. Most
       landlords prefer their tenants
to be over eighteen. We finally

found a weekly where the lady
       in the office didn't look too hard
at our application. The four weeks

up front probably helped with that.
       The room at Lydia's was nicer.
But the drive into the city got old.

At least, that's what we told Lydia
       when we said we were moving out.
In reality, living with her was getting

           old. She could be a real bitch,
              and she was pushing us to do
           stuff besides strip. *You could make*

           a lot more if you'd treat a few
              of your clients to a little touchy-
           feely. Not all of them, of course.

           Just think about it. Getting
              paid for something most
           people give away? No-brainer.

She Pushed Hard Enough

That Alex has actually considered
               doing it. *It's not such a big deal,*
as long as they use condoms.

The thing is, Lydia wouldn't have
               to know. I could do it on the side,
and not give her a cut. We could

save up enough money to blow
               this city. Go somewhere pretty,
like Portland or San Francisco.

When she talks like that, it makes
               me think about Iris. How turning
tricks has used her up. How she

tried to let it use *me* up. Why
               couldn't I have a real mother?
Why did she have kids at all?

Iris used to talk about moving
               somewhere else—somewhere
exciting, like New York City.

Oh yeah, I can just picture
               Iris in Manhattan. Cruising
Central Park. Hustling johns.

When I Think About Iris

I can't help but think about
      Gram. She must be worried
about me. I should probably

try to send word that I'm okay.
      Alive, anyway, "okay" being
a relative term. But how can

I let her know without giving
      away where I am? Letters have
postmarks and phones can be

traced. I just hope she's taking
      care of the kids. Keeping them
safe from Iris. Most of 'em are

back in school. Except Sandy.
      He's still too little. Hope he's all
healed up, chasing balls

around again. Just not in
      the street. Oh God, why did
I have to think about them?

A Mack truck of guilt crashes
      into me. How can I be home-
sick, when I don't have a home?

I Start to Pace

North and south, across
        the grease-stained beige
carpet. Guess the last tenant

kept his moped in the living
        room. The carpet was steam-
cleaned when he moved, but some

black marks can't be excised.
        Alex went to the store about
an hour ago. I would have

gone along, but my period
        this month is major. I'm close
to bleeding out, I think, and

I've downed enough ibuprofen
        to kill a horse. But I've still
got cramps. Maybe that bastard

who raped me made me pregnant
        and God was gracious enough
to let me miscarry. Whatever

the problem is, it has definitely
        put the brakes on shedding
my clothes for strangers.

Which Means a Couple of Things

One, Alex is the only one
        working, so our income
is cut in half right now. Plus,

she's going out by herself,
        which scares the crap out
of me. I know she can take

care of herself and all, but
        still . . . Ah, can't think
about the downside of that.

If anything bad ever happened
        to Alex, I'd go crazy. Except
for Gram, Alex is the only good

thing I've ever had in my life.
        She lifts me, like a double shot
of espresso. I wish she were here

right now, to lift me out of this
        black pit of boredom. My indoor
hike carries me past the bathroom,

where the laundry basket
        overflows dirty clothes. Might
as well wash them as keep

walking by 'em, I guess.
        I gather them up, grab some
detergent, and shovel quarters

into my pockets. The laundry
        room is downstairs and in
the other building somewhere.

This will be my first trip there.
        Jeez, man. For almost October,
it's still hotter than hell. Maybe

ninety in the shade. By the time
        I locate the short bank of washers,
I am dripping sweat. Lovely!

Hopefully, the person pulling
        her own clothes from the dryer
won't get close enough to smell me.

Her Back Is Toward Me

And just in case my ripeness
   doesn't precede me, I say,
"Hello," so she knows I'm here.

She jumps about three feet.
   "Sorry. Didn't mean to
sneak up on you." When she

turns, I can see she's a little
   younger than me. Wow,
her posture made me think

   something different. *It's okay,*
     she says. *Guess I was off in*
   Never-Never Land. Don't use

   that washer. . . . She points.
     Someone's pen exploded
   in it. There's ink all over.

"Thanks." As I put my dirties
   into the other two washers,
she starts to fold her clothes.

I can't help but stare. The girl
   would be beautiful, except for
the dark circles under her eyes.

She reminds me of those
        models—what do they call
them? Oh, yeah. Heroin chic.

I know squat about heroin,
        but my guess is she's using
something. Or it's using her.

        Eventually she notices me
            observing her and jumps on
        defense. *Something wrong?*

"Oh, no. Sorry. You just, uh . . .
        remind me of my sister. I haven't
seen her in a long time."

Not totally true (Mary Ann
        resembles her only slightly),
but it works. The girl exhales

        (was she holding her breath?),
            and her shoulders relax. *Oh. Okay.*
        I haven't seen my sister in a while

        either. Not that she cares,
            I'm sure. Well, I'd better go.
        See you. Poof. She's gone.

The Clothes Are Still Spinning

So I take a minute to duck
        out the door, watch where
the girl goes. Not sure why.

Her room is kitty-corner from
        ours, across the parking lot
and on the ground floor. Wonder

who she lives with. Guy?
        Girl? Relative? She can't be
out on her own, can she?

What is up with me? Why do
        I care who she lives with?
Shit, I really am bored, aren't I?

Bored and bleeding. Sounds
        like the name of a book:
Bored and Bleeding in Vegas.

Okay, Alex, you'd better get
        home soon, or I'll turn into
a bored, bleeding, babbling loon.

Early Evening

And Alex still isn't back yet.
        Where the hell is she? I call
her cell, but the canned voice

that answers informs me that
        she's unavailable, meaning
she's out of prepaid minutes.

Guess I'll have to be patient.
        I fold the clothes, put them
away. Treat myself to a Lean

Pocket. Turn on the aged TV.
        Half listen to *Jeopardy!* while
I go to the window, hoping

to catch a glimpse of Alex,
        coming up the sidewalk.
I don't see her, but I do see

heroin chic going into her room,
        about six paces in front of a guy.
He's older. Balding. Her father?

My guess is no way, or if he
        does happen to be her father,
it's a definite case of incest.

Is Every Girl

In this nasty, stinking city
        turning tricks? Young,
old, at least as old as you

can get without dying
        of some incurable sex
disease? I swear, I will never

do that, never sink as low
        as my mother. My pretty
heroin chic neighbor.

My beautiful best friend,
        who I love so much it hurts.
And I swear, as soon as

I can, I will find a way out
        of this place. Will Alex come?
Or have I lost her to the night?

She Stumbles In

Around nine. Worry turns to
       relief. Then I take another
look at her—hair mussed,

makeup smeared, clothes
       wrinkled and buttons undone.
Relief explodes into anger.

"Where the fuck have you
       been?" I sound like a crow.
"You scared me shitless."

       Alex remains placid. *Been*
          taking care of business
     is all. Someone's got to.

It's more than a little bit
       obvious that the day's
"business" included more

than stripping. The smell
       of sweat and sex hangs
in the air, a storm cloud.

"Alex, what have you done?
       You're not turning tricks
like some hooker, are you?"

A strong memory of Iris
       stumbling in after dark,
perfumed in sex, surfaces,

swims into blurry view.
       Goddamn it, no! "Please,
Alex, tell me you didn't."

       But she doesn't deny. Won't
              say I'm wrong. *It's okay,*
     Gin. . . . It's not so bad, really.

     I mean, the sex isn't good,
            but it's fast, and all things
     considered, the pay scale

     isn't bad. Fifty bucks for
            under ten minutes' work?
     Three hundred an hour!

     Shit, girl, that's attorney
            wages, and you don't have
     to go to school—

"Stop it! We don't need money
       that bad. I'll get off the rag
and we'll go back to stripping.

"Lydia can have her cut. We
          were doing okay like that,
weren't we?" We were, damn it!

          Finally Alex deflates just
                    a little. *Sit down. Please?
          There's stuff you don't know.*

Like how she knew all about
          Lydia's escort service before
we ever got here. Like how Lydia

never invited her to "come stay
          any time." Like how when we
talked about running away, Alex

called Lydia and set the whole
          thing up. Like how Lydia
promised to keep her mouth

shut, as long as Alex went
          to work for her. Like how
Alex's not-stepdad *did* call,

looking for her. But Lydia
          denied knowing a thing.
So Alex owes her, big-time.

Alex Goes to Shower

But not before promising
        again, *It will just be for*
a little while—just until

we can save up enough
        to blow this freaking city.
I love you, Gin. Stay cool.

I love her, too. And I can't
        stand the idea of her being
with a bunch of stinking, nasty

men. If I could bring myself
        to do it too, we could save
up even faster. But I don't think

I could. I'd be no better than
        Iris. Would I? Did she ever
think, *Just for a little while?*

The room still wears evidence
        of Alex's recent encounters.
I go to open the window. Notice

Ms. Heroin going through
        her door again. Followed by
another guy. Not her father, either.

A Poem by Cody Bennett
Door

I once heard an old
saying about things
going all to hell.
It went, "When

                                a door

closes, somewhere
a window opens."
If so, when a train

                                slams

into a Volkswagen,
does a BMW materialize
down the tracks? If you
remember your undies

                                in your

dreams, do you wake
up naked? Okay,
maybe the logic fails.
But hey, let's

                                face

it. Logic doesn't really
apply to old sayings,
either. Does it?

Cody
Logic?

What's that? If it ever applied
to my life, my choices, those years
(days?) have vanished from memory.
I am spinning. Spiraling. Clinging to
the eye of the tornado. If I give up,
give in to the mad desire to just

let go, I know I'll die. But death,
close by, might be preferable
to this dizzying ride. How did I get
here? How did things go so wrong,
so fast? Left? Right? Whichever way
I choose, one thing is very clear—

I can never turn around, never
go back. Twisters only move in one
direction—full speed ahead.
Like Dorothy Gale, I ran from safe
haven, searching, despite the storm
gathering strength behind me.

The Chiefs Kick Off

In about an hour. Still time to place
a small bet. I log on, check out the point
spread. Awesome! So, okay, maybe
a little larger bet. I can pay Lydia back
later. Fuckers better step up to the line
of scrimmage and play fricking ball!

> Guess I'll call Ronnie, if only to hear
> her voice. My cell phone blinks—
> did she call me? But when I retrieve
> the message, it's Misty, grating my ear.
> *Hey, cutie. How about a double*
> *date? And can you bring smoke?*

Misty is the skank who hooked
me up with Lydia. Okay, maybe
I shouldn't look at it that way.
She did me a favor, or at least
we both thought so at the time.
Her boyfriend plays poker

with Vince. One night he was
way too buzzed to drive home,
so he called Misty. I had pretty
much lost my shirt that night,
and when she showed up, I was
looking miserable. Chris still

had a sleeve or two left of his
shirt, and while he was busy
losing those, I invited Misty
to smoke some bud. We got to
talking, and the more we smoked,
the more I confessed, which made

her open up to me. *Yeah, money
sucks, but you can't live without
it. I'm paying my way through
UNLV with a little sex-on-the-side.*
She let that sink in, and it took too
long. *You know . . . escorting?*

"You mean you get paid to . . . ?"
I studied her closer. She looked
like a college student. Nothing
more. Certainly not a whore,
especially not the type I see hawking
their wares from the sidewalk.

*Yeah, and it's not so bad, really.
I mean, if you're going to have sex
anyway, why not earn a little extra
cash, you know?* She took a big drag.
Held it a long while, as if it helped
her think. *I won't trick forever.*

I had never once in my life thought
about having sex for money. Could
finding enough cash to help myself
out of debt be *that* easy? I asked for
details, and when she mentioned
working for an established escort

service, it almost sounded legit.
"Do any guys work there?" My
stupid little brain glommed onto
a picture of lonely middle-aged
women paying for an evening
of companionship, plus some fun.

> *A couple,* she said. *Lydia calls
> them her "boys," but I think they're,
> like, in their twenties. Why?*
> She winked. *You interested in
> a little paid action? I can introduce
> you to Lydia if you want.*

"Let me think about it." Wow.
Sex for money. I still hadn't
considered the possibility of it
meaning having sex with men
when I asked, "Oh. One thing.
How much does it pay, anyway?"

Her Answer

Surprised me. Thrilled me. Who
knew you could make a hundred
bucks an hour (after the service's
cut) for screwing? I thought it over
for at least a day, and even made
a written list of pros and cons.

Pro: Work one hour, get paid more
than eight hours at GameStop.
Con: What if the old babe was really
disgusting and wanted, like, oral?
Pro: My insurance had already
Lapsed, and I had no way to pay it.

Con: If Mom ever even suspected,
she'd flip her fricking wig!
Pro: If Mom ever found out about
the credit cards, she'd lose all faith in me.
Con: People who have sex for money
might end up with some awful disease.

Pro: With enough cash to place the right
bet, I could win enough to fix everything.
Con: What if having sex on the side
meant I couldn't get it up for Ronnie?
Pro: I didn't have many choices left.

Result: I picked up the phone, called Misty.

She Introduced Me

To Lydia, who outlined the rules
and regulations, not knowing
I still had women in mind. When
I finally mentioned that, her smile
slipped a little. But only for a second.
You're envisioning American

Gigolo. *Sorry, but that kind of
escorting is rare. Something you
see in the movies, really. Generally,
when I get calls for young men,
it's older men doing the calling.
You ever been with a man?*

"A man? No!" What? Did I look
gay or something? Sex with men?
Not even a hundred bucks an hour
was worth that. At least, not then.
"So every one of your 'boys' is gay?
Because I'm, like, totally straight."

Lydia shrugged. *No one is one
hundred percent hetero. We are
all bi to varying degrees. It all
comes down to necessity.* Turned
out the statement was accurate. Took
about a week to see things her way.

Sometimes Misty and I

Do have "two-fers" with confused
guys. But not today. "Sorry," I tell her.
"I've already got a client lined up."
In fact, I'd better go. I hang up, pop
a Valium, "borrowed" from a bottle
in Ronnie's medicine cabinet. Fuck.

Stealing pills. I suck. But I'm glad
I have something to push away
the pain, stash it in a compartment
of my brain I don't visit very often.
I cruise slowly, noticing cars
prowling for street-corner hustlers.

Twenty bucks for a backseat blowjob?
At least I haven't sunk that low. Yet.
No! That will not become my future.
Then again, if someone would have told
me two months ago I'd be selling myself
to men, I'd have said they were full

of shit. Necessity is a motherfucker.
And if they would have said I might
even like it, I'd have kicked their ass.
The first time I offered myself up, turned
myself into meat, I ran to the bathroom,
heaved. That guy laughed and laughed.

Lydia said it would get easier.
The first time is always the worst.
Just remember you can always
say no, if something doesn't seem
kosher. Somehow I doubt many
rabbis would bless "Cody meat."

But Lydia was right. The second
time wasn't as bad. At least I managed
to make it through without losing
my breakfast. Every time after was easier
still, except for the guys who needed
a shower. B.O. is a definite bitch.

Once in a while I get really lucky,
when a dude decides he'd rather talk
than screw. They're paying me for
my time. If they want to complain
about their significant others, hey,
I'll listen for a buck fifty up front.

But I don't have to like any of it.
Shouldn't like any of it, and getting
off is just plain crazy. I do this because
I have to. Not because I want to. I need
a good, healthy dose of Ronnie. Only
what if she doesn't turn me on now?

I Pull into Valet

At the Riviera, not the nicest casino
in town, but not the sleaziest, either.
Not that it matters. What I'm going
to do is more than sleazy. It's sick.
But I'll leave with enough money,
even after Lydia's cut, to give Mom

a hundred toward the bills. And,
depending on how generous the guy
feels after, I just might have enough
left over to place a small bet on
the Chiefs. If those bastards do right
by me, I could maybe skip a date

or two. "Date." Why don't I just call
it what it is—a trick. I'm turning tricks.
Can I really have sunk so low?
I'm having sex with men—often married
guys, trying to figure out why
they're attracted to boys—for cash.

I'm not gay! Before a few weeks ago,
I had never even checked a guy out,
let alone thought about doing one.
So why isn't it harder? Why am I
heading into the elevator, going up
eight floors, to room 822?

Two Quiet Knocks

Nothing. Two more, louder. Footsteps
toward the door. It opens. "Dan?"
The guy nods, steps aside to let
me in. The room is obsessively neat,
and a familiar scent perfumes the air.
Gingerbread? Like Ronnie's shampoo.

Dan is fortyish, short crewcut
graying slightly at the edges.
He wears no shirt, and his muscles
are tanned. Toned. Jesus. He could
be an underwear model. Why does
he need to pay for it? Whatever.

As long as he has the cash. "So, Dan.
What can I do for you?" I know the drill.
Lydia coached me in the art of paid
seduction: *Strike the deal up front. Never
give them more than they pay for.
Collect before you start. No COD.*

No cash on delivery, because after
you're finished, they might say you
didn't deliver. I've done this for
a month now, and so far, not one
has made that claim. Customer
satisfaction guaranteed. God!

Dan Has Done This Before

You can take me around the world.
He reaches for his wallet. *One fifty,*
right? He tries to sweeten the pot. *Dan*
will pay extra to go without a sleeve.
He talks about himself in the third
person? No wonder he pays for it.

No condom? It's not the first time
I've had the request. I'd kill for
the extra cash, but I'm not taking
a chance on AIDS. "Sorry. No can
do. Cover up, I'll take care of you."
I pull my T-shirt over my head, watch

him strip off his jeans. His waist
is narrow, his hips straight. Beautiful.
Stop it! What's wrong with me? He's
down to his skivvies. I should have
charged more. He's built like a fucking
bull. "Holy crap, dude, I don't know. . . ."

What's wrong, kid? Never done
it with a real man before? His voice
falls, cold and heavy as hail. *You want*
me wrapped? Do it for me! He pushes
me to my knees, comes around in front
of me. My heart thuds in my chest.

I open the foil pouch, remove
the thin latex protection. *You ever
seen a ramrod like Dan's?* I shake
my head as I roll the condom down
over it. *No, of course you haven't.
Let's see just how good you are.*

I close my eyes, fight not to gag at
the taste of lubricant, not to choke
on his thrusts against my throat.
I think about Cory, locked up
in juvie until a judge decides
he's been "rehabilitated."

Dan decides he's done with Europe.
He pulls me to my feet, moves behind
me, drapes my back with his chest.
His muscles are thick cables, but his skin
is smooth and cool as snake skin. *Check it out.
The little boy likes that.* He reaches down

between my thighs. *Look how hard he is.*
No! How could something so messed
up turn me on? Whatever he does, I won't . . .
His lips brush the back of my neck
and, still folding me into him, he moves
me toward the bed, urges me facedown.

The sheets smell of bleach. I picture
Mom, waiting tables at Denny's. Jack's
life insurance put off the foreclosure.
But not forever. And those fucking
bills just keep piling up. Her meager
tips won't pay them. Something has to.

Down go my boxers. *Oh my. What
a sweet little bottom.* Dan's hands,
moving over my skin, are soft,
and when he lowers himself over me,
a cloud of cloves and apple sinks
around me. Reminds me of . . . Ronnie.

God I love her. She is my spark
of sanity. My light against the darkness,
closing in. She knows things are bad,
but not *how* bad. If she even suspected . . .
this. What I'm doing. What I've already
done, she'd never speak to me again.

Dan is in for a real treat, isn't he?
He presses up against me. I brace
and he pauses. *Do you think it will hurt?*
Let's see. He pushes, but only a little.
A test. *Oh yes, I'm afraid it might.*
And after Dan, nothing else will do.

I Bite Down

On a strange metal taste—a metal
taste of emotions. An odd blend of fear
and . . . excitement. For some fucked-up
reason, I'm excited. I can't want
this! Adrenaline firecrackers through
my body. Blood pulses in my temples.

> *You make Dan happy now, hear?*
> Pain! Oh my God! Nothing
> has ever hurt like this. I tense, beg
> him to stop. But he doesn't stop.
> Doesn't slow. Can't take it. Can't.
> Through the rhythmic pain, apple.

Pressure. Pressure, deep. Oh!
Nothing has ever felt so good.
Exquisite. Exquisite. No! I won't.
No matter what, I won't. This isn't me.
I'm only here for Mom. Cory. I won't!
But I do. And when I do, it's over the top.

I Leave, Emptied

And when I get home, the house
is emptied too. Emptied of life.
Emptied of love. Emptied of . . . us.
I suppose Mom might find another man,
but he can never be Jack. And Cory?
He's already harder. A stranger.

If there's anything left of my brother,
I don't know where it is. I hate to visit
him because when I look into his eyes,
all I find is death. He's a walking,
talking, breathing corpse. Lockup
will only make that worse.

I go into the bathroom, turn the shower
as hot as my skin can stand it. Scrub.
But the universe doesn't hold near
enough soap to wash this filth away.
The slippery lather does what it often
does to me. But when I touch it, I hear,

The little boy likes that, doesn't he?
Scrub harder. I keep at it until the spray
goes cold, shrinking every body part
and raising rows of goose bumps. Can
I ever feel decent about a shower again?
Can I ever feel okay about me?

A Poem by Eden Streit
Shrinking

Do you know how it
feels to be shrinking?
Withering away into

           nothing

more than a memory?
You need to put one foot
in front of the other,

           but

running in place
is all you can do.
How do you overcome

           pain

when it's something
you breathe, a blast
of hot exhaust

           in your

face, something turned
you must eat, or starve?
How do you search for

           tomorrow

when you're mired
in an endless today?

Eden
They Say Freedom Isn't Free

I agree. My bid for freedom from Tears
of Zion has already cost me dearly.

I don't know what will happen to me
if Jerome keeps his promise, unlocks

my door tonight, steals me away from
Father's house of rehabilitation.

I have no clue where I'll end up. Maybe
right back here (please, God, no). The one

thing I'm sure of is, should I leave this
place, I will not touch down in Salt Lake

City. Will not set up housekeeping with
Jerome. I will find a way to escape him, too.

I sit in the dark, heart racing as seconds . . .
minutes . . . hours creep by. Did he change

his mind? Did someone change it for him?
The air in the room grows heavy. I sink

into it. Can't find breath. I start to drown. . . .
Suddenly I wake up. A key is turning

       in the lock. Jerome came for me after all.
       He pulls me to my feet. *Ready?* he whispers.

The compound is dark, everyone asleep.
We sprint across a cushion of sand

to Jerome's Malibu, slip inside. It is old,
but tuned, and starts easily. Still, the engine

sounds very loud from where I sit, looking
for lights to blink on. Not a one. Nothing

but a billow of dust, lifting into the night
sky. Night! It's been weeks since I've seen

the stars. A voice drifts from not-so-distant
memory: *Pretty tonight. Looks like you*

could reach out and touch the stars. I close
my eyes, transported to a sleeping bag

in the bed of a Tundra. Andrew is warm
beside me. *I want what I've no right to take.* . . .

Tears fall freely as Jerome turns south on
Highway 93 toward Wells. He doesn't notice,

so I let them fall. By the time we reach I-80,
the stars are nothing but blurry streaks.

Old Malibus

Aren't exactly fuel efficient. As we roll
into Wells, Jerome slows down, checks

>the gauge. *Better gas up. There's a truck
>stop ahead. Hungry? It's a long way to SLC.*

"A little," I fudge. I've barely eaten a bite in
two days. "Thirsty, too. Any chance of a Coke?"

>*What'll you give me for it?* He snickers
>at the old joke. Only he isn't joking.

He pulls up at the pumps, opens the glove
box, reaches for his wallet. And there, on

a folded road map, is his cell phone. A buzz
like a high power line vibrates in my ears.

>Jerome doesn't seem to notice. He gets
>out of the car, puts his keys in their usual

>resting place on the front floorboard.
>*Do you have to use the bathroom?*

I shake my head. "Not until *after* the Coke."
When he goes inside, I grab the phone.

One eye on the door, I dial Andrew's cell.
This AT&T customer is not accepting incoming

calls. No! Quick. Dial his home. *The number*
you are calling is no longer in service.

Andrew! Where are you? No time to worry
about it now. Not if I want to get away

this side of Salt Lake City. I need to buy
some time. The keys . . . I reach down,

locate them, toss them under the backseat,
just as he comes out the door, goodies

in hand. I have maybe five minutes.
As Jerome starts toward the island, I jump

out of the car. "Decided I should pee after
all," I say, passing him on the sidewalk.

Nerves ping-pong in my stomach. I feel
like I'm going to vomit. But I don't, and

he doesn't seem fazed at all. Over my
shoulder, I watch him go to the car, open

the door. As he leans inside, I duck
around the corner of the building.

It's quiet this time of day, and in the steel
blue of just-before-dawning, a row of semis

waits silently for their drivers to wake. I dash
across the short span of asphalt to the far side

of the trucks. Maybe there's somewhere
to hide behind them. No! Nothing but desert,

stretching all the way to the freeway. What
now? He'll come looking any second!

I run down the row, hoping for . . . ? Can I
hide in one of them? Don't think so. If I try

to open one of the back doors, it's sure to make
a racket. About three-quarters of the way

down the line, I pass a travel trailer, attached
to a big crew cab. Something about it calls to me.

If the owners are asleep in the trailer, maybe
I could slip inside the truck? Could the doors

be unlocked? As quietly as I can, I pull up
on the rear passenger handle. Holy mother!

It opens. I climb up, shut the door,
skooch down on the floor, close my eyes.

He must be looking for me by now.
When he finds me, what will he do?

But It Isn't Jerome

Who finds me. It's the owner of the fifth
wheel. It is light when he opens the door

to let his border collie inside. *What the—
What the hell are you doing in my truck?*

I'm afraid to get up off the floor.
"I'm sorry . . . I didn't mean . . ."

Come on! Think! Something sort of
close to the truth pops out of my mouth.

"It's just that my boyfriend and I got into
an awful fight. I was afraid he'd hurt me,

so I hid in here. . . ." I must have fooled
the dog, anyway. She licks my face.

The man, who's maybe sixty, looks
dubious at first. But something about

my expression makes him go on the alert.
Think he's still here? What's he look like?

Thank you, God. "Short. Thin. He drives
a blue Malibu. I'm really scared."

*You stay right here with Trinket. I'll take
a look around.* He shuts the door.

Relief firecrackers through me in tiny
bursts. I'm stiff. Tired. But maybe okay.

It isn't long before the guy returns.
No sign of a blue Malibu. Where you

headed, young lady? He gives me a once-
over, but if my industrial outfit makes

him wonder, he doesn't say a word.
Think fast, Eden. "We were going to

Salt Lake City. But I want to go home.
And my boyfriend has all our money."

He takes every word in perfect stride.
Okay. And just where is home?

South on 93? Keep going, and end up
in "Vegas." I hold my breath, hoping.

Can't take you all the way there.
But I can get you as far as Ely.

I finally feel safe enough to scoot up
onto the seat. "That would be great.

I can call Andr—uh, my brother to come
get me." And pray he answers this time.

At Fifty MPH

The trip from Wells to Ely takes close
to three hours. I stay scrunched down

in my seat for a long while. Wes notices
without comment. Finally he says,

> *I think you're okay now. Been checking*
> *the mirror. Haven't seen anything blue.*

I straighten a bit. Trinket squirms and yips,
as if happy to see me relax. "Good girl."

> Wes smiles. *You like dogs, I see.*
> *Have any at home, waiting for you?*

I almost say no, that my parents are
much more into God than dogs, or any

of his creatures that don't tithe heavily.
But then I think of Andrew. The ranch.

And, "Sheila. She's a bluetick hound,
just a pup." We talk dogs for some time,

then ranching. Wes has a big ranch,
with Angus and Quarter Horses.

"Andrew . . . uh . . . my brother works . . .
uh, worked on a ranch for a while."

Did he, now? Speaking of your brother,
do you want to give him a call?

We'll be in Ely before you know it.
We should have cell service now.

"I'd like to, but I left my phone in
my boyfriend's car." His phone, actually.

Wes points to the center console.
Use mine. It's right in there.

I dial the well-known numbers,
with the same results as before.

The number you have called . . . Where
could he be? Still, I know Wes and I must

part ways soon. And I suspect he'll worry
if I don't get hold of someone. I pretend

Andrew answers. "Hey. Um, something kind
of bad happened. Can you come get me?"

Where Is Andrew?

What's up with the phones? Is he okay?
What about his parents? Where are *they*?

It's all I can think about. Wes keeps
right on talking, and I try my best

to find answers to his many questions.
But most of them probably don't make

much sense. Suddenly Trinket stands up
in the backseat, whines a little, wags

> her stumpy tail. *We're getting close*
> *to home and she can smell it,* explains

> Wes. *The turnoff's south of town,*
> *so I can get you a little closer. There's*

> *a nice truck stop out that way. You'd*
> *be safe enough there until your brother*

> *comes, I reckon. Most truckers I know*
> *won't let your boyfriend mess with you.*

Sooner rather than later we turn
off the straight two-lane blacktop.

Wes decides to fill up before heading
on home. I leave his company

rather reluctantly, and before I walk
away, I go around and give him a hug.

"Thank you so much. I don't know
what I would have done. . . ."

        He blushes a furious rhubarb color.
        Ah. It was nothing but common

        decency. But tell you what you can
        do for me in return. . . .

Yeah, right. Figures. I can guess what
he wants in return. But whatever.

I owe him big-time. And it's nothing
I haven't already done. "What?"

        Choose your next man more
        carefully. You deserve better.

Oh my God. How could I think . . . ?
My own face flushes, red hot, and

my throat knots as my eyes fill.
"I will," I manage. "I promise."

Eyes Burning

I start away, completely awed by
the kindness of this perfect stranger.

Wes stops me. *Wait one second.*
I turn back. In his hand is a twenty.

*You must be hungry. Have some lunch
while you wait for your brother.*

I could protest, but I *am* hungry.
Starving, actually. I kiss him on

the cheek. "You're the absolute best!"
He drives away and I go inside.

The smell of greasy food almost
overwhelms me. It's been so long!

"Double cheeseburger, fries, and
a chocolate shake," I tell the waitress,

feeling a lot like Pavlov's slobbering
dog. After I eat, I have to get out of here.

Jerome must be looking for me, and even
a half-wit could guess I came this way.

Vegas. Why not? All I need is a ride.
And there are plenty of truckers to ask.

It Takes Three Tries

The first says he's not going to Vegas.
The second one just says, *Fuck off.*

The third, a beefy guy with bad teeth,
looks me up and down. *You running away?*

I had an hour at lunch to figure out
a good story. I use it now. "Not exactly."

He flashes his rotten smile. *Not exactly?
What, exactly, does that mean?*

"See, my parents split up, and my mom
moved me to Elko so she could live

with her boyfriend. I hate that bastard. He . . .
he . . . you know." I look down, acting

all embarrassed. "Anyway, I just want to
go home to my dad's. He lives in Vegas."

*Old story, kid. But what the hell?
I'm going that way. Hop in the cab.*

We climb into opposite sides of the semi.
The trucker swallows some sort of pill,

starts the engine, and as he turns onto
the highway, I say a little prayer of thanks

for my rescue. But we don't get all that far
before rescue becomes something else.

Don't suppose you have any money?
asks rotten mouth. Considering

I'm wearing nothing but a light blue,
pocket-free shift, and carrying not

a thing, the answer should be obvious.
Diesel's getting awfully expensive.

"Sorry. No. Stupid me, I forgot
my backpack. Wish I could help."

*Well, there are other ways a girl
can help out a guy. You know?*

Mr. So-not-nice trucker issues an ultimatum:
Oral sex or a very long walk to Vegas.

Stupid me. But it's not really anything
new. At least I don't have to kiss him.

He Drops Me Off

At a diesel stop on the outskirts of the city.
I don't say thank you. I paid my way.

It's dirty here and surrounded by desert.
Not pretty pinion-studded playa like up north,

or back in Boise. But plain yellowed sand
defiled by houses. Lots and lots of houses.

From here, I can see giant casinos, all different
shapes and sizes. Motels. Chapels. Strip malls.

Traffic clogs a maze of streets and freeways.
Honking. Puffing exhaust. Military jets scream

across the cloudless sky, and commercial
aircraft come and go in regular procession.

It's all ugly. Stinking. A sinkhole of unrealized
dreams, forfeited faith. A girl could get lost here.

A Poem by Seth Parnell
Dreams Forfeited

Diffused by distance,
him a thousand miles
away. Still you feel his

pain.

It's as if you can tune
into him with a psychic
antenna, catch some unique
sonar that carries his

cries

across great distances.
It stops you cold
in your plodding tracks

and you

wonder where he is.
Could he be just
outside? You put your
ear to the door and

listen,

crazy with want,
knowing the front
step is vacant.

Seth
Any Farm Boy

Half worth his beans and
      butter would tell you weight
      lifting and cardio training
      are all about ego. A hard day's
work on the back forty gives

you both, and a crop to boot.
      But Carl insists I stay in
      shape. Guess chubby guys
      stand on the low rung of
the trophy boyfriend ladder.

      Truth be told, he was pissy
         about how he put it to me.
         You know what happens to
         muscle when you quit working
it, *right? I'm not into fat boys.*

      It would be in your best
         interest to invest a little
         time at the gym. It was not
         a suggestion. It was an
ultimatum. One major thing

I've learned about Carl is,
          business or pleasure,
          it's his way or no way
          at all. While I can respect
that on a certain level, when

it's in my face, it's not easy
          to take. He is one hundred
          percent about control. Not
          sure why I didn't see it
sooner. Not looking, I guess.

The strange thing is, I'm not
          the least bit flabby, let alone
          fat. So why? Preventative
          maintenance? Whatever. I have
nothing better to do, anyway.

So Here I Am, Midmorning

Jogging six miles per on
    a treadmill. Going nowhere
    and doing way too much
    thinking about what I've
allowed myself to become—

powerless. Even at home,
    the only time my dad
    dismissed me completely,
    no argument allowed, was
the night he kicked me out.

Remembering him, revisiting
    the farm, stirs up a cloud
    of homesickness. Loneliness.
    I am alone in this place,
despite nightly company.

I don't belong here. I know
    that. But I don't belong
    anywhere else, either.
    And that is at the heart
of the black depression

pressing down on me,
    flattening me. I have
    no place. No home. Sex,
    but no real affection. I am
kept, but not cherished.

I Am Swimming in Sweat

When an amazing-looking
    guy decides to share the gym.
    The way he assesses me
    leaves little doubt that he's
not into girls. Maybe working

out isn't such a bad idea after
    all. He offers a ten-thousand-dollar
    smile, then sets his gym
    bag down on a chair. I can't
help but stare when he strips

off his shirt, revealing buffed
    pecs and a six-pack I'd kill
    for. The guy is a high-priced
    Thoroughbred. And I'm
definitely not talking mares.

He goes straight to weights,
    choosing some machine
    I have no clue how to use.
    When he looks my way,
I'm still staring like an idiot.

    He grins. *What? Did I flash*
        you or something? Hope
        it wasn't offensive. Most guys
        seem to like it well enough.
    He pauses. Gives me time

to formulate some inane answer.
　　　I slow the tread to cooldown
　　　speed, try to quit huffing.
　　　　　"I . . . uh . . . sorry . . . didn't
mean t-to stare . . ." Huff, huff.

"I just started"—huff, huff—
　　　"working out and"—huff—
　　　"I know this is dumb, but"—
　　　huff—"I don't know how to
use all the machines." Heart rate

slowing, I catch my breath
　　　and finish, huffless, "I thought
　　　I'd watch you and learn how
　　　to do it. Uh, use the machine,
I mean." Okay, *that* was inane.

　　　He finds it amusing. *Oh, I see.*
　　　　　Well, I use the machines all
　　　　　the time. Happy to give you
　　　　　some pointers, if you want.
　　　The name's Jared, by the way.

"Seth." I stop the motorized
　　　roadway. "I'd appreciate
　　　anything you can give me . . .
　　　I mean tips. . . ." Shit!
I'm sabotaging myself!

Hang On

Just why did I think that?
        Sabotaging what, exactly?
        I'm not shopping for
        companionship. Am I?
"Tell me to shut up, okay?"

        Jared laughs. *Shut up,*
            Seth. He gestures for me
        to come over to the machines.
        So what are you most
        interested in working?

Now we both laugh at
        the unintended (?) double
        entendre. "Well . . . other than
        that, I want one of those."
I point to his amazing stomach.

        Don't blame you. Okay,
            you can use the ab crunch
            and the assisted pull-up. But,
            so you know, diet is huge too.
        This is all about protein, my man.

"No problem. I can handle
        meat. . . ." (!!) Once again,
        I give his body an approving
        assessment. "And just so *you*
know, I'm not afraid of hard work."

He nods. *Most farm boys*
aren't. At my perplexed
look, he adds, *It's your accent.*
Very Midwest, with a touch
of the South. Kentucky? Missouri?

Oh man. It shows? "Indiana,"
I admit. "I never realized
we had accents, though,
especially not with 'a touch
of the South.'" Really weird.

Not sure why it works
that way, but it does.
Nothing to worry about,
though. I find it kind of
appealing. Come here.

I'm a kid again, called to
the front of the classroom,
not knowing what for.
Will he—shiver—touch me?
But no, all he does is show me

how to properly use the ab
crunch machine. Still, he
stays close, and the entire time
I'm burning gut flab, a word
floats in my head—beginning.

All Worked Out

Tired, sore, I start toward
        the townhouse to shower.
        As I leave, I venture,
        casually as I can, "Hope to
see you around again soon."

        Jared is toweling off
                his own sweat polish,
                and I'm struck again
                by the beauty of his body.
        Hot tub tonight at nine?

I hesitate. I never go out
        when Carl's home. Still,
        he wouldn't object,
        would he? Long as I omit
the Jared part. "I'll sure try."

        He gives me a wry grin.
                Could he know why
                I live here? *If I don't see*
                you tonight, I'll run into
        you here, I'm sure. Later.

I follow him out the door,
        watch his sure gait along
        the walkway, tugged, steel
        toward magnet. It's odd,
really. Usually I'm attracted

to softer men, with the major
            exception of Leon Winkler.
            And wouldn't his football
            jock butt shudder to know
exactly *how* I looked at it?

Don't know why I'm
            thinking about any of this
            now anyway. I'm pretty
            much committed to Carl,
who should be home soon,

expecting me showered
            and shaved, all smooth
            and scented with Armani
            Black Code, his favorite
fragrance. Expensive taste,

not a bad thing. He'll also
            want dinner started. High-
            end meat or seafood. Steamed
            vegetables. Fresh bread.
Never the same meal twice

in any given month. Good
            thing Dad taught me how
            to cook. Hmm. Wonder
            how Carl would feel about
venison sausage and gravy.

Venison Is Not Easy to Find

In Vegas, so I'm working on
  seafood Newberg (recipe
  care of one of Carl's large
  collection of cookbooks)
when he finally arrives.

He is not alone. Neither
  is he sober as he trips
  through the door, laughing,
  accompanied by a friend.
Acquaintance? I have no

idea. This is the first time
  he's ever brought anyone
  home. The guy is maybe
  forty-five, and everything
about him, from the square

    cut of his bangs to the way
     he wears his extreme
     jewelry, screams "queen."
     When he squeaks, *Hello there,*
    he leaves zero doubt about it.

    Carl comes over and gives
     me an ostentatious gin-
     flavored kiss. *Something*
     smells good, and I'm not
    talking about in the kitchen.

He kisses me again, which
        is weird. For all the sex
        we've shared, a kiss from
        Carl is relatively rare.
I almost don't know how

        to respond. Finally he draws
            back. *Oh, how rude of me.*
            Come say hello to my friend,
            Brett. Brett, meet Seth,
    my uh . . . paramour.

        Carl takes my hand, leads
            me to the sofa, where
            Brett has made himself
            extremely comfortable.
        Pretty boy, Brett says. *Very.*

My nerves lift on sharpened
        edge, like when you go
        hunting and suddenly feel
        hunted. I force my voice low.
"Good to meet you, Brett."

        Now, now. Let's not be
            so formal. He laughs,
            and it isn't a pleasant laugh.
            Any paramour of Carl's
        is a paramour of mine, right?

Before I Can Answer

He is all over me. Hands.
        Mouth. Ugh. Tequila.
        I push him away. "Wait
        just one fucking second. . . ."
I step back, look at Carl,

        but he's into the game.
        Refereeing, in fact.
        No need to be rude to
        our guest. He's here by
invitation. Understand?

"Invi—" Carl wants me
        to be with this creep?
        What happened to our
        "exclusive relationship"?
"No, I don't understand."

        With fine diamond clarity,
        Carl explains, *I enjoy*
        a bit of variety from time
        to time. I expect your whole-
hearted participation.

        He pushes me, and not
        gently, toward Brett.
        Now apologize to my
        friend as I hope you
would apologize to me.

He Does Not Mean

With words. And he doesn't
    exactly mean solo. They
    move in unison, and I am
    sandwiched between them,
Carl behind me, moving

sensuously, while Brett dares
    kiss me again. I hold my
    breath against the assault
    of gin at my back, tequila
in my face. A strange tongue

in my mouth. Now Brett
    rests his chin on my shoulder,
    and he and Carl are kissing.
    It's a cobra dance, and despite
what it means, I am charmed.

Seduced by sensual motion.
    Behind me and in front
    of me, both men grow hard,
    and for some horrifying reason,
I respond in like manner.

I Have Never Considered

Three-way sex. How would . . . ?
        Oh. No way will I let one
        of them take me like *that.*
        Like Loren, Carl has always
played the feminine role.

But unlike with Loren (who
        insisted on using condoms),
        with Carl (who refused to),
        I set limits—"Carl, you know
the rule." My rule: hands or

        mouths only. He stops
            kissing Brett, but neither
            man quits moving, writhing
            like mating hooded serpents.
        We're playing by my rules,

        remember? But don't worry.
            I only expect you to give.
            For now. From somewhere,
            he extracts a condom, hands
        it to me, keys to the kingdom.

Don't rush, he orders,
  and don't you dare
  close your eyes. I want
  to see how much you like
it. He moves in front of me,

  strips Brett from the waist
    down, pushes him onto
    his hands and knees. Then
    he drops his own trousers.
  Come on, he urges, positioning

himself inches from Brett's face.
    Shaking, I move behind Brett,
    grab his shoulders. Carl's hands
    cover mine. Brett moans as I . . .
Oh my God! I am damned.

But I don't stop and I don't
    rush. Carl's eyes never once
    leave mine. Finally I beg
    his permission. "Now? Please?"
He nods and I do. We all do.

A Poem by Whitney Lang
Don't Stop

Don't look behind you.
Something is chasing
you, and if you slow

                 down,

it will catch you. Run!
Faster! Through alleys.
Tunnels. Underground.

              Down there

in that dark place,
fear is your friend
for complacency kills

              down where

instinct is survival.
Reach. Find your wings.
Fly away from the

              monsters,

hard on your heels.
Don't stop. Only
then can they win.

              Run!

Whitney
Fighting "Night Time"

Pretty name for the hideous pukes
and soaking sweats of withdrawal.
I understand I have to go through it.
Die if I don't. Maybe die if I do.

I don't want to die. Do I? Fuck,
what if it's better than living half in,
half out of this world? Goddamn Bryn!
Bastard turned me into a zombie.

So why do I sit here, crying to see
him? Why do I love him so much?
He cheats. Lies. Lied about everything,
from start to now. I know it. Don't care.

I want to be with him. Want to make
love with him. Even though that means
waiting my turn. He has other girls.
Other zombies. Killing time in cheap

rooms like this one. Sometimes he comes,
rewards them like he rewards me,
with junk and beautiful sex. Sometimes
other men come. That sex is never

beautiful. It is selfish. Needful.
Fueled by sick desire to get off. Get
even. Get over someone who has
hurt them by symbolically impaling

someone else. So Bryn's zombie girls
stay stoned. Out of our heads
messed up. Eyes closed, we can
be anywhere. Italy. France. Australia.

Jupiter. Hell. Doesn't matter, as long
as we're not *here*. As long as we can
pretend we're still pretty. As long as we
can make believe Bryn still loves us, too.

I'm Not Stupid

I know I'm addicted. Damn it all,
despite the many promises I made
to myself, I mainline now. A needle
in the vein delivers Nirvana

so quickly! And in those first few
minutes, when all the pain is lifted,
I see what Bryn saw in me that first
day at the mall—naïveté. I was stupid.

He knew it. I was crazy hungry
to fall in love. He saw it in my eyes.
And then, when I called him, stinging
at rejection, he so had me. He is very

good at what he does. Recruiting
girls, feeding them a steady diet
of lies and drugs, then starving them
until they submit to his demands.

He is a pimp, plain and simple.
A fucking gorgeous, sweet pimp,
who I'd do anything for. Including
advertising my body: For Sale. Cheap.

He'll come to me soon. I need the Lady
bad and he knows it. Can't send me
out on the streets like this. It isn't pretty.
Probably couldn't even give myself away.

When Bryn's Key

Finally turns in the lock, I'm huddled
in a corner, covered in goose bumps,
shivering through the sweat. At
least I'm all puked out. He takes

one look, nods. *Poor baby. Don't
worry. Daddy has presents for his
beautiful little girl.* He comes over,
sits beside me. Pulls a dime bag

from his pocket like it's made of gold.
Clean rigs, too. *Let Daddy fix it
for you.* He cooks up a perfect spoon,
loads it, plunges it between my toes.

Bryn gives me wings. The sting
is luscious, the awful rush all I need.
No, not all. I need Bryn. And he's here,
all mine right now. His lap is warm,

inviting. I climb into it, slip my arms
around his neck. *Thank you. Better now.*
Oh, so much better. Soaring. Up here
in the clouds, the air is dry. I kiss him,

suck his tongue into my mouth, seeking
moisture. It curls over my own tongue,
sensuous as smoke. Time slows.
Make it stop! Make it stop with me,

here in Bryn's arms. I want him.
Want him to take me higher. Want sex
as it was meant to be, as only Bryn can
ever give it to me. "Make love to me."

He pushes me to the floor. My head
spins, dizzy with anticipation. My brain
screams, kiss me! Kiss all those special
places, just like you used to. I know

he will, but . . . But what? Why
is he stopping? He reaches into
a back pocket. What is that?
A rubber? No. We don't need that.

I'm on the pill. It was one of the first
things we did when we got to Vegas.
"N-no." Is there mud in my mouth?
I can barely cough out, "Why?"

> He stops fiddling with the wrapper,
> but doesn't answer right away. Finally
> he says, *Never know what kind of gift*
> *one of your customers might have left.*

What? My face flushes, hot from
the skag, hotter still with an overdose
of anger. Always, with no exceptions,
"My *customers* use condoms."

I Try to Push Him Away

But even if I were perfectly
straight, my stick-figure body
would be no match for his toned
physique. And I'm not straight.

My vision is blurred, like looking
through a fishbowl, and my muscles
feel like steel cables—much too heavy
to drag around. And the weirdest

thing about all that is how great
it feels. I'll nod soon, and that's when
the pain vanishes. So hell, he can screw
me, if that's all it means to him.

       He boosts himself up over me.
       Tries to look down into my eyes.
       But I stare at the wall. Will myself
       to go limp. Familiar one-act play.

       That's it, he soothes. *No need
       to waste a perfectly good boner.*
       In. Out. In. Out. I close my eyes.
       Float. Pretend I'm with a john.

When I Surface

From my lake of dreams, Bryn
is gone. He left a note: *Stashed
the bag and fixings in the usual
place. Same price. Tomorrow.*

How have I fallen so low? I knew
about junk, even told Bryn no way.
Then I let him talk me into it. Love
is more than blind. It's brain-dead.

My brain screeches, *Fix! Fix!
Quick, before I make you heave.
Quick, before I give you the runs.
Quick, before I start remembering.*

Remembering I once had another
life. Hated it then. Might still hate
it now. But more than I hate this?
Hate what I've become? No matter.

This is all I've got. I cook up a spoon.
Oh yes. That's good. So good.
Clock. Where are you, clock?
There you are. Evening already?

The boys are out, scamming
for play. Shower. Hurry. Night's
tick-tocking away. And I've got
bills. *Same price. Tomorrow.*

Skin Tight Men's Club

Is hopping tonight. Boys go in.
Stay a while, watching pole dancers
and cocktail waitresses, shaking
their boobs for tips. Boys come out,

horny as hell. Some go home
to beat off or bug their wives.
Some look for girls like me,
loitering in the shadows where,

       hopefully, cops cruising beats
       won't notice them. Bryn taught
       me the ropes. *Act interested,*
       but don't push. The girls who

       get busted are in-your-face.
       Dress sexy, but leave some up
       to the imagination. Sexy schoolgirl
       That's the look you want.

       Ask what they want up front,
       and collect before you take
       'em home. Wouldn't want to
       do all that work for nothing,

       and believe me, plenty of guys
       got nothing, especially if they
       overspent inside. And if some
       dude seems hinky, say no.

I've said no a couple of times.
It wasn't because they were fat
or bald, but because of what I saw
in their eyes. More accurately,

what I didn't see in their eyes:
life. Sharks, that's what they were.
Dead cold scary. No way was I
chancing a swim with them.

Most johns are more mackerel
than great white. Cold slimy bait
fish, quick to jump into the net,
especially when what they're

jumping in after still looks fresh.
Don't know how long that can
last. Hooking uses you up fast.
Figure in hyping, I'll look thirty

before I turn seventeen. I turn
sixteen day after tomorrow,
not that one single person in
the world gives half a damn.

Why Did I Have to Go

And think about that? Damn!
If I were still in Santa Cruz, I'd be
planning my Sweet Sixteen party.
Daddy would insist. We'd have it

at the club, and we'd have a band,
and Paige would be there and maybe
even Kyra. . . . Oh my God. What
have I done? Daddy must think . . .

What? I'm dead? Mom hopes I am.
But not . . . Daddy. I'm sorry. Shit!
I sit down hard. Sidewalk cement bites
into my butt, which is naked beneath

a short denim skirt. My head tilts
against my knees, and my eyes trickle
tears. Heavy. My head is so heavy.
The H wants to take me away

and I want to go. Away. Far. Where
nothing hurts. Nothing . . . Eyes on
me. Are there eyes? Don't look. Have to.
To know . . . Who? Can't lift my head.

> Roll it sideways. *Are you all right?*
> The eyes are talking. No. Not eyes.
> Lips. Stupid. Eyes can't talk.
> *Do you want me to call 911?*

"N-no thanks. I'm o-o-k-kay."
So okay I can't even say okay.
For some messed-up reason,
I start to hiccup. "Ju—" *Hick.*

"Just think—" *Hick.* "Thinking
about my b—" *Hick.* "Buh-birthday."
Hick. Hick. Hick. Somehow
I manage to focus my eyes.

> The guy isn't pretty, but his
> expression is kind enough. Maybe
> even concerned. *Are you sure
> you're okay? You been drinking?*

Can you get this screwed up
from alcohol? Looney Tunes laughter—
hick-hick—spits from my mouth.
"Sorry. No, don't drink much."

> Now I can see the wolf in his eyes.
> No surprise. Even nice enough
> guys go on the prowl. *Okay. What
> do you do that's fun, then?*

I Swear Until This Moment

I never even noticed his hand
creeping up my leg, ever closer
to my semi-exposed crotch.
Eyes can be deceptive when

they talk. I crack up again.
This time, at least, the hiccups
seem to have disappeared. But
I'm starting to ache for a rig.

Bryn's words settle through
the fog. *Leave something to
the imagination.* I give the guy
a quick feel before pushing

his hand away. "Oh, I for sure
know how to have fun." Game on.
Wait. Bryn again. *Ask if he works
vice.* "You a cop or what?"

>He grins. *Or what. I'm not even
>from around here.* He stands, pulls
>me to my feet, steadies my wobble.
>*Live close? I'll walk you home.*

It Isn't Far

Just eight blocks. The guy chit-
chats the whole time. Something
about Omaha. Cornhuskers? He
played for them? Bets on them?

Oh yeah. Sportsbook. Won five
big ones. (How big? Hundreds?
Bigger?) I can't concentrate on
what he's saying. All I can think

about is a syringe full of magic.
How fast can I do this guy?
We swing into the parking lot,
cut across to Building Two.

Key. I need the key. It's in my
purse somewhere. Too much crap
in here. Like, why do I carry it,
anyway? Just to irritate myself?

We reach the apartment and I hear
Bryn again. *Look around before
you open the door.* I do. A car
is parking a few spaces down.

And going up the stairs of the other
building is that girl I see sometimes,
mostly in the laundry room. Copacetic.
Cool word. Where did it come from?

I unlock the door, start to turn the knob,
when more words fall into my brain.
Business before pleasure. I turn.
The guy is so close, we're almost

attached. I give him a little shove
backward. "Before we go in, we
should talk about what you want
and how much that will cost you."

> *Cost? You want me to pay for it?*
> He pushes me inside. *I don't pay*
> *for sex. Even if I did, I wouldn't*
> *pay for you, you junkie bitch.*

He is all predator now, and on me.
Scream! But his hand is already over
my mouth. I shake my head, look
into his eyes. This wolf has mayhem

> on his mind. He takes me down.
> So okay. Give it to him. I go limp.
> *No!* he screams. *Fight, you goddamn*
> *whore! Fight, or I'll kill you.*

No fight left in me. Fuck me. Kill
me. Don't care. He wants both.
His penis stabs me, his hands lock
around my throat. Air. No air. Black . . .

Air!

My lungs grab it suddenly. I float
up into gray light, roll onto my side,
vomit. Only nothing comes out.
Noise. Someone's screaming.

> *Get the fuck out of here, you son*
> *of a bitch. I'm calling the cops*
> *right now, so you'd better run.*
> *Come back, I'll kick your ass.*

My throat throbs. The wolf! I sit up.
Too fast. My head is a merry-go-round.
Down. The carpet stinks. Saved.
I'm saved. Bryn! He does loves me.

Watches over me. "Bryn? Where
are you?" Footsteps across the stinky
carpet. Not Bryn's. Too soft.
Someone leans over me. The girl

> from the laundry room. *Just lie still.*
> *I think you'll be okay. He's hurting,*
> *though. I hit him with a book.*
> *Good thing you read big ones.*

She smiles. Sad. She's sad. *Should*
I call the cops? Didn't think so.
I'll stay with you for a while if you
want. I'm Ginger, by the way.

A Poem by Ginger Cordell
I'll Stay

Right or wrong,
I'll stay until
you tell me I have to

                                    leave.

Until you can look
into my eyes, swear
you no longer love

                                    me.

It would be a bitter
cup of broken-
promise tea, but

                                    I'll

swallow it if you say
I must. If I go, sad
sweet dreams will

                                    follow

me, weighting my days,
strangling my nights.
Sad, sweet dreams of

                                    you.

Ginger
Sadness

Encircles me, a black halo.
        It's this city, this dried-up
desert well, sucking hope

like sand. People come here,
        hoping. Hoping to get rich.
Hoping to get laid. Not many

go home richer than when
        they arrived. Easier to get
laid, as long as they have

a few bucks in their pockets.
        Then there are the people
who move here with big

dreams. They dream of stand-up
        comedy, of playing rock and
roll. They dream of dancing lead

in some steamy casino show.
        If they're talented and lucky,
they might end up in a chorus

line or drumming with a bar
        band. But lots of them wind
up just like me, selling pieces

of themselves. Pieces they can
　　　　never have back. There's this
girl who works for Lydia.

　　　　Her name is Misty. *I won't do
　　　　　　this forever, she swears. *Just
　　　　until I get my degree. Then*

　　　　the world is my apple pie. . . .
　　　　　　Okay, metaphor isn't her best
　　　　thing. And neither is school.

If she gets her degree, it will
　　　　be because she slept with
the right teacher. Or three.

Every time I run into Misty,
　　　　a little more of her is gone.
I can see it in her eyes.

When you sell your body, you
　　　　also sell what's inside. Piece
by piece, you sell your soul.

Now Here's This Girl

Who almost lost everything.
        She let her guard down. Plain
and simple. If I hadn't been

doing my usual nosy thing,
        checking out the neighbors,
she'd probably be lying here

waiting for her pimp to call
        the coroner. Yes, I know who
her pimp is. He's the only guy

who comes around almost
        every day. Collecting money
and delivering sustenance—

food, trinkets, and substances.
        Heroin. I was right about that.
I watch her now, plunging

        a syringe full of hot amber
                liquid. Her head rolls side-
        ways and she fixes me with

        sleepy golden eyes. *Want
                some? I don't have a whole
        lot, but I kind of owe you one.*

"No thanks. Not my thing."
        Her body visibly relaxes as
relief pumps through her veins.

Suddenly she clutches her
        stomach, runs into the bathroom.
"You all right?" I yell at the door.

        She exits seconds later, pale
                but smiling. A very bad smell
        of voided body waste trails her.

        Doesn't embarrass her at all.
                Sometimes the Lady makes
        you sick. But it's good sick.

        There's room on the couch,
                and a vacant chair, but she sits
        on the floor, as if afraid of falling.

        Now she rocks herself. Forward.
                Back. Forward. Back. *Thank you*
        for . . . wait. How did you know?

"I dunno. Guess he just looked
        like bad news. Then he started
yelling crazy shit. I usually

mind my own business. . . ."
　　　　Yeah, right. "But my 'little
voice' was screaming. Good

thing you never shut your door.
　　　　Even better, he was too busy
trying to choke you to notice."

　　　　Her hands rise protectively
　　　　　　toward her neck. *I thought
　　　　I was on my way to hell for

　　　　sure. She strokes the raised
　　　　　　scarlet finger marks gently.
　　　　Hurts like a mother. Is it ugly?

I have to say, "Pretty ugly.
　　　　You might have to take a few
days off. Most guys won't want . . ."

Too familiar. Then again,
　　　　I just watched her shoot up.
I repeat, "Take a few days off."

I Expect Surprise

That I know how she makes
        her money. Or anger at me,
because I've been such a snoop,

or at herself, because she's
        made it so obvious. I get neither.
Nothing but silent acceptance.

Is it the heroin? Or is it just
        her? Probably both. I want to
ask where she came from. What

kind of parents she has, if she
        has any at all. How she hooked
up with her so-called boyfriend.

That's, no doubt, what he calls
        himself. Want to ask, though
I know the answer, if he's the one

who started her on the junk.
        Her head sways forward
as the drug carries her toward

Dreamville. She'll be totally out
        of it soon. I'll ask something
easy. "What's your name?"

At the sound of my voice,
her head jerks up. *Oh. It's you.*
You tell me your name first.

Wow. She's pretty out of it
already. "I told you before.
It's Ginger, remember?"

She giggles like a little kid.
A stoned little kid. *Oh, yeah.*
Hey, Ginger. I'm Whitney.

Somewhere in her sudden
animation, I catch a glimpse
of Whitney, the way I imagine

she used to be before . . . him.
She nods again and I hurry,
"Are you still in love with him?"

Yo-yoing in and out of now,
she is coherent enough to know
who I mean. *Bryn is everything.*

It's the Last Thing She Says

Before dropping all the way
        into whatever dark narcotic
place the junk pushes her toward.

I swear I'll never venture there.
        Lately I don't even feel like
drinking much. All it does

is make me stupid and sick.
        It doesn't make me forget.
In fact, sometimes, the drunker

I get, the more I remember.
        I remember the kids, how
annoying and entertaining

        they could be. Do they miss me?
                Have they even asked, *Where
is Ginger? Why did she go?*

I remember Barstow, the armpit
        town where I first made a friend,
first got decent grades. Ms. Felton

        even told me once, *You're an
                excellent writer. You should
        think about it as a career.*

Writer? Me? And what am
　　　I doing instead? I remember
Sandy, a ball in the street,

　　　　and Mary Ann's face, scrunched
　　　　　　with pain. *I'm sorry. I should
　　　　have . . .* Only the blame belonged

to me. Which always brings
　　　me back to my very favorite
memories, all centered around

Gram, deceptively petite, while
　　　so driven. Tireless. Completely
devoted to a pack of kids she owed

absolutely zero devotion. All
　　　because of her giant capacity
to love. Does she hate me

now for taking the easy way out?
　　　Would she ask me to come home
if she could? Did she mean it when

　　　she said, *You know where I live.
　　　　No matter what, I want you to
remember this is always your home.*

Tempting as It Might Be

To get back on the bus, see
          if she would welcome me,
uglier memories intrude on

that sweet little daydream.
          Since the revelation about
Iris sicking her snarling dogs

on me, other faces—other
          mutts—materialize when
I least want to recognize them,

often just as I sink into an
          alcohol-fueled stupor, praying
it will let me sleep, dreamless.

I was so young the first time,
          I didn't know what it meant,
only that nothing had ever hurt

so bad. Walt tore me up and I bled
          and bled and when I screamed,
nobody came. And he laughed.

That's it, little baby. Scream
          for your daddy. Only he wasn't
my daddy at all. My daddy was

a brave soldier, fighting far away.
          Iris told me so. I still believed
the stuff she told me then. When

          I told her about the man, not
          my daddy, she said, *He was*
only making you into a real girl.

I didn't understand. But I made
          myself believe her. I was a real
girl now. But what was I before?

Walt Was the First

There were others. Nameless.
        Faceless. I figured out how to
close off my brain when they did

it to me, to withdraw into a dark
        little room inside my head, where
I couldn't see them. Couldn't smell

their sweat, their stagnant breath.
        Couldn't taste the tobacco coating
their tongues, or the beer tainting

the spit they left in my mouth.
        Couldn't feel what was down
between my legs. But now they

revisit me. Is it because of what
        I'm doing? Because of these
nameless, faceless men watching

me? Even without them touching
        me, I feel dirty about what I do.
Alex does even filthier things

but says it all washes off with soap.
        I don't believe that. I think it all
leaves stains. Indelible stains.

I Wait for Her Now

Wondering where she is, what
       she has done today, if she'll come
home. Lydia called. We've got

a bachelor party at ten. It's nine
       fifteen already, and no sign of
Alex. I tried her cell. Went straight

to voice mail. The battery must be
       gone. If she doesn't show, I'll have
to go alone. Won't be the first time,

and she knows how scared I am
       to work by myself. I still love her,
but I feel her slipping away, bit

by bit, every day. Finally the door
       opens. She's a total mess—makeup
smeared, hair like a rat's nest, clothes

dirty and torn. I rush to her side,
       "What happened? Are you okay?"
I try to hug her, but she shoves me

       away. *Don't touch me.* Tears spill
          from her eyes, tracking mascara
       down her cheeks. She sinks down

on the sofa, puts her face into
　　　　her hands. *Bastard screwed me,*
then robbed me. Took everything.

Again I try to hold her. This time
　　　　she doesn't pull away, but she is
like sandstone. Hard on the surface,

crumbling beneath. "It's okay.
　　　　We'll be okay." Then, an afterthought, "How much did he get?"

　　　　Her head sags against my chest,
　　　　　　　wetting my shirt with tears, snot.
　　　　Not sure. Four or five hundred.

Anger flares suddenly, but not
　　　　because of the money. Because
of what we've become. "We've got

a goddamn bachelor party,
　　　　clear across town. We'll barely
make it if we leave right now."

　　　　She looks up at me with ringtail
　　　　　　　eyes. *I can't . . . please. I'm gonna*
　　　　be sick. She runs to the bathroom.

I follow, put an ear to the door,
　　　　hear the definite sound of puke
splash. "Okay," I call. "I'll take

this one by myself. But when I get
        back, we have to talk." For once,
I'm not afraid to do the gig alone.

The whole cab ride over, I think
        about what it is I want to say.
I arrive at a few minutes after ten.

The guys are young, not much
        older than me. Good. They won't
ask for many extras. I handle

the business end, promise a lap
        dance to the groom, who looks
excited and scared at the same time.

And for the entire hour I'm taking
        off my clothes, shimmying and
writhing and faking "sexy," my mind

is on one thing. I don't know
        how, where, or even with whom.
Just know I have to get out of here.

A Poem by Cody Bennett

Don't Know

Who I am anymore.
I was sure once, not long
ago. Knew where I came
from, and where I was

          going

to. Now I don't have
a clue who puts on
my shoes in the morning,
nor what direction he's

          going

when he closes the door
behind him. He looks a lot
like me. But his flame has
been extinguished, buried

          too far

beneath his soil to find
air enough to smolder.
It is no more than a vague
memory, all oxygen

          gone.

Cody
How Do I Find Myself Here?

Not even a year since everything
started a snowball roll toward hell.
It's a place I'm starting to know well,
a place I deserve. I mean, I couldn't
stop Cory from fucking up. He was
set on it. And Jack wasn't my fault.

I didn't make him get cancer, did my
best for him when he did. Hear that,
Jack? I wanted to help you! Couldn't.
I'm not God. What happened is between
him and you. Can't you do anything
up there to help me out down here?

Okay, maybe I'm not worthy
of your intervention. Maybe you're
just plain grossed out. Pissed off.
But if you help me, you'll help
Mom, too. She can't make it on
her own. Damn it, you promised!

And dude, if I can't worm my way
out of this crazy place, I'll have to
consider that medicine chest, still full
of pain meds and sleeping pills. Mom
would only miss me so long. The rest
of the world wouldn't miss me at all.

That Includes Ronnie

Oh, she claims she misses me now.
I only see her at school, and I'm not
there a whole hell of a lot. I should
be, of course. Just started junior year.
If I really want college, really want
more, I need to focus not only on

attendance, but on getting good
grades. Impossible. Too much
going on. Too much going down.
Hard enough, just surviving.
Trying not to think about Cory.
Not to think about Lydia, etc.

I get to class late, or not at all.
Can't find interest in any of my
classes. English? I talk good enough.
Math? Let me give you a point
spread. History? Want to hear
mine? Chemistry? Girls or men?

And Ronnie? She pleads for attention.
*Can't you please come over, spend
a little time with me? C'mon, Cody.
I miss you so much. Remember . . .*
Then she'll try to convince me,
bringing up one of those special

(God, yes, they *were* special)
times we spent in bed. Oh, I do
miss holding her close. The satin
of her hair. The luscious full curves
of her body. But sex means something
different now. I can't tell her that.

So I lie. Tell her I have to work. (For
a temp service, so she can't track
me down any certain place.) Tell
her I have to drive Mom somewhere.
(Usually to visit Cory.) Tell her
I'm just too freaking tired. (No lie.)

Sooner or later, she'll get sick
of the excuses and find another
guy. I only hope it's someone
who deserves the perfect girl.
Not an addict. Not a boy whore.
Not a fucking loser like me.

The Only Thing

I've won at lately is a few games
of chance. A hand or ten of poker.
And the Chiefs have been on a roll.
I've tried to keep the bets reasonable,
but the problem with winning is,
once you've got a bigger bankroll,

you want to make bigger bets. Got
a whopper riding this week. Enough
to let me skip a couple of "dates,"
if my luck holds. I have been smart
enough to pay my car insurance
for six months, help Mom with

the power and phone. She thinks
I'm working at a temp service too.
Since they place you in jobs
temporarily, according to different
businesses' need, it provides
the perfect excuse for sometimes

having money, sometimes not.
For being away from home odd
hours. And, since those jobs tend
to be manual labor, Mom doesn't ask
why I so often plunge straight into
the shower after coming through the door.

On a Positive Note

I've managed to make small credit
card payments. Not enough to pay
down the principal, but enough
to cover the interest, anyway. Only
one problem. As had to happen,
I couldn't keep intercepting the bills.

Mom called me into the kitchen. *Cody,
what are all these charges to Int-Gam,
Inc.?* She stood there, hands on hips,
waiting for my confession. How
could I tell her "Int-Gam, Inc."
was Internet Gaming Incorporated,

and that I had been using the cards
for months, losing money hand over
fist? "I'm not sure, Mom," I lied,
looking her straight in the eye.
"But just so you know, I found
those credit cards in Cory's things."

I can't believe what a liar I've become,
and lying about Cory was a way low
blow. But she bought it. Why not?
Her youngest son is a criminal.
Not much of a stretch to think
that he might also be a thief.

Credit Cards

No longer being an option, sports bets
will have to be laid down through
local bookies. Vince knows one or
two. And there's always poker.
Hey, I've got a stake—a few hun
saved up. Anyway, I've got spending

cash, thanks to Lydia. Mostly it's
from men. Thank God, I haven't had
too many experiences similar to the one
with crew-cut Dan. I can't seem to excise
that night completely from my head.
I've questioned a lot of things about

myself before. The gambling. Booze.
Drugs. Lying. But, despite sleeping
with men for money, I've never
questioned my sexuality. That's
the core of any man, any person.
How can I be unsure of that, especially

considering the pain and humiliation?
Maybe Lydia was right, and we all
swing both ways to some degree. *It's
all according to necessity,* she said.
Does that mean if every woman
disappeared, I'd actively crave men?

Not Craving Any

Of the guys at Vince's tonight.
I glance from face to face, chest
to chest. Nope. Not a single twitch.
Maybe there's hope for me after all.
Now if Lady Luck will just decide
to climb into my lap, hang out.

> *Hey*, says Vince. *Anyone bring
> smoke?* He looks straight at me,
> not expecting me to say yes. It's
> been weeks since I had enough
> cash to score. My connection had
> almost given up on me too.

I surprised him, and I surprise
Vince now. "Actually, yeah, I do."
I hand over a couple of big blunts,
light another, pass it on. Only way
to convince Vince to introduce me
to his bookie friends is with generosity.

Meanwhile, it's poker. The key
to winning this game is properly
assessing the competition. I know
most of the guys at the table—Vince,
best player here, a regular bluff master,
not afraid to lay down a major bet.

Justin is an elementary school janitor.
Can't afford to bet big. Never ups the ante.
Sitting down is Shaun, UNR freshman,
innocent-looking, but knows how to bet.
Finally, there's Misty's boyfriend,
Chris. He's a total jerk, and wasted.

> A fair bit of coke has been passed
> around, but I'm guessing he's been
> smoking ice. Maybe even crashing,
> despite the cola. His mood is mean.
> *Fucking deal already, would*
> *you? Haven't got all night.*

> Vince stares him down, trying
> to decide, no doubt, if he's going
> to have to deal with Chris some
> way other than nicely. He starts
> with nice. *Take it easy, man.*
> *Where you have to be, anyway?*

> Chris grabs the cards, now in
> a pile in front of him. He sorts
> them one way, then another, shoots
> eyeball arrows around the table as if
> we're all just waiting to give our
> hands away. *Got a date with Misty.*

Fact Is

I've got a date with Misty. Well,
not with her, exactly. We both have
a date with some sexually confused
out-of-towner. Three-ways aren't
quite so bad. Misty isn't the brightest
girl. But she's got a killer bod to focus

on. It's okay to be turned on by that.
The evening's little snort party will
help me out too. In fact, we might
even have fun. But, far as I know,
Chris isn't coming along. "You sure
you're hooking up with Misty tonight?"

> The table falls silent. Not even
> a minimal buzz as Chris gives me
> an odd look. *That's what I said.*
> *Why? You know something*
> *I don't?* He throws three cards
> on the table. Waits for more.

And also for my answer. "Uh.
It's just I thought she had to work
tonight. You know. For Lydia."
I draw two cards. Dig way down
for composure. Lady Luck is definitely
rock 'n' rolling with me. Full house.

Chris doesn't respond. For some
reason, that bothers me a lot. I look
over at him and he's staring at me,
head tipped as if listening to something no one else can hear. Little
voices in his head? Schizo, too?

It's all lost on Vince, who draws
last. One card . . . C'mon, Lady,
don't trade partners now! His face
gives nothing away. But when
he bets, we all gulp in breaths.
He tosses some chips. *A hundred.*

Justin folds. Shaun considers quite
a while, finally calls. Chris swears
softly, breaks out in a sweat, trying
to figure out if Vince is bluffing,
decides he must be. He calls. I call.
We show our cards. My full house

wins the pot! Six-fifty! Oh, yeah.
Lady and I are doing a full-on mosh
now. One thing I've managed
to learn, "Thanks so much, gentlemen,
but it's time for me to go." It *is* time,
in fact. My date is in twenty minutes.

Hot Damn

I am feeling good. I stop at the bank,
make two deposits. Into my account.
Into Mom's account. Not much, but
enough to help out a little. I'd cancel
my three-way, but I promised I'd do
it. Lydia is expecting me to. And so

is Misty. Who I really want to see
right now is Ronnie. First time in
a long time I'm feeling the need
for a long, healthy roll in the hay.
I give her a call, half expecting
her to be out with somebody else.

        But she answers immediately.
        Hello? Oh God! The sound of
        her husky voice lifts me even
        higher. *Uh, hello? Is somebody*
        there? When I let her know it's
        me, she is standoffish at first.

"You can be mad at me. I deserve
it. But Ronnie, I swear, I'm so sorry
for pushing you away lately. Things
have been . . . uh, bad. We can talk
about that later. I get off in an hour
and a half. I know that's pretty late. . . ."

Zero hesitation. *No! Come over.*
I'll stay up, however long it takes
you to get here. She pauses, and I
can imagine her voice growing
thick in her throat. *Goddamn you,*
Cody, she sputters. *What took so long?*

I haven't cried in a long while,
not since I mostly got over Jack.
I pretty much thought my tear
machine was broken for good.
But no. I can barely choke out,
"I don't know. But I do know

I love you. See you in a little while."
I can't get her off my mind as I drive
to the address Lydia gave me. I feel
awful. Feel wonderful. And for
the first time in a long time, I feel
hopeful. A few more dates, a couple

of big wins, I'll get out of this
business for good. I'll find a real
job. Put money away. Help Mom
somehow. Stay in school, work my
ass off and get into college. Oh, there's
the motel. First things first.

I'm a Little Late

Usually Misty waits for me and we
go in together. Guess she didn't want
the guy to think we weren't coming.
I check the room number. Twice.
One time I knocked on the wrong
door. Was that guy ever surprised!

This time when I knock, Misty calls,
Come on in, baby. I do, find her
already mostly naked. The guy,
who's a totally forgettable middle-aged
nothing, is completely naked.
Jeez, man. I'm only five minutes late.

The dude, who isn't much down
there either, despite it being at full
mast, turns his attention away from
from Misty, focuses on me. *What
are you waiting for? Time is money,
you know.* Like it's going to take him

much time at all. But whatever. It *is*
his money. And less time is better.
Misty distracts him with her yummy
boobs and I start to pull my T-shirt over
my head. Suddenly the door explodes
behind me. What the . . . ?

Something—bear or bulldozer—
knocks me face forward to the floor,
forcing my breath into the carpet.
    Misty screams and Nothing Man
     yells, *What the fuck,* as my right
kidney takes two massive punches.

My shirt is still over my head and
I can't see a damn thing as I fight
for air. But I hear *crack-crack-crack.*
And the room goes silent, except
for strained breathing, right above
me. And then I hear . . . sobbing.

    You fucking whore. It is Chris's voice.
    You promised . . . no more . . . you
    said . . . and you . . . he means me.
    His boot takes out two ribs. Oh
    my God. Is he going to kill me?
    Jack! Didn't mean it. Don't want . . .

Snap! Lightning? White-hot. Electric.
Shattering. My back. Pieces. Bone.
Dark. Darker. Cut through the black,
blinding light. What? Buzzing. What?
Suck air. Where? Can't . . . No, please.
Ronnie? Sorry. So sorry. Ron . . .

Light Floats

Just beyond my eyelids. I want
to open them, see the light, but
the darkness is comforting. Not
much here. Beyond the nothing
(nothing? Nothing. Nothing Man?),
something. A hum. A whisper.

Wake up. Can you wake up for me?
Motion. All around me, movement.
Pressure. Wrapping me. Pressure.
Air. Saccharine air, pumping
into my lungs, through . . . plastic.
Plastic? My eyelids stutter. Light!

Sunlight. I am outside. Can't move.
Tied? Strapped. Strapped to a gurney.
Parking lot. Red and blue lights.
Oh my God. I remember. I roll my head,
see another gurney. "Misty?" A cloth
covers her face. "No." It is a whisper.

Best I can do. A second gurney
carries another still figure. Nothing
Man. Gone. Both of them gone.
But I am still here. "Thank you, Jack."
A paramedic asks what I said. "Phone,"
I tell him. "Call Mom. And Ronnie."

A Poem by Eden Streit
Still Here

At least I think so,
what's left of who
I used to be

a shadow

on the sidewalk.
I look up, try to find
a rainbow, but the only
thing there is

a lone cloud,

stretching thin
and thinner, clear
to almost not
there, across

an upside-down sea.

I lower my gaze into
a puddle, close my
eyes at what I see.
Don't want to believe

that ghost is me.

Eden
I Am Less Than a Ghost

I am a corpse, sleepwalking the streets
of Las Vegas. Sometimes I think

I should just head on out into the desert,
lay down on a soft mattress of sand,

close my eyes against the diamond sun
and circling black wings. And wait.

It might be preferable to this cement bed
behind a 7-Eleven Dumpster.

> There are lots of us living on the street.
> They say Vegas is easier than Reno. *Warmer.*

> *There are shelters,* I've been told, *where*
> *you can eat free. Shower sometimes. Sleep.*

But I'm afraid of the questions. Too many
questions. So when my stomach offers up

its acid, when I can't stand the hollowness
for another second, I sell one more slice

of my soul. One slice, twenty dollars. I've been
here three weeks. Not much left of my soul.

As for My Body

It's battered, scraped, bruised. The Tears
of Zion shift looks about a hundred years old.

I did spend a few bucks at the Salvation Army.
Bought a used skirt, two tank tops. Underwear.

I hate to think who used them, or why they gave
them away. But they only cost a dime apiece.

I stink, too. I've managed four or five showers,
when the man of the hour wanted to spring for

a motel room. More often, it's the seat of his car.
Quick and easy, five minutes or less. No emotion.

No pain. And the weirdest thing is, I'm not
the least bit embarrassed about doing it anymore.

That's the worst part. That, and when my brain
insists on remembering Andrew. Thinking

about how he held me, rained his love down
all around me, brings devouring pain.

So I'll think instead about the coming night, where
I might peddle the remaining tatters of my soul.

Rush Hour

The freeways are bumper to bumper,
so surface streets jam with commuters.

A few of the pushier girls go straight
up to them at traffic lights, knock on

their windows. *How about a date?*
Most of the guys shake their heads.

Some of them look close to panic. Afraid
they might catch something through the glass?

But every now and again, one of them
opens the passenger door and the girl slips

inside. The car takes off, and minutes
later, comes back around, business done.

I watch a girl get out of an older Cadillac.
At least they had plenty of leg room.

She steps to the curb, stares me down
with steel eyes. *What are you looking at?*

For some crazy reason, I shatter.
"N-nothing. I m-m-mean I d-don't know."

Her gaze softens. *New to the biz, huh?*
Well, sweetheart, this is a real bad place

for tears. Those guys are freaking sharks.
If they smell blood, they'll chew you up.

"I know. I'm sorry. It's just that you're
the first person who's even talked to me

since I got here. I mean except to tell
me to suck harder, or . . ."

She cracks up, and so do I. *Yeah, well,*
I know exactly what you mean. Uh, don't

get me wrong, okay? Her nose scrunches
up. *But you could really use soap and water.*

"That bad, huh?" My face actually heats.
Doing disgusting things with gross men

doesn't embarrass me, but her observation,
no doubt deserved, does? "I'm on the street."

She reaches into a pocket on her skirt,
pulls out a thin fold of bills. *Here's fifty*

dollars. Get a room and some food.
And listen, from the looks of you, this

*isn't the right business. Get smart. Call
home. You don't belong on the street.*

I shake my head. "You worked for that,
and I know what you had to do for it."

*Everything about her hardens. I told
you to get smart. Take the money.*

*I don't know what you ran from,
but living like this can't be better.*

*Funny, but my girlfriend, Ginger, keeps
telling me the same thing. I never wanted*

to listen before. Maybe now I'd better.
Her nose wrinkles again. *Call home.*

But shower first. She turns abruptly.
Later, she snorts over her shoulder.

Good Samaritan

The words pop into my head. That
is the second time someone I didn't

know and will likely never see again
handed me money they couldn't afford

to give away. I don't understand. Why
me? Other words surface from a place

      of deep indoctrination: *Whatever they*
      do for the least of my children, they do

      for me. . . . I wander along the overbaked
      cement, sucked into a cerebral vortex.

When it finally spits me out again, I am
on the sidewalk in front of a church. Guardian

Angel Cathedral. Catholic. I am struck
by the beauty of the angular architecture,

and by the amazing artwork above my head—
Jesus, hands extended in welcome, to one and all.

I've never once walked beyond the doors
of a Catholic church. But I am drawn inside

this one. I enter, a stranger to the faith.
To the God of this faith and every other.

Friday evening, no worshippers, I find cool
solace inside. I slide into a seat at the rear,

fold my hands. Close my eyes. Do I remember
how to pray? "God, you know I have done

terrible things. I don't want to do them anymore,
and ask for your forgiveness. I am so sorry. . . ."

My voice catches in my throat. Was I speaking
out loud? Just a little more. "Thank you

for good Samaritans. And please, God, please,
if it's your will, show me the way out."

A sense of peace blankets me, and a gentle
voice whispers, *How can I help you?*

God? No. There is shallow breathing, too.
I open my eyes. A priest sits beside me.

He reminds me of Andrew—handsome,
and fresh, with compassion in his eyes.

"I don't know how, Father, but I do need help."
Need his help, and God's help, to be saved.

A Poem by Seth Parnell
No Way to Be Saved

No way to hit reverse,
turn around,
go back home.

          No

chance at forgiveness.
The shale cliffs of

          redemption

have crumbled,
surrendered to the sea.
How do you look

          for

miracles when you
deny belief? How can

          someone

formed of bone and sin
trust his weight to wings?
How does a man

          like me

find innocence again?

Seth
I Don't Remember Innocence

Not, I guess, that I need to.
> Nothing innocent about
> how I live now. Nothing
> naive about being a toy.
That's what I am now. A toy.

But, hey, what are my options?
> I thought about trying to go
> home. Once I even swallowed
> every ounce of pride, put
in a phone call to Dad.

> His raspy voice lifted
>> memories, good and not so.
>> *Hello? Hello? Who the hell
>> is this?* Then he thought
> a sec. *Seth? Is that you, boy?*

Don't know if it was the "boy,"
> or just remembering his words
> the night he sent me away,
> but I couldn't say a damn
thing. I slammed down

the receiver, retreated into
          a murky cave of depression.
          It's a place I've visited
          more and more lately.
The only thing that seems

to yank me away from there
          is working out. Sweating
          poisons of body and soul.
          Having Jared around to help
me sweat isn't so bad either.

          In the few weeks since he
                    started helping me, I can
                    see a vast improvement.
                    He agrees. *Much better form.*
          Both your lifting, and your body.

He is really close, and the smell
          of his sweat beneath his leathery
          fragrances reminds me of a tack
          room. For some reason, it is
desperately turning me on.

Despite my ballooning
          attraction, I have yet to overtly
          put any sort of moves on Jared.
          He might be taken. And I am
under ongoing ownership.

But no way can I lie back
        on this weight bench without
        that traitorous part of my body
        totally giving me away.
I inhale like I can't find air.

        You okay? he asks. His own
                breath falls hot on my neck,
                and the stable smell becomes
                almost overpowering. Tack.
        Sweat. I remember something.

I was little. Playing at Grandma
        Laura's. Hiding in the tack room.
        Hiding with my cousin, Clay.
        He touched me. There. And it
felt good. So good. So . . . "Oh."

I turn to Jared. What the hell?
        "I'm okay. Except . . ." God!
        "I totally want you." There.
        Said it. He can laugh at me now.
But he doesn't. He kisses me.

We Are Alone

In here. The workout room
      is always deserted midday.
      Still, I might hesitate, but
      Jared is in total control.
    Come on. He leads me into

the sauna, but doesn't turn
      it on. Now our sweat scents
      mingle and the combination
      is heady. There is no need
for words as our bodies link.

He is strong. The first strong
      man I've ever been with, and
      this time I don't give. It is new.
      Frightening. Exhilarating.
But somehow I trust it to be

all right. And it is more than
      that. A piece of my puzzle
      falls into place, a piece I didn't
      know was missing. Fifteen
minutes to Seth, reinvented.

I'm Still Trying

To sort it all out in my head
        when Carl gets home. Early
        for once, and with no company.
        "Oh. Didn't expect you so soon.
I'll start dinner right now."

        Don't bother. He goes into
        the living room, pours himself
        a drink. Does not pour one
        for me. *So tell me. What
did you do today?* The look on

his face explains way too much.
        Something nasty bubbles up
        in my belly. But I'm not
        ready to confess—not yet.
"I read. Swam. Worked out."

        *Sounds like a pretty easy day.
        You have it easy here, don't
        you, Seth?* He doesn't wait
        for my reply. *So why in the hell
did you want to go and blow it?*

Okay, he knows. But how?
        And what does that mean
        to me? And how much,
        exactly, does he know?
"What are you talking about?"

He advances, sipping his drink
　　　　like he doesn't have a care.
　　　　*You know exactly what I'm
　　　　talking about. Did I give you
permission to pick up some*

*guy in the workout room? Slip
　　　　into the sauna for, shall we
　　　　say, an afternoon quickie?
　　　　Did you think I wouldn't keep
tabs on you? All you young fags*

*are alike. Simon's philandering
　　　　taught me a lesson—never trust
　　　　a boy toy. And here in Vegas,
　　　　there is no shortage of pretty
faggots, willing to do just about*

*anything to earn an extra dime.
　　　　That includes acting as bait.
　　　　I didn't expect Jared to follow
　　　　through and actually do you,
but whatever.* I start to protest.

Carl holds up a hand. *Shut
　　　　your mouth. You have twenty-four
　　　　hours to pack up and get
　　　　the hell out of here. Be gone
when I get home tomorrow.*

He Will Not Allow

Explanations or arguments.
        He's had his say and I am
        to leave. He doesn't give a damn
        where or how. Won't even front
a few bucks to send me on my way.

I wander into my room, turn on
        my computer—the computer.
        It belongs to Carl. I've got
        less than a day and zero capital
to start completely over.

I have exactly one resource—
        a better, buffer body than when
        I arrived. I'll have to barter
        it more carefully. It's the only
one I have, after all. I go to

Craigslist, Las Vegas Personals.
        Click on Men 4 Men, scan the ads.
        Here's a Help Wanted ad for Have Ur
        Cake Escorts. Just in case, I jot
down the number. But what I'm

really looking for is another Carl.
        There are a few possibilities.
        Can't be too picky. I send
        out several e-mail intros, wait
less than patiently for a response.

A Poem by Whitney Lang
Less Than Patiently

The Lady waits. Pretty
China White demands
I listen, and hold her in

                     my arms.

She is my only friend,
my one ally against
the low, throbbing

                     ache

inside my brain,
against the loneliness
my heart was not
prepared

                     to hold.

Will it break beneath
the obscene weight of

                     him

not loving me? How
is it possible I could
have been so very wrong

                     again?

Whitney
No Love

In this world for me. No hope.
No future. Nothing but plodding
through each day, not quite
surviving. I am not alive

except when I'm fresh off a plunge,
that first rush after a hot shot.
Then, for scant minutes, life
rages through my veins, a river.

Bryn comes later and later each
day, if he comes at all. Sometimes
I wait, barely hanging on,
wondering if he's back in Santa

Cruz, combing the mall for a new
Whitney. Then I get mad. Not only
because my body is twisted with spasms
of need, but also because I should

be there. Not him. I belong there—
used to belong there. Don't belong
there or anywhere like this. Waiting
for maintenance. And so, I've come up

with a plan. Bryn isn't the only supplier
in Vegas. Sometimes they hang out
at strip clubs. And, I suspect, I can find
one who might be up for a trade.

I watch from a distance as a car
pulls up against the sidewalk, a block
down the street from Skin Tight.
Don't know if the deal was set up before

or if this is a regular haunt for the guy
who goes to the window, collects
some cash, and tosses something at
the passenger. The deal is down in less

than thirty seconds. I can't be sure it
was H without a little scamming of
my own. The guy, who is pretty much
a stereotypical Latino deal-meister,

turns back toward Skin Tight. I sidle
up, flash some thigh. "Hey, honey.
You looking for a little fun?" Already
broke one of Bryn's rules. But this guy

def isn't the heat. He is high himself,
but not on junk. His pupils shout "crystal."
My heart sinks. I start to back away.
More reasons than one for rules, I guess.

The guy grabs my wrist, pulls me
into him. *Hey, now. Where you going?*
You ain't a whore and *a tease, are*
you? 'Cause that might make me mad.

I've gotten a whole lot better at reading
guys since my little choking incident.
This is not a guy I want to make mad.
"No, baby. Just a whore, and a good

one." Might as well play the game
for money if the Lady isn't on the line.
But I'm not giving up on that yet.
"I was just hoping maybe you had

a little something in your pocket."
I run my knee up over his bulging
groin. "Something besides that, I mean,
and something to take me down."

His turn to assess my eyes, looking
for lies. What he finds is a junkie.
He shakes his head. *Don't got no bonita,*
baby. But I could maybe get some.

That's the crystal talking. He wants to
get off, not an easy thing, high on meth.
I hate doing guys on meth. Takes too
long. But hey, this was my deal.

We Agree on a Time

To meet, and a corner three blocks
from my apartment, just in case
Lorenzo can't score. Not having
some crazed meth fiend thinking

he's getting laid with nothing
coming back the other way. After
Mr. Omaha, it was days before I'd
let a john come through my door.

> Bryn was patient. For maybe one day.
> After that he was all, *Get over it already.*
> *Odds are you'll meet up with a creep*
> *once in a while. You had your once.*

He promised to check in more often,
to keep a better eye on me. But it hasn't
happened that way. Ginger has showed
more concern, and I don't even know her.

> She knocks on my door at least
> every other day. *Just making sure*
> *you're still breathing,* she says.
> Doesn't come in very often.

But that's okay. Not like we're best
friends or anything. Girls in the business
don't really have friends. Our lives
are all about acquaintances.

I'm Supposed to Meet

My latest acquaintance soon. Don't
know if I can make it three blocks
without a little help. Please, Lorenzo,
score! I'm getting so low. It's only

been a few hours since my last visit
with the Lady, but I'm shaking like
it was yesterday. Just a small fix for
now. If Lorenzo doesn't come through,

maybe Bryn will show. I only know
I've got to stop the knotting in my belly.
Ah! Better. Have to go while my brain
can still tell my feet to walk. Three blocks.

Lorenzo! Right on time. Fine quality
in a dealer, right? Sexy. Look sexy.
Forget the schoolgirl part. This guy
isn't shopping for innocence. "Hey, doll.

Find what I'm looking for?" He smiles,
takes my hand, slides it down into his
pocket. Not one bag. Two. And,
farther down, something else.

> No problem. It's part of the deal.
> *My guy says dis stuff is pretty good.*
> *You wanna pay for one and fuck*
> *for one, or what?* We start to walk.

I have a little cash stashed. Don't tell
Bryn about my "extra" deals. A little
extra cash for a little extra service.
"Sounds good." Meth or no meth,

though, we have to go quick. I'm on
Bryn's clock already. "Before we start,
show me the stuff." He does. It isn't
white or even brown. "What's this?"

> You never seen black tar? Baby,
> it's the best. Believe me, those boys
> in Mexico know their shit. Now come
> over here. Take a taste of this.

I've heard of black tar Mexican.
Never tried it, but guess I'm gonna.
Ol' Lorenzo gets a ride around the world.
Doesn't take as long as I thought.

By the Time He Leaves

The Lady is singing a siren song
to me. Might as well try the black,
see if Lorenzo's acquaintanceship
is worthy of long-term cultivation.

Two bags stashed, might as well take
a real rocket ride. I cook a massive
spoon. Don't even bother to look for
a vein more concealed than on my arm.

Five. Four. Three . . . Whoosh!
Incredible. Lorenzo, I love you, baby.
Rush! Waves of pleasure flood my brain.
It's a regular cerebral orgasm.

Wait. No. Too much. Down I go.
And oh, the noise. The noise inside
my head. Pounding. Blowing.
Exploding like a hurricane.

Close my eyes against the wind.
Spinning in my brain. Air. Need air.
Suck it in. Thick. Can't breathe it in.
Damn stinking carpet. Again. Slow.

Slow. Slow. Heart. Beats. Slow.
Wind. Spins. Inside my head.
Don't like this. Bad wind. Hurricane.
Slow. Sleep. Slow. Sleep . . .

A Poem by Ginger Cordell
Wind

Shuffles autumn feet
across November sand,
stirring grit like

                ice

chips. Crystal white.
It blows along
deserted sidewalks,

                crusts

lonely avenues. Where
has she gone? Panicked,
I search for

                her

in familiar places.
Restaurants. Theaters.
Alleyways adjacent the

                heart

of the city. I call out
her name. It returns,
hollow, an echo.

Ginger
Late Night Last Night

Three outcalls, one post-midnight.
       It was a good night for tips, so Alex
and I celebrated with fine Italian

dining and people watching on
       the strip. I slept in this morning,
lay in our bed, still perfumed

with our lovemaking. We don't
       do that so much now. I've missed
it. But more and more, Alex flinches

when I touch her. Not just me,
       I think. But anyone. Everyone.
It took twenty minutes of gentle

kissing and easy massage to arouse
       her even slightly. And while she had
no problem pleasing me, nothing

I did could bring her all the way.
       Sex for Alex is nothing but a job.
It isn't in my power to fix that.

It's strange, really. Strange
       and sad. When we first got here,
it was me who shrank from touch.

Alex taught me the joy of skin
       against my own skin. She showed
me how to feel without fear.

Now she's the one afraid to feel.
       I wish that I could change that.
But she's built a fortress around

her. A sand castle. It's bound
       to crumble. And when the sea
rushes in, I'm afraid she'll drown.

It's Almost Noon

By the time I yank myself out
       of bed. "Alex?" I call, but my
intuition tells me I'm alone.

I check the bathroom, wander
       into the living room. No Alex.
Damn, damn, damn. She can't be

out turning tricks already! What
       is wrong with her? We don't need
the extra money. I don't get it.

I want to find her, drag her
       off the street or out of whatever
car she has gotten into. But Vegas

is a big city. Alex could be
       anywhere. Still, she has a few
favorite places. I clean up,

get dressed, call a cab, head
       out the door. Damn. What's
going on across the parking

lot? Looks like a garage sale.
       Oh. Whitney. An ambulance
took her away a few days ago.

Guess the landlord decided
          she's not coming back and neither
is her sleazy pimp boyfriend.

A small knot of people stand
          around watching the landlord
haul her stuff out of the place.

Sounds like the creep is taking
          offers. I go up to an older lady.
"Everything for sale, huh?"

          The woman barely looks at
                    me. Too busy checking out
          bargains. She shrugs. *Guess so.*

Poor Whitney. How far
          did you run this time?
"Why? Did she . . . is she . . . ?"

          The lady shrugs again. *Don't*
                    know. But hey, those junkies
          are the walking dead, anyway.

Junkies and Whores

Whitney and Alex. No life
       force left behind the lenses.
The walking dead. Spot-on.

      My cab arrives. Not a driver
             I know. *Where to?* he demands,
      tapping the steering wheel like

      he's got somewhere better to
             be. When I hesitate, he drops
      the flag. *Where you want to go?*

I'm not in the mood for snippy
             cabbies. "Just drive down Las Vegas
Avenue. I'll tell you when to turn."

It's my dime. I'll spend it how
             I want to. I have him cruise in
circles, in an area known for

its strip clubs and accompanying
             activities. "Slow down. I might
want you to stop." Feels good to be

the one giving orders for a change.
             I see several working girls. A few
guys. One or two in the "not sure"

category. There. That's her.
Right there in the plain light
of day, hustling. "Stop here!"

He pulls to the curb, and I hand
him two twenties for a thirty-two-dollar
fare. He looks at me. *Change?*

"Goddamn straight." No tips
for smart-assed cabbies. Off
he drives in a huff. Good.

Alex doesn't notice me right
away. Too busy working a guy
in ugly purple Bermuda shorts.

I tap her shoulder. "What's up,
girlfriend? You're not thinking
about doing this guy, are you?"

Alex jumps. *Ginger! What
the hell?* She looks at Bermuda,
who is seriously checking me out.

He licks his lips. *Well, hello.
You're not really her "girlfriend,"
are you?* Meaning, are you two,

like, lezbos? "Actually, I am
        her girlfriend. Why, you want
to watch?" You effing pervert.

I can't believe how pissed
        I am, or how submissive
Alex is acting. I expected more

                of a reaction. Bermuda reacts
                        for both of them. *Hell yeah!*
                How much to do the two of you?

        Don't say anything, Ginger!
                Alex warns. Who the hell
        died and made her boss?

If she can hustle guys, so can
        I. This one won't get off cheap.
"Three hundred for all you can eat."

                Right on. Bermuda reaches into
                        his back pocket. But it isn't money
                he shows. *Vegas vice.* He flashes

        a badge. *You're under arrest for
                solicitation.* Then, an afterthought.
        How old are you, anyway?

A Poem by Cody Bennett

Afterthoughts

Why can't an afterthought
be forethought?
Where does

                                  hindsight

take you if you're
focusing behind you?
What important

                                  is gained

when the lesson
defies recollection?
When Alice stepped

                                  through

the looking glass,
did she see herself
backwards, or did
the whole rabbit hole

                                  experience

simply make her
close her eyes?

Cody
Don't Want to Open My Eyes

If I do, it will mean I admit I'm still
alive. Right now, I think, I could
choose to let go, say a silent good-bye,
and join Jack on the Other Side.
Do I want to do that? Don't think so.
But what if it's better? Until I decide,

I lie here, churning in an anesthetic
sea, inhaling antiseptic air. I'm on
my stomach, and want to turn over,
but something won't let me. And when
whatever painkiller it is they've got
me on starts to wear off, my back catches

fire. While I wait for more, praying
they hurry, a tide of voices rushes in.
            Whoosh: . . . *he should have*
regained consciousness by now. . . .
            Whoosh: . . . *suspect was the girl's*
boyfriend . . . haven't found him yet. . . .

            Whoosh: . . . *know what the boy*
was doing there or his relationship . . .
            Whoosh: . . . *leave me, Cody. Don't*
you dare make me lose you, too.
            Whoosh: . . . *Colts, fourteen; Chiefs, ten.*
Figures. Goddamn loser Chiefs.

Eventually the Tide Recedes

One voice remains. Even if she wasn't
talking, a steady, downstream flow,
I'd know it was Mom by the hills
of her hands. They stroke my face,
gentle my hair from my forehead.
Carry me back to when I was little.

> *I don't know what you've gotten*
> *yourself into, Cody boy . . .* just
> like when I was little . . . *but you*
> *can work your way out of it . . .*
> just like when . . . *I don't know*
> *if I can help you, but I'll try. . . .*

Work my way out. But it's such
a long way out. I don't know if
I'm strong enough. Not even with
your help, Mama. Easier to just say
good-bye. Your hands feel good,
though. I love your hands. . . .

> There's a weird noise. A loud hum.
> *No! Cody!* Footsteps. Running. *Cody,*
> *you come back here right now!*
> More hands. Motion. I am on my back.
> Shit! That hurts. Different hands.
> Pressure. Something covers my nose.

Air. Sweet. Why is it sweet?
In and out of my lungs. Breathing
for me. The hum changes to a steady
blip . . . blip . . . blip . . . Hey, just
like in the TV shows. *Blip . . . blip . . .*
I know what that means. I'm still here.

Mama? Don't cry, Mama. Rub my hair
again. I'll stay for a while. Promise.
Goddamn! My back's on fire again.
But I can't say so. Can't open my eyes.
Can't promise I'll stay. That would
be lying. And I'm so, so tired of lies.

     Voices. Decisions. Voices. I'm okay
     for now. One voice I haven't heard.
     Ronnie, I understand. Hope you know
     I'm sorry. You . . . are . . . are . . .
     Mama's voice again. *His pillow is wet.*
     Doctor, is he crying? Doesn't that mean . . .

Yes, Mama. For now. Don't know
how long I'll stay. If I come back,
I'll try my best to change. Mostly change.
Feels good when you rub my head,
Mama. *Blip . . . blip . . .* Odds are good
I'll come back to you, Mama. . . .

A Poem by Eden Streit
If I Come Back

If I come back to you now,
can we be what we were

          before

life's uncertain rhythms
tore us so far apart? If

          I return

today, will your arms
gather me in, or will

          I

be wrenched away,
snatched by a riptide I

          have

no power to resist?
If I find my way

          to

you, one man standing
in a crowd, will I even

          know

who you are?

Eden
Off the Streets

Safely sheltered by the kind people here
at Walk Straight, thanks to Father Gregory.

What is it with me and good Samaritans?
I never believed so many really existed,

never guessed that any of them would ever
reach out and yank me away from hell.

That's where I was. Hell isn't some fiery
pit "down there." It's right here on Earth,

in every dirty city, every yawning town.
Every glittery resort and every naked stretch

of desert where someone's life somersaults
out of control. Satan—Evil—doesn't have

horns or poke you with a pitchfork. His power
doesn't come from full moon sacrifices, and he

doesn't go out looking for new recruits. He
doesn't have to. All he has to do is wait.

Walk Straight

Is an amazing place, a rescue for teen
prostitutes who want to turn their lives

around. All they have to do is ask. I didn't
know to ask, but Father Gregory did.

It's run by an exceptional woman,
he told me, an ex-prostitute herself.

When she got out, she wanted to help
other young people get off the streets.

You'll have a place to live, an education.
They'll help you decide how to shape

your future. If you have a pimp, they'll
encourage you to testify against him,

and they'll go to court with you so you
don't have to be afraid to put him away.

When I got here, they cleaned me up,
fed me, had a doctor run some tests.

I'm not pregnant, didn't catch some
horrible disease. I was a little anemic,

but that will change with good nutrition.
I didn't eat nearly so well at Tears of Zion.

My Caseworker

Is named Sarah. She's really nice, but
she does ask a lot of questions, some

of which I'm not prepared to answer.
Sarah: *Where is your home, Ruthie?*

Okay, so I haven't been completely
honest with them. I'm afraid if I give

them my real name, they'll find some
kind of all points bulletin out for me.

So I used my middle name—Ruth. Sarah
added the "ie" to make it "feel friendlier."

I didn't exactly lie when I answered,
"Las Vegas has been my home for a while."

Sarah: *Okay, then. Can you tell me
how you ended up in "the business"?*

More mostly truth. "I never wanted to.
I just didn't know any other way to survive."

Sarah: *I understand. And what about
your parents? Will you tell me about them?*

"They're dead." That was not a lie.
My parents *are* dead. To me.

Boise, Idaho

Is a bittersweet memory, and Tears of Zion
is a wake-up-shivering nightmare. My parents

are zombies, death-walking through both.
I would die before I'd go back, and I'll have

to tell Sarah all of that very soon. Because I did
find a way to get hold of Andrew. His mom is still

a professor at Boise State. And, duh, professors
have e-mail addresses. We have computer access

here at Walk Straight. I e-mailed her two days
ago. She got back to me yesterday.

> *Eden! Thank God you're okay. We've been*
> *so worried! Andrew has searched and*
>
> *searched for you. He pestered your parents*
> *so much, I thought they'd have him arrested*
>
> *again.* . . . She gives a long story about
> the first time they had him arrested, and how

they and some of Papa's congregation
harassed Andrew until he had to have

his phone number changed. *He'll be so*
relieved. How can he reach you?

I Insisted on E-mail

A phone call would mean somebody
knows and cares I'm here. I'm not

ready to confess that yet, not ready
to think about talking to Pastor Streit

and his not-nearly-as-sweet-as-she-seems
right-hand woman. She will never be Mama

again. I don't know how much I will ever
be able to tell Andrew about the past few

months. I'm changed, and he'll know
that. But does he have to know why?

If he finds out I'm here, I guess he'll figure
out why. I go to the resource room,

> open my Gmail. Oh my God. It's here.
> *Eden,* he writes. *I can't believe it's you.*
>
> *Every prayer answered. When can
> I see you? When are you coming home?*

To the point. All Andrew, in cyberspace.
I type a to-the-point reply: "Not sure

when I'll come home. Lots to talk about.
Just know, now and always, I love you."

A Poem by Seth Parnell
Home

Simple word. Four letters,
two consonants, two vowels,
one of them silent.

                                            Home.

You wish you could walk
through a familiar
door, shout out

                                            the word,

in a simple two-word
sentence:"I'm home!"
But that door

                                            has

been closed to you,
slammed shut in
your face, and

                                            no

amount of pleading
will open it again. Two
consonants, two vowels.
One word without

                                            meaning

when you don't have
a home.

Seth
Always Believed

There would be a way back
    home eventually. Figured
    sooner or later, Dad would
    come around, accept me
for how I was born. Part Mom,

    part him. But no. I did finally talk
        to him on the phone. For all
        of three minutes. *You come
        to your senses? Asked
        the Lord for forgiveness?*

"That's between him and me,
    Dad. And anyway, I never had
    much sense to begin with. I'm
    still who I am, though, no more,
no less. Want you to know I love you."

He didn't budge. Didn't
    say okay, son, come on
    home. Didn't say I'm good
    with you, just how you are.
Didn't tell me he loves me.

I Also Messaged Loren

Found him on Facebook.
   Seems everyone has one of
   those now. "Moved to Las Vegas
   with a friend," I wrote. "Things
didn't work out, so I'm looking

for another place." I hoped, of
   course, that he'd write back,
   confess how much he misses
   me, ask me if maybe I'd like
to give upstate New York a try.

I didn't hear back for quite
   some time. So long, in fact, that
   I was beginning to think he
   was going to ignore me completely.
Finally, though, I got a reply.

Seth. Great to hear from you.
         Glad to know you wound up
         somewhere cosmopolitan.
         I've got some news of my
own. Hope you'll be happy for

me when I tell you I hooked
         up with someone really
         special. You'd like him,
         I think. In fact, he reminds
me a whole lot of you. . . .

Don't Know Where

I'll wind up in the future.
        I have no way to leave Vegas.
        Not for a while. So for now,
        I'll stay here, living with David.
Met him through a friend of a chat

buddy, and so far, so good.
        He choreographs major shows,
        and with over thirty years in
        the business, is something of
a Sin City icon. His house has

ten bedrooms. You could call
        the decor garish, with marble
        statues and white furniture.
        Paparazzi hang around outside
his parties, which are regular.

I have no more with David
　　　　than I had with Carl, except
　　　　for amenities. My life is still
　　　　not my own. But it may never
be. One thing I did take away

from Carl is to try and earn
　　　　a little money of my own,
　　　　save up a small nest egg. Have Ur
　　　　Cake Escorts is my way of doing
that. When David isn't looking.

A Poem by Whitney Lang
When You Weren't Looking

The child became a woman,
though she wasn't ready
to. Don't ask how or

         why.

Those questions are not
the important ones.

         Can't you

see you didn't

         care

enough to notice?
How will you feel
if we have no

         more

time together? I wonder
if you're sorry now

         about

the way you locked your
heart, access denied to
the beggar at your door.
She's nobody, only

         me.

Whitney
Almost Died

That's what they told me. Ninety
percent of me wishes they would
have let me go. Easier than battling
the vicious onslaught of withdrawal.

Easier than coming to terms with who
I was when I almost died. I don't even
know that girl. She's an esoteric
someone, like a movie character

you can't quite recognize. Even
with my head just about straight,
she seems like a caricature—a cartoon
rendition of one of the living dead.

Throughout a week of intensive care,
I drifted in and out of the almost corpse,
not quite warmed by hospital flannel.
Then there were several more days, mostly

conscious as they pumped sustenance
into my veins. Sustenance and heroin
substitutes. Easing me off the Lady.
Pretending they didn't want me to hurt.

I Can't Tell You

Exactly how many days I hovered
somewhere between this world
and another, or which was the scariest.
But the first face I saw, when I decided

I might as well open my eyes, didn't
belong to a doctor or a cop. Or Bryn.
I can't remember ever seeing it so full
of compassion. Who was this woman?

> *Oh, Whitney,* she said. I expected
> a *How could you?* but instead I heard,
> *Thank God you've come back to me.*
> To her? Did I come back to her?

Did I come back at all, and if I did,
would I stay? The jury was still out.
Still is today, a month later. No matter.
That day, her concern surprised me.

Pleased me. Overwhelmed me, though
I'd never admit it in a trillion years.
I pretended indifference. "Nice to see
you, Mother, I guess. Why are you here?"

> My snotty tone should have drawn
> a barb. But no. She came over to
> the bed, took my hand. *I'm so sorry.*
> *If I would have lost you forever,*

I don't know what I would have done.
Please, Whitney, whatever your reasons
for leaving, for . . . for . . . She actually
started to cry. *We can work through this.*

Daddy came in later. Angry.
And Kyra, on semester break.
She was upset that I might have
damaged her reputation. Whatever.

But it has been Mom chipping away
at me, trying to convince me we can
maybe—maybe—become a family
again. I don't know if I want that.

First I have to make it through rehab.
It's a pricey place, with a pretty staff
and lots of mindless activities. The shrinks
even pretend to be nice while they're

picking at my brain. I tell them just
enough to make them believe
they're fixing me. I'm probably
unfixable. But hey, you never know.

A Poem by Ginger Cordell
You Never Know

When a passing cloud
might meet another,
and together unleash

           lightning

on thirsting ground.
One insignificant spark

           strikes

bone-brittle tinder.
Buoyed by the quiet
breeze, an ember

           smolders until

evening wind blows,
carries smoking wisps
upon its wings into

           the forest,

sighs into crackling
summer leaves until
the canopy

           burns.

So take note of every
passing cloud, because
you never know.

Ginger
Don't Know If It's the Same

Everywhere, but Vegas has
      its very own teen prostitution
court, complete with a special

judge who says he believes
      that underage hookers (my
term, not his) are the victims

of this particular crime. After
      watching him deal with a long
lineup of young tramps (my term

again), I think up to a point,
      he's right. Pimps and johns
are most definitely the criminals

here. The problem is that most of
      the girls in the courtroom, including
Alex and me, were willing victims.

Whatever. We are damn lucky to
      have a judge who cares even a little
about what happens to any of us.

His choices for what to do with
       us are limited. Juvie. Group homes.
Treatment programs, for those

who need them. Hard-core
       repeat offenders spend time in
Caliente, a lockup in mid-nowhere,

Nevada. And for the few
       lucky ones with families
who still care and will take

them, the chance to go home.
       Turned out for once in my
life, I was one of the few.

When I called Gram, she
       freaked. Good freaked,
I mean. All the bad of what

       I've done started spewing
          from my mouth. She shut me
       up right away. *We can talk*

about that later. Right now,
        tell me what I have to do
to bring you home. She didn't

yell. Didn't cry. Not until
        she told me about Iris. *She's*
dying, Ginger. Advanced HIV.

Gram and the Kids

Really need me now. Iris, too.
           She's wasting away. Docs
say she's got maybe a year.

I tried to get Alex to come
           back to Barstow with me.
She's not budging an inch

from the group home her social
           worker assigned her to. A group
home for pregnant teens. She said,

        Me and the baby will be just
              fine. The program will find
        me a job, help me learn how

        to be a mom. She vows to be
           a better mother than her own.
I just hope she's better than mine.

I'll miss her, of course. She's
           been the biggest part of me for
a very long time. But truth is,

the biggest part of me should
           be me. Just have to find her.
Maybe she's even a writer.

A Poem by Cody Bennett
Have to Find

The courage to leap
the brink, let myself fall
beyond the precipice
most people call

life.

I've grown tired of
stumbling, skinning
my knees. If flight

is

possible without
the sting of growing
wings, let me fly

a-

way, above the madness,
to a place where
there is nothing to

gamble

but another go-round.
And, win or lose, there
is a chance at something

after

the penultimate decision.
Because life, and maybe
death, will always be
a gamble after

all.

Author's Note

I am often asked how I decide to write about a certain topic. This one was inspired by a statistic I came across. Did you know that the average age of a female prostitute in the United States is twelve years old? This book doesn't explore the base reason for that statistic—young children are imported into this country from places like Thailand and Africa to serve as child prostitutes. Other books do address that issue, and I may too, one day. But for the purposes of this book, the statistic piqued my interest in teen prostitution. *Tricks* looks at a handful of reasons that might drive a young adult to sell his or her body. Here, and in real life, almost always you can distill the reason to survival.

Prostitution is not a glamorous profession. Even high-priced call girls often end up addicted, abused, or worse. No one deserves the kind of mistreatment often perpetrated by "johns" and pimps. Whatever the reasons for resorting to prostitution, whatever has happened in someone's past, the future is theirs to shape. The first step is to find a way out.

If you or someone you know have reached that place, and are under the age of eighteen, there is help. A wonderful organization called Children of the Night will take you off the street and help you start over. All you have to do is ask. Their hotline number is 800-551-1300. But if you can't remember that, dial 911. Local law enforcement can put you in touch with them.

What happens in Vegas stays in Vegas ... or does it?
Discover if there's a way out in *Traffick*.

TRAFFICK

The sequel to *TRICKS*

Ellen Hopkins
The # 1 *New York Times* bestselling author

A Poem by Ginger Cordell
Will I Walk

Away from here, this dirty
city, where people come
in search of Lady Luck,
certain she'll guide them to
the fortune she owes them,

or

to shed their skins, reveal
the extraordinary creatures
beneath, aliens they struggle
to conceal from spouses,
ministers, their local PTA.

Will

I walk away from her?
My best friend turned lover
before our tumble from
enlightenment, if such a thing
ever belonged to me. Can

I

excise her from my heart
as easily as she deserted me?
If I opened my arms, begged
her to return, would she come
back, or would she turn and

run?

Ginger
How Can I Leave

Here without her—Alex, my sweet
Alex. At least, she was sweet until
Las Vegas claimed her, made her
its bitch. This city is a pimp, selling

fantasies. For a time, Alex and I
were a fantasy duet, working for
Have Ur Cake Escort Service,
despite being a couple of years

underage. "Eighteen" isn't necessary
to participate in a business that
props up the underbelly of Vegas.
It was not what I had in mind when

I ran away, but then again, I had no
plan, and sometimes it comes down
to survival. We survived, stripping
for pay in hotel rooms, mostly

working bachelor parties, two for
the price of one. I insisted on that,
refused to do more than take off
my clothes and dance. But Alex

couldn't care less about spreading
her legs and accepting foreign objects,
as long as the dudes were willing
to pay the going rate. Then she got

greedy, started working the streets
so she wouldn't have to kick back
Lydia's commission. I found her out
there, soliciting some guy wearing

ugly purple Bermuda shorts. That
pissed me off, but in hindsight,
looking for revenge by offering to let
him buy all he could eat, double-decker,

wasn't the smartest move. Turned
out, he was a cop on a trash run, prowling
for teen hookers. Vegas has issued
stern orders: get 'em off the sidewalks,

    bust their pimps and even their johns.
    Detective Bermuda Shorts was only
    doing his job. *Tell me who's sending*
    you out, the court will go easy on you.

Alex and I didn't roll on Lydia
or Have Ur Cake. Luckily, Judge
Kerry was sympathetic anyway,
an honest-to-goodness do-gooder.

    Nevada considers trafficking
    children a serious offense.
    This is not a victimless crime,
    and you, young lady, are a victim.

Nothing He Said

Made sense. How can a willing
participant be a victim? No one
tied us up at the end of the day
(although a few of our customers

offered). And we weren't trafficked,
as far as I knew then. No one kidnapped
us and smuggled us to the foreign
country of Las Vegas. Now, thanks

to my recent interaction with law
enforcement, the courts, and social
workers, I understand that three
things define trafficking: coercing

someone to turn tricks, transporting
them for that purpose, or in any
way threatening or encouraging
an underage person to sell their body.

Oh, and how good ol' Iris collected
money for allowing men to force
themselves on me? Uh, yeah. That,
too. Then, there's Have Ur Cake.

Since Alex and I haven't reached
the age of eighteen—that magic
birthday that supposedly makes
you an adult—Lydia was definitely

guilty of pandering minors for sex.
She arranged our "dates," and
collected a hefty fee for her trouble,
so technically she was our pimp,

though we asked for the work.
She never had to twist our arms.
But she totally knew how old
we were, and that we'd run away

with a minimal bankroll. Plus,
she did, in fact, put us in her debt
by letting us stay with her when
we first arrived in Vegas. When I

appeared before Judge Kerry, though,
I didn't understand all that. "I don't see
myself as a victim, Your Honor. I was just
trying to make enough money to survive."

> He looked at me with such sadness
> in his eyes. *I understand survival,*
> *but this is not a good way to earn*
> *money if you truly want to survive.*

I Guess I Was Lucky

I don't really know
what all Alex faced
when she did outcalls
solo. She refused to talk

to me about it. I only
did a few gigs alone,
and I never exactly felt
threatened. Together,

there were a few times
when I thought a client
might hurt us, and one guy
forced Alex to jerk him off.

More than once, we got
stiffed for payment, and
then we owed Lydia
anyway. She never really

bullied us. Convinced
is more accurate. She had
a way of doing that, although
she never could talk me into

stuffing condoms into my bag
and earning a hell of a lot more
money. I'm a dancer. A stripper.
But I'll never be a whore.

Now My Stripping Days

Are over, at least that's what Judge
Kerry said. After my advocate
determined Gram does want me
back in Barstow, they sent me

to stay in a group home until
Gram can arrange to come pick
me up. The law says I can only
be released to a "custodial adult."

Hey, at least I have one of those,
unlike Alex, who ended up in
a different group home—one that
accepts pregnant teens. Pregnant.

If she got that way, it means
she wasn't using protection, and
God forbid she picked up anything
else besides sperm. The father?

Some anonymous trick, and who
knows what color the baby will
be, or what defects it might inherit
from its paternal side? So sad.

Then again, everything about Alex
makes me sad—her childhood;
the things she's allowed herself to do;
the fact I might never see her again.

Our Goodbye Was Bittersweet

Bitter, because it *was* goodbye.
Sweet, because it meant she was
safely off the streets. I spent many
hours pacing our apartment,

pining for closeness and a return
to sweet adventures in bed,
wondering when she'd come home.
If she'd come home. She always

did eventually, but every time
another little piece of the Alex
I loved was missing. Tricking chews
you up from the inside out.

We had a few minutes together
while waiting to see the judge.
"Gram says she welcomes me
back, believe it or not."

> *I believe it. The one thing about*
> *you I've always been jealous of is*
> *how much your grandma loves you.*
> *No one's ever loved me like that.*

"What about me? I still love you,
Alex, don't want to live without
you. Please come with me. I'm
sure Gram will let you live—"

No. Are you kidding me?
She's got six kids to take care
of, plus your mom. You expect
her to add me and a baby?

"We can work out something.
Get jobs, our own place. I can
still help Gram with the kids,
and . . ." It sounded ridiculous.

Aw, Gin. I want you to go back
to school, get your diploma,
head off to college. You can
legit make it in the real world,

and do it all on your own. You
don't need me holding you back.
She reached out, put one hand
on my cheek. I directed it to my lips,

kissed each finger. "I don't know
what I'll do without you, and I'm
scared for you and the baby."
Her hand fell away, never there.

Don't worry about us. We'll be
just fine. Besides . . . She forced
her voice cold. *I've been thinking*
and I've decided I prefer men after all.

DISCOVER NEW YA READS

READ BOOKS FOR FREE

WIN NEW & UPCOMING RELEASES

RIVETED

YA FICTION **IS OUR ADDICTION**

JOIN THE COMMUNITY

DISCUSS WITH THE COMMUNITY

WRITE FOR THE COMMUNITY

CONNECT WITH US ON RIVETEDLIT.COM

AND @RIVETEDLIT

FROM THE *NEW YORK TIMES* BESTSELLING AUTHOR
Ellen Hopkins

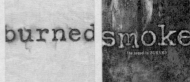

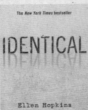

CRANK
"The poems are masterpieces of word, shape, and pacing . . . stunning."
—*SLJ*

GLASS
"Powerful, heart-wrenching, and all too real."
—*Teensreadtoo.com*

FALLOUT
"*Fallout* is impossible to put down."
—*VOYA*

BURNED
"Troubling but beautifully written."
—*Booklist*

SMOKE
"A strong, painful, and tender piece."
—*Kirkus Reviews*

IMPULSE
"A fast, jagged, hypnotic read."
—*Kirkus Reviews*

PERFECT
"This page-turner pulls no emotional punches."
—*Kirkus Reviews*

IDENTICAL
★ "Sharp and stunning . . . brilliant."
—*Kirkus Reviews*, starred review

TRICKS
"Distinct and unmistakable."
—*Kirkus Reviews*

TILT
"Graphic, bitingly honest, and voluminous verse."—*SLJ*

RUMBLE
"Strong and worthy."
—*Kirkus Reviews*

PRINT AND EBOOK EDITIONS AVAILABLE
From Margaret K. McElderry Books | simonandschuster.com/teen

EDEN WAS ALWAYS GOOD AT BEING GOOD.

Starting high school didn't change who she was. But the night her brother's best friend rapes her, Eden's world capsizes. And she buries the way she used to be.

A *New York Times* Bestseller

★ "This is a poignant book that realistically looks at the lasting effects of trauma on love, relationships, and life.... Teens will be reminded of Laurie Halse Anderson's *Speak*.... An important addition for every collection."
—*School Library Journal*, starred review

"Don't let a book of this magnitude pass you by. Pick it up and read it because Eden's story demands to be read."
—*Once Upon a Twilight*

PRINT AND EBOOK EDITIONS AVAILABLE
From Margaret K. McElderry Books   simonandschuster.com/teen

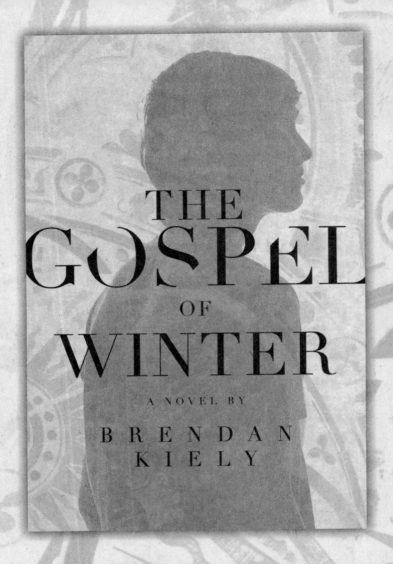

She thought she had grown up enough by now and knew enough by now not to be surprised by anything anymore.... But she was wrong.

★"An important work."—*School Library Journal*, STARRED REVIEW

★"Will linger with readers."—*Publishers Weekly*, STARRED REVIEW

★"Gritty, graphic, and shatteringly painful to read . . . A masterfully told, unforgetttable tale of what hope looks like in desperate circmustances and of the struggle to find power in one's voice."—*Booklist*, STARRED REVIEW

Dime is pulled into the life so smoothly that she doesn't even realize it. Soon she's making choices and doing things she never thought she'd do. Losing herself piece by piece, until it feels like she's barely got anything left inside. But what if the tiny part that does remain is enough to help her break free?

PRINT AND EBOOK EDITIONS AVAILABLE | SimonandSchuster.com/teen